The Ass's Tale

John Farris

Unbearable Books / Autonomedia
Series Editors: Jim Feast and Ron Kolm

UB – 1: *Spermatagonia: The Isle of Man,* bart plantenga
UB – 2: *Negativeland,* Doug Nufer
UB – 3: *Neo Phobe,* Jim Feast and Ron Kolm
UB – 4: *Shorts Are Wrong,* Mike Topp
UB – 5: *The Hotel of Irrevocable Acts,* Carl Watson
UB – 6: *The Ass's Tale,* John Farris

Forthcoming
UB – 7: *Some Heart,* Deborah Pintonelli
UB – 8: *This Young Girl Passing,* Donald Breckenridge

The Ass's Tale

John Farris

Unbearable Books / Autonomedia

Book design: Jim Fleming
Front cover illustration: Shalom Neuman
Back cover photograph: Andrew Castrucci

First American Paperback Edition
ISBN: 978-1-57-027-221-9

NYSCA
New York State Council on the Arts

This publication is made possible in part
with funds from the New York State Council
on the Arts, a state agency.

Unbearable Books are published and distributed by
Autonomedia
POB 568 Williamsburgh Station
Brooklyn, NY 11211-0568 USA

info@autonomedia.org
www.autonomedia.org
www.unbearables.com

Printed in the United States of America

*O*nce my ass got lost: I had been riding it and had just gotten off at the house of a friend who had promised to feed and care for it, but when I looked around the thing was gone, just like that! Being that I had arrived at that town on it, I had no way of leaving, as it took a good foot to negotiate that terrain, rocky and craggy as it was in the mountains. I had thought myself more familiar with my surroundings than was actually the case, the light in those parts playing tricks on the casual traveler so that what could appear as good road might actually lead to a ravine or a dark cave there would be no way out of without the consummate skill of a spinner who had spun some good yarn he had trailed behind on his entrance like the yarn Ariadne gave her lover to help him get out of the labyrinth. I am afraid I did not have that foresight.

CHAPTER ONE

I was bound to meet with trouble in my life as my nose could never be kept clean, not even by Alice, my maternal grandmother, a tyrant if ever there was one in her passion for the suffering of her Lord and Savior, intolerant of anything that wasn't stripped down and bleeding, bearded, as I found myself many times at her hands. "Petronius," —I don't know why they named me that or exactly who did it—she would say, "look at you! Come here, boy, I'm go havta pick that nose!" and get a rag, me at the end of it; she wiping (a symbolic attempt, as it were, to clean my slate), although pick and rub as she might, I could never come clean, guilty before that terrible Lord, a little snot everywhere and in grown people's business. My mother'd had a hand in it too, picking at me for lice and lint as well, and feathers. I was always full of feathers due to there being a hole in my pillow that would always reappear, as if by magic, no matter how many times it was sewn up. She said I looked like a bird, and "Would I please not eat like one" was one of her favorite expressions with me. I guess I did eat like one for all we had around there, so what did she want from me? I flew the coop early or was pushed out by my brother, who was younger than myself although a great deal larger, but I survived by landing in a junkyard where I scavenged copper wiring from the rotting bodies of automobiles, a penny a pound. Nineteen pounds of wire, one pound of bologna; eleven pounds, a loaf of bread; twenty pounds, a lump of cheese. A good living, but I was kept busy, the nose to the proverbial. I lived in a rather snappy green Hudson that was probably a lemon or that had been stolen by someone and abandoned, and that miraculously had a radio that played classical music and some jazz I didn't object to—Benny Goodman and "Sing, Sing, Sing," but, hey, beggars can't be choosers, can they—and a nice plush back seat I could fall onto after a hard day of stripping and just pass out after enjoying my bologna sandwich or my ham with a bit of cheese and my quart if I had been particularly industrious that day, and dream of events that were vague then, but that would shape me as sure as I lay there dreaming; me, drifting on a reed like Moses or Charlie Parker, encountering strange tongues, odd voices coming at me from the radio; but how was I going to get there, a snotty-nosed kid with no ass to speak of?

CHAPTER TWO

How I found out about my ass was this way: Having
stripped whatever material that was available, I was
hanging around the junkyard waiting for a new ship-
ment of carcasses to arrive as they did every two or
three days and listening to some jazz I thought was inside my head but which was coming from that miracle, the radio, it having been one of those rare days somebody had slipped a real disc on
the locals, one of those old whiney blues with a real jump chorus on
Vocalion, when I heard a noise that sounded like a scratch. Aside from
the shipments, I had never seen anyone at the junkyard. The car bodies usually dropped from metal cranes like heavy water in a storm and
I had had to learn early on to avoid being struck, or I would have been
mashed as flat as a coin. Can you imagine my head on a silver coin or
even copper? Chrome? Nickel? Maybe nickel, but I would have been
anonymous, I would not have been myself: me, Two Feathers, ugh—not
even a dog— but here was one at the window attached to a beefy gentleman in a well-worn uniform with a stick. To judge from its snarling
and slavering, the dog did not appear to be too friendly. The man said,
"Git yore black ass out of there now! A stripper are ye? I thought I
was missing some of my coppers, hey, Rudolph?"

Rudolph was the dog, a beast if there ever was one.

"Can you hear, nigger? I said git yore black, jazz-lovin' ass out of
there, pronto. Quick! Now pronto. That there is Spanish. Quick? That
there is English. Now I bet you these boots I'm wearin' (call 'em clod-
hoppers if you wants to) you understand one o' 'em."

My mother called me "pet," the diminutive of Petronius. My grandmother called me "pest" —a sinner, a hewer of wood, a drawer of water.
By now, there was water in my drawers. Nobody had ever called me
"nigger" before, at least not in that tone. The dog looked positively fe-
rocious. It scratched menacingly at the window like a well-worn record.
The announcer's voice came on: "And that, ladies and gentlemen, was
Victoria Spivey. And now, the Casa Loma Band." The Casa Loma Band
went into some insipid number with a lot of legato saxophones in uni-

son, something like, "Roaming Through the Gloaming."

"Whut are you waitin' for, nigger? Git your black, copper-stealin' ass out o' there, now! Don' lemme havta come in after yuh!"

So I had an ass, and it was black.

Was this how the Tainos felt?

The man said, "Got any gold?"

Now, I had some gold. I wasn't in that copper mine, that cemetery of wrecks, for nothing. I was in it for the material. The man couldn't help but to see I had gold unless he was a fool; there was gold stashed everywhere—under the hood, in the glove compartment, around my neck, in my teeth. I'd had some little bronze figurines cast as weights to make sure I got proper measure from my stripping, big men on little asses, women pounding yams. Smelting had not been invented in China, smelting for war.

"Git outta there," he said.

There was no way in this god's world I was going to stay in any Hudson no matter how miraculous, without some precaution: Before I had begun to realize any profit from my stripping, before I'd bought the first slice of bread, I'd invested in some carbide locks and some bullet-proof glass for the windows. The Hudson—well, it could take care of itself. There was no way that bitch—it was a bitch, I could see six little teats—the man either, was getting in there at me without a tank, with a six-inch shell.

I didn't see any tanks.

That stick might have been battery-charged, but this was the Hudson, circa 1949. The Casa Loma Band again, some watered-down Latin American number. Still, I was scared. I'd heard about those dogs. I said, "What d'ya want?" Wishing I might hear some good music, not this hillbilly stuff.

"What?" he said, turning purple, eyes starting to spin like he was in a laundromat. If he'd had a nuclear device, I would have been gone, but I could stand a small siege. I had some food. I had my ass some water, spring water, as I had dug a well beneath the Hudson and piped some in from a spring that ran below it. "Look out, Rudolph!" The man took a swing that would have broken teeth, smashed skulls. The stick bounced harmlessly off the windshield and would have broken his skull except that he was wearing a hardhat; still, the force of the blow knocked him to his knees. The dog yelped excitedly as if now it really was going to get some blood. The man took another swing that sent him sprawling. He looked at me in disbelief. He looked at his stick. It was broken. I had heard it crack on his hardhat. He pulled himself quickly to his feet. He walked slowly to the Hudson. He looked down at his stick and then at me. "What are you, some kind o' smart nigger?" The predictable.

I said nothing. Who knows, they could have sold me some bad glass, some faulty steel; after all, it wasn't my manufacture. I would have been like the Negus Tewodrus of Ethiopia with his German gun against Victoria, but it worked. He stared down at me "Do you hear me talkin' to you? Are you ignoring me?"

I didn't know what to say: I didn't know if I was a smart nigger or not.

I supposed my eyes were as round as saucers.

"Nigger, your eyes are as round as saucers."

I supposed my teeth were as white as pearls.

"Nigger, your teeth are as white as pearls."

I supposed I was sweating.

"Nigger, how come you ain't sweating?"

I felt my brow and under my armpits. I wasn't sweating. My ass felt secure. He said, "What's your name?"

I had decided to change my name to Lucius, Lucius Apuleius. I don't know why. Something I'd read or heard somewhere. I was tired of all that "Pet" business. I told him, "Lucius Apuleius."

The man said, "What?"

I told him again.

He said, "That ain't no nigger name." He asked me if I had changed it recently and, if I had, why I hadn't taken a name like "Wole" or at least "Yahya" or "Muhammad." I told him I could take any name I wanted to, as was my constitutional right, the First Amendment. Naming yourself comes under "Free Speech." I thought he was going to have a fit. The dog pranced nervously, looking up at her master and whining. The announcer said, "That was the 'Tennessee Waltz' by Tennessee Ernie Ford."

I hadn't been listening. I was watching that cracker.

"How come you been stealin' my copper?"

I told him it wasn't his copper. The dog started to growl. He said, "Shut up, Rudolph." The dog stopped growling and started to whine. He said, "Calm down, girl." The dog licked her chops nervously, looking from her master to me. "What do you mean, it's not my copper?"

I said, "You have been leveraged out." Obviously he had not read *The Wall Street Journal* or *Crain's*. He asked what I meant. I said, "Just that. Leveraged out. Taken over by a hostile company."

He asked how I knew that.

I told him I had read it in *The Wall Street Journal.*

"Goddammit," he said.

He asked where I had got all that gold.

CHAPTER THREE

With me, it was as if life had its evil twin. If indeed there was a light and a dark, then what did that make me—a black man with a black ass? Why had my name been Petronius before Lucius? Bravado aside, why had I named myself Lucius? Was it a lack of imagination on my part? A lot of my friends at school had been named Lucius: There'd been Lucius Clay and Lucius Williams as well as Lucius Brown. There were more, all belonging to an exclusive club called the Lucans, but I can't remember them so well, coming at me as they do through a mist. It was so long ago that I attended that school with all those tens of thousands of Luciuses, but I do remember that everybody called them "Lucky" (which brings to mind another character whose name had a "Luc" root, and another, which for reasons that might seem obscure I won't go into now), maybe I wanted some of that luck to rub off on me, and maybe I was just grasping at straws to feed my ass. Until this time, there has been nothing lucky about me. As the saying goes: If it hadn't been for bad luck I wouldn't have had any luck at all. My old grandmother had taught me that as she had taught me about the Lucayos (she herself being another extinct Bahamian) and how they had allowed themselves to be pushed into somewhat of an evolutionary cul-de-sac, having not been lucky enough to be born in the correct time and place. Lord, Jesus Christ, what could Huracan have done but get them blown away. Lord, how that woman could go on, a preacher, who would have put to shame ten thousand Buddhas. "Hey Grammy," I would want to say, "in paradise, who needs you?" But she would have slapped my mouth and made me go cut a switch, with what she'd never have understood as malevolence, waiting for my eyes to go saucer-white and wide with surprise, with what she had to consider the impertinence of a devil she was going to beat out of me, some devil who had done this to her, sat her daughter down and convinced her to produce a me. Lord, eyes rolling and switching for all I was worth, according to that Lord. Lucky me, for this small correction; I should just wait and see if she could be wrong on something so lucent. I would bite my tongue; bite it clear off.

What was I doing in that junkyard? Okay, I was making a living, but was that all I was cut out to be—a junky?*

Who was this man outside my window?

I said, "What can I do for you?"

*That's what we called people who collected junk—with the "y" rather than the "ie" used to denote "users."

CHAPTER FOUR

How I got my ass out of there was as follows: It simply got tired of sitting and broke out doing sixty. There wasn't any chance of that cracker or that dog of a dog catching that donkey. It was all I myself could do to keep a grip. After that, whenever I wanted to go anywhere, my ass would run like hell, although being on the run certainly did have its consequences.

The most immediate consequence of flight was that I could no longer strip for copper as every time I would find a fresh corpse I would see that cracker coming in his uniform with his dog and a fresh stick, trying to sneak up on me. By now I'd gotten a remote for the Hudson so I would no longer have to fiddle with a key on entering or leaving, and as long as this wonderful, new-found friend of mine—my ass—had confidence in itself and in me, I felt good, and daily found myself roaming farther and farther afield in search of fresh opportunities for our maintenance, feeding and caring for ourselves. I was a specialist in metals, my ass in grass. Oh, how that animal did love itself some grass! As much of the stuff as it could get its hooves on; I myself was amazed by how much it could consume, being such a little burro, and I soon found that the more it got, the faster it could go, so we spent a considerable amount of time searching it out as well looking for the stuff I needed for my craft. And what was my craft? I was thinking of going into jewelry. Having had all that gold, I felt I had an affinity for it and other precious metals and stones, as well as the copper, which if I would have come across in my travels, I was certainly not turning it down. It was around this time I discovered my cock.

We had stopped in a little park in the middle of the city so the old ass could pull on some grass, a new and succulent variety it had uncovered in a little copse and delighted in, when I heard footsteps coming up the path leading to this very patch, and wary of the man who was always after me, alerted the burro (who was pulling away happily with a dreamy look in its eyes) to the noise in case we would have to split quickly when it suddenly ceased its intake and looked up inquiringly. "What is it, John?" I said. (By this time I had named my ass John.) It gave out a large bray that was followed by a snuffling sound. A similar bray and snuffling sound soon followed, as if in answer from just outside the copse. Feeling the strangest apprehension, I said, "Steady, John boy," and over the rise that dropped down to us appeared a most extraordinary sight, the daintiest little ass I had—up until that time—ever seen. John brayed excitedly. The little burro—accompanied by what it explained was a female—brayed back. She laughed, showing the most beautiful white teeth and pointed toward my genital area. "What's that?" she asked, "your beautiful cock? Got any grass for my ass?"

I offered her some of the grass. She played with my cock. "Nice bird," she said.

I said, "Nice ass."

CHAPTER FIVE

So now I had a cock and an ass —all three of us unemployed, as in me, myself and I, three-in-one. What was I to do? I had to find myself another yard and quick. I was looking for anything, but they were all occupied by men, of all races, but still men, and all in the same well-worn uniform as that man who had wanted my gold, and who had claimed the world's copper as his own; I knew out of experience to avoid them. I'd initially been attracted by a flickering light issuing from one of the yards I in my naiveté had assumed to be the light of a television set, a then-new phenomenon of technology said to be capable of changing how people viewed one another, and, curious about this, I stopped to have myself a look-see, though I did make sure I stayed carefully hidden. A man was saying, "Do you know why this place is so great?"

Another said, "No, why?"

The man said, "Human beings hang out here."

The other laughed. He said, "We kin have some fun."

I heard a laugh track; some snickers. They were standing around an oil can at which they appeared to be warming themselves; curious, as it was not a cold night. I noticed they were carrying guns as well as sticks; in fact, they were armed to the teeth, daggers everywhere, bandoliers slung from their shoulders for automatic fire. What happened next was chilling enough. Some Indians appeared: Plains Indians, Assinaboine, I believe, and pre-Spanish contact, as they'd no horses, just dogs to which they'd attached drag-sleds for their wickiups and their cooking pots and whatever; nomads with women and children. The man who had spoken first, who had said, "Do you know why this place is so great," now said, "Ready, boys." The other men laughed and said they were ready. They shouldered their weapons. The man said, "Fire!" and they shot the Indians dead: men, women and children. Then they advanced on the dead Indians —people, really—scalped them all, and made a movie out of it. There was real blood, lots of it; lots and lots. I realized being pre-Spanish contact "Indians" was a misnomer, but what else was I to call them; I didn't know their names. Some Chinese came on, and they shot them. Some Japanese came on, and they shot them. Some Russians came on, and they shot them. Some Koreans came on, and they shot them. Some Vietnamese came on, and they shot them. Some Cambodians came on, and they shot them. Some Laotians came on, and they shot them. Some Serbs came on, and they shot them. Some Croats came on, and they shot them. Some Cubans came on, and they shot them. Some whales came on, and they shot them. Some Afghanis came on, and they shot them. Some Jews came on, and they shot them. Some Germans came on, and they shot them. Some Iraqis came on, and they shot them. Some Kurds came on, and they shot them. Some Syrians came on, and they shot them. Some Egyptians came on, and they shot them. Some rabbits came on, and they shot them. Some birds came on, and they shot them, turkeys. Some bears came on, and they shot them. Some deer came on, and they shot them. Some Mexicans came on, and they shot them at the Alamo. Some Greeks came on, and they shot them. Some Hindus came on, and they shot them again and again. Some cows came on, and they shot them for beef. Some Latvians came on, and they shot them. Some Grenadians came on, and they shot them. Some Panamanians came on, and they shot them. Some Romanians came on, and they shot them. Some elk came on, and they shot them. Some chamois came on, and they shot them for sport. Some elephants came on, and they shot them for ivory. Lastly, but not leastly, some niggers came on, and they shot them, laughing. They were cartoons, with lots of shooting in them. Lots of blood. They shot a huge panorama of the Napoleonic Wars and everybody died. They shot everything and everybody, and made a movie out of it.

I don't know why I had thought I wouldn't have seen them on TV or that they wouldn't have been watching it if, in fact, that had been what it was, but I'd just seen something in the paper about that business and, being on the run all the time as I was, I wasn't getting to hear much music. I was just plain starved for some communion and had thought I might find Nat Cole or Dizzy, maybe on Steve Allen or Jack Paar. Milton Berle wasn't even funny, though I did like Sid Ceasar because Imogene Cocoa had such a big mouth. Rochester was a scream, and Amos and Andy, and Charlie Chan. Peter Lorre got killed because he was an evil motherfucker, and Orson Welles. I will never forget that laugh track as everybody died. Then the Romans came on, and crucified my grandmother's lord. I wondered what she thought about that; if she could watch something like that.

The men were bored just standing around during the crucifixion, so they shot themselves. Some people came on the L.I.R.R., so they shot them. Some people came on the subway, and so they shot them.

Some people worked at the Post Office, so they shot them, the workers. People at fast food restaurants, on college campuses—Kent State, the University of Texas— on the sides of highways, from apartment buildings and in shopping malls. Then they blew themselves up with plastique to seventy-two millimeters, one hundred five millimeters and put it in high definition, with suppurating wounds. Then they made a bomb and dropped it on themselves at the box office so everybody left. *Heaven's Gate*, I believe it was called. Came crashing down. On them. And everybody died laughing. So many, there was nobody left; nobody at all, just empty seats, but I couldn't stay there because it was so sad, plus it was radioactive. As I was leaving, some women came on, in interviews and on soap operas. They were shot in action.

Creeping away, I looked out for my ass and played with my cock.

CHAPTER SIX

The Hudson was being outgrown, as was everything. I no longer liked that music they played on the radio. I mean, Benny Goodman was all right insofar as he had had enough insight and appreciation for what was happening to hire a young and innovative Charlie Christian and a Lionel Hampton, but did that make him the king of anything? Certainly not of swing; not with Fletcher Henderson out there, Count Basie. C'mon, for my old grandmother's lord's sake, Gene Krupa and Panama Francis? Harry James and "Hot Lips" Paige? Don't give me that. King of the cash box, maybe, as they had claimed to be the kings of copper. My ass. Look how patient it was as I twisted knobs and spun dials looking for what I wanted and so rarely got; Mario Bauza, Machito, El Sexteto Nacional, knowing as I did that if I got them at all, they had been signed to a bad contract. Seven hundred and fifty dollars from Allan Katz at Decca for "One O'Clock Jump," plus twenty-three other tracks, an exclusive signing for three years with no royalties to anybody, not even Count Basie's ass, or Lester Young's, or Herschel Evans', while Barbara Streisand would get twenty million dollars for playing two nights at Las Vegas! I mean, come on, who was handing out the money, and why? Who was doing the programming? And where was James Moody? For that matter, who was James Moody? That was the problem. Everybody knew who Tchaikovsky was (the big 'T' again), but nobody knew who James Moody was. If you don't know who he is, how can you find him? See. He could get lost just like that.

I knew who he was.

I was going to find him.

Still, I needed some information to do it, and I wasn't going to get it in that Hudson, as big and plush as it was, on that radio, miraculous as it was. I had to have some wax; some vinyl.

Libraries were discouraging, but I found a little record shop off One Hundred Forty Seventh up in Harlem where the proprietor said he could oblige me. It was a strange little place; dusty and seedy, with some black heads in the window, turbaned and made of plaster, around which was arranged a group of tiny pyramids, a little diorama bearing the legend, "THIS IS A REMINDER OF THINGS TO COME." Black turbaned heads made of plaster—tiny pyramids—things to come? Odd.

The proprietor himself was rather odd as well, with the fine brown hair and light skin of a Caucasian, though he told me most emphatically that he was indeed a black, and produced an alto saxophone which he said he played, demonstrating a tone and a rhythm I wasn't all that impressed with, but the thing about it was this guy was right around my age, maybe a few years older, and he was playing the saxophone; I hadn't known young people could make music like that. Oh, I had heard some rocking at my grandmother's Pentecostal church, but that was nothing like this, with strange chordal inversions in which the tonics were where the fifths should have been and flatted, and a B minor 7 chord could suddenly become dominant as if by magic, simply because of someone whose name the kid said was Thelonius Monk: Thelonius: see—that was like me—Petronius, only that was another story. Anyway, the kid said it was called bebop and that he knew Bud and Ritchie Powell, who lived right around the corner. I didn't know who they were. He wasn't all that impressed with me, but he did tell me many things I needed to know, like what *klookamop* meant and *reetapooty* and *vous said swing, alreet, crazy, baby, you dig, prez?* I had thought I was 'hep' but the kid was 'hip,' and knew all the 'ladies' Lester knew. He said 'hep' was just 'help' with the L missing, but 'hip' was the love, did I dig it? 'Hip' was the joint, 'hip' was the straight dope. He agreed to let me go through his records, to just browse his discs; the discs that were sure to contain everything I needed to know to get closer to this, this thing, this enigma, this jazz. He had some Beethoven too, the piano and violin sonatas that would come to this. He looked high.

He said his name was Jackie and that he knew Charlie Parker. He wouldn't tell me what his last name was. He said, "In case you are a narc."

I asked him what a narc was.

He said a narc was "the man."

I said, "The man?"

He said, "Rreety-o-roony, solid, Jackson," and that I was probably too stupid to be one.

The man? Was it the man who was after my copper?

The name Jackie rang a bell.

Jackie said, "Don't worry about it. If you don't know who I am now, you will one day, prez, if you ain't a complete square, and if you are really hip, you will find James Moody."

In those days all the hip (as I was being taught to say) record stores had booths in them which you could hear a demonstration of whatever record you happened to be interested in, but another strange thing about this one was that it didn't have one of those; Jackie said he could play anything I wanted to hear, and proceeded to do so. He played "Chelsea Bridge" and "A Nightingale Played in Berkley Square," and, wonder of wonders, "Moody's Mood for Love" by James Moody, and then he played, "A Long Drink of the Blues."

Other than how he played the blues, as I said, I didn't like his tone all that much, and on that alto saxophone I didn't hear much Moody — even though, it was well known, or should have been — that Moody played the alto as well as the tenor. The alto saxophone has a strange sound, being pitched all the way up there in E flat and, as far as I was concerned, only certain cats could get to it, like Johnny Hodges, and later, Ornette Coleman and Marshall Allen. I told him so. He got mad and threw me out. Landing ignominiously on my ear and pulling myself to my feet, I asked about Moody, what he knew about him. He looked me up and down contemptuously. "What do you want to know for, square?" he asked, his tone acid, pitched somewhere above E flat as if he had produced it by using alternate fingering — alternate, hell — downright false. False fingering. A melody out of a fake book.

I continued dusting myself off as I imagined Steve Martin would later, or Charlie Chaplin might have, straightening the creases in my short pants before meeting his admittedly cool gaze. "Jackie," I said, "you are answering a question with a question," hoping for a bit of lead in my own tone, hoping he found my own gaze as cool as his; hoping he would find me not cool; hoping he would find me as cool as death. "Star Eyes" as played by Charlie Parker. That cool. Cool, cool. As cool as what Mahdabuti would be talking about — "refrigerator cool."

Jackie laughed, mirth shaking him like a blues guitarist shakes an E string, and when he stopped laughing, when he stopped shaking, he leveled that cool gaze on me before cocking his head like the hammer of a six-shooter and regarding me as a Westerner might a stranger in a box-back suit with a twenty dollar gold piece on his watch chain, a stranger who had wanted more gold, while the Westerner had wanted the twenty dollars and the stranger to get out of town before sundown, or else. "What's your name?" he asked spitting the question out like a lean, mean cobra; an unusual species of snake for these parts — the parts of the simile. In the simile, this was Needles, California, in Death Valley. You had to be cool or you'd die, even if you had big ears like a bat. You had to have big eyes like a nighthawk or an eagle. Where were my feathers now, hey, grandmother?

I said, "Lucius. Lucius Apuleius."

His head jerked upright even more. He said, "What?" and shot a glance at my ass, who had been patiently pulling at some grass, and who now looked up at me apprehensively. He said, "And your ass?" I said, "John." My ass and cock were ready. To fly.

He said, "Look, you know I don't want any trouble, going around talking bad about my tone and such, my sense of rhythm. I know I'm just a blues player; I know I'm not Charlie Parker; I'm just a fifteen year old kid; what do you want from me, kid? So what if I get high? Why don't you just take your ass and git outta here *muy pronto; andale, hombre—avant, avec moi—marche!*"

I didn't know why in this particular sequence of the scenario, this motif, with this particular mise-en-scene, he felt he had to speak French to me. The Spanish I could dig, as the vernacular was Mexican and more appropriate to the approximation of Needles, the Sonora Desert being so close. Still shaking dust out of my pants, I said, "Hey, I'm not the Lucius you think I am. There are lots of them, maybe ten thousand Luciuses."

For some reason, he wasn't buying it. He said, "But there is only one Lucius named Apuleius, and further, I happened to know there is only one ass named John."

John brayed nervously.

Jackie said, "The man is after you. You could bring heat. You are not cool by any means."

I said, "I am, by any means necessary," I showed him the X on the baseball cap I was wearing.

He said, "That ain't cool, man, that's just Spike Lee."

I showed him the X on my ass's right haunch. The brand. The fire-brand. Jackie blanched. He could do that, being almost Caucasian. He said, "I told you I recognized your ass! That's John X. He is wanted. He is a renegade and a hophead." The kettle was calling the pot black, or was it the other way around; I forget.

"Jackie," I said, "The man is after my gold; he thinks my ass is gold. Look over there, Jackie. Does that ass look golden to you? No, it is not. It is as black as me. It is as black as night. As black as jazz, as black as Buddy Bolden."

He asked where my ass picked that up. Heartened, I said, "What are you referring to, Jackie?"

He said, "That sound! That sound like Buddy Bolden, 'Funky butt, funky butt, take it away...'"

I informed him gently I knew that was Jelly. Jelly Roll. Lord Jelly. Jelly Roll Morton. Lord.

He said, Lord.

It was funny, I had been thinking about that Jelly. That Jelly Roll. "One and the same," I said. "Lord Jelly Roll Morton. Lord! What my grandmother thought of that I don't know, but my ass picked it up somewhere all on its own. Actually, Jackie, I'll tell you the Lord's honest truth, I don't know where I picked him up, but it has a little Bunk Johnson in it. It could have been mixed in with some hay; hey,what do you think?"

"Or with some pod," Jackie said, laughing. He relaxed.

My ass made him feel good and it had only farted. And I had been so worried about that animal I was going to shit a brick. I asked if the man had been around lately.

"No," he said, "I ain't seen him in the last few days..." He raised his eyebrows. "Got any gold?"

"Not so much, Jackie," I said. "Not anymore." I reached into a pocket of my short pants and took out a twenty dollar gold piece. I flipped it to him, watching the coin spin through the air like a tiny sun before arcing into his palm. "Next time we can dispense with the six-shooter bit."

"What six-shooter bit?" he said slyly. He pocketed the coin, looking around furtively. "I really dug the bit about Needles." Grinning, he said, "I dig California."

I pulled some more gold from one of my teeth and tossed it to him. He snatched at it like a cat. "All right, Jackie," I said, "what about Moody?"

He asked if I didn't see anything in the record bins I could use.

"Jackie," I said, "seeing something is not the problem. I have to hear it."

I explained to him about the Hudson and that I'd nowhere to put any equipment in any case, the car being small. He showed me a 9x12 glossy of a chocolate-colored gentleman who wore black horn-rimmed glasses. He held a tenor saxophone by the neck as if he were going to wring it so hard it would scream, "Music! Music!" Underneath this image was the legend JAMES MOODY. I had never seen anyone hold a saxophone like that, tenor, alto, soprano, baritone, C melody, whatever.

He said, "When you get time, go see the President."

Who did he mean, Truman?

He must have been reading my mind like a bebop chart. "No man, Young. Prez."

I had almost forgotten about Lester, who held his instrument like he was crossing the Delaware and trying to keep it dry. The President.

He would have something to say; he always did. It was rumored he could give a six hour lecture on his instrument without once repeating himself. If Lester was the President, James Moody was Lafayette. Jackie told me I might catch Lester at a dive on West Fifty Second called Kelly's Stable or at another joint he usually frequented called the Three Deuces. He handed my ass a fresh packet of grass. He told me to be careful, they were mob joints, I should watch out for my own ass, and cover it carefully at all times. It was good advice. Usually wherever the mob was, the man was not far behind. They usually worked hand-in-hand or hand-in-glove or hand-in-pocket, in everything like Mantle and Maris or MandM's, only they didn't melt anywhere, not in your mouth or in your hand, they just took, and whatever they took from down there they fought over like mad dogs, but siblings, sending wreaths to each other's funerals and such, guarding the families of informers. Informers: they had spies everywhere. You couldn't take a piss without being spied on by the main man down there in Washington, D.C., J. Edgar, who had personally put a bug in everybody's ear, in everybody's toilet, just so he could watch. He would announce over the radio in the Hudson that it was his pleasure to watch, to serve in this way, loving golden showers as he did. Gold again. They were always after your gold, trying to fuck you, that was why I had to cover my ass well, keep my cock hidden from the monitors he had had put in the halls everywhere, especially in the schools where the Lucans hung out, and in the clubs. It was well known on the street that he had a relationship with Luciano, having used him to prepare for the Allied invasion of Sicily only a few years before, let out of jail after more than a million murders—a million and one—and deported for just that purpose. They didn't call him 'Lucky' for nothing, but that was not my immediate problem. My problem was I was too young to get in the clubs. My ass was too. It was downright embarrassing.

CHAPTER SEVEN

Rummaging through a certain yard, I came across a television set that was as dead as the corpses of the cars I stripped for a living, but having seen some television, I liked it better dead than what I saw on there when it was working because when I looked at it, I noticed right away that it reflected my ass in the little screen; it reflected me. I had found out one thing in this world: you can't be straight. You have to get yourself a shtick, an act. If I was going to do this work, I was going to have to get an act, and I would certainly have to get my act together: in this old dead television that now reflected me, I saw a way to do just that. Strapping it to my ass, I hauled it back to the Hudson, where I installed it over the front windshield where the rear view mirror should have been and would sit for hours, watching myself make faces at my ass, squinting, pulling my lips taut against my teeth and grimacing, baring my teeth and snarling, snorting like a horse. I could see my ass on television. It was great incentive and a fabulous acting technique that I pioneered though Feldenkrais would later claim it. I could sing and dance too; oh, I wasn't the world's best singer or even the world's best dancer, but I could certainly entertain myself. I would catch whatever radio I could; on great days, air checks of Duke Ellington from North Dakota or somewhere, and my ass would join in with its braying, like Cootie Williams, like Cat Anderson, but always, always like Buddy Bolden. It was much better than the *Merry Mailman* or *Mr. Rogers' Neighborhood* (*Sesame Street* had not yet been invented), and much better than *Pee Wee's Playhouse* would be later. At least I was not a pervert who wanted to seduce my ass subliminally, being strictly an entertainer; in other words, the greatest joy in my life was derived from just hamming it up; the elasticity of my own expression simply fascinated me: I was better than Boris Karloff in *The Man with a Thousand Faces*. I was as good as James Cagney at hitching up my belt with my index finger extended and my thumbs up. I was as good as Humphrey Bogart at saying, "Here's looking at you, kid," I could be as good as Robert DiNiro at imitating James Cagney, as good as Anthony Hopkins in *Silence of the*

Lambs. Since I didn't have to sell myself on anything, since I did not need or want to sell my ass, I even made better commercials, right there on my ass; Alexi Gente, the Marlboro Man; on my ass. Who else could do that, what art director, what producer, better than I?

I was busy hamming it up in this manner one day and dreaming of that day (which, in my naiveté, I hoped was not far off) when millions of people all over the world would be watching me, talking with me on all the talk shows (I could talk my ass off) and talking about me in all the newspapers, not only for being a great stripper or a great actor, or a great one with jewelry—metals and stones and other junk—but also and most of all for being THE MAN THAT DISCOVERED JAMES MOODY, that would be like Columbus discovering America, when I saw on the dead screen something quite animated that was not myself, that was not my ass, and it was a good thing too that it was there in the Hudson safe with me, or so I thought. Superimposed on that cadaver of a cathode ray was a vast array of America's superheroes all led by that villain, the man (the French say a 'villien' is a peasant, and all peasants are supposed to be good for something when there is a levy on the population for a call-up or simply a ball or a tournament or a marriage, the notices tacked up all over town, attached to trees all over the countryside saying, GOOD CITIZENS, YOUR LORD NEEDS YOU TO PRODUCE WHAT I WANT NOW).

This man was a peasant, what was it he was producing?

Paul Whiteman, Howdy Doody, Superman, Rin-tin-tin, Roy Rogers and Gene Autry, Hopalong Cassidy and Lash LaRue, Zorro, the Lone Ranger and his town Indian Tonto—these two obviously needing silver for the masked ranger's bullets—Kukla, Fran, and Ollie, I Love Lucy with that guisano Desi Arnez (Babalou, Meester), the Nelsons, Bing Crosby and Bob Hope, McCarthy and MacArthur in a show that couldn't last, "Mc and Mac," Betty Boop and her Dog Nobody Could Know Was a Nigger, Buck Rogers and His Rocketeers in the Twenty Fourth Century, Farmer Gray, Lawrence Welk, Steve and Edie Gorme, Perry Como, Stan Laurel and Oliver Hardy, Betty Crocker, Harry Truman, Estes Kefauver (and all those characters he would call up and hang out with, make deals with at chop houses near the Senate Building), the Masked Marvel (a lot of them were masked), Disney, the Pope, the Wizard of Oz.

"Look," the man said, pointing to a scowling kid who looked about fourteen, fifteen years old, a really surly type teenager, "it's Elvis. He has got all your moves down, nigger, you might as well give it on up— I mean, give up—we have got you covered, partner!" He turned to the one called Elvis and said, "G'wan show 'im, kid."

The kid called Elvis went into his moves. He had me covered. He sang, "YOU AIN'T NUTHIN' BUT A HOUND DAWG," wiggling his hips slowly, jerkily. I was immediately transformed into a hound dog. My ass looked at me in disbelief. I howled and howled as Elvis howled back. It was up to my ass now.

Now, hey, I will be the first to admit it, I have on one or two occasions been an asshole in my life, but up until that time I had never been a dog (a "blood," but never a "hound") and in my consequent panic hit the remote control device that slid back the carbide bolts, allowing the reinforced doors of the Hudson to swing wide open and these characters, led by the man, the producer, to swarm in on me and my ass. Fuck, I tried to dog them but there were just too many, image after image, overwhelming me, Paul Whiteman, Gene Autry and *I Love Lucy* (et tu, Desi). I tried to use my teeth, but in my innocence wouldn't go for the throat, and wary of their crotches, snapped ineffectually at their ankles. Those cowboys were all wearing boots. It was all I could do to keep their horses from trampling my ass, jumping all over it. The poor thing shot me a look of complete disgust as if to say, "Some protection you are." It seemed worried about its chops and quickly stuck a mute in what was, as it were, the bell of its instrument. Peter Lorre was in there too, his eyes half lidded, sensuous as he whined, "We got 'im now, hey Boss?"

Fucking immigrant.

The man said, "Shut up, Peter. Get out of the way."

Peter Lorre muttered a characteristic "Aww." He scowled, moving reluctantly.

The man said, "Get 'im outside ..."

They hustled us outside, my sore ass and I by the forelegs, me snapping ineffectually at their wrists, ineffectually because, of course, they wore fringed cowhide gloves, rough side out. The fringes whipped at my eyes until, blinded and exhausted, I lay there seemingly, if not totally, subdued. The man said, "Okay, yuh dog-eared nigger; thought you wuz smart; whar yuh got it hid at!"

He was an American, and I could not catch his accent. My ass was mute.

If I hadn't been thinking "man" at that time, I would have thought Andy Devine, but if you can understand it at all, I was not in my right mind, to say nothing of my body.

The man said, "I guess you sold off all the copper, didn't yuh, yuh Reginald Lewis-assed motherfucker, thought you wuz ahead o' yore time," and fetched me quite a kick in the ribs. "Whar is der gold, der gelt, hund?"

Rudolph was with him. Rudolph smirked as if it filled her with a particular glee to see me kicked and beaten, reduced to a dog-like state. Turning to Lash LaRue, the man said, "Hey, Lash, let me have your lash." Lash LaRue let him have it, a smart one, across his back. The man jumped to attention, screaming. "Ow! I didn't mean for you to give it to me; I meant for you to let me have it!"

Lash LaRue didn't talk much. He let the man have it again, pretty much in the same spot, like Robin Hood splitting an arrow he had previously sent dead center of a bull's-eye. The man groaned, snatching the whip. He said, "You fool," and slapped Lash LaRue. LaRue punched him in the eye, knocking him down. The whip-wielding cowboy jumped on him, pummeling him until the others managed, after some struggle, to pull him off. "Sorry," he said, "I'm not used to taking orders from anyone."

The man said, "Dumbkoff! How do you think empires are built and maintained; through rugged, pseudo-individualism like yours? Not on your rusty-dusty tintype. It takes direction! You are working for this company or you are not working! We're dropping you!" Lash LaRue disappeared from sight. The man turned to the company of American heroes. They had gotten very quiet, as if afraid one or all of them would disappear next. Desi Arnez attempted a "Babalou," and was told by Lucy to shut up. He said, "Hey Lucy, thees ees bery uncharacteristic of you, dear. Do you want a divorce right now?"

The crowd shushed him. The man said, "You artists have simply got to understand that I want you to interpret only what I want interpreted, do you understand?"

The assembled company stirred uncomfortably, murmuring and muttering among itself. The man slapped the now-dropped Lash LaRue's whip against his thigh like a quirt: "Do you?"

Rudolph growled, baring her fangs. The group muttered uneasily, milling about, unsure of what to do. Finally, Kukla of Kukla, Fran and Ollie stepped forward. "We do, Boss." He looked back at the crowd. "Don't we?"

Nobody said anything. I hadn't noticed Charlie McCarthy. He stepped forward with Mortimer Snerd. "We ain't dummies, Boss. We understand perfectly!" Edgar Bergen made them do it.

The man said, "Good."

Rudolph relaxed. She looked at me expectantly, almost grinning. Turning to me, the man said, "Whar you got it hid?"

I couldn't say a word. That was the way I was brought up. I was not a pig and I would not, could not squeal, particularly on my own ass. Using the whip like a sap, the man cracked me across the left ear, breaking my eardrum. I can't hear out of that same ear today. I yelped, but still could not utter a word. As I said, it was not in my tradition. He might beat me like a dog, but I could not squeal. That's not the way I was raised.

"Where, nigger?" He brought the handle of the whip down again, across my rib, cracking it, reminding me of my grandmother. He said, "Search it, boys!"

They searched the Hudson, coming up with nothing, as the only gold I had left was in my teeth, perhaps why my bite had been so ineffective. They searched my ass and found the bag of grass Jackie had given it. The man said, "Aha, nigger, this here is our lucky day." Rudolph leapt around excitedly, baying to beat the band. The man said, "Git him, boys!"

They got me. They got me good. They beat me unmercifully. They beat me like an Arab would a dog, and then, to top that, they kicked my ass over and over, my poor ass who bore it silently as well, stoically. Stubborn as a mule, my little burro. They beat it pretty badly too and after they had had enough of that, they hauled us off to the hoosegow, my diminutive ass and I. Then they hauled us off to Treblinka. Then they hauled us off to Dachau. Then they hauled us off to Auschwitz. Then they hauled us off to Bergen-Belson. Then they shipped us off to Babi-Yar, then they hauled us off to Goree Island, through the "Door of No Return," from where they shipped us off to America, where they stripped the stripper. I had been as naked as my ass, but they unclothed me. Then they hauled us off to Angola. Angola, Louisiana, and then they hauled us off to Parchman Farm. Old man Parchman was long since dead, and I suspect I know how it happened: his farm was a killer. Then they hauled us off to Sing Sing. Then they hauled us off to Attica, New York, to the Storm King Correctional Center as it was to be renamed later, as the name "Attica" would bring too much to too many people's minds. It was to be a dog's life.

After stripping me of my dignity and beating me, maybe it was the other way around, the next thing they did was to separate me from my ass, after which I was given a haircut and a number: 221903. As far as the authorities were concerned, John no longer existed for me. I don't know why they bothered with the haircut, they already had me by the short hairs, but I couldn't complain. A waste of the taxpayer's money, though it was said to be a way of assuring recidivism.

CHAPTER EIGHT

Upstate New York is very beautiful, but it can also be very gray. The skies over that place were as gray as it got, and everything was the color of the sky itself: the trees outside the walls that bore the grayest apples, the forty foot high wall that was as thick as the fat heads of the Dutch and those Germans that had resettled the region (replacing an indigenous population that had either been exterminated or shipped off to gray, remote areas called reservations, where, if lucky, they became tourist attractions), the six machine gun turrets with their rifle-toting guards that stood above the wall, the eyes and faces of the guards, though their uniforms were the darkest blue (blue as that night sky) with black stripes streaking down the leggings like black lightning, uniforms that were no newer or better kept than the man's who had brought me here (who told me as he was leaving that if I ever got out of there he would hunt me down and find me), the large yard that euphemistically served as a recreational area, the bleachers where convicts sat watching the most desperate games or gambling, or mumbling in gray tones to each other about the grayest matter, or simply sat staring darkly off into space (maybe pulling on a cigarette while watching the gray smoke curl skyward, creating the cruelest illusion of freedom and lightness as the mind itself was stamped indelibly with the fact that one was a convict, a number, a dog); the food—always potatoes that in winter were gray with frostbite, the bits of beef or non-generic, free-range poultry served twice a week—the buildings where the convicts worked, ate, and slept their guarded sleep.

I was given a gray uniform, a shower, and afterward, a lecture by a huge, pear-shaped cracker called the captain whose waist was so large it took three lengthy belts to encircle it while his head was as tiny and pointy as Zippy the Pinhead's; he was that surreal. Besides the gray, the only other colors in that entire place were the blue of his pants with their black stripes, his white shirt and the red, broken capillaries in his face. His condition was probably plueritic as he moved his legs with great difficulty, hauling one up and hurtling himself forward with each step. The brown cigar lit with the orange of hellfire was jammed between his teeth like a turd; his thick lips pursed around it as he puffed and puffed like a devilish cherub. Four gold bars were pinned to his white shirt, two on each shoulder, and a gold badge. The lecture he gave was this: "You are not men. Yous are convicts. You have no rights. You are numbers. You are animals. Some of you are dogs." Here he looked directly into my brown eyes of a whipped hound with his steel-gray ones. I looked around uneasily. It was true, we were animals, made so in most cases by transformation and conditioning. We were dogs and snakes and coons and possums with numbers instead of names. I thought I recognized a Lucan. He was a snake, but I thought I detected a faint glimmer of recognition in his gray, rheumy eyes.

The captain said, "Listen dog, look at me when I am talking to you! What is your number?"

I tried to say 221903, but try as I might, I could make no sound other than a whine. I pointed to the numbers on my chest.

He said, "Well, dog 221903, I suppose we can expect trouble from you, hey? Good, you surly cur." He wrote something in a little notebook he carried in a back pocket; incongruous, this little notebook, as he was so large. Having finished his lecture, he waved to some guards who led, or rather herded, us off to our cellblocks, slithering, loping, crawling as best we could in lockstep. The Lucan was taken to A Block while I went to C Block where I was assigned #C32, A 5. I had been given six numbers: I was in a hell of a fix.

The journey from the reception area to C Block was the most reluctant one of my life. I had been sent to school by my grandmother, and to the store for things I didn't understand: roots and stuff, but here was the most irrational transportation imaginable: there I was alive in the body of a dog in a shell of a building with huge blocks going to a cell, a gray cell, 5x8, and barred in that same dreary color, the monotonous color of lead. A building with no random entrance and no random exit, everything was quite by design. C32 was on tier two. A guard whose name I would come to know well later threw a lever like one on a die press, opening and closing the doors behind us. Everything here was organized around a single idea: the conditional maintenance of a kind of life. Though each and every cell was individual, there was nothing singular about any of them. Oh, there was a picture here and there of a particular face pasted to a wall above a seatless toilet, but all bore the same gray look of uncertainty, as if at any moment they could go sliding down into the watery vortex below ... another picture might be tacked up though it too could only be an enigma, never quite the same, always with the same gray hangdog look of certainty, of expectancy:

nothing was to be uncertain, not one speck of dust. On the way to my own cell, in #25, I thought I saw another Lucan; he a snake as well. Slithering up to the door of his cell, he had watched me pass, curiosity in his gray, rheumy eyes.

As I said, my cell — I called it mine — was the same dreary affair as the others, with a tiny cot, a seatless toilet bowl with a washstand above it, and above that, a metal mirror that distorted what it reflected, three solid walls, the fourth, a barred aperture from which could be viewed this gray, dreary world and which, in turn, allowed others to watch. A small metal table extended from the wall opposite the cot, attached to which was a metal seat. Besides the uniform, I had been given two sheets, two pillowcases and two gray wool blankets. I arranged these on the cot and turned to face my new world. There was not much to see; through the bars and across the void: the gray seasons. In winter, the eternally gray snow; in spring, the gray leaves; in summer, the gray heat; in fall, the gray mist rising from the faintly discernible hills outside the walls. A further amenity was piped-in music, Mendelssohn, played badly and incessantly by the prison orchestra. This was the ultimate and eternal torture: I could hear no jazz. After receiving a cracked rib and a broken eardrum, I was now to suffer culture shock, the purported aim of which was my rehabilitation and retraining, but which was only punishment.

I had always had a working knowledge of Morse code, and was surprised to hear, under the Mendelssohn, a tapping sound organized to spell my old name, Petronius. "Petronius," it went, "hey, Petronius! Is that you, old buddy? Use the cup on your sink to answer me."

There was a tin cup on my sink. Picking it up in my mouth, I tapped back, "Lucius, is that you? If so, you are not my buddy." The Lucans had always been mean to me. Really, in my estimation they had always been snakes; shadowy, venomous.

"Forget that, Petronius," the Lucan tapped back, "this here is a totally new situation, and, hey, we's all in it together."

"My name is not Petronius anymore."

"What is it?"

"It's Lucius."

The Lucan tapped out a laugh. "You had to come on in, din't you. The Lucans is what's happening, ain't they?"

I told him I hadn't changed my name to be a Lucan. I asked why they had never let me hang out with them and why they had stuck me up a couple of times. He said I should let bygones be bygones, but that, anyway, they had done it to raise funds for their movement to finance themselves.

A movement to finance themselves? "Why?" I asked.

"Romance," the Lucan sounded out, "romance without finance is a nuisance. Mah baby said I had to git out and git her some gold..."

Everybody was after it! As I said, I had never trusted the Lucans. Instinctively I pulled my upper lip down over my teeth and, like a monk, took a vow never to open my mouth in that place except to eat. They were not going to pry it out of me.

The Lucan tapped, "Whut is yo' beef?"

I said, "My ass got caught with some grass."

The Lucan laughed again. "Some grass!" A raucous guffaw from a snake if there ever was one. "Where is yo' ass now?"

I told him I didn't know. It was true. I didn't know where my ass was, and if I had seen it in the state I was in, I doubt seriously if I'd have known it from a hole in the ground. "How many Lucans are here?" I asked.

He said, "Five percent of the population. Five percent of the people is righteous."

I rapped, "What about the others?"

He said, "Eighty five percent of the population is ignorant."

I asked, "And what about the ten percent?"

They were the guards, he said. They knew the truth and refused to reveal it, even to themselves. He said the Lucans were organized on the fact that the truth would make them free. It would stop the gold diggers arrayed against them.

"Gold diggers?" I tapped; I hadn't known about them. I had known about strippers and miners, but, with all my gold, I had never heard that term. "What are they?"

He said, "Is you a fool? The man is a gold digger, the warden is a gold digger, the guards, and mostly, your professionals. Is you got a dentist on the outside, is you had anything done to yo' teeth lately?"

I could hear his snake-of-a-head cock in anticipation. Where we come from people went to the dentist for one thing: to have gold put in their mouths. I stopped tapping, unsure of what was going to happen next, what to say to make him not want to look in my mouth. He tapped a laugh, then spelled out, "Naw. I remember you, you and yo' brother, y'all wuz some po' ass nigguhs; you ain't never had shit and wouldn't do nuthin' to git nuthin"

I didn't tell him I didn't think sticking up my grandmother was "doing something," even if she did follow "the Nazarene," as the Lucans called her professed lord.

He said, "You could have joined us; you wuz always too scared, you old weak-kneed nigger! Got caught wif some grass on his ass. Ain't that a scream." He tapped a guffaw. I had imagined him slapping his snaky knees when I heard him hiss sharply. Neither of us had heard the guard approach. I found out later the guard had opened up his gate and gone in on him. Tapping was strictly forbidden and any one caught doing it, I found out later, was severely punished. I never saw him again any of that first winter.

CHAPTER NINE

My ass was lost, I was a dog, but I still had my cock: my transformation had done nothing at all to diminish me in that concern, it having become as thin as a stalk of asparagus with the characteristically cone-shaped head of that vegetable, though instead of being green, it had acquired a fiery red color and had, as a result, become the only bright spot in a world of gray, the steel-gray of gunmetal and battleships and storms. When the man and that horde of characters descended on the Hudson, it had, clever bird, hidden in a fold of skin in my groin area, as not being of the Jewish faith but that of Hagar's children, these women had not had me circumcised, though I am almost certain this had less to do with what my old grandmother might have wanted and more with my mother's free thinking, as much as my grandmother might have seemed to enjoy chipping away at my manhood. Except for being marched (or rather driven) to the chow hall (or the mess) or taken to the laundry room and the showers twice a week (symbolic enough), those first few weeks we were left pretty much alone, to our own devices.

Just under my cock and precisely where my ass liked to sit when we were together, I had, tucked away, two rather large and wrinkled balls that, although I am sure they must have seen them, the guards had let me keep. I played with these often. My cock would pop out of its convenient sheath and join me in the game I taught it — or it taught me, I don't know which — where I would send the two balls flying towards it and it would slap them both back to me simultaneously, a sort of cricket: it being the batman, I being the hurler. What a hurlyburly! Whack! And how those two wrinkled spheres would fly, back and forth, back and forth, back and forth, back and forth, back and forth, back and forth, back and forth, back and forth, for hours. Back and forth, back and forth, back and forth, though I found that if we played the game for too long or too hard, my little cock would get so excited it would throw up. It usually did this all over me; all over my thighs, all over my hand, the hand I hurled with, a hand that became so sticky and wet we couldn't play much after that, as my hand would start to stick to the balls so they couldn't fly effectively unless I would quickly wash it, and cold water seemed always to have the effect of making me lose my concentration so I would not want to play anymore, the bird either. It would just lay there between my legs limp with exhaustion and in a slight state of shock from the cold. When this happened I would rub it down briskly with a coarse towel. This toweling usually had the effect of restoring its vigor, and it would want to play again and again.

Although we ate plenty of the gray, frostbitten potatoes, I lost a lot of weight during that period. Sometimes playing thusly, I would think about that girl with the pretty ass, but more often than not I just thought about my bird and the balls, and that was enough. I had more than enough to deal with right there without driving myself crazy thinking about some girl I hardly knew just because her ass was beautiful. I could not afford to think about her that much. Once while we were thusly engaged, that guard almost surprised us, but I heard—or maybe smelled, being a bloodhound my sense of smell had become acute—him coming and tucked them away between my legs, quickly zipping up my pants. I had barely done so when he passed. I must have looked guilty, because he smirked and asked me what I had been doing, though being the sorry, dog-eared creature that I was, I couldn't answer. He seemed to know though, and passed on, smirking. But if he had known, he should have confiscated both them and the bird right there on the spot, as leaving me my balls eventually proved to be the method of my escape, and after a manner of speaking, that guard's downfall.

Being interested in metals, I was eventually assigned to the machine shop. The machine shop—or the metal shop, as it was referred to—was in a corrugated tin shed across the big yard from the dormitory buildings and the mess hall where we slept our guarded sleep and ate our puffy meals. Every morning at six a.m. we would be awakened and marched to the mess hall for our sickly gray mess of powdered eggs that had to be consumed rapidly, as exactly ten minutes after we had been directed to a table and told to sit, we had to stand again, with whatever in the indented trays we had been expected to eat with our clumsy, round metal spoons (that for some reason reminded me of those my grandmother used to measure the buckwheat flour for her Easter cakes) and digest, finished to the last morsel, our trays to be stacked with the suspicious metal spoons on some carts under the watchful gray eye of a guard, after which we would line up for the forced march back to the Big Yard where we would be counted, told to queue up for our work assignments, and marched off to our shops. There was a Lucan in mine who recognized me right away. It seems they were all snakes of the type this one was, a coachwhip. I knew some sign language, and we managed to communicate though silence was a strict rule, he speaking it with his forked tongue, I somewhat clumsily with my nubby paws. I asked him how he had been transformed.

"By some cracker kid named Elvis," he said.

I said, "I was too."

He asked me if I liked it. I told him, "Hell, no." I told him I liked Moody. He said he liked James Moody too. He asked if I was ready to do anything about it. I asked what he meant by "doing something." I wanted to believe him.

Tongue undulating like the Atlantic Ocean, only in a sense more primordial than that, he signed, "Never mind that right now, if you is interested, when the time comes we go let you know." His tongue became suddenly becalmed. He added cryptically, "We will know you by your works."

Wanting to know more, I signed, "What works?"

"Just do it, gates," he said, and signaled that the guard was coming. In a series of silky motions he returned to his assignment, which seemed to me to be making donuts out of metal plates with a die press. He was also used as a drill, his cord-thin body made to spin at fantastic speeds, up to two thousand revolutions per minute! It turns out he was the best in the shop, drilling plates of incredible thickness in seconds. I was often made to wonder how he did it without getting dizzy, more, how he went through the plate without burning himself to a crisp, but he simply could, and that was why he was the best.

What "works" had he been alluding to? I sniffed dejectedly, a tear falling from a baleful eye. The guard strolled up like he'd all the time in the world. He stood looking down on me with his arms akimbo, a thick club dangling from a leather thong around his wrist. He let some time go by and said, 'What's your number, animal?"

I pointed to the number stitched into my shirt front.

He said, "You're some kind of bloodhound, ain't you?"

"Well," he said quite irritably, "what the fuck is a bloodhound doing in a machine shop? What the fuck is wrong with those people up there in that office? What kind of forced labor, I mean, labor force is this! You are just a dumb dog! You can't even push a broom, can you?"

Indigant and all this being new to me, I wagged my tail.

He said, "Oh, a friendly one, hey?" He looked at me appraisingly. "Well, I guess we can always tie a broom to your tail." Giving me a familiar pat on the head, he directed a gorilla that had been operating a hydraulic drill to tie a broom to my hapless tail. He said, "We'll give you a try anyway. See how you do. If you work out, who knows? You could have a career here." He sauntered back to his post, inspecting the progress of various workers as he passed.

So I was to be set to sweeping up the metal filings and bits of casting from the floor of the shop. What ignominy! This was the final indignity. Me, Lucius Apuleius cum Petronius whose beautiful black ass was John, an expert in metals and particularly the precious ones: gold, silver, copper; bronze and brass; chrome and bauxite, a specialist in stripping and casting scrap, fit to do no more than sweep the floor of the machine shop. Hearing this, I let out an involuntary howl that reverberated mournfully through the shop, bouncing off the grim gray walls of the building, as if resonating from the gray stone itself. I hadn't known I could sound like that, not to say, "sing." Immediately there were other, answering howls of pain and sadness. It was like being in the same room with Robert Johnson, Furry Lewis and Huddie Ledbetter all singing at once, as if a hell of a lot of people had been dogged by the man and could only find relief in this mournful howling, the baying of ten thousand bloodhounds. The guard's response was immediate. There were two buttons next to his post, a red one labeled PANIC and a black one labeled ALARM. He hit the red one hard. All hell broke loose. I was hit hard by a flying wedge of his cohorts, and when I came to, I was in a place black as hell must have been before the fires were lit. I was certainly as sore as hell. I can't tell you how long I lay there like that, sticky with my own blood, swollen and sore to the touch, with no medical attention because in that place it seemed not to be about time, as the poet once said, being completely dark and monotonous, impermeable, inaccessible even to the Mendelssohn. This black monotony was broken only by a pale reach of incandescence that seeped in under the door through a space between it and the floor used to slide a tray of tasteless gruel and tepid water through at various intervals without having to open the door, without having to provide contact. I tried counting between the intervals in an attempt at establishing a linear sense of reality, but would invariably slip out of consciousness and lose count. Beginning again, I found them so irregular as to be meaningless, incalculable, without rhythm. As at first I couldn't move, I lay there in my own excrement, my own urine, sore and stinking. Why didn't I just howl some more? They would have beaten me to death. That would have been better that this nothingness of a whipped dog, but I was too bruised to even howl about it. I experienced chills and a burning fever during which I imagined I was myself again, talking to that pretty girl with the beautiful ass and I could feel my cock wanting to play. I was hardly in any shape, but it kept slapping against my thighs with a wonderful life and will of its own in an attempt to reach the two balls so that instinctively, I began to play the game, at first half-heartedly, and then with more vigor, until I was completely into it. When the bird spat up, I lay there exhausted but the image of the girl was so strong in my head of a dog that the bird wanted to play again and again. I thought I was going to die: back and forth, back and forth, back and forth with the bird spitting up, me wiping it off and starting over again.

I thought I was going to die, but I didn't. It was a good exercise, good for my sore bones and bruised body, and the more I did it, the better I felt, until soon I felt strong enough to lap up the tasteless gruel and sip a bit of the tepid water, some of which I used to clean myself as best I could, and passed the time thusly, even happily, thinking about the girl and her beautiful ass playing with my bird. From time to time I thought about my own ass and what might have happened to it.

One day after who on earth knows how long except the captain, the warden, and whatever other authorities as were in possession of that information, the door was flung open and a rush of light came flooding in, almost blinding me. It was excruciating, and I almost howled with the pain, but remembering what had gotten me here, settled for a mere whimper. A guard said, "Come on out of there, dog, the captain wants to see you."

He marched me to the shower where he stood disinterestedly watching me clean myself, and then to the captain's office. "Being hauled before the captain," it was called. Rapping on the door with his stick, the guard said, "Captain, it's that dog."

The captain said, "Send him on in."

The guard said, "You heard him dog, go on."

I went in, unsure of what was going to happen to me now.

"Come on in, dog," the Captain said, "and shut the door behind you."

He was seated behind a huge mahogany desk with a green blotter, and what looked like a timetable and an hourglass on it. There were also a death's head pencil holder, a photograph of Adolph Hitler, Joseph Mengele and Rudolph Hess that was obviously taken back when they were buddies, in their school days (when they hung around the smoky cafes of Vienna, Munich and Berlin together, discussing the future of Germany and the world) and a file with what looked like my number on it. He pointed to the photograph and said, "Do you know the Warden? No? He is away now, but he will be back as sure as your grandmother's lord." He pointed to the file on his deck: my file. "Your grandmother was a Christian, wasn't she? I know you can't talk, though I understand you sure can howl and you can sign, can't you. All you niggers can. It's like dancing with you."

I made the sign of a Heirophant of the 23rd Degree and asked him why he referred to my grandmother in the past tense.

The captain looked at me with surprise. He said, "You mean you didn't know? Your grandmother is deceased. Dead. She and your mother. They died in an automobile accident. They were on their way up here to try and break you out, but they hit a tree at Cobb's Corners and the car immediately burst into flames. There was nothing left but their charred bodies and the black box that contained their plans. They were going to drive clear up to the next country, rent a helicopter, fly it on over here, and bust you out. Did you ever hear anything so primitive, so naive? It was insane, and wouldn't have worked anyway, what with you being down in the hole and all, how would they have found you? Finally, all they got for their plans was cremated. Is that Christian, cremation? I had thought it pagan, Hindu or something."

I felt sick. So my sweet if somewhat madcap mother and my old Jesus-quoting, Bible-thumping grandmother were dead. And they had died trying to rescue me. Strange. I could believe my beautiful mother might have tried something like that out of love for me, but my cane-cutting, switch-hitting grandmother? I had had her figured wrong all that time. It was a blow I all but staggered under the weight of, and a tear fell from my red eye of a hound. I felt like howling, but I didn't. I don't know why I didn't; perhaps it was the thought of my ass perhaps playing with that girl's one impossible day.

The captain said, "But that's not why I had you brought up here."

What else was there; how much more could I take?

The captain said, "I like the way you howl. You could be a good dog if you would let yourself, a good hunter. How about it?" He leaned forward, expectantly.

I signed, "What do you mean, Captain?"

"I want you to howl for me," he said. "You are not supposed to do it, and I'm not supposed to like it, but I do. You go to bat for me and there could be something in it for you, some extra rations, and not that questionable pigeon or that Riker's Island seagull that passes for poultry around here, but some real sirloin. How about it? I'm offering you a deal."

I could not believe my ears. He wanted me to be a dog for him, to howl; an offense I had nearly been killed for, and now he wanted me to do it for extra rations. "Would that be like squealing?" I asked.

He said, "Nah, that's different, squealing. That what pigs do. This here is baying. That's what dogs do. See, I like the truth. I like to hunt for it. I think you could help me with that. Plus, I just plain old like the way you do it, I swear I do. I like it so much more than that kid they are bringing out, that Elvis Presley. It's more authentic. How about it?"

I was stunned. In a sense, this man was asking me to sing for my supper. I signed, "You mean, be a canary?"

He said, "Naw, nigger, a dog! I want you to be a dog! What's wrong with that? You are a dog aren't you, or am I wrong? Look at yourself."

I looked down at my short coat.

"I know you are no canary. C'mon, canaries sing, you howl. That's what I want you to do. I want you to howl for me."

Okay, so he wasn't asking me to sing. He wanted me to howl for my supper, and what I'd get in return would be a few extra steaks, a few extra chops. It actually sounded good. Hell, as the man said, I was already a dog, wasn't I, it only remained to be seen what kind I was, as the saying goes, and hey, he wasn't saying I'd have to swing anyway. So what the hell; he wasn't blind, so I wouldn't have to be his eyes and as rheumy as mine had gotten in that hole, what could I see to tell him, or so I rationalized. I suppose I was just hungry and confused by the news of my beautiful mother and my old verse-spitting grandmother.

"You won't have to work."

It was a final clause, a bonus. "What would I have to do?" I signed.

He said, "Oh, you just take a walk around the big yard; you visit the shops; you stroll through the cell blocks and anything unusual you happen to see or hear out there, you just beat it on back here to me and sit yourself right down there and bay your big brown heart out the way all the really great bloodhounds did back in Africa for Mungo Park and old John Hawkins, you get my drift? That is some pedigree you got there. The nose you got on you, and though your hair is short, it is straight and reddish as if you had some white man in you, those big floppy ears, where'd you get 'em?

I told him I didn't know.

The captain said, "Hey, as good-looking as you are, I could have been your dad. Nah, I'm just joking. Actually I never fucked around with no darkies, though I do have a younger brother who liked to sow all his oats wild, here and there and everywhere, and I got a cousin, say, is your name actually Weber?"

Burning with shame over this familiarity with my mother's memory, I signed that he had my files and could see what my name was.

"Anyway," he said, "you are my kind of dog. How about it?"

I said, "I need a chance to think." I hadn't noticed it before, but there was no Mendelssohn here.

"No thinking," he said. "I am not going to pay you to think, and I will do all of that. Do you understand? If you do not, you can go right back to that hole and stink."

That stinking hole! The bird was nice, but I had the bird anyway.

I thought about my mother and grandmother, who had died for me as surely as her Lord had done so for her. I had deep thoughts about my ass. I signed, "And what about my ass?"

The captain looked at me shrewdly. "Nigger," he said, "you sure drive a hard bargain." He took a puff of the cigar and let out a cloud of evil-smelling smoke. "Okay," he said, "if you are really good, I will let you see your goddamn ass. I have never at all seen anything like it, how you niggers love your asses."

I signed that if we didn't love our own asses, who would?

"You had better not get too smart, too big for your balls!" He grinned, leering knowingly, his mouth open, fat cigar stuck obscenely to his thick lower lip like a turd.

The prospect of seeing my ass was the final push: being reunited with my ass was just too much. I signed that I'd sign.

"Good," the captain said, and pulling a blank sheet of foolscap and an inkpad from his desk, he pushed them toward me. He said, "Sign here."

Not without some trepidation I stuck a large, nubby paw into the inkpad and pressed it on the foolscap. He snatched it eagerly, inspecting it. "Hey," he exclaimed, "this ain't half bad. I'll tell you what, I will assign you nominally to the print shop. There are a couple of rats over there I want you to meet and get together with, maybe come up with a design for your project. You will still have the run of the place, but I want you to get me on something, and I want you to get me real clear, do you hear me?"

"What?" I signed.

He said, "It's just art, and you don't have to think about it too much. The more you think about it, the more trouble you're gonna get into, do you understand?"

I signed that I did, though, in point of fact, I did not. I stole a glance at the print. It looked good even to my rheumy eyes. That was how I started making prints. I asked how soon I could see my ass, my little burro.

The captain said, "Right away," and pressed what must have been a button under the surface of the desk. A guard appeared. The captain said, "Bring his ass on up here."

The guard disappeared, returning about ten minutes later with my ass in tow. I was overjoyed. O my poor, sweet little ass; it looked sorrier that I did.

That night, back in my cell sleeping my guarded sleep of a convicted dog, I dreamt about my mother and grandmother. It seemed they were trying to tell me something but it was in a language I couldn't understand, as I hadn't the right ears; grandmother pinned to a huge golden crucifix, my mother seeming to pray to her, to beseech her for her forgiveness when it was apparent I didn't understand. I had the ears of an ass and the mouth of the bell of a trumpet. I grew more mouths: a cornet and a flugelhorn that all had mutes around which no sound could be produced, so that the more I blew, the bigger and more round my cheeks and neck got until my embouchure was finally as huge and swollen as Dizzy Gillespie's, and the bells shot straight up to my grandmother, but there was yet nothing coming out of any of them that she could hear; she just kept shaking her head as if to say, "No! No!" My mother alternately pointing to the cross and praying, as if my grandmother were the god crucified by her mother's desire to make her more perfect, more acceptable in her own eyes. My grandmother would fall down from the cross and the captain would nail her up again, her ears, nose and lips pierced by a soldier's lance, or was it the captain my mother pointed to, my grandmother shaking her head, "No! No!" Oh, mother, I am trying to say, why hast thou forsaken me, and et tu, Granny, but it comes out blues: "Aunt Hagar's Blues," or "Bessie's Blues" or "Billie's Blues" or "Blues for Mr. Day" or "Blues for Mr. Knight" or "Blues for Blind Lemon" or "Blues for You," but my crucified grandmother and my beautiful mother can't hear me because of the mutes in the trinity of my bells and if I am playing the blues and nobody hears me, does it mean I am playing or not playing, am I serious or what; and if they speak to me, my imploring, bereaving mother and my grandmother, and I can't understand them as I never could, is it because I have the ears of an ass and three mute mouths made of brass or is it because my grandmother has no ears that aren't pierced through with the lance of proverbs from the Old Testament because, as everybody knew, she much preferred gospel? Later I dreamt of that girl again, the one with that pretty little ass, and she was a leprechaun who needed some gold in her pot and a new rainbow as someone had stolen all the gold from her little pot with the result that her little rainbow had gone gray, and I said, "Baby, when I get out of here," I said, "if I ever do, I will get you some gold. Do you believe? Do you hear?" And she said, "Yes," and laughed. I could feel my familiar cock growing restless, but I did not play with it, not in the dream, because she showed me her delightful little burro and asked me if I liked her little burro, and I said, "Yes, yes, yes," delighted she would show me her wonderful little ass. "Well then," she said, waving me toward them, "why don't you come play with it," and me, pushed further and further away from her the more I tried to move in her direction and I woke up with my cock lively and wanting to play the game.

CHAPTER TEN

The Big Yard, hemmed in on four sides by the great, gray wall with its six turrets and machine-guns, each manned by a rifle-toting guard, and its bleachers where the convicts sat watching the games they played on each other, or sat gambling, or sat simple-mindedly watching the gray smoke of their cigarettes curl skyward, was dominated by a large softball diamond, while the gray wall itself was divided into smaller areas of privilege where more games were played on each other, the gambling went on every day for years; for shirts, for socks, for cigarettes, for shoes, for sweaters, for cans of tuna fish, for lives. The plotting that went on here was to determine who was who in the hierarchy of the prison, a hierarchy dominated by those among these wretched animals who by dint of the sharpened spoons they managed to hide in their mouths, ruled. This was nothing more or less than natural selection at work: the big cats were first, being predators; next came the poisoners, and after, the stingers. The Lucans were not on top, being snakes, though the place was full of them. Lions, tigers, and the wolves were on top, and they preyed on the sheep. The Lucans had to make do with small rodents scurrying desperately around the diamonds, the scared, defenseless rabbits. This was what I was told not long after my impressment into the captain's service by a Lucan that recognized me, and they were resentful that the predators were walking away with the big game; the Lucans wanted more of the action, which translated to having more wall space. There were too many of them to be kept to the Great Diamond, as the softball field was called. I asked if a lot of them weren't diamondbacks. The Lucan said they weren't all diamondbacks, some had muscle, like anacondas, for example. They were not all poisoners, and they meant to take more, at least half the privileged areas along the wall that were called courts that had been given to them by Divine Right, the Lucan complained. They were ready to show those cats a thing or two, they had people who could spit in a lion's eye at twelve feet and blind him. The Lucan from the machine shop showed me a shiv he had secured in his mouth, a special one he had made for

throwing that was so balanced its point could be driven home to someone's heart from clear across the Big Yard.

I had to ask the point of the whole thing.

"Steel," he said. It was as hard as that. Set in stone.

A big cat told me I should definitely stay away from the snakes. He
said they were exactly what they ate: rats, rabbits. He went on to say
they were no more than second-tier boys and could never be anything
else. He said as far as I was concerned, the only thing the cats had
against dogs was they hung around the man too much. He had rheumy
eyes with which he stared hard into my rheumy eyes. This was my arena.

The captain's face was not flushed with broken capillaries for nothing; he liked his double shot of whiskey, and he ran the place with the
discipline of a drunk. He was a paranoiac who was obsessed and his ob-
session was the coons. It was rumored he had one as a houseboy and
chauffer once that had, on his release, run off with the captain's wife
and his nineteen-year-old daughter, as pretty a blonde as anyone in Ul-
tima Thule would want to see. He hated them, and would pump me
daily for anything I might have on them: what coon was up to what,
where, and at what moment. His biggest fear was that one of "them"
would escape from there with his other daughter: a raven-haired, fourteen-year-old whose beauty was said to be a drug; it was rumored that
she even liked them. It was said this fourteen-year-old whose beauty
was like a drug was named, of all things, Drusilla, 'Silla for short, and
Dru' because she was in the habit of drawing up the drug of her beauty
that was supplied by the rumors circulating among the convicts into
her young, healthy veins in large doses, and that every day at a certain
time she stood at the window of her little room in a turret over the Big
House with her long, black, wavy tresses like Rapunzel's, waiting for
someone, anyone with enough conviction to say, "Rapunzel, Rapunzel,
let down your hair," like in the fairy tale so she could let down her hair,
or like a raven-haired Juliet waiting for her con coon of a Romeo to
find his fate with her, to seal it with a forbidden, heady kiss from the
Shakespeare in the prison library. "What are them goddamned coons
up to today?" he would say, focusing his steel-gray eyes on my snout of
a forlorn dog while pouring himself a stiff one, and each morning or
each week I would say, "I don't know, Boss."

"What do you mean," he would say, "you don't know?"

"It's hard to tell," I would say.

Year in and year out, season after season, his retort would be,
"What in the hell do you mean, 'It's hard to tell'? How much am I
paying you?"

"What, three, four steaks a week?"

"Six," the captain would say, hurriedly tossing down another. "Six. I pay you six steaks a week. Once a month, prime rib."

I took a chance once and said, "But sometimes the ribs are fatty."

He had me thrown back in the hole, though having decided for whatever reason he couldn't do without me, soon had me hauled out and back before him. "What do you mean, 'hard to tell?' You are a bloodhound and should know all about coon business, their sharp accents as if they had spoons hidden in their mouths and slick talk for the unwary, shouldn't you?"

"Boss, I don't know." (I could act and accent like a coon even signing.) "These coons is so mixed up these days I swear it is gittin' harder an' harder to even tell who they is with all this race mixin' goin' on."

The captain winced. He took a drink of his whiskey and said, " Don't remind me." His look was forlorn.

"I'm going to listen out for it carefully, Boss! Coon business ... there must be some record of it out there."

He looked at me with renewed interest. "You will, Lucius?"

He had called me Lucius! Imagine that! The whiskey made him see me, and not a number!

The captain said, "No, really," he began to blubber, "with that reddish-brown hair you have, you could almost be my son. And your nose is so sensitive! He felt his own blood-shot organ as if by way of comparison. He flattered himself if he thought we looked anything alike at all. The truth was, the captain looked worse than a broke-dick dog. "Nigger," he said, suddenly his vicious self again, this creature of his own caprice. "have you heard the one about the farmer's daughters?"

Wary of a trap and wanting to appear as naive as possible, I said no, but I was pretty sure I had heard them all.

He said, "Then you better listen and you better listen good: Looking for a motel, a traveling salesman made a wrong turn off a main road late one night and had come to a farmhouse. Knocking on the door, he asked the farmer who appeared if there was a motel in the vicinity.

"The farmer said, 'Motel? Not for a hundred miles.' He asked the salesman where he was headed for, and when the salesman told him, said the younger man must have made a wrong turn somewhere. The salesman looked somewhat distraught, so the farmer, a kindly man if somewhat mistrustful of strangers, told the salesman he might pass the night there as he'd an extra room; the only problem being he had three impressionable daughters he did not want the salesman fooling around with, so he would have to put a shotgun in the salesman's bed that would go off if the salesman moved, to insure against any hanky-panky.

The salesman said that was alright with him, he just wanted to sleep, and he would be on his way in the morning, at first light. This arrangement being made, the salesman was nearly asleep when he was awakened by a 'Psst!' He was quite surprised to see the farmer's daughter lifting up her dress underneath which she wore no panties and pointing to her crotch. In somewhat of a panic he pointed frantically to the shotgun. 'Oh pshaw,' she said, 'it ain't loaded,' and without the slightest hesitation and not the slightest blush, climbed into bed with the startled salesman, where they made violently passionate love, after which the girl left, her finger to her lips. The salesman had no sooner got to sleep again when he was awakened by another 'Psst!' much like the first, though more husky. It was the farmer's middle daughter, pointing to his prick. Surprised again, he pointed to the shotgun. 'Oh Pshaw,' the girl said coquettishly, 'it's not loaded!' and climbed into bed with him where they made mad love right away, after which the young woman kissed him endearingly and left. Exhausted, the salesman soon fell asleep again but after only a short time was awakened by a third 'Psst!' Reluctantly, the salesman pulled himself awake. Sure enough, it was the farmer's eldest daughter, a ravishing beauty if ever there was one, and she was pointing to his prick. 'What the hell,' said the salesman, pointing wearily and almost by rote to the shotgun. 'Oh pshaw,' the farmer's eldest daughter said eagerly, 'it ain't loaded,' and boldly and purposefully crawled into bed with the salesman where they had their way with each other lovingly after which the girl gave the salesman the lightest, sweetest kiss on the cheek and left, whereupon the salesman fell again into a somewhat troubled, though exhausted sleep, the kind of sleep sure to produce a maelstrom of dreams. To be sure, after a short while the young man was awakened by a fourth 'Psst!' this time from the farmer's wife who was pointing to his genitals. It was quite impossible to believe that such a gorgeous, youthful woman could have three grown daughters, but the salesman, thoroughly drawn from both his trip and his earlier activities was compelled to say, 'Please, lady, give me a break!' Shocked, the farmer's wife fled the room crying. Not a moment later, the farmer himself, quite agitated, appeared. 'Young Man, young man," he shouted, 'Wake up now! Haven't I,' he shouted, "given you of my hospitality and shown you great respect?' Startled and thoroughly ashamed of himself, the young man was forced to concede that he had. The farmer continued, shouting, 'Well, for me, I am thoroughly aggrieved and insulted! First you fuck my youngest daughter, then you fuck my middle daughter and my eldest daughter, after which you refuse to fuck my wife! What's up with that!?' 'I'm terribly sorry, sir,' the salesman said, 'to have insulted your wife, but after all of that,' he continued pointing to his groin, 'it wasn't loaded.' The farmer said, 'Well this is!' and producing a pistol, shot the salesman dead.

The captain said, "I hope you get what I'm driving at."

"I am sorry," I signaled, "but I am not quite getting the connection except to say that your, your ..."

The captain said, "Anecdote."

"anecdote was rife with violence and passion."

"Does that tell you anything?"

Confused, I said, "I'm not sure."

The captain said, "Nigger, you can't be that stupid. I am telling you this because it's my tradition. I do not like my hospitality abused!"

I would have preferred not to have had to suffer his hospitality at all, but I couldn't tell him that.

He went on: "I suppose you have heard I have a daughter."

I said quickly I had not.

He looked grateful—relieved even—and said, "Well, I do. And I want you to help me keep those coons away from her. I do not want them filling her up with dope about how beautiful she is, because she is not. My other daughter was the only beautiful one. A blonde with a capital B. The Aryan ideal. This one is raven-haired, but she is all I've got left. I would like to keep her safe and sound until a good marriage can be made for her, preferably with a baron, a land baron, so one day she can have her own prison and some nice kids she can keep there for the future. I cannot do it alone. It's rough out there. It's getting rougher all the time." He started to blubber again, and took another drink. I felt like I needed one. He said, "Can I count on you; will you help me do this?"

"I will surely do my best, Boss, I will try."

The captain gave me a look that pierced me clear to my humanity. "No, no," he said. "Please, do it for me, please!"

"Okay, Captain," I said resignedly, "I will. I will give it my best shot."

"Oh thank you, thank you," he said. "Thank you! Give me your paw on it. Let's shake."

It was a poignant picture and a wonderful photo opportunity; the very human captain shaking with a dog, his dog, after which he threw me a bloody piece of sirloin that I devoured quickly, greedily. Taking full advantage of this opportunity, I again asked about my ass, having no idea—though I had spoken with it—where it was being kept.

The captain said, "You don't have to worry so much about that. The State is taking good care of it. Do I look like a careless person to you?"

"But, but where is it being kept?" I asked.

"That is a secret," the captain said slyly. "It's insurance. Keep your ass from running away. Having to send the paddyrollers after it.

The rats in the print shop were a set-up, having been instructed to give me information just to see if I would pass it on to the captain, but they sold to the highest bidder, for in this game of predator and preyed-upon, the very lives of these rats were at stake. Never very big (except in the case of the dull and defenseless capybara), always mangy and hungry, always shifty-eyed, the rats were at the very bottom of the prison hierarchy, for, as everybody knew, they would turn on you and squeal in a moment, hurt you bad if there were more of them than you, and there almost always were, for they usually traveled in packs. They were, in point of fact, the most ubiquitous of all the prison population. Indeed, it was they who constantly scurried around the diamond as though on a wheel that had been compressed on four sides into a lop-sided square, and who could be heard throughout the big yard and the cell blocks and all the shops (wherever it was permitted) squealing in their intermittent, high-pitched whistles under the Mendelsohn, the whistles, the squeals that their lives depended on, but which, conversely, also placed them at high risk of discovery. Catching and killing them was a favorite sport of the Lucans, who, due to the ubiquity of the rats, were in a ratio proportionate to their numbers. Lucans were always up to something, and the rats were always squealing on them with the re-sult that their tiny skeletons and pelts littered the big yard and the blocks where the Lucans devoured and regurgitated them. The place was washed down regularly so it would not stink of their feral fetid odor, the odor most given off when they squealed; and now here were two of them telling me some monkey was fucking the captain's daughter and some gorilla was feeding her a lot of dope about how pretty she was. How I knew it was a set-up was this: the captain had no younger daughter; he had only the one; this one was no more than a figment of his besotted imagination, a compensation for the loss of his actual child. Who told me this was the Lucan from the machine shop. He said he didn't know ex-actly what kind of game I was playing, but was sure I was not as stupid as I appeared to be, being the captain's runner and all; not to say "dog." He said he knew I was wondering how he knew all of this, but Lucans were everywhere people least expected them to be: in the ground under their feet, in the ducts of their offices, in their very hearts and souls.

The rats squealed their cheap gossip in unison. It was all I could do to keep from laughing in their faces. This cheap P.R. ploy, this design-ing chatter; their sharp beady eyes dulled by double-dealing.

"And the coons," I asked. "What about the coons?"

I was surprised by their glibness, their readiness to lie: "Coons? That girl ain't got no time for coons, that gorilla is on her back and that monkey has got her going! Tell that to the captain."

Sauntering over to the inkpots, I grabbed one, pulled a sheet of paper from a nearby stack, and made a print of the rats' behavior, an impression that would last forever. The next day one of them was found dead, his throat cut with a spoon. The other one, alone in the shop now, was more furtive than ever. "Tell this to the captain," he said, "There is big doin's goin' on."

"What sort of doin's," I asked, not really wanting to be seen talking to him.

He said he didn't know exactly, he would try to let me know later.

Two days after that he was found dead as well, his throat cut; the spoon that had been used to do it perfectly balanced, a throwing spoon sent so accurately it had sliced through his carotid, nearly severing his rodent head from his furry neck. This was too much like a Raymond Chandler mystery: someone was getting rid of the squealers and I had a good idea who it was; all I had to do was follow the plot, the grid, the dots, stick to it carefully and I'd have a whole book about it, but it was not going to be easy; there was a dark turn of mind at work here: voodoo? Almost as if to prove it might have been, I thought I saw, across the big yard, a gorilla strolling with what looked like a raven-haired beauty. The daughter? Was she a figment of my imagination or the captain's? What was real, and what was not? I seemed to see a little monkey on the poor girl's back: a gray monkey, but a monkey to be sure; and the captain was worried about coons. What was clear through the gray mist of that fall morning was that they were the least of his worries. Everything seemed normal in the shops; they hummed with their usual activity; the laundry went out on time, the cobblers repaired what they could of the inmate's worn soles, the cooks turned out their usual soufflés of gray, frostbitten potatoes from the winter before, but added to the usual grayness of the big yard with its great diamond was an aura of ominousness, of impending calamity. For one thing, the Mendelsohn was speeded up as if a record made to turn at 45 revolutions per minute had been suddenly put at 78, with the result that everything seemed jumpy, everybody: the inmates, the guards, the captain. He went through his usual bit about the coons.

I said, "Captain, I don't think it's the coons."

The coons had been a catch-all, a scapegoat for his personal problems. There was a look of abject fear on his face. "Not the coons, not the coons? What do you mean, you stupid cur, it's not the coons; it's always the coons! If it were not for them there would never have been such a thing as crime, and I would be out of a job; but I am not out of a job, am I? Look at me; I'm the captain, aren't I? So it must be them, it must!" His voice was tinged with a pink hysteria that contrasted strangely with the gray. "Oh god," he said racing for and pouring himself a drink, "I wish the warden were back. He would know what to do about all of this for sure!" He drained his glass and quickly poured himself another, downing that shakily.

I decided to take advantage of this turn: "Captain," I said, "begging your pardon, but what about my ass? If I could be more in touch with it—"

A guard burst in at that moment. "Captain, Captain," he said, "there is trouble in the big yard! A guard has been killed. Others have been taken hostage. There was no alarm, because they said if one was sounded they would kill the others!"

The captain's face turned gray, then white. "Who's involved?"

"I don't know, Captain—" the guard said, "at least one big cat is in it, and, I believe, some snakes! The Lucans, they call themselves."

I wondered if there was one in the ducts now, listening. I seemed to hear, over the frantic, speeded-up Mendelsohn, a slithering sound, like hissing from a well-worn record.

The captain said, "What about my daughter?"

The man gave the captain a startled look. "Sir, your daughter?"

"Yes you fool, my daughter. Is she safe?"

"Sir, you don't have a daughter, at least not since I've been here, and that's been over five years ..."

"I don't, I don't have a daughter?"

"No sir."

So it was true. The captain did not have a daughter. Then who—or what—was that apparition I saw in the big yard with the gorilla, and the monkey on her back? The captain began to sob. "They have taken my child; what do they want?"

The guard looked worried. "They have not presented any demands as of yet beyond our not sounding the alarm, not contacting the State Police, the Governor or the National Guard. We don't know what they want."

"Why don't they stop playing that music!"

"You ordered it, sir!"

"Well, now I'm ordering them to stop it!"

"Sir, I don't believe they will. They say they are not taking orders from you, sir."

The captain turned an apoplectic red: "What! Not taking any more orders from me? Well, who is taking the orders! Suppose I want something to eat; suppose I need some liquor; some fine wine for the governor, because," he said, pointing to me, "you can bet his sweet ass His Excellency will be here when he hears about this—but wait, wait, I could lose my job—wait, we'll take care of this ourselves. See what they want."

A second guard came running in, quite out of breath. "Captain, Captain, they want you to send out the dog!"

"The dog?"

The guard caught his breath. "Yes, Sir, the dog! They want you to send out the dog! They have already killed Schmidt! They say they will kill the others if you don't send out the dog!"

The captain said, "Huh, Schmidt. The others. They got my daughter already, what can the others matter? Tell them I'll give them the dog all right, only it is gonna be as dead as Schmidt and the rest of them. A dead dog, that's what they're gonna get! You tell them that, you hear?" He had gotten up and started towards me in a drunken rage, a Mauser in his ham fist.

"Wait, Captain," I signed, desperate.

He leveled the Mauser at my chest, over where my heart was, the heart of a dog. "Wait? Wait for what, you miserable cur. Say your prayers, dog!" It was a desperate move, but then, I was desperate. "Captain," I signed, "Captain, I have seen your daughter!"

The effect of those words on the captain was immediate: dragging his monstrous pear-shaped bulk over to me, he grabbed me by my lapels, the muzzle of the Mauser dangling towards my genitals. "My daughter," he said imploringly, "you have seen my daughter? Where did you see such a thing; tell me!" He dropped the gun. I kicked it away, but he didn't notice. "Where!"

I said, "In the big yard." Where else? That's what the bastard thought. I was telling him what he wanted to hear. He had me sent to the big yard under a white flag of truce.

There was fighting everywhere in that place. It was a free-for-all in which any and all grudges were being addressed now that the guards in their towers, under orders not to shoot, could only stand helplessly by, watching the action below. A Lucan met me at the gate. "Be careful, Sir," he said, handing me a helmet, "you could get hit, mushroomed. We can't control the snipers." Threading through what he said was a minefield, we made our way to a tarp set up behind the bleachers as a sort of command post. The body of a large capybara, stiff with rigor mortis and bloated with maggots, lay outside. Inside, the Lucan from the machine shop appeared to be in charge as a host of them slithered in and out with messages to and from him. The group surrounding him made way for us as I was brought up. He saluted, and greeted me bravely.

"How you doin', brotha," he said. "Salaam-alaikum. We are not Muslims, though we do give the greeting. We just leave the 'as' out."

"The ass?" I said hoping for some word on the condition of my own.

"No, not the 'ass,'" he said, allowing himself a fanged grin, "the 'as,' as in the beginning. We intend to change that."

"The 'as'? To what?" I asked.

"Because," he said, "that is our objective."

I didn't get it. "Because" was a qualification of "why." He sounded more than a bit like the Red Queen. "I admire the Red Queen," he said, seeming to divine my thought.

Perplexed, I asked, "Why 'because'?"

He said, "Because they wanted to keep that capybara out there. The big cats wanted it, the jackals wanted it, the wolves wanted it, the hyenas wanted it, the grizzlies wanted it."

He said my observation was quite correct. The scavengers and predators had joined together. This had never happened before, and was why they were having a bit of a problem.

I said, "But they are fighting each other!"

He allowed himself the fanged grin again. "That's the way they fight. That's why we think we can beat them."

I looked at the bloated body of the capybara. The big cats might have wanted it, the jackals might have wanted it, the wolves might have wanted it, the Lucans might have wanted it, but it looked like the maggots had it. Again, the Lucan seemed to divine my thought. "We can take care of the maggots," he said.

I had never seen the type of snakes they were dealing with. The capybara was a six-footer, and bloated.

He said, "The big boys are in on this: the boas, the anacondas. Don't you understand? We're going against the established order. That out there is the established order! We are fighting against fascism."

I looked out at the various groups fighting each other and among themselves. It was true the Lucans alone seemed to have a sense of purpose, fighting as a unit; as one; never mind that as big and bloated as the huge rodent was, it could make a meal for only one large snake; that was if the maggots didn't finish it off first. I felt a profound sense of disconsolation. Where was my ass in all of this? I asked him the question that was most on my mind: did he see my ass in any of this, and if so, where exactly?

He looked at me cooly, his eyes half-lidded, almost concealing the gray film of rheum. "Your ass," he said appraisingly. He suddenly became tired and looked away, at the fighting that was raging outside.

"Your ass is out there somewhere," he said wearily, "in the big yard."

"Thanks for the information," I said, unable to keep the sarcasm out of my signing.

"You're blaming me? Don't blame me," he said, and "don't blame us. We didn't transform you, we didn't send you up here, and we certainly did not separate you from your ass. You seem to be forgetting that. We are not the perpetrators here, we are the victims of others' encroachments. We are addressing that. We want what is ours, and we are not letting any absurdist get in the way of that goal. You want your ass back? Well, I am afraid you are going to have to bite the bullet."

There were bullets flying everywhere. Was he asking me to bite one of those? They weren't exactly protein. A mortar went off somewhere to our left. A few seconds later a shell burst through the tarp, creating a hole through which we could see daylight, but not doing much more damage. It was full of sharpened spoons. Lucan spoons. The fire was either misdirected, or the front had suddenly fragmented further.

"Who is on that mortar there; whose position is that?" the Lucan demanded.

Another sputtered out a name like "Arnold, Benedict Arnold." The Lucan in command said, "Well, tell that bastard to redirect fire! Tell him to get his goddamn aim straight." Another shell filled with sharpened spoons—Lucan spoons—came crashing through the tarp. This time two of the Lucans went down, spoons sticking out of them like quills on a porcupine. The commander, whose name it turned out was Luke, said, "Something stinks and it is not this capybara. Arnold knows we are here, and he knows goddamned well how to count, to allow for windage." A Lucan slithered in and confirmed Luke's suspicion. A sharpened spoon in his back had all but cut him in two. "Arnold's turned," he gasped, and died.

Luke was visibly shaken. "Boys," he said to those gathered around, "we are in worse shape than we had thought. Arnold's gone over. But to who?" he mused.

Another shell came crashing through the tarp, taking two more Lucans down. Some predators were advancing on our position from the direction of the mess hall on the right.

I said, "Why don't you just give up the rat?"

"It's much too late for that now," Luke said. "Those bastards are certainly not going to bargain."

He had hardly gotten the words out of his mouth when who—or what—should come staggering in looking dazed but my sorry ass. I was overjoyed.

Luke said, "Sorry brothers, but every tub has got to stand on its own," and to me: "Well, are you coming?"

I only barely had time to bark before he went into his high-speed drill. Grabbing my ass, I stepped into a vortex of concrete and blackness behind him.

Where we came out was in a copse of gray wood some five hundred feet or so beyond the wall. There we split up; the coachwhip going his way, my ass and I, our own.

CHAPTER ELEVEN

Of course, there was nowhere to go but back to the Hudson. We had been away some years, but there it was, squat and thick as a tank, doors yet flung open as wide as when those kidnappers had dragged us out and hauled us off kicking and screaming or, at least, howling and braying. What struck me immediately and most about it was how incredibly green it was, and it took my eyes some time to get used to it; not much else was the same. It had been stripped as I had once stripped the junkyard itself; the radio was gone, and the wire that had conveyed the miracle of jazz through the speaker and to my ears was gone, as was the speaker itself. The seats were gone too, and what had been the well was just a hole in the floor. The piping had been pilfered along with the gold I had hidden under the hood under what had been the battery, and in the trunk, and under the interior overhead light, and the precious and semi-precious stones, the lapis lazuli. Whatever I had left was in my teeth; that around my neck and in my ears and through my nose gone long ago, confiscated.*

Still I was glad to be back, the rusted floor another spot of color I could enjoy once I became used to it. Needless to say, I was glad to have my ass back. The problem was, what was I going to do now? I was yet a dog, a state of being I had no idea of how to function in the world in, as having been remanded by the State immediately after my transformation, I had always been fed and told what to do by what were, in effect, my masters. Now I was out on my own, and hunted by at least another agency, though as I soon found, there were so many stray dogs in the city I would not stand out particularly, and where people were soon used to seeing my ass, even on Forty-Second Street, hustling change for the movies or whatever. Mine was just another ass in a great peep show; albeit a black one. Every once in a while someone or other would feed me and try to seduce me into going home with them but I always shied away from these enticements, preferring a little act with

*Years later, some of this would appear on "Mr. T"

my donkey; my ass braying and dancing, I baying and dancing, to raise change. We were like Freddy Keppard or Louie Armstrong, with a little Thelonius Monk thrown in to appease the modernists. Reduced to the state of a lower animal myself, I could understand the animal better than ever, and we made the changes easily; someone could call out any tune in any key at all, and immediately we were on it. I was definitely an entertainer. The more people clapped, the more I would buck and dance and bay, though the truth was, they didn't give us very much money; more than the penny a pound I had gotten for stripping the copper, but what with the way inflation had risen during our stay in prison, you had to say we were barely nickel and diming it; a dollar was rare, and nothing cost a penny anymore. Still, we were making music. At any rate, I must say I did not miss the Mendelsohn, and it was not long after making our escape that I heard some incredibly wonderful news: that place had imploded on itself. There were no known survivors. At least I was not being pursued from that quarter though I could not help thinking I would now never know whether or not the Captain did indeed have a daughter. Actually, given her reputation and all, it would have been much better for him if he had not.

In point of fact, everybody on Forty-Second Street was some kind of whore: my ass and I sold our music; the concessionaires nestled among the movie houses sold every kind of flesh. If I had had to be transformed, I was glad it was into a dog and not a pig or a cow or a chicken or a fish, for those were offered everywhere in sausages, in patties, in breasts and thighs; and in the movie houses that littered the street themselves from Sixth Avenue to Eighth with their marquees as brightly lit as Luna Park, everybody loved a pig or a cow or a chicken or a fish for all the wrong reasons. Everybody on The Street was after a piece of the action, chasing it down, consuming it with fried potatoes when they had caught some of it, washing it down with a fifteen-cent soft drink or a twenty-cent beer. Oranges were sucked into little round receptacles, or square ones like heads with mouths wide open, waiting. There was so much trash it could hardly be contained, and it spilled out of the receptacles onto the street at every step. The pavement was painted, sticky with the jism of the residue of countless paper cups of coffee and Coca-Cola and Pepsi-Cola and orange and grape soda and pina colada and papaya, nature's miracle aid to digestion. It was a Wall Street of the senses, and night and day brokers strode up and down through this jism that was the detritus of their trade in their shiny purple sheath dress or their red faille miniskirts with red six-inch heels, always the mavens of fashion; or they stood arms akimbo under their fake fur coats, hips thrust forward in attitudes of studied insouciance, calling, cajoling.

John Farris

I did not like The Street much and when we had finished our act, my little ass and I, and had gotten enough change for a pattie and some hay or some grass, we would head back to the Hudson to sleep or, if we weren't too exhausted, work out our little routine for the next day. And James Moody? I was no closer to him than I was before, as dogs were certainly barred from the clubs. That Elvis Presley character had definitely fucked me up, and I realized that if I was ever going to get to Moody, I was going to have to get past him. He said I was "nuthin' but a hound dog," and I had immediately become one. Was that even relevant? What was the key to all of this? It wasn't F sharp, it wasn't in G, that was bobby-soxer shit, it wasn't in G flat; it had to be in E or A, or C, or some flat in this sprawling city. In order to find it I was going to have to B sharp, and the problem with that was there was none, at least in the mode I was in. I would have to invent the god-damn thing. My ass and I would have to explore all the intervals. We would have to come up with what might very well be a new pitch: a mi-crotonic. It seemed to be working. We would be on The Street play-ing some number and someone would invariably say, "Say, who is that ass over there, that one on the trumpet?" and someone would invari-ably say, "That ass over there, you mean the one on the trumpet? Why, that's John!" and someone else would say, "The singer? I don't know. I don't know the singer's name, but he is a dog for true, ain't he?" and maybe they would toss me a nickel or a dime, and maybe they would chase us away, in which case we would find ourselves another spot, set up, and go through our routine all over again. If the money wasn't fab-ulous, the exercise was great. If I was ever going to be natural again, I was going to have to find that key. Once a gang of Irish kids— I guess from nearby Hell's Kitchen—kicked my ass, but when I snapped at them, they ran away. The street was teaching me one thing if no other: if I was going to survive, I would have to put plenty of bite in my bark. My ass and I toughened up quite a bit, and soon those kids in that neighborhood learned not to fuck with us.

A couple of girls on The Street actually liked us and would pat my ass or allow me to lick them. They were good customers, and when I would see them coming, I would go into something special, like Moody's "Lover's Conversation." My ass would get real loose and I would throw an extra lick or two in there just for them. It wasn't long before they were making requests like, "Lover Man," and "Our De-light," or "Pent-up House," the last which I could scat pretty good, being so pent up myself.

One day as we were wrapping it up, these two appeared and re-quested "Woody'n You," and, after, "Valse Hot." With the chops I had now acquired, I could do a pretty good job of imitating the young Sonny Rollins, and my ass could almost approximate the brilliant though not long for this world Clifford Brown. When we finished the last number, one of the girls said, "Hey, why don't you come home with us?"

The other one said, "Yeah, we don't know about your ass, but we sure do like you!"

Asking them if they understood, and receiving a "solid," as they called it, I signed, "Fuck you, I don't go anywhere without my ass and it doesn't go anywhere without me."

The one whose name turned out to be Woody said, "Hey, don't get sore about it; it's just that we live in a hotel, and we don't know how your ass would look going in there."

I signed, "Well, don't make my ass sore and I won't be. If you can't accomodate him, hey, what can you do for me?" I had, by now, learned to be just that cold; to say what I meant, and to mean exactly what I said.

"Okay, Pops," the other said giggling, "like Woody said, 'Don't get sore!' We will see what we can do to accommodate the both of you, hey, Woody?"

Her name was Peck.

She gave my ass a little tickle. Woody let me lick her hand.

By now, my cock—which must I must say I had not felt since our escape—had begun to stir.

Woody said, "Hey look at this beautiful bird; how brilliantly red it is, how beautiful! I'm going to play with it. I hope you won't mind."

"Gee," said Peck, "you are making me wonder what his ass is like."

The girls lived a couple of blocks away in the Mayfair, a huge megalith of a building that was, while being staid, actually pretty discreet. No one even raised an eyebrow as we went in, not at the front desk nor at the elevator as we waited to go up. I suppose the reason for that was that the girls had given their profession as "circus performers"; thus the management and clientele must have assumed my ass and I to be just a couple of their tricks, which oddly enough, in terms of their actual professions, was not too awfully far from the truth: both girls would turn out to be fabulous contortionists.

When we got to their suite, Peck asked if my ass liked grass. I laughed. My ass brayed a G.

"Hey, let me see your bird," Woody said. Peck slapped my ass playfully.

The five of us had a good time; my cock and Woody and I, and my ass and Peck. Nobody got jealous and we all had fun making a five-pointed star. Later, we made pretzels. God, they were talented.

Both of the girls were from out of town; Woody from California, Peck from Chicago. Both had come here feeling that New York could offer them more opportunity for their work. They had both grown up with animals and, having neither family nor friends here, wanted nothing less than to adopt the both of us. I could not believe our good fortune—they were both quite beautiful—and, as I have mentioned, proficient at what they did. A team, they usually required little from us except that we help them work out their routine. My cock grew to love Woody—a six-foot redhead with a penchant for sucking like a Hoover with a romantic attachment and the fine long legs of a Rockette. She was only twenty-seven, but had been working at her craft for over twenty, having been schooled by an uncle before she could read. There was nothing she did not know about it. Peck, a freckled blonde with the fresh-scrubbed look of the Ivory Snow Girl, was the amateur, in that this was only her first year "in the life," as they called it, having been brought out by a man whom she said no more about than that he was a pig, really. She was her partner's junior by a few years, but worked at learning her new vocation with a vengeance, absorbing all and everything in Woody's book until she had acquired every trick for herself. Eager beaver. I too was a willing pupil, but just when I thought I had learned everything, Peck would come up with something else. "Around the world" was her specialty; Around the World in Eighty Minutes. Jules Verne had nothing on her. When we had gone through variation after variation on these required exercises, we would take in films like *Naked*, *Snappers*, and *Farewell, My Concubine*, that Woody said were good training aids, though being a film about pedophiles, *Snappers* made her cry.

They worked at home, and when they did so, it was our job to hide in the closet, and if there was any "trouble," not to say anything "unusual," to bark and bray. Why I say "not to say anything 'unusual'" is because they specialized in the unusual; what went on in there was hardly your "usual" bedroom stuff, with the result that we were privileged to watch some pretty outrageous things, even bizarre. Being specialists, they had a clientele that came to them from all points of the globe, and, as a general rule of thumb, the farther they had come, the more important they were; and the more important they were, the more they would require of the girls, as further, *importance was usually kept at pace with by impotence*, so that the equation was this: order of impotence is commiserate with importance, so that the King of some Middle Eastern state, Saudi Arabia, say, would only want to shake out the carpets and air dirty laundry about the young princes of the Sultan of Brunei, while some kid from New Jersey, who had gotten lucky gambling, would be an all day sucker. Consulted by the high and the low with no distinction beyond price, their agendas were always full. Woody told me the first measure of equality was in the bedroom. A typical session might have gone like this: "Good afternoon, Senator. [Woody, ushering in a portly southern gentleman.] "And how are you today?"

The senator: "Oh, tolable, Woody, tolable."

Woody: [Straightening his tie] "Oh? A big, important man like you, sweetheart? Why only tolerable?"

The senator wipes his brow with a snowy handkerchief. "Woody, they can't not want me anymore!"

Woody runs her long fingers through the senator's shock of silver hair. "Of course, they want you Senator! Everybody does. You know that."

As Woody removes his coat, tie and shoes, Peck brings him his slippers. Woody lays him gently back on the bed.

The senator says, "Woody, for the first time in twenty years, I am seriously being challenged. Can you believe I have got a less that 20 percent approval rating?"

Peck, who has disappeared into her bedroom, reappears as Little Bo-Peep. She is carrying a shepherd's crook. Woody motions her over. Peck says, "Senator, do you know this crook?"

The senator squirms, declines to answer on the grounds that it might tend to incriminate him.

Peck says, "Do you?"

The senator says, "I do."

Peck says, "Senator, I am going to shove this crook up your ass. Would you like that?"

The senator says, "By God, yes, Peck, I would love that."

Peck shoves the crook up the Senator's rear-end: this is symbolic of the senator's relationship with crooks, of the relationship of victims to sheep. In this episode, Peck is known as "the Shepherdess." The Senator shits himself, lays for a while in his own filth before the girls bathe, powder and diaper him. The senator says, "I am losing my hair. My opponent has hair. Lots of it. People like hair. They associate it with vigor. Virility. It dates back to the Old Testament. The sun-god, Sampson. It's part of the Jewish conspiracy. While a lot of my constituents are not, they are, in very subtle ways, influenced by Jewish thought. I am going to have to get a hair weave."

Woody says, "Would you like a hair weave, Senator?"

The senator says, "By God, yes, Woody, I would like a hair weave."

The girls give him a hair weave. The senator leaves feeling good about himself.

In this manner—through the peep-hole—my ass and I saw Whitaker Chambers, Joseph McCarthy and J. Edgar Hoover, who asked for a witness. Chambers stepped forward, swearing foully. It was supposed to be a hearing. An assistant Secretary of State went down on Woody and Peck. Hoover wore a calico dress and a sun bonnet like Marlon Brando would wear in *The Missouri Breaks*. Brando would say later his character was influenced by the F.B.I. director. Nixon, too, came dressed as a pumpkin. When Peck brought out the crook, Nixon screamed, "Oh no, I am not a crook. Absolutely not." He would give this speech to the American people.

It was a good life. Woody bought me a rhinestone collar and Peck bought my old ass a vicuna oat bag. We made music less and less. The girls liked to show us off, and when nothing else was going on, Woody would get out the old red leather leash with the old rhinestone collar, Peck the old vicuna oat bag, and we would go out for a stroll along The Street. People loved us, and going through the lobby was a trip: the six-foot redhead with the huge bloodhound with a rhinestone collar and the red leash, and the freckled blonde with the nice ass. Even the old ladies liked us, commenting on John and ogling my cock. The gentlemen would tip their hats and smile. Sometimes they would tip us too, having heard John bray and me sing on occasions we did have to come out of the closet. We did though, one day, have a most curious experience: comic, actually, if its consequences would not have been so tragic. We had been strolling to the elevator as per our usual, when we were approached by a man who looked vaguely familiar. He wasn't wearing a uniform, though he did look that familiar.

"Hello Woody," he said.

Woody tensed. She appeared shaken. I had never seen her like this: cool Woody, with a whip-hand. Instinctively, I made myself very small, covering John as best I could. "What, what are you doing here," she said, "I-I thought—"

"I had to come, Woody," the man said. (I was sure it was a he.)

"Why," said Woody.

The man said simply, "I had to, Woody, I just had to."

Woody said, "You would "just have to," wouldn't you. How did you find me?"

"Photographs," he said. "It was easy, really. There are pictures of you everywhere; didn't you know that?"

"I'm a model now. A model of virtue. That how I make my living, no thanks to you. I thought you said you would ..."

"Would what, Woody?"

"Leave me alone, that's what! You said you would, didn't you?

What do you want from me now?"

I could feel the hairs at the back of my neck rising. It was him, I was absolutely sure of it, though he was so occupied by Woody he seemed not to notice me. He did not have Rudolph with him, a fact I was glad of. Could you imagine that dog sniffing around my ass?

He said, "I couldn't help it, Woody, all those pictures only reminded me."

The woman, who had become angry, said, "You had to come. I'll bet you did! And now I suppose you're gonna be wanting me to go somewhere with you. Well, I'm not gonna do it, not this time! Hey, I've got some pictures too, since you love them. Do you want to see them?" Pulling a wallet from her bag, she produced some photographs.

The man blanched.

"My lawyer's got the negatives," Woody said. "I do have a lawyer. Do you want to know her name?" She gave the name of a lawyer whose address was nearby, on Eighth.

The man drew back. He resembled nothing so much as a fox, surprised by a feisty crab. "Woody," he exclaimed, hurt in his voice, "I know that lawyer, she is a specialist in child abuse!"

For some reason, she had him going. She said, "That's right."

The man said, "But you were not a child!"

"I was too! I was only six years old, you bastard!" she said, flinging the pictures at him, "And you were supposed to be my uncle!" He cringed at this. "But you were so special, Woody, special, I loved you so much. Don't you know that?" He was almost crying. Almost. While one eye was tearing, the other appeared to be watching to see what effect this confession of affection was having on the girl.

"Shit, Sam," she said, "if you don't get the fuck out of here, I'm going to call the police. No. You are the police. I'm going to set my dog on you, you goddamned pervert!"

I wished she had not said that. I did not need any undue attention from this character, no matter what their relationship was, and I turned nonchalantly from them to inspect a small painting that hung at my back, but not before I noticed his sudden interest in me. "That dog?" he said, peering at my ass. "Woody, where'd you get that dog? He looks kinda familiar."

My heart leapt into my mouth. He started towards me.

She looked from the man to me and, sensing trouble, said quickly, "Sam,-Sam …"

He turned reluctantly from his investigation of me. "What?"

"What was so special about me?"

The man forgot about me. "Everything, Woody," he said, plaintively. "Everything, you were so precocious, so fresh. I knew you did-n't love me then, but I wanted you to grow into it. I figured you would. I haven't done too badly by you, have I? Look, think about it. I got you started in this business, didn't I? You seem to be doing well; where else could you have gotten the training you got from me, some third-rate Third-World country? You bet your sweet ass you couldn't have. You ought to be more grateful. At least pay your taxes. When was the last time you did that?"

Noting Peck for the first time, he said, "Hi! I've seen you in pic-tures. You are gonna look good in film, but I bet you a fat man you'll look twice as good in the flesh. Why don't you give your old uncle Sam a kiss?"

"Sam," Woody said, "you are a pig! Don't you forget I have those negatives. Don't you think I won't expose you for what you are? Don't you think that for one minute! I am not afraid of you anymore!"

A look of resolve crossed the Man's face. He said, "Okay, Woody, Okay, it looks like you've got the upper hand for now, don't it? But I'm gonna tell you something: don't you underestimate me, you hear? I will be back, do you hear me, Woody? I'll be back when you least expect it and you'd better have your tax files ready." He shot a glance at Peck and said, "You too, sister," before disappearing into the elevator, which arrived miraculously at that moment.

That painting was etched into my brain; a naked woman descend-ing a stair. I was not familiar with the artist, somebody named Duchamp. Marcel. I have never liked the name "Marcel." It sounded like something black people did to their hair. So the man was Woody's uncle and his name was "Sam." Or supposed to be her uncle. That was ironic. I had an uncle whose name was supposed to be "Sam" though in point of fact it was "Obideke."

A couple of days later, Woody came in hysterical. Her lawyer had been killed, savagely mutilated, and the negatives were missing. The authorities said it looked like the work of a pervert. Woody said we couldn't stay there anymore. The next day, we moved out of the May-fair and into a seedy hotel on Sixth Avenue, near Twenty-Third Street, in the flower district. What could have been more seedy than that? I was aware of being hunted again. We could not even go out for fear of being discovered, like Columbus discovered America, or Stan-ley discovered Livingston, or Ponce de Leon discovered Florida while looking for the Fountain of Youth or Cortez had discovered Tenochti-tlan, where the great, feathered Montezuma lived on his magnificent floating island of maize and beans and tomatoes, or like Balboa dis-covering the Pacific, so we would send out for rice and beans and chorizos or chuletas with aguacate, or one of us would go quietly down to one of the Greek joints on Sixth and take something out; meatloaf with mashed potatoes and string beans, usually Peck or I going, as Woody was petrified she'd be seen, and my ass never knew where it was headed at any given time. We didn't stay there too long. Peck soon found us a place in the Village that was more suited to our needs; off Seventh Avenue, at Forty-Two Morton Street. The entrance was recessed behind a row of brownstones with an imposing iron gate and a little cobblestone courtyard where we could keep John if he was being too cantankerous (who in the world knew about stubborn asses better than I), and they didn't mind dogs. Why we had moved so abruptly from the Twenty-third Street address was that one day Peck had gone down to the Greek's to get us something to eat and had seen displayed on a lamppost a leaflet offering a reward of one hundred dollars for information leading to the whereabouts of John and I. It described me to a T, right down to the rather prominent knot in the crown of my dog of a cranium and my huge, upturned snout; and in case anybody didn't get that, there was a picture of my black ass. Woody went down and called the number the leaflet advised anyone with information to call and told the person on the other end she had seen us in Key West waiting for a boat to Cuba, but it didn't work; no sooner than she had gotten back upstairs than the intersection was converged on by a platoon of squad cars.

What was good about the Morton Street address was that everybody in the area looked like us. The landlady was a little old six-foot, red-headed lady whose companion was a little blonde, freckle-faced old lady who looked just like the Ivory Snow Girl after ten thousand porn flicks, who told us to come right in, she loved animals. She had had a dog, she said, just like me, who had just died who had hung out with an ass like mine named John. To beat all that, she said the donkey had just died, and we were most welcome! Peck asked if she had seen any leaflets around that looked like us, and she said she had, because something was always getting lost around here: dog, cat, child, monkey, snake, cockatoo, but she said we shouldn't worry as there was so much of everything getting lost the chances of anything being ever found was practically nil. Once in a while, she said, something or somebody would be picked up, but that didn't mean the poor things had been found, could it? Did it? Anyway, she said, even if we didn't choose our lives, we still had to live them didn't we, we still had to take our chances, young people like us, healthy animals and all. She asked if we were healthy. Ever the class act, Woody and Peck produced certificates, and the old lady was satisfied. She said she ran a respectable house and was sure we would come up with the rent, which was worth more than any hundred dollars to her.

The old lady's talk heartened us, though the part about the snakes interested me; were they Lucans? Anyway, we soon felt confident enough to go out for strolls again, though not above Fourteenth Street or below Houston except for an occasional foray into Chinatown, avoiding Little Italy like the plague as our kind was not in vogue there. If they didn't like "your kind" down there in those days, they would try to creep up on you and kill you, and if they couldn't creep up on you and catch you themselves, and you were into anything at all they knew about, they would definitely fink on you. Exactly like those predators I had encountered in that episode upstate, they wanted everything for themselves, particularly all the blondes and all the redheads. They didn't like you to say it and would get mad at you if you did, but they were all gangsters down there; gang business was how they thrived, and those that knew enough not to say would bless them absolutely, forgiving them for whatever, sins, whatever; so we definitely avoided them. Woody said that in her business she had learned that the highest measure of respect a gangster can give you is to ignore you, because if he ever does pay you any attention, one day he is going to come to collect. She said her uncle had told her that. They were like the I.R.S., and he certainly knew. So we avoided them. It wasn't so hard; our new neighborhood was a huge area that offered lots of diversion within its limits. It was true that the notices were everywhere, but it was also true that nobody seemed to notice them. Although being a dog was hardly my natural state, it was nice to see others here like myself; unmuzzled, free. Their asses were not black either; some were yellow and some were pink, some were brown, some were gray and some were dappled. The thing about it was they were always changing themselves, making themselves over to look like somebody else, so that while one ass might be pink today, tomorrow it would be brown, and if it had been yellow yesterday, tomorrow it would be red all over, and if some ass were gray today, you could bet your sweet ass that tomorrow it would be dappled.

Into all their game, seeing Woody and Peck and my black ass, the very next day, every ass in town was black. It was about fashion, and fashion that expressed the individual; not Madison Avenue, which everyone called simply, "Mad." These colorful individuals were all artists of some sort, and the colors were actually codes that functioned as signals depicting craft, so that if an ass was red all over, that ass was probably a poet, while a dappled ass was most likely a painter. Pink was for dancers and choreographers, while brown and gray and yellow were for actors. Most of the black asses were musicians, so mine was the right color. They wore red, too, because down there in those days, everyone was a communist. Everywhere were harlequins and saltimbanques; and being contortionists, Woody and Peck fit right in. A picture of me had been found, and it was nice too, in a way, to see pictures of my ass everywhere. It was like I had become famous, although some of them were mutilated where someone had taken a pencil and blackened an area over a front tooth, altering my appearance so it appeared I was in need of dentures, or giving me a moustache or a beard and spectacles, or a black eye, and, if not me, then John. I have no idea why they did this, other than to amuse themselves or to disguise themselves, but I soon saw they did it to everybody, so I really didn't mind too much, it was rather fun. Woody and Peck liked it so much they went out to a novelty store and bought moustaches and dentures and spectacles and black eyes for us, which we would wear when we went out. This had the effect of disguising us even though as I pointed out to Woody one day after some people had pointed to us laughing, it also enabled people to recognize us. Woody said it didn't really matter as down there everybody was always pointing at everybody and laughing; it was how they communicated, and everybody looked like us anyway, or some strange variation of us; maybe with a one-sided mustache or a van dyke with a monocle, or maybe with two teeth blackened instead of one, or round spectacles with buck teeth and slanty eyes, which my ass was fond of, it was a party.

Everybody hung out at one of two squares—both named after U.S. Army generals, Sheridan and Washington—much as in New Orleans people hung out in Jackson, which was a minor puzzle: if everyone was so hip, why the squares? And did they name the squares after U.S. Army generals because these people were squares or were the squares round? In some cases it was down from the heights (as in the case of Washington) or up from Georgia (as in that of Sheridan), but always through Washington, having had to pass through D.C., or having come all the way across the country from Washington, that was the usual route, though as I say, it was a minor problem. Underneath all of the gaiety and all the abandon in these squares was the visible specter of authoritarianism: there were replicas of these generals everywhere—standing with their swords drawn, on horseback with their swords drawn, charging or with their horses at rest, swords in their scabbards, in stone, in bronze, in concrete. Reflecting, as if they had come down right out of the concrete or the bronze or stone over the bridges and down from the heights or up from Georgia and points west were the town's policemen mounted on their chestnut geldings, batons drawn, ever ready to charge the populace and coming up every once in a while with some poor, hapless dog or some ass that didn't cover himself well enough or some poor dog with a hopeless ass or some six-foot, redheaded whore with a freckle-faced blonde, who looked for all the world like the Ivory Snow Girl fresh from her bath with a John. Still, like the six-foot, redheaded landlady with the blonde, freckle-faced companion, who looked like the Ivory Snow Girl after ten thousand porn flicks, and the old dog who had just died had said, nobody was ever found, as in the case of one huge red ass named Brown, who would as regularly as clockwork, get into fights with the local Italians and get hauled off to jail by one or another of the replicas, though he would be back out soon enough, dressed in a red toga and a red leopard skin loincloth with leather thong sandals, sporting half a moustache with a monocle and dentures with some of the teeth missing, declaiming his poetry, which insofar as I could tell was pretty god-awful, though he did have his admirers. I later heard he got killed in a fight out in Los Angeles, but not before he had convinced somebody or other to produce a recording of his work, which was, in my humble opinion, exactly as I had suspected earlier, pretty bad. Still, he was something magnificent to see, striding up and down whichever square, huge arms with their bulging muscles folded across his mighty chest, reciting in his stentorian voice. He was a bit of a plagiarist too, as most of what he recited was what we called "toasts" that followed a ballad form with two rhymed feet in every line and a similar rhyme at the end of every other line to complete the stanza, like, "One dark night when the moon was bright, etc." that I had heard when I was in prison. I do not think he made them up.

Too, it was perfect for music, though everybody carried a guitar whether they played it or not, and as everybody only liked the guitar, we had to incorporate them into our act; and every day, disguised as we were, we would troop dutifully down to the mathematically precise circle in the square, find ourselves an abutment to the fountain at about three o'clock (zodiacally, the twins), park ourselves there and go into our routine (with Woody playing the tambourine and Peck on maracas or castanets if it was a Latin-American or a Spanish number), high as we could be on pot or Benzedrine. When we couldn't get any benzedrine, we would send Peck, who was pronounced the most unimpeachable of us with her well-scrubbed, innocent blonde look of the Ivory Snow Girl, to the pharmacy for Vick's inhalers, which we would crack open like squirrels or monkeys that had found some plastic nuts with fabulous writing on them, extract the cotton that had been dosed with the mentholatum and chew, howling to beat the band next to us, all the bands that circled the square around us.

There were Lucans.

People carried them around their necks like exotic collars; diamond-back rattlers, cottonmouths, corals, black mambas, anacondas, boa constrictors, coachwhips. A girl was strangled by her boa right in the square not many days after we had gotten there, in mid-afternoon, before all the bands and all the replicas, before all the generals, and nobody made a move to stop it, nobody; they couldn't, fascinated as they all were by the sheer drama of it, the girl's breath being ever so slowly squeezed from her by her own collar—choke-collar, as it were—the girl unable to utter a gasp, the snake tightening its grasp of her long and exquisitely slender neck with each constriction until her eyes became bloodshot and bulged as though they would pop out of her skull, and her face turned red (she had been a blonde, a freckle-faced blonde with the fresh, well-scrubbed look of the Ivory Snow Girl), and then purple and black. When she did finally die, the whole square clapped. There were shouts of "Bravo!" and "Encore!" Relaxing itself, the constrictor stood up from the girl's prostrate body and made a graceful bow. Searching the crowd with beady eyes, it asked if there were any volunteers for the encore. A six foot redhead with the long graceful legs of a dancer stepped forward and the constrictor repeated its performance to the gasps of the delighted crowd, offering the snakes for sale. Woody and Peck decided never to buy one.

One day as we stood around howling, high on benzedrine or the inhalers, I forgot which, I heard a "Psst, hey brotha!" and, turning around, I saw a coachwhip stand straight up next to me, its posture suggesting that if it had had hands they would have been in the pockets of a raincoat, the collar turned up. It was wearing black, plastic-framed sunglasses, the kind beboppers wore after Dizzy Gillespie, and a beret, and was the Lucan from the machine shop. "Salaam-a-laikum" he said, giving me the greeting.

"Lucius, who is that?" Peck asked.

"It is a friend, Peck," I said, a little disturbed by this apparition.

"Friend?" Peck said raising an eyebrow. "You have strange friends, Lucius."

"Everybody has a strange friend or two, Peck," I said.

She eyed me a little narrowly. "Who do you mean, me and Woody?"

I was annoyed. I said, "Fuck, drop it, Peck." And to the Lucan, "Hey, how you doin'?"

The Lucan said, "You can't give me the greeting?"

I didn't remind him I was never a Lucan nor had I ever any intention of becoming one. Instead, I said, "Alaikum salaam," and repeated my question.

He pointed to the girls and said, "Get rid of them."

"What do you mean, get rid of them?" I said, "These are my friends!"

Woody said, "Yeah, Buster, who are you!"

Peck said, "You get lost!"

The Lucan, in a sudden motion, showed them his drill.

"Hey," the girls said.

"Get rid of them," the Lucan said again. "Tell them to take a walk or I will."

I told them to go back to the house. Muttering and protesting, they left. "Okay," I said testily, "what is this? Those were my friends you pulled your drill on!"

He said, "Hey, it's me, Luke, don't you remember me?"

"Sure I remember you," I said. "How could I forget?" It was true; how could I have forgotten that place: the captain, us going through the wall into the blackness, the stench of the rotting corpse of that capybara. Memories came flooding in like rain, my bird in the hole. "But what's that got to do with anything? I told you, like I said, those were my friends!"

Luke said, "I helped you, didn't I?"

I didn't know if he had helped me or not. I was a fugitive, wasn't I? I said, "Yeah, in a way. You helped me in a way."

"Now don't be equivocating, Brotha. Did I help you or not? If you can say no after what I did for you, well, that's the kind of dog nigger you are!"

I supposed he had helped me, yet I couldn't help thinking, yeah, and I know what kind of snake you are. I said, "Yeah, you helped me ..."

He looked at me for a moment with what seemed a beady desperation. What he said next made me desperately wish I had not said he'd helped me, ever. "I need a place to stay."

I was a dog who hung around with an ass and a couple of whores, but I damn sure did not want to live with a snake—a Lucan—an escaped convict. Who knows what he had gone up there for? I knew he was a murderer or at least an accomplice to it; I had seen his boys kill rats like they were garden slugs. I said, "I live with those girls. I'm sorry, you shouldn't have gone through your little act with them."

"Square it with them," he said.

"For how long?"

"Indefinitely."

If there had been a ceiling, I would have hit it, but there was only the infinite blue. Indefinitely. It sounded like a California sentence: one day to life. I said, "You need to stay with me indefinitely? How long is that? What happened?"

The Lucan looked a little paranoid. He said, "They're after me!"

"Who is 'they?'" I asked.

He looked at me as if I were positively stupid. "Don't you know?" he asked exasperatedly. "They is everybody!"

I said, "Shit, man, 'they' is after me too! Don't you have any friends? Where is, I mean are, your boys?"

"The Lucans? Scattered."

"What do you mean, 'scattered'? Look, don't you see them out there? There are Lucans everywhere!" I pointed to the snakes in the crowd, working it, their slick moustaches, missing teeth. The black eyes they sported. On certain days, they all sported black ellipsoidal eyes, or green, I thought, with envy. With avarciciousness, with spite; black with hatred.

He said, "Look where, Brotha?"

Another performance had begun. (I had learned to call it "performance.") A snake was exhorting the crowd for change; another in a sandwich board was declaiming a kind of poetry; "skunk" they called it, I think because it stank. Another was wheeling a baby carriage with old clothes in it. Still another had rolled itself into a hoop and was racing madly around the circle; a circle around a circle. "There," I said, "and there, and there!" I was pointing like a compass.

His glittering eyes were piercing behind the sunglasses, taking what would have been a step back but which for him, being a monopod, was a hop, a hip hop. He said, "Lucans? Brotha, do you think you is really seeing Lucans? Look again."

I looked again. Nothing had changed; not even with their asking for it, demanding it. A quarter here, another there; nothing more. Another snake took another encore; someone took pictures of it. This time a replica of the generals, a town policeman hauled it away. I said, "What's changed?"

The Lucan said, "Seeing is believing. Believing is being."

The benzedrine or the mentholatum or whatever it was had definitely kicked in. The Lucan continued: "'Being' is not always what it appears to be. Gerunds change things."

Something had me going. I didn't know if it was the drug or this snake. "What you see is not to be believed." What kind of shit was that? He sounded as if he had been reading the *Bhagavad Gita*, which had become quite popular.

Something flew past the Lucan's ear. It was a sharpened spoon. He went flat and slithered behind an abutment. After a moment he peeked out and when no other missile was forthcoming, straightened up and popped back. "Brotha," he said, "those are not Lucans!"

Reluctantly, I led him out of the square and over to Morton Street. My ass didn't like it one bit, and Woody and Peck didn't either. There was trouble right from the start. First of all, I became disoriented and could not find Morton. Leaving the park at the Third Street entrance, there seemed to be no way west of Sixth Avenue, and I kept bumping into the Waverly Cinema; Bergman, *The Seventh Seal*, *Virgin Spring*. Luke was no help for, as it turned out, except for his little sojourn upstate, he had never before in all of his life been out of his neighborhood and had never heard of Bergman. He was more confused than I. Turning left off Sixth onto Cornelia, we would run into Bleecker (which had never seemed so bleak) where for some reason that was beyond me, I kept turning left again back onto Sixth, the cinema (nothing had changed there either), Cornelia, Bleecker (still bleaker), and back onto Sixth. Wishing to break this pattern that was ridiculous even to me, I headed us east again on Waverly where we circled the square a few times. Circumambulation seemed important somehow, and I was just settling into a groove when Luke asked if I knew what I was doing, to which I responded, "I think so. The sun is there, or would be if it weren't night, right? I think if we keep the sun on our right—our rights, as it were, whatever—we might be able to make something happen. I don't know what, but I think we'll see." I had suddenly become aware of infinity, and was glad we had made the sign for it.

Luke asked if I had any more gum. He had to repeat himself, which I thought was wonderful. "Gum?" I asked absently, "Gum? Do you mean chicle?"

I liked the way that sounded and let the syllables roll off my tongue again. "Chicle?" and again: "Chicle," giggling before breaking into a paroxysm of laughter. When I had pulled myself together again, I said, "Chicle? I don't chew it."

I liked the alliteration and said again, "Chicle? I don't chew it." More laughter. When the fit subsided, I became suddenly glum. Aware of being glum, I realized it rhymed with "gum." That seemed to be terribly important. "Glum gum, I said, I don't chew it."

Luke pointed to my jaws. "What do you have in there, Brotha?"

I was grinding my jaws like an exotic dancer in a coffee mill, slowly, sensuously. I couldn't even spit. What came from my mouth was as dry and white as cotton, so light it could be wafted on a breeze out into the traffic on Third, where it bounced off the windshield of a Chevy and disintegrated into a hundred tiny spheres, each lighter than air. Seeing where it came from, the driver yelled, "Hey, you, keep your goofball spit over there where it belongs, wit' da rest o' da freaks!"

Throwing the Chevy into park, he slung the door open and leaped out, shaking a fist as big as a basketball. I tried to say "Fuck you," but all that came was hoarse bark. He seemed to understand, and started for us. Some people's perceptions.

"C'mon, Luke," I said, and we broke into a run.

CHAPTER TWELVE

We didn't get home until daybreak. Woody and Peck were asleep. I motioned the Lucan to a couch and my ass and I slid into bed. The way I ground my jaws that night is why I don't have any teeth today. Every shadow was an asp or an adder facing off against cottonmouths. They fought with sharpened spoons and lances, always aiming for the heel or the groin, and spat streams of venom that burned to the touch, and blinded. Melding, they crushed each other with the weight of their mergings and fell ponderously apart or darted or glided; silent moccasins and rattlers that could have made the sound of a mambo, mambo with mambas. Descarga for cobras in hoods, anacondas; blind shadows. I awoke I don't know how much later with a splitting headache and Peck screaming, "Lucius, what is that goddamned snake doing in here?"

Had I not been hallucinating? Was it real? I had cottonmouth. My tongue was swollen with the venom of puff-adders. I said, "What snake?" It was difficult, but I got it out.

I was astonished, but Peck was in shock. "What? What was that you said?" she asked, hands over her mouth, eyes wide as a paranoid's. "Woody!" she screamed, "Woody!"

Woody woke up pawing the air. Her eyes yet shut, she licked her lips. "Wha—" she said, "Wha— Wha—"

"Lucius can talk," Peck said.

Woody said, "C'mon Peck, I'm sleeping here!"

Peck said it again: "Lucius can talk!"

Woody ran her thin, large knuckled fingers through her tousled hair. "Come on, Peck! What are you, crazy? What are you on? I know what you're on, you know."

Peck says, "I'm not on anything, you redhead bitch, I said Lucius can talk! Go on, Lucius, show her. Say something now!"

It was my turn to be in shock.

"And do you know what the first thing out of his mouth was?"

"What, Peck?"

"A lie," Peck said. "Wouldn't you know that from a goddamned dog? He tried to pretend he didn't know there was a snake out there! He said, 'What snake?' with that hangdog look he gets when — I realize it now — he is lying!"

"Lucius," Woody asked amazed, "is this true? Can you talk?"

I was truly speechless. I don't know by what extraordinary effort I was able to say what I had said, but it was a fact that I could not get anything at all out now, not even a whimper. During the girls' exchange, I had tried to signal Luke to leave, but he had either ignored me or was yet asleep. Woody said, "Is there really a snake out there?"

"And guess what," Peck said. "It's not just any old snake, Woody, it's that one that pulled that thing on us!"

Woody said, "Is that true, Lucius?"

I was reduced to signing. I don't say "reduced" out of any feelings of superiority over mutes or the deaf, I just mean "reduced" in that one moment I could talk and the next, Pow! just like that, nothing, and that's what I mean when I say "reduction." I signaled that I could explain.

"Woody," Peck said, "why don't you go see for yourself! The goddamned thing is out there stretched out on our couch like he owns it! I thought we weren't going to have any snakes over. Not only are they too kinky, they are downright dangerous! You saw what they were doing out there."

And I had a headache!

"Let him explain, Peck," Woody said. "Is that true, Lucius?"

"Yes," I signed.

"What is he doing here?"

I explained that I owed him a favor.

Peck said, "What kind of favor?"

I had never told the girls anything about my past, not that I was hiding anything, but just as I had never probed their background, they had never really asked me about it. I guess being a dog and all, they had just assumed I didn't really have one. Hesitatingly, I explained our relationship as best I could, from the beginning. I went through the school shit up to our spectacular escape.

Woody said, "So you are not a dog!"

I communicated that in actuality I was not.

Peck seemed to have acquired some venom of her own. "Yes, he is, Woody," she said. "Look at him. He is a lying dog, just like the rest of them. And that one over there on our couch is a snake!"

I thought I saw two fresh puncture wounds on her neck just above the shoulder. She sounded a little hoarse.

Luke woke then. He asked where the shower was.

"There," said Woody, pointing to the bathroom. "Show him where the towels are, Peck. I suppose you are a 'he,' aren't you?"

"Do you want to see my thing, slut? I already showed it to you one time!" Luke was indignant.

Woody, ever the lady said, "Lucius, tell him he doesn't have to be so rude."

The Lucan huffed off to the bathroom.

"Lucius," Woody said, "how long is he going to be here?"

"I don't know, Woody," I said. I thought I saw two grim lines settle around her mouth.

Peck said, "Woody, why don't you ask him why he tried to lie?"

I didn't like the insinuation in her tone though I was too depressed to deal with it. Luke took his time in the toilet. Peck said, "Shit, he's going to use up all the water; what's he going to do; use up all the water? Shit!" Peck liked her time in the bath; still, I had never seen her so bitchy. I had never seen her talk to Woody this way. And I hadn't been "lying." I had only been evading the truth. I had simply been unable to distinguish between what was the truth and what I wished were the truth. It was a depressing feeling.

Woody said, "Well, what's his name?"

"Luke," I said, "his name is Luke."

"Luke. That's the diminutive of 'Lucius.' That's like yours, isn't it?"

I said, "Sort of."

She wanted to know where I had gotten it.

I was not in the best of moods. "What do you mean, 'Where did I get it?' It's a name! Where do people get names from?"

"People give them to them," she said simply. "Who gave you yours?"

I thought about my beautiful mother and my old grandmother who had named me Petronius. I had not thought about them in a long time. I felt really guilty about that and how they had died. Depression settled on me like a curtain. I signaled that I did not want to talk about it.

"Get him," Peck said, "he doesn't want to talk about it."

"What's the matter, Peck, my ass not fucking you enough; you're not getting enough of my cock? As much as I bark around here and bay I have got as much stake in that couch as you do!"

Peck bristled. "Lucius," she said, "are you calling that limp bird you have been carrying around with you lately a cock? It is more like a wet hen!"

I looked down. My cock lay between my sorry hind legs of a hound like a snail. Its color was not good. Instinctively, I slapped at it. It bounced against my balls and lay there, exhausted. My ass was yet asleep. "Go on," I said, "why don't you wake my ass up, Tell it, it doesn't satisfy you anymore! That is all you have got to do, you know."

Peck realized she had gone too far. "I don't know, Lucius; it's just that that thing out there is an escaped convict."

I signed, "So am I, Peck." I felt so tired.

Peck would not give it up. "You're so different, Lucius."

"Peck," I said, "we are all on the run."

The Lucan emerged from the bathroom wearing a new skin that fairly glistened from the result of his cleaning exertions. He had always before spoken rather formally as if he were making a speech from a soapbox, but now he used dialect, a vernacular I suppose he thought Woody and Peck, being whores, would understand: "Intraduce me ta da bitches. Whut's happenin'. Whut's goin' on baby," he hissed to Woody. "I'm Luke."

Peck said, "Shit," and went to the bathroom. A moment later she screamed and came running out nearly hysterical. Her chest was heaving like a racehorse. Her scream woke my ass.

Woody: [Running to her.] "What's wrong, Peck?"

Peck: "What the fuck is that in the toilet!"

Woody: "What, Peck?" [She runs to the bathroom. My ass beats her there. The tub is full of scales, as is the washbowl. The toilet has spilled over with them. In a way, they look like jewels.]

Peck: "What the fuck is that?"

The Lucan says, "Whut da fuck is wrong wid you?"

"That," Peck says. "What is that!"

"Shit," the Lucan said, "better git used to it. Good fertilizer."

Peck: What is wrong with this … this …"

The Lucan: "You gonna need a shovel. I don't see one here. Go git one." [Produces a bill.] "Go git one."

Something had happened to Peck. I had never seen her speechless. She appeared to go white. She dropped her shoulders dejectedly, resignedly, and went as if in a trance to the closet where she extracted a light coat, donned it and went out the door still in her bedclothes. She returned in a short while with a shopping bag, from which she extracted a small shovel. "That's not big enough," the Lucan said.

Peck, shoulders drooping in further resignation, trooped obediently back to the door and out, still without a word. None of us moved, awestruck by her deference to the Lucan, the degree to which she had fallen under his influence, how quickly it had been affected, almost as if she had been hypnotized by his dark eyes. When she came back, she had a larger shovel. She appeared to be in a trance. Perhaps we all were, and we watched in fascination as Peck cleaned up. What she did with it all, I don't know, but pretty soon everything was put right again, every tile gleaming, all the porcelain. We stared at our glistening reflections in the mirror with amazement. "There," Peck said, her voice sounding hollow.

Luke said, "Yas indeedy! Don'cha feel bettah now, baby?"

"I do feel better. Yes, I do," Peck said rather woodenly. I hardly knew what to make of it.

The Lucan said, "What's f' breakfast?"

Pretty soon we were all sitting down to a hearty meal of sausage and eggs and French toast and a steaming pot of coffee. Luke made Peck go back to the store for some grits, and we had those as well with cheese and bacon and butter. Woody found some grass for my ass, which it pulled at musingly, an uncharacteristic moody look on his face, though soon he was mellow enough. Peck even washed the dishes, after which she went to take her shower. A short while later the phone rang; odd, because since the girls had had to give up their tricks, we had given no one our number.

The Lucan said quickly, "Don't answer it."

The phone rang all day as if someone knew we were there and not answering. We decided it was not a good idea to go out.

The Lucan's takeover wasn't even subtle. We ate grits the rest of that day; and the next, he made Peck cook some chitterlings he produced from somewhere as if by magic. It was truly amazing; he had only been on the scene some twenty-four hours and already he had us eating chitterlings. Peck balked at first, which was understandable since they smelled like shit. The Lucan coaxed her patiently, telling her that the stink was inescapable because that was what was in the meat, more shit than had been in the bowl. He explained that what he was levitating before him was the large intestine of that ignoble and filthy beast created from the rat, the cat and the dog on the island of Patmos by the big-headed scientist, Yacoub, namely, the pig. He explained it had been created as slave food, but it was in actuality transforming, as it had — filthy as it was — allowed the slaves to survive and had become an article of faith to the Lucans, who used it in their sacraments much as the Catholics use the wafer, and, besides, he liked the taste of them. Better than any wafer, that was for sure. He said all she had to do was clean the god-blessed things properly, rinse them in a little vinegar and some onions and peppers in a pot of water and cook 'em on down, skimming off the fat as it rises bubbling to the top. His forked tongue played excitedly around his lipless mouth as he explained, and his beady, glittering eyes rolled heavenward. He seemed to pat his scaly stomach, a stomach remarkably trim, the plates of skin over it stretched taut, hard as carapace. "Mmuh," he said, "sho am tasty."

Peck said, "C'mon," she didn't want to clean any more shit, but soon the whole house was smelling like it, and the chitterlings were bubbling away merrily, if foully, on the stove.

Woody suggested we open a window, but the Lucan said no, that would draw attention to our being there. In fact, he said, clothes or rags, whatever, should be stuffed under the door so people living in the building or randomly entering or leaving would not be aware of our presence. Protestation was of no avail, and soon bits of rag and articles of clothing were stuffed around every aperture of the apartment with the result that, after a short while, the apartment became unbearably stuffy, rife with the aroma of excrement, of ordure, of offal, which the Lucan said was a recreation of the physiology of the pig (who was without sweat glands) and of the life condition of the slaves themselves. He said we shouldn't worry; they would be ready soon enough, and in the meantime he would demonstrate for us a little dance that was to be performed during the ritual eating called, the "Ophidia," or simply, the "snakedance." To prepare for the dance we had to rub ourselves down with a snake-oil he produced that he said was made from snakeweed and snakeroot (a compound held together by snakebird fat) while he built a little snake fence around the small snakepit where we would do the dance. Afterwards, he produced a pink bog orchid called snakemouth from a small snakeskin bag worn around his neck like an amulet or talisman, placing it in the center of the pit, after which he began the dance, a dance in which images of snakes are handled, invoked or symbolically imitated by individual sinuous actions. After maybe a half-hour of this, he asked if we would progress single file, in a serpentine path around the pit. This, he said was known as "the Procession." He showed us a pretty hip step called "snaking," where he wound his way around the little pit in the manner of a snake, then dragged himself along like a log. He crawled, he moved sinuously, extending and contracting himself silently. He imitated the hellegramite, the flight of the dragonfly, the hellbender, hissing like a hellcat. Hell-bent, he removed some hellebore from a hellbox and a hell brew, which we were instructed to drink while imitating the call of the hellhound, a short series of barks that I was particularly good at, and the Lucan congratulated me here, as he said he himself could never manage more than a short series of hisses. It was like a hellhole in there, a netherworld in which the dead continued to exist; the nether realm of the devil and demons, where the damned suffered everlasting punishment, of error and sin, producing a state of torment in which wickedness and destruction prevailed over everything, all abuses and turmoil. In this dance we were called helots. It recalled, too, the miserable condition in which our people had to exist during slavery. Both the girls were really good at it, and it was not long before we were "snaking" with the best of them, snapping our jaws and making sharp, cracking sounds at anything that moved—which was after all, only ourselves—our movements more and more abrupt, with indiscriminate deliberation.

All of this culminated in the most frustrating orgy I have ever participated in in my life.

To judge from the sounds Woody and Peck were making, the Lucan must have been pretty good at it, and I think my ass got a little jealous. It was amazing. Woody looked like she had a big black tongue forked like a snake's that kept darting in and out as she writhed and convulsed as if she were Erzulie, the blue Haitian goddess of the sea, while the Lucan took on the appearance of Damballah. And Peck? She seemed to have become his slave! She did everything he asked her to, including shoving him up her butt as well, until he reappeared in her mouth like a forked, black tongue. My cock was nowhere near that big, so I had to be content with the more conventional in and out, the rapid lap of my broad, rough tongue of a bloodhound, which, to be truthful, Woody had liked well enough, though I could not now escape the suspicion that she was faking it with me; her "Ow, Lucius," more by rote and cute than the frankly uncontrolled screams escaping from her while entwined with the Lucan; as when she had shoved him, twisting up her butt, as when his black head of a snake had emerged from her pink mouth and she appeared possessed by all the gods of Haiti, as if that little snake were as huge as a horse. I could imagine the maracas as they made sound; mambo for mambas, decarga for cobra in hoods; anacondas.

Both girls looked drawn and dazed when we finally wound down and the Lucan told Peck to serve up the chitterlings, saying it was best to eat them now, before we showered, while the funk of sex was yet on us. An entranced Peck served up steaming piles of the porcine entrails over rice and collards upon which we were instructed to pour liberal doses of G. McCauley's Red Devil hot sauce and salt. The girls devoured them greedily, regaining their vigor as they ate, chattering away. They kept asking for more, and soon the whole pot of the accursed things was gone. It's a funny thing about chitterlings. The closer you get to them, the less you tend to notice the smell, and that, I believe, was what finally led to the trouble.

The Lucan must have had a hundred pounds or more of the entrails secreted about his person, for he produced them frequently, demanding that they be prepared, and had taken to wearing a strand or two around his neck. They must have been frozen because I hadn't noticed any odor. Each time we ate them we were required to do the dance, which was followed by an orgy that became more and more frenzied; an orgy of dance, an orgy of sex, and after, an orgy of eating. It was too much for my own personal taste, but the girls were just wild about it, going into each session with more gusto, performing the dance with more abandon, more and more greedily. My ass did not mind it too much, but as I said, I myself was not too crazy about it.

The phone kept ringing. We did not answer.

CHAPTER THIRTEEN

One day—or night, as the blinds were kept constantly drawn, I don't know which—there was a knock at the door. I had been imitating the sound of the hellhound. The Lucan froze. He gestured for silence and made a move for his drill. The knock came again and again more and more insistent, and the voice of six-foot, redheaded old lady whose blonde, freckle-faced companion had the fresh-scrubbed look of the Ivory Snow Girl after ten thousand orgies, ten thousand porn flicks, said, "What's going on in there? Is everything all right? It smells like someone has a cancer in there or has already died from it! If you don't open the door right now, I'm calling the police. You know I don't like to do that, but my other tenants are complaining. The whole neighborhood is complaining. Open up!"

The Lucan motioned Woody to the door. He told her to answer without opening it.

"Hi, there," she said as sweetly as she could manage. She sounded tired.

The landlady insisted. "Open the door," she said. "Are you all right?"

"We're fine," Peck said airily. "How are you? We're just a little busy now. Do you mind?"

"Yes, I do mind," the landlady said. "Open up. Right now. This is my house and I have every right to know what goes on in it. You open up this minute!"

The Lucan slithered into the next room motioning Woody to open the door.

Removing the towels and bits of rag and clothing we had stuffed around it, she opened it a crack. "Hi," she said, sanguine.

Falling back, the landlady uttered an "Arrgh," and covered her nose with her apron. "What are you doing in there, making whiskey? Don't tell me that, because I know what mash smells like. What is it, dope?"

Woody said, "No Gertrude," — the landlady's name was Gertrude after Gertrude Stein— "we are not making whiskey or dope."

"You let me in there right now," the landlady said. She pushed her way in, staggered, and promptly fainted.

When she came to, she gasped, "Smelling salts!"

Peck said we had none.

Gertrude said somebody would have to run next door and get them or she would die. Saying she had a bad heart, she gasped and appeared not to breathe. Her eyelids fluttered and her eyes rolled up in her head. Running out, Peck returned with the smelling salts, the landlady's companion. Alice B., close behind. The companion was named after Alice B. Toklas, though even after ten thousand porno flicks she was nowhere near as ugly, as dark as that one who baked hashish cookies and ate them with the greats: Alfred Jarry and Andre Breton, Apollonaire, Picasso, Duchamp, Ernst and Hans Arp, who made everything black or square or arranged things according to the laws of chance. The companion was a blonde, as freckled and freshly scrubbed as the Ivory Snow Girl after ten thousand porn flicks and a few thousand orgies. Peck applied the salts to Gertrude as Alice promptly fainted. As rapidly as Peck applied the smelling salts to one, the other would faint, so we had to remove all the rags and bits of clothing we had stuffed in all the apertures, raise the blinds, and throw open the windows, whereupon people fell out all over the neighborhood. All afternoon the normally shady quiet of Morton Street and its environs was broken by the insistent screams of ambulances ferrying the elderly and people with respiratory problems to St. Vincent's Hospital. When those beds were filled, they were taken to Beth Israel and Bellevue, and when they could no longer be accommodated there, to Mother Cabrini, NYU Medical Center, Roosevelt, Metropolitan, St. Luke's, Doctor's, Harlem, and Columbia-Presbyterian. The situation was labeled pandemic, though later, when what had happened actually came out, all the Negro leaders, including those from the NAACP, would label the hoopla racist.

When Gertrude finally woke up, she said she knew what that smell was, a smell she remembered from her childhood in Kentucky. It was chittlins, she said, chittlins; pronouncing it just like that, chittlins, as if she had invented the term—if not the substance—long ago. She said someone was cooking chittlins in her house, and in all probability doing a snake dance, a dance which, as everybody knows who does it, is hypnotic, producing hot flashes that provoke orgiastic fantasies. She said the odor had the same effect on her then as it had now. She had fainted dead away and, when she came to, she had wanted some (which was why her parents had hustled her away from old Kentucky, to get her away from those Negroes); she meant, she said, the smell of those chittlins and their Negroes, taking her first on a grand tour of the Continent and then settling her here in New York. She asked if she might have some.

"Well," Woody said, "they aren't mine, but I suppose you may."

Alice did a little jig and whooped. She said she had been hearing about some ritual attached to the consuming of them and asked if we'd a real Lucan to lead the dance. She giggled. "I've heard," she said, eyes fairly glittering in anticipation, "once you have snake, you never break," and she certainly could use some as she had been feeling a little brittle as of late.

At which point the Lucan slithered in. Hearing what was wanted of him, he looked at us in disgust. "Hey," he said, "them old bitches looks lak bulldoggas!"

"C'mon, Luke," cajoled Woody, winding her hips slowly, sensuously, in an impromptu little hootchie-cootchie.

"C'mon what?" said Luke. "They ain't that much chittlins in the whole world."

Gertrude said, "You must!"

The women pleaded with him with the result that we had to stuff everything up once again while Peck put the pots on.

The way they danced was hilarious, their rhythm off, their steps awkward, stiff. They made the single-file part pretty much all right, but the serpentine path was jagged with abrupt right angles and other geometrics that were old twists on an old story, a song of love and glory. Entranced himself, the Lucan broke the line to explain that their movement had a history, it was a variation done by an order of the codont, and when it came to snaking, they were a complete travesty, being so wooden. Getting pretty drunk on the hellbrew, they did the log a lot better. By the time we got to the "sex" part, I was ready to give up but they were quite ready for it. When the Lucan suggested he be applied to her rectum, our landlady screamed, "Sooeee!" like a champion hog-caller, tore off her old-fashioned calico dress with the high, ruffled collar, like Alice Toklas used to wear, and in a twinkling had the visage of a snake, the forked tongue, the writhing tail of the coachwhip. My ass grabbed Woody and slipped the grand pipe of a donkey to her, while my wet, red cock entertained both Woody and Peck. I myself performed listlessly, disinterestedly; something—I don't know what—in the back of my head, tugging. Maybe it was the phone calls, which had not stopped. I was going to ask Gertrude if she had been phoning when I realized how stupid that was; the ringing was going on at that moment and they were here with us, engaged in unspeakable acts and preparing to eat chitterlings. Instead, I asked Gertrude if she had ever been to the island of Patmos.

Woody, who had the visage of a snake, hissed, "Lucius! What is wrong with you?"

"Wrong with me, Woody?" I said. "What do you mean?"

She uttered an "Ow," in response to some movement Luke made inside her. "I don't know, Lucius," she said. "You seem listless. Oww." Her eyes half-lidded, tongue slithering in and out wetly.

"I don't know, Woody, I can't put my finger on it."

"Owww, that's just it, Lucius, you can't put your finger on it. Ooh, you haven't put your finger on it in some time, umph!"

"I don't know Woody. It might be because I don't have any fingers. I haven't had any in some time. Have you ever thought of that? Look at these paws. What can I do with them? I can't put my finger on anything."

"Oww," she said, ecstatically. "I don't know, Lucius, you might try something. Ooh, look at Luke; he doesn't have any fingers either, but look at what he can do with his tail! You do have a tail, don't you? Ooooh!"

The Lucan slid out of Woody's mouth and up Peck's waiting behind in a rapid fluid motion. "Ooh, do it, Luke, do it!" She screamed like a banshee.

My ass was stroking Alice in an attitude of pure bestiality. My cock had Gertrude pinned against the wall of the pit, slamming it to her like a piston. She almost lost her teeth. "Whoo," she stuttered through slipping dentures, "r-r-ride 'em c-c-cowboy!"

Though I did take the tip from Woody, I found my tail nevertheless had neither the suppleness nor the extraordinary length of the coachwhip's, and did not nearly enough for her six foot body. "You're right, Luke, " she said pushing me away, "you're just not into it."

Fortunately, it was just then time to eat. The Lucan's orgy was over.

"Marvelous!" Alice B. was saying.

"Fantastic!" Gertrude said, "Why, this is everything I had imagined it to be! The dog, truthfully, is a little disappointing, but everything else is superb!" She slurped an entrail down with unfeigned gusto.

I had slammed my napkin to the table and was slinking off to a corner when there was a sharp rap at the door. "Gertrude, Alice," a voice said, "Are you in there? Is everything all right? Open this door right now. Let us in!"

We froze.

"Oh, that's all right," Gertrude said from around a mouthful of chitterlings, "that's just George Sand and a friend. She is a good pal. I told them, if I wasn't right back, to check on me. They're cool. You'll see. She is a writer. Her friend is a model, who sat for famous artists. Do you know Marcel Duchamp? She sat for him once. Her name is Mona Lisa."

Removing the rags, Peck opened the door, and George Sand came in accompanied by a strikingly beautiful, dark-haired girl who wore half a moustache.

They all came after that; first the lesbians and then the lavender boys, who daring as they are, can't keep anything quiet. A secret, yes, but not quiet; and then everybody. Forty Two Morton became the scene; I don't know how, because though people called, we never answered the phone. Still here they were, all crazed, all wanting to eat chitterlings and snake. I became more and more glum each day. Nobody seemed to notice the absolute control the Lucan exercised over the group, requiring them to give him all their money for chitterlings or hellebore or for the hellbrew or whatever, and if I would say something to someone, they would laugh and say I was just jealous of the Lucan's knowledge of the ritual and his big prick. It was useless to remind them that no snake has a big prick. All the guys were into Woody, Peck, and Mona Lisa with her beautiful half-a-moustache, which meant that no one paid any attention to me; not even my cock or my ass. They were all enthralled by that Lucan, the snake; though as it turned out, I was not wrong to have been so nervous about everything.

Billed in the *Guinness Book of Records* as the longest party ever, with people eating chitterlings and snaking and such, with our pictures in all the dailies and all the weeklies and all the magazines, like *Life* and *Look* and such, with all the A-trainers making their way down from the Heights, with all the tourists from everywhere in the world taking snapshots, as I look back on it now, I do not wonder that not long after the *Guinness* entry, we were visited by a young man in a uniform. "Look," someone said, "that guy is taking pictures!"

"So what," said someone else, "somebody is always taking pictures! That's the way you get to be a star. People see you in all the newspapers and all the magazines, and some director says, 'That face! I want that face!' and somebody rushes out and gets you with this fabulous offer for the movies or Broadway or somewhere!"

"I'm from the gas company," the young man said. "Don't mind me. Someone reported a leak. Is there a leak? It sure smells like it. In fact, it stinks, and while some of it might be gas, I do not think that is all it is. There is too much of it and nobody is blown up. Nobody blew up when I rang downstairs. One of the characteristics of a gas leak is, you blow up. This smells like chitterlings."

He continued: "Let me tell you something about taking pictures. I heard someone talking about the First Amendment of our great Constitution. Well, my right to take pictures is covered by that, being considered 'free speech,' which was found to be good for the citizens of our country. It is the first of our rights. Does everyone here know their rights? You have the right to remain silent."

The room remained silent.

He went on: "You do not have the right to eat chitterlings, or 'chittlins,' because they lead invariably to 'snaking' and other antisocial acts that are not good for our constitution, the imbibement of a tincture of hellebore and the imitation of the hellhound." He looked directly at me. "Devil worship. I can see the snakepit, the bits of snakeweed and snakeroot. I can smell the snake oil. You have been participating in the 'Ophidia.' Uttering the four letters of the tetragrammaton hidden in the word 'ophidia.'" He fainted, coming to with the tongue of a snake. Someone introduced him to tetrahedrocanabinal, after which he was given tetrachloride and tetracaine, tetratomics, and tetter.

That was not the end of it. More of them came, and more, ostensibly to read the meter. After the "meter readers" came the fire department and the health department. All fainted dead away, awakening only to join the revival. Finally, a man in a well-worn uniform showed up; a familiar man with a familiar dog: Rudolph.

"Do you smell anything, Rudolph?" the man asked.

Yelping, Rudolph fainted. The man did, too. When they recovered, the man said, "You are all under arrest. For subversion, to say nothing of the Mann Act."

"Oh, my god," screamed one of the lavender boys, "oh my god, it's the Man!"

Another said, "And would you look at those arms, that wood he is carrying; he's got the whole world in his hands! I surrender, dear!" They sang that song.

The man tried to arrest us but was so woozy everybody scattered. Some of us escaped.

It was a stampede as mindless as panicked as any in Isaac Dinesen's *Out of Africa*, the Tarzan pictures of the period, *Bomba, the Jungle Boy*, that diverse. Each animal kept to its kind in flight, the winged with the winged, the hoofed with the hoofed, though the cloven-hoofed were kept separate from the ungulates. This was a matter of Rabbinical law and a tenet of religious faith covered by the First Amendment. Fleeing was free expression, and they each did it according to their ability: they slithered, they crawled, they trotted, they galloped madly, they leapt like gazelles, they made the house shake like pachyderms, their white eyes of panicked animals rolling in fear. They ran this way and that, lumbering, sprinting after themselves like cheetahs, biting at each other's heels in a headlong frenzy of escape. As I said, some of us did. My ass and I hit the ground running after having tumbled out a window. People went running past us, but I saw neither Woody nor Peck nor the Lucan. I was worried about them—at least about Woody and Peck—but figuring it best not to tarry, made my way east on Bleecker, my ass behind, my cock and tail between my legs. I was right too, about tarrying, the man was hot on our heels; we could feel his hot breath of a raw onion on our necks as we ran pell-mell, his long arm of some terrible law casting about for us. While justice might be blind, sometimes the law is not; it is more like a raptor, more like a bald eagle with thirteen arrows in each of its talons. If there is any olive, it is the olive-drab of an army, and this terrible law with his eyes of a raptor that represent this terrible law with thirteen teeth in each talon says, "There they are; git 'em, boys; a reward o' ten talents to the first man-jack o' ye as hits 'em and bring 'em down, and a few extra coppers under o' his feet! How's that me buckos, hey, me pretties?"

The ensuing army roared, hurling its terrible darts. We heard them hissing past my ears, whistling past my naked ass, whining like so many angry bees as they ricocheted off the pavement around us. The man yelled, "After 'em!"

Bleecker was a jumble of Italian sausage shops and bakeries where fresh loaves of prosciutto were sold, and barrels of roasted peppers in olive oil and vinegar, along with bone-white loaves of provolone, gleaming cases of gorgonzola, mortadella, ricotta and mozzarella, shelves of breadsticks, sundried and crushed tomatoes, fennel and rosemary, basil, oregano, pine-nuts, and pasta of all kinds, bow-ties and rigatoni, semolina and spinach. My ass wanted to stop and get something—some basil, or oregano, I forget which—but I said, no, certainly not now. I swear, sometimes that animal seemed to know no danger! Sprinting past a pizza shop, we ran into trouble of another sort.

"Hey," someone said, "Look, look at dat jackass! What is it doing on Bleecker Street?" "Someone" being a young bravo from the neighborhood with a nose like a banana or even of Pinocchio after he had not gone to school and had told many, many lies. "Hey," this new trouble said, "ain't dis Bleecker Street, ain't it?"

He was speaking to his lieutenant, who said, "Hell, yes. Dis is Bleecker Street. It is, ain't it?"

"Well," said banana-nose, "is Bleecker Street ours?"

"Yeah, it's ours," another bravo said from around his toothpick. "S'posed to be anyway. Dat's whut duh ol' moustaches tol' us, ain't it?"

"Well," says Pinocchio, "If it's Bleecker Street and it's ours, we don't allow no jackasses on it, do we?"

"Not wid no dogs," said a bravo, sniffing.

"Well, let's get 'em," says banana-nose.

So now we had the whole block after us as well as the Man. Bleecker was never bleaker. We turned right onto Thompson in a hail of missiles: arrows, stones, bottles, whatever came to hand came to mind and was hurled at us, books, even the *New Testament* (which I didn't understand), by a young priest in a black cassock, as we sprinted past St. Anthony's. "Cave canem" he intoned like a bell, and after a moment, "The ass in the manger. It is separate from the flock!"

Unable to decide whether to go west or east, I indicated we should continue straight. John looked at me as if I were crazy and sped east on Houston as fast as his spindly legs of a jackass could carry him. Afraid I would never ever see him again, I flew south, past the priest. His cassock flew up, revealing a walkie-talkie where he should have had a penis. His balls were tattooed to represent the hemispheres. Shaking a fist, he screamed, "Vai alla valle dei cani!" It sounded as if he were talking to God. I figured that was what the walkie-talkie was for; but then why did he cross me? Why was he saying, "alla"? Why wasn't he saying "Tutti"? He tried to stop me with a "tout," but I knew he wasn't French; not with that prick, not with those balls.

I shouldn't have listened to him at all, for in the few seconds it took me to make sense of his testimony, the man had completely closed in on the south. Pinocchio and his bravos converged from the north. It had gone dark in the east, so I headed west. As used to running as I had become, I had never experienced anything like this: the world had begun to spin, and I was seeing the stars in all their constellations; Orion the Hunter and the Drinking Gourd, though as they encircled me, I could not name a star in Orion's belt, nor could I hold the Gourd steady, Copernicus was a Pole coming at me from Brooklyn: where was Brooklyn? A famous jazz musician from the west would ask that question later, every bit as lost and out of breath as I was, the blood pounding in my temple. Which temple? Had I one or two? Why was I faced with this? It wasn't a mirror; I couldn't see myself anywhere, I wasn't big enough, I couldn't see over the counter in most places in my short pants. Everything was as grand as the stars and as out of reach. Stumbling to the pavement, I felt myself tumbling into the dark. Backlit from the lights of the Empire State Building, lit from the front by the spot I was in, my inquisitors advanced on me from the north. Backlit by the lights of the Battery in the harbor, lit from the front by glee and the anticipation of action, my tormentors moved in on me from the south.

CHAPTER FOURTEEN

"P sst!"

I had slipped into the vortex of the ritual.

"Psst," the voice said again, "in here!"

I thought I was hearing things. Being dragged. Drugged. "Don't hit me," I said, eyes closed so I would not see my antagonizers. "Just don't hit me!"

"You're hitting me! Don't hit me." The voice sounded hollow.

"I'm not," My voice sounded hollow, as if it had come from a cave.

The voice said, "Do you want me to repeat?"

I had not yet caught my breath. "Repeat?" I gasped.

"Repeat?" the voice sounded tired, patient; as if it had heard this many times.

"Repeat? Repeat what?" I was groggy; I felt I was not getting enough oxygen to my brain. I couldn't move.

"I'm a little tired of this."

"Of what?"

"Of what?"

My lips were not moving. Opening my eyes, I saw I was in the Stygian darkness of a cave. I couldn't see a thing. "Where am I?"

"Where am I ... Where am I ... Where am I?"

"I don't know! I can't see. What's the matter with me?"

"What's the matter with me? I'm blind."

"What's the matter with me. I can't see a thing! Am I blind?"

"Wait," the voice said, "let me put the light on. I don't use it when I'm by myself. Think it's a total waste of my energy. I don't really like to waste energy. Not like that. Hell, no."

A light came on suddenly.

"There," the voice said, "is that better? Was that a good idea? I can't tell you know. Not anymore. It wasn't always like this, but now my lips are sealed. While that might not be a good idea, nevertheless, it is true."

I didn't see anybody. "Where are you?"

"Where are you?"

"If your lips are sealed, how come I can hear you?"

"I'm not saying anything."

Yet a little weak from my run, the force of my fall, and, above all, my creeping terror of this new unknown, I said hollowly, "How come you sound so hollow?"

"How come you are so hollow?"

"I'm not hollow." It sounded hollow as I said it. "Who are you?"

"Who are you?"

"Why don't you answer me?"

"Why don't you answer me?"

"Why won't you answer me!"

"Why won't you answer me?"

It sounded obvious, but I said it anyway: "Because I asked you."

"Did you?"

"I did."

"I don't believe you did. I did."

"Look," I said, "I don't mean to sound rude or ungrateful but I'm a little tired of this."

"Ah, you see," said the voice, "I have told you something. I'm a little tired of this. Would you like to leave?"

That was the last thing I thought about. I said, "Leave?"

"Leave." I thought about the bravos upstairs and the man and Rudolph. I thought about the gas inspectors, the tax collector and the health inspectors. I thought about the fire inspectors, the possibility of giant orange flames; fighting them. I started to sweat. "Leave?"

"Leave."

"I don't think so."

"I don't think so either. That would not be a good idea, would it?"

"I don't think so."

"Then let me shut off the reverberator."

"The what?"

"The reverberator. It's what creates the resonance you hear. I'm an engineer, oops, I wasn't supposed to tell you that." I could feel the thing flinch, as if in anticipation of some punishment. "Oh, no matter. Would you like me to shut off the reverberator?"

"The resonator?"

"That's another name for it, yes, the resonator."

I don't know quite why, but I didn't think that would be a good idea either. "No, please don't shut off the resonator!"

"Ah, please, aren't we polite. I don't think that would be a good idea. Tell me, why do you think that?"

I was sweating profusely now. I wasn't hot, in fact, I was rather cool. I wasn't thinking. I couldn't. I didn't even know where my ass was; maybe a hole in the ground. I started to miss it. "I don't know how!"

"I don't know either. I don't know why you think so much."

"What makes you think that?"

The thing laughed a hollow laugh. "I was joking," it said. "My thinking days are over. I haven't thought about anything in a long time, though I do like my little jokes. Sometimes they are terrible. I've been told that. Do you think I'm terrible?"

Though I felt an unreasonable fear, I made the decision to lie. My skin felt cold, clammy, maybe from the darkness of the cave. "No, I don't think you're terrible."

The thing seemed to appreciate my terror; to feed off it. I could feel that that was what is was, a thing. I took a deep breath. The thing said, "You're wrong. I am not a 'thing.' I am nothing, and that's what you are. You suspect you are a dog. Isn't that what you are?" Its tone had turned menacing, and made the hairs stand on the back of my neck.

"No," I growled, "I am not a dog!"

Laughing again, the thing said, "That is the funniest thing I've heard in ages. Look at you. You look like a dog."

I looked down at my four paws, my tail, my shaggy coat in short pants. I heard myself bark, "I am not a dog!"

The thing stopped laughing. "Not a dog. You are not a dog. I am blind and I can see that. What are you? Don't answer, I can tell you. You're frightened, aren't you."

This time I couldn't lie. "Yeah," I said. "And you, does that make you feel good?"

"Don't be silly," the thing said. "How could your fear make me feel good? Or bad? I'm afraid I don't feel. Nothing to feel with."

I felt calm as it said this. What was there to be afraid of, a voice? Nothing I could see, just this terrible hollowness I did not want to end.

"How did you get here?"

"I fell," I said, "I was being chased; you dragged me in here—"

"Do you know where you are?"

I signaled that I didn't know.

"I have to tell you," the thing said. "You are in trouble. You seem to be in a coma. I may have to eat you, but I don't know how. Look at you, too meaty for a salad and too rangy to fry. Maybe I will bake you or broil you."

I had a vision of desert, each grain of sand, a minuscule shell of a bit of a being. Mine. Heat radiated in shimmering waves across a glowing horizon. The sun as a red yolk.

"You wouldn't make a good soufflé. Oh, I don't know. I don't know what to do with you, to tell the truth. Maybe I'll have a party. Invite some friends. We'll dress you up. I don't know how, but you'll be good, I am sure. Maybe sauté you with garlic and onions. Do you like peppers? Jalapeños? No, we can't have you smelling like garlic. Some of the best people will be here, heads of state, great kings and queens. Emperors like Charlemagne. Caesars like Augustus and Julius. Octavius. Popes like Borgia. Stellar lords and ladies like Sheng and Josephine. Though they won't come together. He is too old for her. Much too old. She will probably come with Marat, or Sade, or even Napoleon and oh! What inventors, with what inventions! It will be your party. Everyone will partake of the host!"

I could not move!

"What do you think now. Would you like that? Sure you will. Everyone will love you, you'll see. I'll make you a hero. That's it, I'll do that. You could become a hero, couldn't you? Let's see, a little ham, that's all it takes, and you could be a real Disraeli. I know you can't move now, caught as you are in your little helix, but, hey, it's a web of your own making. I bet you're full of baloney, too."

I sensed something poking at my stomach, arcing over a paunch that grew as the force of the thing moved over it. I had never had a paunch, but there it was, a mound like the Ohio Indians used to make for their burials.

"Just look," it said, "and there's nothing you can do about it. If you stuff yourself, you stuff yourself, and if you can't move, you can't move. You see, that's something every good soldier knows instinctively, how to be absolutely still."

I could move my eyes, but that was it.

"The pickle you are in is this: I have laced you with some strychnine. You can't feel it, of course, because it numbs you. Numbness is the first step in your preparation, because you feel too much. Disassociation, that's the key. Oh look, one of my guests has arrived already! Lucius, I wish you could say hello to Edward Teller, but you can't. Edward, as you might know, is the father of the hydrogen bomb. Now there is a man that loves his child, but do you think he would touch him with a ten-foot pole? Not on your liver! The boy went wrong somewhere."

The thing laughed. Teller joined him sheepishly. "That boy could blow up the world, the way he was raised." Teller and the thing laughed uproariously, rolling in the blinding light, Teller's laugh like a bad wind.

"Ten times, and he still would not be happy," the thing said. "He is kept in check only by his murderous rages."

Teller, looking like Peter Lorre in *The House on Green Street*, muttered, "Aw, Boss, he's ahead of his time. Maybe that's why he is like that. Anxious. Depressed. Explosive."

The thing said, "Where is he now, Edward?"

Teller shrugged.

The thing said, "Somebody is going to bury him one day, but I'm almost sure it will be too late. He is a real monster. Much, much worse than *The Thing*. Tell me, Edward, exactly how did you do that?"

Teller pulled himself straight as a Prussian general, took a monocle from a breast pocket and wiping it with an immaculate handkerchief, placed it over an eye. He cleared his throat, as if ready to give a speech and said simply, "You have to be very, very serious."

A youngish man with half a beard and half a head of hair entered. Sporting half a moustache and one eyebrow, he looked vaguely like Mona Lisa. "Hello John," the thing said. "Lucius, let me introduce John Frazier, John Linley Frazier. John, I wish you could shake hands with Lucius, but you can't, because he hasn't got any. He will be the host tonight. The hero. What do you think of that, John?"

The newcomer clapped. "Bravo," he said.

"John is an auto mechanic-cum-ecologist. You might say he is somewhat at odds with himself," said the thing. "Oh look, it's Fritzy, Fritzy Hermann! He is the Ogre of Hanover, a real butcher with an eye to gain in the grandest capital manner. Fritzy sold his victims as horsemeat and peddled their clothes as a sideline. He would have made a million if he hadn't gotten caught. As it is, he lost his head. Fritzy, say hello to Lucius."

Hermann had a surprisingly deep voice for someone who had lost his head, having been beheaded by the German government in 1925. It came from somewhere deep in his chest. "Hello," he said. "Forgive me if I don't take off my hat, having nothing lately to put one on. Oh, Mnemsomyne, oh Echo, you have outdone yourself this time. He looks like a hero!"

"Oh, good, good!" the thing said, "Look who's coming! It's Henry, Henry Lee Lucas. Glad you could make it, Henry. What have you got to say for yourself: what have you been up to?"

"Oh, I've done some bad things," the man said in a slow Texas drawl, "but so far they can only prove I killed my mother. What's for dinner?"

The next arrival was Edmond Kemperer. Kemperer's claim to fame was that after killing his mother, he had surgically removed her vocal cords and stuffed them down a garbage disposal. "My mother talked too much," he said, "and most of what she said was garbage anyway."

The thing said, "Hear, hear!"

Next came notorious Texas rightwinger Joseph Zinn, who had gunned down a leftist activist as the latter was on his way to work in a convenience store. He was a specialist in matricidal dismemberment as well, having chopped up his. He hated politics, and the thing discreetly suggested I not mention the subject.

Following Zinn at a somewhat respectful distance was a particularly good friend of the thing's as his passion was injecting people he didn't like with slow-acting toxins. He was Marcel Petiot, strong-arm bandit, heroin-dealer, and ex-mayor of the town of Villeneuve-sur-Yvonne in France, who used his position as a respected medical doctor and politician to lure Jews to a torture chamber he had concealed beneath his house with promises of concealment from the Nazis. "Good evening, Doctor," said the thing, "how are things going?"

"Slow," the doctor said, "you know, the war and everything."

"I might imagine," the thing said. "Is there anything I can do?"

The doctor looked depressed. He said, "Not really, well, it's female trouble."

The thing said, "You, Doctor, female trouble?"

Petoit seemed not to appreciate the joke, in fact, he appeared not to be given to humor of any sort, though he did brighten a bit when he saw Teller. "Hello, Edward," he said, waving.

"So what is it this time, Marcel, somebody wouldn't fall for your line?"

"You know everything, don't you Edward," Petoit said uncomfortably. "I might as well tell you. The Borgia girl had agreed to accompany me, but at the last moment, I tell you the very last, she begged off saying she had forgotten a prior engagement with her father."

"Are you still chasing her, Marcel?" said Teller. "I've heard she has all her dinners with her father, if you know what I mean. I think it's a hopeless cause."

"What are you saying?" said Petoit. "I'm afraid I don't know what you mean!"

"Not the Pope," the thing said, mischievously.

Petoit's look was murderous. "Slanderer of the Catholic Church, you are worse than a murderer!"

Teller turned red by degrees. "I am a scientist, you pony doctor. I would be more careful if I were you, you hear?"

Petoit pulled a syringe. Teller pulled the hydrogen bomb.

"Now, now boys," the thing said, "this is a party."

"I'm sorry," Teller said.

"Then, for my sake, put that thing away."

Teller hid the bomb from view, in some secret place.

"And you, Petoit, put away that syringe."

Relaxing, Petoit unscrewed the needle from the instrument and placed both in a little black bag he carried. "I'm sorry," he said, "but I love that woman, and Edward knows that."

"Ah," said the thing, "love ... but is that reason for an international incident?"

"I'm sorry, Lucius. I'm sorry, Edward."

Teller didn't look sorry at all.

There had, in fact, not been any women, though the next arrival was Christa Lehman, a madcap, good-time girl of about twenty-two. It turned out that she had been adulterous, and when her husband found out about it, she fed him truffles stuffed with poison. Her father died of convulsions not long after, after leaving her home. Finding that she liked making candy, she gave some to neighbors, and was apprehended after a dog and a neighbor died. People loved her candy so much a spate of suicides soon followed, using the poison she favored. Though she hadn't invented it, she was viewed as something of an innovator and benefactress to mankind. I was afraid of her because she had killed dogs.

Petoit told her he was interested in her method. Teller said her technique was primitive. They started to argue again when a second woman arrived. Teller was immediately distracted. "Ah, Donna Maria," he beamed.

Donna Maria Alvarez, the daughter of a prominent banking family in Mexico had revived an ancient Aztec method of mummification. Married to a respected rancher, she embalmed four children she had by the lover she shared with her sister. Admitting to the crimes, the ensuing trial became a cause célèbre when her husband went berserk as she held their child in the courtroom, stabbing her to death and almost severing the child's arm from its body in the process. The citizenry, citing an ancient code, felt justice had been done. "At no great expense to the state, and I might add, rather swiftly," the thing said. It is said the bodies are on view to this day in a glass-enclosed case in a museum in Saltillo.

Teller asked how she was. "Thirsty," she replied.

The next to arrive was strange even by these standards, having killed at least a dozen people with an axe in New Orleans. What was unique, even endearing, about him was that he had written to the *Times-Picayune* that he was crazy about jazz and would axe no one that played it in the living room. This curious creature, from the bayou, dressed in a zoot suit, said, "Who's playin' Baby."

"Lucius," the thing said, "this is the Axe-man of the Big Easy. We do not usually do him the honor of inviting him. Axe-man meet Lucius. Lucius is playing tonight. Say hello to Lucius and don't call me 'baby,' it's vulgar."

The axe-man said, "Cool. Wha's goin' on, Lucius, where ya at? Hey, looka dere, he ain't got no hair! He's a real houn' ain' he. Tell me Hometown, does you play jazz?"

"The Axe-man is a solipsist, Lucius. He is crude and loud. Hardly refined enough for our company."

Teller applauded. The Axe-man slid into a corner. "Too bad he don' play jazz," he muttered, "too bad for him!"

The next arrival outdid Axe-man in appearance, being a red mass of pulpy flesh resembling road kill wearing glasses and a beard. "My," said the thing, "tonight it seems we are well represented by the medical profession! Dr. Goldstein, what an unexpected honor, really! What brings you back in time for our party? Lucius, Dr. Goldstein killed fifty Arabs at prayer. How about that for a devotion? Dr. Goldstein, say hello to Lucius Apulius!"

Goldstein's response was lost in his bloody flesh.

There was a loud commotion at the door. A booming voice said, "Of course, I am invited here. How could there be a party without me? Those are my wives!"

The thing said, "That must be Amin Dada. He belongs. And how is the General tonight?"

The personage that entered, a huge grinning man, wore an olive-drab uniform with red epaulets after the fashion of the Soviet army. He was accompanied by hundreds of women in riotous patterns of color. After them came an entourage of general officers from all the armies of the world, kings, emperors and presidents. Adolph Hitler came with Eva Braun. Amin paid court to Catherine the Great, telling her his organ was as great as any horse's. Everybody threatened to send huge armies against everybody.

"All right everybody," the thing said, making a sound like clapping, "let the party begin!"

They played War. I was not having a good time. Nobody could really dance; they all seemed repressed.

"I want to get fucked by a horse," Catherine said.

The Dey of Algiers offered her a fine chestnut stallion that fucked her so hard it killed her. "Did you like it, Catherine," the Dey asked, clasping his pudgy hands.

"I loved it, dear Dey," she said. "Oh yes. Slay me."

The Dey laughed so hard, he fell off his throne. "Laughing powder," Allen Dulles said. "Oh, look, here's Hoover."

I hadn't noticed the little gray cleaning lady with the face of a Boston bulldog.

"Marita fucked Castro," said Hoover.

The crowd hooted.

"It was a fair swap," said J. Edgar. "Guevara for Marita."

The crowd rolled.

Doing a little two-step with Dulles, Hoover said, "I'll give you the other side, if you'll put in another nickel."

Someone in the crowd dropped him a dime. Retrieving his mop pail, he adjusted his kerchief. "The dirty communists are after us," he said into his pail.

The crowd whooped.

He said, "The British are coming! The British are coming?!"

Dulles raised an eyebrow. "No," he said, "it's not the British, it's the commies!"

"No no," said Hoover, "it's the nationalists; it's the imperialists; it's everybody! Quick, get out the horse!"

Somebody produced a horse that looked like it was ready for the glue factory. Christa said she had gotten it from Dr. Petoit. Never mind that it looked sorry, she said, it would give anyone a run for their money. J. Edgar's mop had gotten wringing wet. Wiping it with his kerchief, he said, "Good. Now let's play a game. You shoot the horse and I'll catch you, okay? Dr. Petoit will tie you up."

One by one the crowd let Dr. Petoit tie them up as they shot the horse, everybody except Teller, who stood surveying the crowd as if wondering how much it would take to kill them all. A few keeled over. "Say, Dr. Petoit," asked Hoover, "where'd you get this?"

Petoit looked guilty. "From Chiang," he said. "I got it from Chiang!" Hoover, glaring at him with his cheeky glare of a Boston bull, said, "Chiang? Chiang Kai Chek? This gentleman?"

Chiang had just walked in with Joe Stalin. "Me," he said inscrutably.

"Oh, Chiang, Chiang," Hoover said, "what am I gonna do with you? I guess it's all right."

No sooner than Petoit would tie someone up, they would get real loose, nodding. It was a horse race. The communists weren't even in it. Stalin couldn't take it. "What is everybody doing?" he asked. "Committing suicide? Stop that!"

Dulles, who had been dancing a mad dance with Hoover, pulled the FBI director behind him, as if to protect him. "You're dead, Joe," he said. "Dead in the water. It's our world and we can do what we want. Kill anybody. Even you. Get him, J.J.!"

Hoover looked intimidated. "Why, Allen," he said, "that's your job! You get him."

"Thanks, J.J.," said Dulles. "All right Joe, that's it. You are getting a penalty."

Teller gave the point to himself. "Okay," Hoover said, "you've been playing long enough, Dulles. I've got stuff on your brother!"

Dulles looked at a brown, foul-smelling stain on his version of the old-boy tie and gagged. "I'll get you for that, Hoover!" he said.

It had threatened to turn into a melee when the thing clapped for order. "This," he said, "is Lucius's moment! Quiet everyone, please! Voila!"

I had been feeling a rumbling in my stomach as if something was stirring in there. It was the first I'd felt since the development of my paunch, and the feeling was accompanied by extreme nausea. As the thing said, "Voila," it burst as Roman candles and a few pinwheels shot out, followed by a flight of white doves, a pheasant, and some quail. Then came a nude dancer with the breasts of a honey cup. The other stuff I might have eaten at one time or another, but she came as a complete surprise; I had no idea I'd had her in me. I felt much better with her release, as if she had been so much gas I had had to expel. The group, narcoleptic, nodded. The thing seemed to nod along with the band, the others.

"Speech, speech!" Teller said, sniffing.

The Axe-man said, "I wanna axe 'im if he don' play no jazz."

"All right, Lucius," the thing said, "I suppose you will have to have your speech. You tell us what you've got to say for yourself."

"This," the Axe-man said, "had better be good..."

"Don't kick," I heard myself scream. I had my speech back.

The thing said, "I'm not kicking. I can't. Look. Look at me."

What I saw in the glare of the building's white light dancing before me looked like nothing so much as a simple mound of a white, powdered substance, though on a certain scale it could have been a mountain; snow-capped.

"I'm just junk," the thing said. "That's why I can't kick. You are kicking yourself."

I was surprised. The stuff in the yards had been a lot different.

CHAPTER FIFTEEN

I woke up on the F train harnessed to a leash held by a blind man. How could I mind? It was actually the perfect disguise for me, given my peculiar circumstances. Who would suspect a seeing-eye dog, even if he was an oversized hound like me? At Thirty Fourth Street, I got up from his feet where I had been laying and, cocking my huge floppy ear of a bloodhound, listened intently to the metallic clicking of wheels traveling the rails; I could count each revolution by the sound they made as they passed over a particular section of track.

"Ah, Lucius, we must be at Thirty Fourth," said the blind man, rubbing my floppy ear. "What would I do without you? I does not know how you does that."

It wasn't the least bit difficult, I could hear the different pitches as the wheels struck the track. Pulling into Thirty Fourth, we crossed the platform for the D, changing at Fifty Ninth for the A just because the blind man liked it. I liked it too. All the way uptown I could hear Duke Ellington, the A train, if I wanted to go to Harlem. A newcomer, Ornette Coleman "Ramblin." I was feeling pretty good as the train pulled into One Twenty Fifth, but the first thing I noticed leaving the subway sobered me up pretty quickly: FUGITIVES FOUND MURDERED! read all the headlines of all the newspapers at the newsstand there at St. Nicholas, and underneath, pictures of what I was sure were the bodies of Woody and Peck. Luckily, my newfound master wanted some gum.

"Lucius," he said, "is we at the newsstand yet? I wants to get me some gum. You knows I likes to chew my gum, doesn't you, Lucius."

The "Arf" I gave was like that of Little Orphan Annie's Sandy Warbucks. I wondered where her daddy had gotten that name, "Warbucks." A cute little redhead with button eyes.

"Well, it's better than chewin' terbakker lak' you does. Tee hee."

It seems that somewhere along the way I'd picked up the tobacco habit, chewing it of all things! "Arf!" I said excitedly, "Arf, arf!"

The blind man said, "Good boy!"

While he bought tobacco and the gum, I hurriedly and with growing dread perused the *Daily News*. "Fugitive hookers found with throats torn ... "Mauled pretty savagely. ... Too savage an act to have been committed by a human being. ... Too heinous for any but the worst sort of savage ... Suspect is a missing dog."

The article went on to say Woody was indeed the long missing child of Daddy Warbucks. She had been kidnapped and was believed dead all these years, kidnapped possibly by the same dog suspected of the murders. It went on to say that Peck too was from a prominent family, meat-packers from Chicago, and had been long missing as well. The perpetrator of this outrage committed on humanity could not go unpunished. Fortunately, the picture it ran of me was badly out of focus; I was as unrecognizable as Woody and Peck were. It had happened the day before. I wondered how much time had passed since I had last seen them; how long had I been this blind man's dog.

"Okay, Lucius, I guess we's ready, ain't we ol' boy."

However long, I felt more comfortable than I had in a long time. It seemed like he liked me. I hadn't been called that in a long time.

One Twenty Fifth Street, the commercial artery of Harlem, was a maze of clothing shops displaying sharkskin suits and lizard shoes, jewelry shops offering gold watches and rings with diamonds in them large enough for any king, any emperor, stores offering furs luxurious enough for any queen of any persuasion: foxes, lynxes, leopards that had once coughed terror into hearts that could now afford to purchase them like so many rags; raccoon, lamb, mink, ermine; some admittedly fake, but some as real as the pain of their being torn from those living bodies that had provided them; beauty shops and barber shops, schools that taught the art of sartorial manipulation, how to straighten out the kink and hot curl it. "IF YOUR HAIR IS SHORT AND NAPPY, KONGOLINE WILL MAKE YOU HAPPY! read signs in these establishments, a picture of some woebegone African princess in the coif she woke with, labeled BEFORE, and next to it, labeled AFTER, a picture of a transformed lady of nearly European demeanor, smiling her smile of a radiantly transformed African princess in a way to wake the sun; the implication being she will probably be dancing tonight, her partner diamond-toothed, pompadoured, sharkskinned after having been an elevator operator all day; an elevator man who will take her up, up, up; keep her up all night dancing how they could dance, dance, dance; dance halls, law offices, movie housed that did double-duty as concert halls, the most famous of these being the Apollo, owned by Leo Shifrin (strange, an establishment in Darktown bearing the name of a Greek sun god owned by a Jew that offered the hottest black talent: Cab Calloway, who could shake his silky tresses with the best of them,

Billie Holiday, Sarah Vaughn, Dinah Washington, Billy Eckstine, Peg-leg Bates, Butterbeans and Suzie, Moms Mabley, The Five Blind Boys, Red Foxx), and tabernacles. Bishop Daddy Grace's House of Prayer, where every Sunday, the trombone section rocked the house.

I led the blind man instinctively past these many emporiums to Seventh Avenue where we turned right, past the Hotel Theresa, which housed these kings and queens of show business, to One Twenty Fourth where we crossed Seventh, entering the basement of one of the many brownstones dotting the block, One Thirty Two West One Twenty Fourth Street. I will never forget that number as long as I live. It was pretty dark in there, darker than it had been in the cave by far; not strange in and of itself though, this being, after all, Darktown.

"Does you need the light, Lucius?" the blind man asked, breaking my reverie. "There you is." He lit a small lamp. "You might want to read something. Don' ask me how I knows. I knows you does that. What I do not know is how. My goodness, Lucius, you sure is one smart dog. Probably the smartest ever! Oh Lucius, like I has told you many times, I sure is glad you is mine. I ain't never going to let you go; not ever. Not till you dies or I does! You don't mind, does you, Lucius, does you boy. I'se good to you, ain't I?"

What choice did I have but to go "Arf!" to avoid barfing. "Never" was a long time. The blind man was without the slightest doubt good to me, and, as I have said, being with him was the best disguise I could have asked for, under the circumstances. Still, all I knew was Woody and Peck were dead, I was a suspect, and I didn't dare let this man know I could talk or he would have had me in a three-ring circus in a minute, front and center. The Apollo. The Paramount Fox in Brooklyn. Busted.

The soft light of the lamp revealed a moderately sized room with a low ceiling that was sparsely furnished and dominated by faded linoleum carpeting that was worn through in spots, exposing the black petroliated underside, and clean, clean, clean, scrubbed daily by the blind man until every corner shone as though he could see. A double bed with a maroon comforter, an old, overstuffed easy chair, a small table on which stood the only lamp and an AM radio made up its spare accoutrements. Off this was a small kitchen with a Formica table, two chairs, a cabinet and counter that contained the sink, a stove where he prepared his tea, a waist-high refrigerator, and off of this, the bathroom. While he would sit at the kitchen table to sip his tea, he would feed me in the living room, as there was no light in the kitchen, he having no need of it. The bathroom was dark too. "I guess you wants your ter-bakker now, doesn't you, Lucius," he said, shoving a plug of the filthy leaf into my mouth. I didn't like the taste of it and didn't know where or how I had acquired such a habit. "Now lemme git the pepper before you chews."

Shuffling off with that speedy gait the blind have when sure of their surroundings, he returned in a moment with some cayenne pepper he unceremoniously dumped into my mouth along with the tobacco. "Okay," he said chuckling, "now chew, Lucius, chew. That's a good boy."

The tobacco and pepper made me gag. The tobacco and the pepper made me mad. The tobacco and the pepper made me spit up into a canister he placed beside my feeding dish for this purpose. "Go on, boy, gag, spit, git mad," he chuckled. "Tha's right. Now you jes' let somebody 'er terother come foolin' 'round yere wid' a blind man. You'll git 'em, won't you, Lucius." He patted my head, drawing his hand back quickly, expertly when I snapped at him.

So that was how I had acquired the filthy habit of chewing tobacco, and my taste for pepper, which persists to this day. Not only was I his seeing-eye dog, I was also his watchdog; given the tobacco and the pepper because it made me mad. Well, that was all right; given the situation I was in, I was certain a little anger couldn't hurt.

Each day after he'd scrubbed the floors at least three times, we would head up One Twenty Fifth to the Independent line down to the Lighthouse For the Blind where he said he'd picked me up, making the same way back, past the newsstand where he would purchase his gum and my tobacco, east on One Twenty Fifth to One Twenty Fourth, from where we would head out again the next morning, past the spiny backs of the grand emporiums to the Independent. It was a circuitous route and one that made no sense to me at all, as for my part, it should have been clear even to a blind man that the IRT on Lenox was closer and would have put us closer to our destination, but he was my master and I was only his eyes, whatever direction he chose, I had to follow. If anyone approached us on our circuit, it was also my job to determine their intent, whether their approach was neutral or threatening, and if the latter, to snarl. Snarling became my way of life. The blind man was what is referred to as a "Geechee" from South Carolina; these were a sullen, soft-spoken people said to come from the west coast of Africa, who would cut you as soon as look at you. The plan was this: if I were to snarl, then growl twice and snarl again, he would commence to cutting. We didn't have too much trouble. After I would snarl and growl, and he would shift into his knife-grabbing stance, your usual "thief-off-a-blind-man" type marauder would quickly back off.

As prominent as the families of Woody and Peck were, and as heinous as their murders had been, there was not one word more about the case in any of the papers, not even the trade ones. It was as if suddenly there was a blackout. There were plenty of others, though: JACK ZANGRETTI, GUNSHOT VICTIM! HANK KILLMAN'S THROAT CUT! GRAY UNDERHILL COMMITS SUICIDE! ROSE CHERAMIE HIT AND RUN VICTIM! DOROTHY KILL-GALLEN DEAD OF DRUG OVERDOSE AFTER THREATEN-ING TO BLOW JFK CASE WIDE OPEN! UNKNOWN CAUSES KILL MRS. EARL SMITH: KNOWN THAT MRS. SMITH HAD BEEN SEEKING UNKNOWN! LEE BOWERS DIES IN FREAK ACCIDENT! RUBY DIES OF BERYLIUM INJECTION! (I thought of Dr. Petoit) DAVID FERRIE DIES OF BLOW TO NECK! ELADIO DEL VALLE AXED AND SHOT TO DEATH IN MIAMI! REVEREND JOHNSON SHOT TO DEATH! CIA DEPUTY DIRECTOR OF CARIBBEAN OPERATIONS COL-LAPSES AFTER PHYSICAL! CRITIC OF ASSASINATION RE-PORT, HALE BOGGS, DIES IN MYSTERIOUS PLANE CRASH! J.A. MILTEER DIES IN FIERY EXPLOSION! SAM GI-ANCANA STITCHED SIX TIMES AROUND THE MOUTH WITH .22 CALIBER PISTOL WHILE IN GOVERNMENT CUS-TODY! COMMITTEE WITNESS JOHN ROSELLI FOUND CHOPPED TO DEATH IN MIAMI! GEORGE de MOREN-SHILDT FIRES SHOTGUN BLAST INTO OWN MOUTH! NICOLETTI PULLED DEAD OF BULLET WOUND FROM BURNING CAR IN CHICAGO! SHOTGUN VICTIM CARLOS SOLLARAS RULED SELF-INFLICTED! NUMBER THREE MAN IN CIA SHOT AND KILLED BY SON OF COP WHO MISTOOK HIM FOR A WHITE-TAIL DEER! SHOOTER GETS PROBATION! CHIVINGTON LET OFF WITH SLAP ON WRIST! QUOTED AS SAYING, "NITS MAKE LICE... KILL ALL, BIG AND LITTLE, AND DAMN ANY MAN WHO TAKES THE SIDE OF THE INDIANS! THE ASP DIES IN SPECTACU-LAR CRASH! The old Asp himself! Even he couldn't save Little Or-phan Annie Warbucks. He wouldn't save anybody ever again.

One Twenty Fifth was a raucous babble of sounds, a riotous carousel of color. Loudspeakers blared the music that had wound its way here from the port towns of the African continent, snaking up from the Caribbean Archipelago in all its many meters; sons of the mountains, sons of the valleys. Mambo bebopped, it rhythm and blued, it rocked and rolled in hues; and when you walked on One Twenty Fifth, you dressed down. The blind man dressed down in a double-breasted blue serge pin-striped suit, a tan gabardine windbreaker, black high-topped kangaroo comforts and either a tan Borselino or a Stetson hat. He always dressed down in one of three starched white shirts with the same black, clip-on bowtie day in and day out, to go down One Twenty Fifth, to go down-town. All the men wore some version of this outfit; maybe with a single breast, while the women wore their flips and their polka dots until they could afford their furs and their lizards. How they usually acquired these was through their own version of the tontine, the boleta, the "numbers." Black mathematics. The random chance of the alignment of certain num-bers with others arrived at through dreams and portents, as in, "I stumped my toe the other day," a citizen says to another.

"Oh yeah?" says the other. "Well, you know, I thinks I is gonna play me a five," and they are considered wise beyond their years when they, oh, roll down One Twenty Fifth, oh, dressed down in their ocelot and their lizards, even the men in their fox box-back bennies, because they'd had the foresight and enough communion with the Holy Spirit to put all their few, meager savings on a five and have it come off. Hit all the numbers or a combination thereof and drive a Lincoln or a Cadil-lac across One Twenty Fifth to church because, if the good lord had not wanted it for this favored citizens, it would not have happened, would it? Buying branches of the rhododendron leaves they called "lucky" from the florist, placing their bets with runners that danced across One Twenty Fifth. The only deviation we made from our route would be to go to the florist next to the IRT station on Lenox to place his own; and I soon found out why he never wanted to use that station. It was simply this: down at the florist's, along with the "lucky" leaves and the boletas, was a young lady the blind man was in love with. "Lu-cius," he said, "never mind not letting your left hand know what your right is doing, never, never let a woman know what it is you does every day if you is in your right mind and wants to keep her."

I didn't know if that was sound advice or what, but I did know I did not like that woman. I don't think she played fair with him. I think she switched his nunbers and kept his hits. I thought she was a Lucan. A lady to be sure, but a Lucan nevertheless. I thought I saw her switch them a couple of times, but what in the world could I have said with-out revealing myself? Anyway, it was not my problem. It was only love, and what is wrong with that other than we are too selfish with it or we are too giving? My problem was something else. I had to stay hidden.

She detected my suspicion right away: "Geech," she said calling him by a pet name, "Geech, where'd you git dat dog?"

"Why, I got him down to ... well, I was on my way somewhere ... I was, you know, jes' goin'," and a voice says, 'You needs a dog! You knows you needs one. Take this one,' and I got him jes' like that. Does you like him, Lil'? You cain't pet him, though, because he is really a one-man puppy, but I kin teach 'im Lil', I kin teach 'im over time ter love you, Lil'. Lucas, say hello ter Lil', Lil' Eva, the finest Lil' flower in the whole shop! Ain't it the truth, Lil'?"

What could I do but whine and bark?

"I don't know, Geech," the woman said. "I don't know. I don't know about that. I just do not like dogs as a rule, and him in particular. A mean ol' dog bit me once. He might bite me."

"Bite you?" said the blind man, "Oh no Lil' Eva, he would never do that! You is my friend, you is my dearest friend, Lil' Eva, and any friend of mine is a friend o' his. Ain't that right, Lucius."

"But he's so big, Geech. If he wanted to bite me, you might couldn't stop 'im!"

The tobacco had me going, salivating and quivering.

"I could too. Lil'. Besides, I wouldn't have to, bein' he is my dog and he does what I says, don'cha Lucius." Patting my neck and rubbing my ear, he expertly drew back when I snapped at him.

"I don't know about that, Geech. See, if you didn't have him, I might could let you see where that dog bit me that time."

"Gee, Lil'," the blind man said, "that would be nice, but ... but ... gosh, Lil', you knows I cain't see!"

"That's right, Geech, you cain't see, can you. I forgot. You would have ta feel it, wouldn't you ... hmm. Well, I might could let you feel it, you know, jes' to let you know what dem dogs kin do to you when you ain't lookin' at 'em!"

"Git rid 'er Lucius? Gosh, Lil', I might do anything for you, but this here is Harlem; a blind man has got to have him a dog anywhere in the world, but here in this neighborhood, he needs a big dog, all these crooks and robbers they got aroun' here! You see what I mean, don'cha, Lil' Eva?"

"But you don't need 'im aroun' me, does you honey?"

"Oh no, Lil' Eva, not you, —I never thought that about you!"

"Well, I'll tell you what honey," Lil' Eva said. "You think about it, big boy, but don't you think about it too long. You know what they says, don't you Geech, 'You study long, you study wrong!' Seems like it's true, don't it."

One reason I will never forget our address is that the blind man played it everyday in an infinite variety of combinations, none of which ever came out. "You knows what I wants, Lil' Eva," he said, handing over what was for him a sizeable hunk of cash. "That is a mighty tempting offer, too. I sure will keep it in mind."

"Well, I might not be here forever, Geech. Just remember what I said," she remarked coquettishly, taking the money.

"I sure will, Lil', honey, I sure will." He steered me towards the door. "I will see you later; maybe we will hit today, huh?"

"Never can tell, sweetie, you never can tell, can you?" Her look following us was one of pure avarice.

When we had gotten a few steps away, the blind man said, "I knows you doesn't like her, Lucius, and I thinks I know why. You thinks she manipulates my combinations and switches my numbers. Well, maybe she do, Lucius, maybe she do. But you know what? I likes her and that's all there is to it. I just like hearin' her voice, and if I pays for the privilege of hearin' it, who kin blame me for doin' it? Even if I is a blind man, I is a man, and ain't that what mens do?"

The blind man had it bad, and like the song said, that was not good. Snarl and snap and growl at the passing marauder as I might, here was a thief that had her hand in the blind man's treasury with his consent. What could I say about it? I could not advise him. Still, I was sure she was a Lucan. There had been one named Lil' Eva back in elementary school though, as she had been a couple of grades behind me, I never got to see much of her. Lil' Eva, Lil' Eva, the frail so nice they had to name her twice. The gossip back then was that she could sure put some steam in the pipes. The only problem with her being a Lucan was there was never just one of them anywhere; if you could set your eyes on one, you could bet there were bound to be more. That was what the blind man should have been betting on, though with that woman as the croupier, I'm not sure he would have won even then. I thought it wouldn't be long before we started seeing Lucans everywhere. The thought raised the hackles on my neck. Paranoia? No. It was experience. What they did, they did in concert.

The blind man had lost his sight in one of the imperial wars forever being waged by the imperial state and was compensated for it by benefits due the disabled veteran in the form of a couple of hefty checks a month. These and the dividends from a few modest investments he made left him pretty well off in relation to the stiffs around him before the dream hit or those like me, unable to work at anything meaningful due to their status as fugitives of the state, or the undocumented, those branded lazy and inept and who were forced or just disposed to create their own economies. The blind man had a purple heart and a couple of other medals for exceptional valor and service. He was afraid of no man, but when it came to that little Lucan, he wore his heart on his sleeve. Oh, he could justify it to me in any way he wanted to, but as far as I was concerned, his little flirtation with that woman was just plain stupid. The jill was a thief and he knew it; having already stolen his heart, the money part was easy. Can you imagine that? I mean, she stole the poor man's purple heart and there wasn't a thing in that world I could do about it! What was I going to do: growl, snarl, snap? He would have gotten rid of me in a minute! It was the saddest thing when he said to me one day, "Lucius, my heart is gone," because I had seen it coming; I had seen her when she did it. I had never felt so vulnerable in all of my life, not even when I was in the prison. The amounts of money he bet with her were staggering for a blind veteran of many wars, or for anybody. His response was to scrub the floor even harder, give me more tobacco and pepper, to become more surly with strangers, more sullen. I stopped chewing the mixture altogether after a while, only pretending to chew, and spitting it into the toilet. He stopped eating. He stopped drinking his tea. He wouldn't even change his shirt. Oh god, I wanted to give him some advice, but he wouldn't have believed it, not even coming from me. Seeing is believing. I thought he was going to scrub himself to hell.

Returning from the Lighthouse for the Blind one day, I noticed a hot dog cart at the corner of One Twenty Fifth and Seventh that had not been there before. The vendor was a Lucan, I was sure of that. I hadn't just fallen off of the watermelon truck parked innocuously in front of the Hotel Theresa. The guy hawking watermelons from it in his sing-song voice, the guy on the stepladder exhorting the crowd, which had collected like water in a basin, to wake up, to throw off the yoke of servitude and oppression, was a Lucan, a clever one to be sure. The crowd was used to preachers and he was pretty good at it.

"The white man is the burden," he was saying.

"Amen, brotha!" came the response.

"He got the nerve to say you is his burden, but he is yours!"

"Ain't it the truth!"

"Hey, if you was his burden, he ain't takin' proper care of it; he ain't liftin' it; jus' look at where you are and look at where he is! Is you on Park Avenue?"

Somebody in the crowd said, "To be a maid!"

"Is you in Westchester?"

"No!"

"That ain't entirely true," a man said, shaking his head, "I got an aunt what's got a house in Westchester. In Yonkers, on Warburton!"

"I ain't talkin' about like your ol' aunt got, brotha, I'm talkin' lock, stock and county here, big acres! Now am I right?"

The crowd said, "Teach, Brotha, speak!"

The speaker said, "Who is in the White House!"

"He is," the crowd said. "He is!"

"Why does they call it the 'White' House? Because he want it 'white,' that's why, and he is not gonna let you in there 'cept to shine his shoes or to cut his hair, or to cook his food! Hey, brotha, you with dat aunt in Westchester, what do your aunt do?"

Sheepishly, but with some pride in his voice, the fellow said, "She were a cook for a white woman. Hey, my aunt cook so good, that white woman give her that house. Cried when she left. My ol' aunt cried too."

The crowd laughed and hooted derisively. The old lady left muttering, "Hm, if we don' cook for him, who is we gon' cook for, and if we don' cook for nobody, how is we go to eat? I cain't stand 'roun' yere listenin' ter you trouble makin' niggers. I has got ter go and cook. I has got ter feed myself."

The speaker, warming to his subject, preaching to the converted, said, "If he can, the white man will make a dog out of you; and if he can't do that, he will make a monkey out of you; and if he can't do that, he will give you a monkey!"

Lucan or not, I knew by my very existence the truth of what he was saying, and if that truth be told, that little old lady muttering as she left looked like nothing so much as a little wizened monkey.

The blind man sighed. "Oh Lucius," he said, "goodness me, I ain't got time fer all this here, I got me a personal problem."

His problem was indeed personal, and because he had it, I had it too. Two types of Lucans was what Luke had said. Thinking back to when that snake Arnold had turned on him and that incident in the square, I knew what kind Lil' Eva was, but where did this guy fit? Who were these people on the corner selling watermelons and speaking? But then who was Luke; why was I taking everything he said for gospel?

When we got back to the house, I knew something was definitely wrong. There were footprints all over the place for one thing; now why should that have been with the blind man scrubbing like a minor leaguer, I could not see. Of course the blind man couldn't see it either, but he did notice right away that things had been moved, so imperceptibly I couldn't see where, but the blind man said quietly, "Aha, Lucius, does you see what I sees? Somebody or terother has been in here, snoopin' around this house, hey, boy?"

I snarled twice, growled and snarled again. Pulling his knife, the blind man commenced to cutting. I could hardly get out of the way in that tight space. He was thorough, and cut in a grid like a painter, but it did him no good this time, there was nobody there to cut but ourselves; the place was eerily, ghostily empty. "Did I git 'em, Lucius?" he asked, panting mightily from his exertions. "Did I git 'em; did I git dem rascals?"

I barked, growled and whined, the signal that there was no one there.

"Shit," he said, testing the blade of his knife with a thumb callused from so much scrubbing, "I'll git 'em. I knows what they thinks; they thinks I got what I gots hid out here somewhere and they kin jes' bust on in yere and git it, hey, Lucius? Well, they sure is fools, ain't they? That is jes why I keeps my money down ter de Lighthouse. Jes' why I invest in dem govment bonds, and iffen dey comes back 'roun' yere messin' wid me, I sure knows what ter do wid 'em." He made a few practice slashes with that knife. "I'll slice 'em too thick ter fry and too thin for ter boil! Now does you see why I gives you dat terbakka and dat dere pepper?"

He gave me some more, removed a whetstone from the kitchen cabinet and, settling himself at the table, began to sharpen the knife as if it could have been made any sharper without disappearing. Finished to his satisfaction, he stood and made another practice slash. A house-fly, drifting lazily by, was severed neatly in half. Putting the open knife down on the table, he returned the whetstone to the cabinet, and reaching under the counter for the pail and brush with, which he used to scrub, filled it with soap and water and began to work. I had spat out the mixture when I noticed the note on the bed. "Hello Lucius," it read in an uneven scrawl I was unfamiliar with, "how are you and that foolish blind man we know you are staying with? We know he thinks he is tough, being a veteran and all, but we'll see about that. Hey, your ass is missing, isn't it, dog ears? How about that! Well, we just don't want you to think it is safe, okay? You will be hearing more from me. If you don't, I'm afraid that will be because it is all over for your ass. How does that strike you?" This note was signed, incredibly, A PAIN IN YOUR ASS.

Fuck. So my ass was in trouble again somewhere, possibly being tortured. That part about pain didn't sound too promising. A gloom settled on me darker than all of Harlem. I wanted to tell the blind man that somehow his love life was tied to my destiny, but how could I do that? And anyway, I didn't even know if that was really true; all I knew was somebody was drawing heat here and my ass was involved. After he had finished his scrubbing, the blind man sat down to wait—in vain as it turned out, as nothing more happened that night, and in the morning we set out as usual for the Lighthouse for the Blind. The janitor who was sweeping the platform of the station had the lean, vigilant look of a Lucan. They can look like weircats. The conductor of the train was a weircat in his vigilance. When we reached the Lighthouse, the new guard at the door had the brown eyes of a weircat, and the new receptionist had the glittering ellipsoidal eyes of a snake, made to look so perhaps because of the horn rimmed glasses she sported with little rhinestones in them that glittered strangely in the fluorescent light as she moved her long neck. She spoke with a lisp, due perhaps, to her cleft tongue. She looked at the blind man with what I thought was predatory interest and her cursory glances in my direction seemed more than a passing look. I wanted to snarl and growl and snap, but I was quite sure that if I did, my career as a blind man's dog would have been over. I was sure, too, that if the blind man had pulled that knife in that place, he would not have been the victor. She had said, "Name, Sir?"

"Sue?" he asked, starting at the unfamiliarity of the voice.

"Not here anymore," said the receptionist, "transferred to another state."

The blind man was incredulous. "Since yesterday? My, that were kind of sudden, weren't it?"

"As I understand it," she said in that peculiar lisp that made her 's's fairly hiss, "there was something about an illness in her family. She asked to be transferred rather suddenly, and it was granted just as quickly. Name, please?"

The old receptionist, Sue, and the blind man had been friends for many years. It had been she who had helped him through his application for the services of the institution. He said, "I didn't know as she had no family..."

The receptionist repeated her question: "Name, please?"

"Hm? Oh, yeah," the blind man said distractedly.

After he gave his name, we were admitted into the waiting room. There weren't many people as it was our custom to arrive early and, after a moment, we were ushered into an unfamiliar cubicle by a woman I had never seen before, and I can't say that if she looked like a Lucan I wouldn't have bolted out of there, but she didn't appear to be — the look in her cold blue eyes was one of concern. "Good Morning," she said, adjusting steel-rimmed glasses and pointing to a folder on her desk, "I'm Mrs. Peabody. I have been going over your files and I am afraid I have some bad news for you. It appears you are overdrawn to where it would take more than your life expectancy would reasonably allow you to cover." She cleared her throat and went on: "I say 'reasonably,' because your account is overdrawn to an amount roughly the size of the national debt. A lot of money!"

"Overdrawn?" The blind man blinked uncomprehendingly. "What does you mean?" he asked. "Whatever I got outa' here them these bonds I got sure oughter be more dan enough to take care of. Dat is just why I got them things, doesn't you remember, anyway dat is what Sue said when she tol' me ter git 'em. My 'security blanket,' she called it."

Peabody picked up the files, glancing through them. "Bonds,

bonds, bonds, let me see," she said, her voice singsong as she said "bonds." "Oh yes, bonds. I'm afraid I have to tell you a lien has been placed against those bonds." She chewed nervously on a pencil.

"A lien? What is you talkin 'bout here, lemme see!"

Pulling herself upright in her chair at this, Peabody said, "If you can see this you are violating the rules of the Lighthouse and defrauding the government of the United States. It is not in Braille."

"Lucius, " he said, "git on up dere and see!"

"Dogs do not read either," she said, "and even if they did, what method would they have of communicating what they read to you? That is not what seeing-eye dog means."

The blind man said, "Lucius can," defiantly tugging at my harness. "Lucius, git on up dere and see what dat thing say."

I did not want to make him look like any more of a fool that I thought him, so I did not move. I pressed the floor with all the weight of my one hundred and forty pound frame. Whatever it was we were caught up in, I was not going to admit anything. Luckily, he seemed merely desperate.

"You are confusing that animal," Peabody said. "Weren't you trained in what to expect from one? Haven't you taken our course?"

"Cose, cose ...?" he said, tugging at me, "Cose I took yo' cose!"

"Then you should know not to expect them to be able to read. Have you been abusing that dog? If so, I'm afraid I'll have to recommend it be taken away from you."

He stopped tugging. "Lien," he mumbled, "lien ... on me ... tell me, who in the world kin lien on me like dat?"

The woman sighed and shrugged her shoulders before clasping her hands cathedral-like under her chin as if she had seen too many cases like this, of blind people who know nothing at all of the intricacies of the bond market, who hadn't the slightest idea of what was happening to them or why as far as their money went. "Well," she said exhaling air like a balloon, "the federal government is the only agency that can put a lien on this type of bond, the IRS. Have you been paying your taxes?"

"I is in good standing wit' de government," the blind man said indignantly, "Cose I pays my taxes!"

Cupping a chin with a meaty palm and tapping a fingernail against the desk for emphasis, she said, "I'm not saying nor are they that you in fact do owe them anything more than what you actually owe them, but until this matter is litigated, your account is frozen, is that clear?"

"Dey must be somebody I kin see about dis," said the blind man.

"There is," said Peabody, "the IRS. I'm sure you'll be hearing from them."

The blind man looked like he had been struck by lightning in steel-rimmed glasses. "Somethin's funny here," he said, "but it ain't really funny, if you knows what I mean ... dere must be somebody I kin see. I'se a veteran and I knows my rights. Come on Lucius, we is goin' ter der V.A."

CHAPTER SIXTEEN

There was nobody at the V.A. he could see. He was informed most emphatically that if he insisted in his attempts he would forfeit whatever benefits he could ever have as an unsighted veteran. When he protested, a guard was called. The man inquired curtly, "Sir, are you insisting to see someone?" The blind man's shoulders slumped. He let out a long sigh. I led him away as quickly and quietly as I could. The guard wore a uniform as wrinkled as skin that made him look as though he'd been born with it. I didn't doubt for one minute he'd a friend with a dog named Rudy. The train took a long time to come, and when it did, the wheels echoed the blind man's words: "What is we gonna do now, Lucius?"

I did not want to go home, but we were on a treadmill. Our fates had lain a heavy hand on us; there was nothing I could do but lead him back along our circuitous route. When we got to One Twenty Fifth, I led him stumbling behind me past the emporiums: past Frank's Steak and Chop House where the hinsty and the white folks ate, past the Baby Grand, the House of Prayer, past the world famous Apollo, where looking up I was astonished to see in huge red letters the name JAMES MOODY, and underneath, in black letters slightly smaller, LITTLE JIMMY SCOTT AND HIS RHYTHM REVUE. He was here. James Moody was right here on One Twenty Fifth Street at the world famous Apollo and we could not afford to go see him. Talk about a blow; my whole purpose in life was to discover this man, and here I was totally unprepared to do it! I wanted to suggest that the blind man get a cup. Hell, I wanted to get one. That would have been good for a laugh, a seeing-eye dog with a cane, dark glasses and a tin cup. As much as the breed does for mankind, I wondered how many of them would throw me a bone or, better, a measly three bucks so I could go and see the great James Moody at that moment, an event I was so sure would be the equal of Columbus's discovery of America, if I could name him and all of his parts, discover him for myself. We didn't have a crying quarter, as I used to hear my old grandmother say.

When we had gotten to Seventh and turned south, I noticed the frankfurter vendor was gone. The speaker in front of the Theresa was still there hanging, cajoling, but the Lucan that had been hawking watermelons was gone, too. Maybe both just happened to have Tuesdays off, but maybe they didn't.

"I got an idea, Lucius," the blind man said and, instead of turning onto One Twenty Fourth, he directed me to lead him to the florist's.

Lil' Eva was dressed rather elegantly for a shop girl. "Aww, Geech," she said as we entered, "you still ain't got rid of that dog?"

I almost growled.

"Naw, Lil' Eva," he said, "I ain't got rid o' him. It look like he de only thing I got, and I doesn't know right now how is I gonna keep him."

She was in a teasing mood. She smelled like she was wearing a new perfume whose name was "money." Its scent was as thick as musk. He could smell it and he sniffed suspiciously. "Why not, Geech?" she said batting lashes she could have snatched off a mink.

"Well, it ain't fer de least o' reasons dat suddenly he is all I got left," he said, pulling me to him defensively and cocking his head as though trying to see where all this new money was coming from.

"You coulda had me, Geechie," she said. "Now, it's just too late. I'm goin' away tomorrow, baby."

"Goin' away, Lil' Eva; where is you goin?"

"Brazil."

The blind man said, "How?"

She giggled. "On a air-a-plane, silly!"

"Wid what? Where is all dis yere smell o' new money comin' from?"

"Aw, Geech," she said feigning surprise, "you ain't hear yet? I thought it would be all over the town by now."

"Heard what?"

"I done hit the number, baby, all three of them digits and I combinated it, too, for some loot. I am goin' to Rio! Too bad I can't take you."

He said, "Ah, dat is great, Lil' Eva, thanks, but I couldn't go nowhere no way. I is in litigation. I cain't go nowhere but ter cote. Somebody is got a lien on me."

"Lien on you? What do you mean, a 'lien' on you? Who you let 'lien' on you like that?"

"The IRA, I mean, the IRS. I ain't lettin' 'em do it; they is doin' it all on they own. I cain't even see what dey got er who is got it! Dem people is like haints down dere; you cain't really even see who dey is until dey gits right up on you, and den it seem it's too late, dey done got you liened on, litigated, and in cote, and if you is a blind man like I is, you cain't see 'em even den. Effen I had me some eyes, I'd have ter say dey was playin' tricks on poor me. As it is, I has jes' got ter wait and see what happens. In de dark."

"Gee, Geech, that is too bad." Her voice sounded like she had a long face, but her look was a study in indifference. Her yawn was stifled by a newly manicured and painted hand. "So what else is new, Geech, what is you gonna do now?"

He hesitated, preparing himself for something he obviously found repugnant. "Well, Lil' Eva," he finally said, "how long is I been playin' wid you?"

"I dunno, Geech, 'bout six months?"

"And you and I is fren's, ain't we, Lil' Eva?"

"As long as the sun shines, Geech."

"Well, Lil' Eva, I thought I would ask you effen you would do me a favor."

"Why goodness gracious me, Geech, a favor? What can yo Lil' Eva do f' you baby?"

"Well, Lil' Eva," he said, seeming to choke on his words, "since I has played my number wid you every day, sometime twice, for six months, and I ain't got no money now on account o' bein' in litigation and all, what I wants ter know from you is," he hesitated and went on, "would you put it in f' me and combinate it f' ten dollars for me; you knows my number, one, three, two, and, well, since you done hit and everything, could you loan me ten against if I hit er dey liens up offa me in cote?

Eva looked flabbergasted. "Why, Geech ..."

The blind man broke in, his words tumbling out in a rush, "I knows Eva, I knows it is a awful thing fer a gennemun, such as I considers mysef' to be, ter stoop so low as ter have ter ask a lady fer a favor such as I is askin' you, Eva, but I ain't got a cryin' quarter, I ain't got a dime!"

"Oh Geech—"

He couldn't stop, his hurried words almost lost in his shame, "And it ain't only me I has ter consider now, even if I doesn't eat fer a couple o' days, I has got ter feed Lucius; dat dere were one o' de rules down to de Blind. I knows you doesn't like him much, but he is my eyes; effen I didn't have him, den what would I do?"

Lil' Eva's tone was saccharine: "Sugar, of course, I will put your number in f' you. Ain't you been playin' it f' almost seven months? But you know, as for that other thing, Geech, you know, it might seem like it the way everybody talkin' and all, but I swear, after I give the banker a tip, pay f' my ticket and a cabana, I won't have nothin' left, not a dime! Everybody think I got so much money, but don't you tell 'em nothing, Geech, 'cause it ain't none o' their business."

Banker? If there was a banker, I'd have to bet a blind man in love it was Eva's pocketbook. All the air went out of him. "Thanks, Eva, anything you kin do." He tugged at me. "C'mon, Lucius."

She said, "Anytime, Geech, anytime. Goodbye, baby. Stay warm and take care o' that dog, you hear?"

I wanted to bite her, rip out her cunt so no man would be taken like that again by one, not even a blind man, but that would have been too much like Mike Hammer in a cheap Mickey Spillane novel. I was not a misogynist nor a literary front for monopoly capitalist interests; I was just Lucius Apulieus, some poor slob, who had been turned into a dog by some squirt named Elvis. I loved women too much for that even if they were crooks. Instead, I led him through the intersection now named African Square back to the house with great trepidation. As we left the florist's, Lil' Eva had said, "Hey, Geech, whyn't you git a cup? You, that dog and a cup would be perfect, you would probably make a million in no time. You might be able to send for me!"

"No thank you," the blind man said resignedly, "I does not like to beg."

All the lights were on back at the apartment, not just the one in the large room, which in our haste to leave we might have neglected to put out, but also the ones in the kitchen and bathroom. There were footprints everywhere. If I hadn't known better, I might have thought they belonged to cockroaches being all over the place as they were, could be, even on the ceiling, but the blind man was too clean for cockroaches. He noticed right away that the furniture had been moved again. "Sompin' smell funny ter you Lucius?" he asked, his voice low, cautious.

I snarled twice and growled, but, to tell the truth, not having had the tobacco nor the pepper in some while, my heart was not in it. He whipped out the knife and started cutting. In vain. I just managed to avoid being cut open from chin to spleen by scrambling from corner to corner. "Did I git 'im, Lucius; did I git 'im?" he asked excitedly. I whined the disappointed whine of a hound. There was another note on the bed.

As soon as the blind man had calmed down a bit, I crept over to the bed, plucked the thing up into my jaws, opened it with my snout, held it down with my paws, and read the same uneven scrawl as before, I HAVE GOT YOUR ASS FOR REAL THIS TIME! It was signed now with merely the letter 'A,' and the word, 'PAIN.' A. PAIN, as if I didn't have enough of those in my life already. I let out an involuntary whimper.

"What's wrong, Lucius?" the blind man asked.

Barking heartily to reassure him, I shoved the note into a handy pocket. I had the feeling I would just have to work this one out for myself.

"I kin smell trouble Lucius; I just cain't see it, and I cain't put my knife on it. Look like de thing be's movin' jes dat fast, like nagual. Lucius, boy, does you believe in de power of de animal spirits? I know wid your seein' eyes and all, you might done seed some o' dat stuff somewhere. Some o'dese people will change into things on you, pigs and snakes."

Something was indeed moving through the air. Something chilling. It hit the blind man like a cold spark of inspiration. If he had had eyes just then, they would have been narrow with suspicion. "I sure wishes you could talk; I bet you'd have a whole lot say. Can you, boy? Talk fer me!"

I barked like a fool. I barked like I was trying to wake the neighbors.

"Okay, okay, shh-shh, calm down boy, calm down," he said, patting my flank and rubbing my ears and pulling back expertly when I pretended to snap at him. "Nah, you cain't talk, can you? Your vocal chords and lips was not made fer de romance languages. But, boy, wouldn't dat be sompin if you spoke Chinese. Yoruba. Igbo. Anything somebody terother might could unnerstand. Oh, wouldn't dat dere be de most splendiferous way outen all our troubles. How 'bout dat, huh? Lucius de talkin' dog. Hee hee. Me and you would be better den Edgar Bergen and Charlie McCarthy 'cause you ain't no dummy. We wouldn't have ter worry 'bout nothin'!"

I was sorely tempted to trust him, to tell him why that would not be the case, but what would that have gained us, some time? That would have been about it, an eternity in the dark earth with the worms; nothing appetizing unless you were an annelid with a skin like Archimide's screw.

"Dey is sompin' goin' on Lucius; I kin hear it."

In the kitchen, over the stove, was an air duct. I thought I heard a rustling in there, less like the rustling of leaves than that of cattle. Their dry bones. Of Lucans.

Silent as death he oozed in under the door through a crack so small it admitted little light, forked tongue making no sound as it slithered in and out of his lipless mouth with all the elasticity of rubber. His eyes bored hypnotically into mine, eyes with the ellipsoidal, dagger-like pupils of a snake: Luke, whom I had last seen with Woody and Peck, my warm-blooded companions, who had suddenly stopped breathing. The blind man stood transfixed, as if mesmerized by the total silence of his progress. As he slid boldly up to me, the blind man cut him in half.

He was so fast he could have fooled me, too, he'd only been waiting his chance. Twin jets of black blood spurted everywhere as if from a pair of fire hoses with no human hand to direct them. The Lucan, writhing and contorting, threw out black blood like spray paint. "Lucius," it wrote, "Lucius, Lucius, Lucius, why'd you let 'im do this to me?"

I signaled rather frantically that I hadn't let him do anything, I was more or less transfixed by that way he had of staring and, anyway, how could I have stopped the blind man who had only done what it was he'd been trained to do: kill anything that moved unannounced. I asked him why he had broken in on us like that. With the sprayed blood of a snake, he said he hadn't "broken" into anywhere, he had simply oozed in through a crack in the door. Having been made a snake, what could he do but behave like one? Could I be other than a dog?

"Did I git 'im, Lucius, did I git dat rascal?" the blind man asked excitedly. "Felt like I got me sompin'!"

I needed to talk to the Lucan some more without his interference. I made a baying sound and whined plaintively, the signal that meant I wasn't sure, if there was any quarry I would nose it out. I hoped none of the spraying blood would hit him before I got the information I wanted. He positioned himself into a "horse" stance and waited.

"What's going on here!" I signaled to dying Lucan.

"What do you mean," he sprayed. "What does it look like? I'm dyin'!"

"I can see that," I said, "and I am really sorry about it, but why did you come here, and what happened to my friends?"

"They are dead," he sprayed.

"I know that," I said. "Did you do it?"

"Brother," he said, "murder ain't my game. I am strictly a thief!"

So he didn't do it; of course, he could have been lying, but I believed him; what would he have had to lie for as close as he was to his maker? "How did you find me?" I asked.

"It was easy," he sprayed, writhing and convulsing. "If you remember, this is my neighborhood. I saw you crossing the intersection and I followed you."

Prodding the note from my pocket, I held it up for his perusal. "Do you know anything about this?" He had been "a pain in my ass" on more than a couple of occasions. "This note. Did you write it?"

"C'mon, does that look like my handwriting?"

Although messy from the abundance of sticky stuff, it did not look like his. I almost wished it had, because if he hadn't done it, then who had, and who was in that air duct, the man? "Why did you come here?" I asked.

"To warn you," he said. "They are after you ..." he seemed to be getting weaker, the blood coming in spurts.

"Who?" I asked. "Lucans?" I was afraid his little speech had gone on too long. I watched helplessly as the two halves of him convulsed. The rustling got louder, so loud I could hardly hear the man's voice over the megaphone outside.

"Them and that man," he sprayed limply. "Lucius, listen to me. Do you see this?" He pointed to the little bag he wore around his neck. "Eat what is in there, quick!"

Outside, the man said, "Come out with your hands up! Send the dog out first!"

"Hey, hey, " the blind man said. "Looka yere, soun' like de cavalry done come once more in de nick o' time, how 'bout dat!"

Willing to grasp at any straw, I pulled the bag from the dying Lucan's neck, opened it and swallowed the contents, which tasted even worse than the tobacco and the pepper. I almost retched.

The last thing I heard from Luke before he died was, "Keep it down, Lucius, keep it down."

"Come on, Lucius," the blind man said, steering me out the door, "I guess we is safe now!"

Outside we were faced by a battery of cops headed by the man. "Where is that dog?" he said. "We want the dog!"

"I sure is glad you fellers is here," said the blind man. "Sompin mighty funny is goin' on!"

"The dog," the man said. "Where is he?"

Here I was standing right next to the blind man and he couldn't see me! Was he blind too?

"We will give you one last chance," the man said. "Where's the dog?"

I looked down at myself. I did not see a thing. It was as if I was not there at all. It took me a moment to figure it out. Whatever had been in the Lucan's bag had made me invisible. "Here 'e is," said the blind man, "standin' right next ter me. What does y'all want wid 'im?"

I walked away and left them standing there arguing.

CHAPTER SEVENTEEN

That night I slept the troubled sleep of an invisible hound, beneath a viaduct along the Harlem River and dreamt of an island of iron and salt and sun surrounded by a ruddy, storm-tossed sea. There was a tingling along my nerves as if something were nibbling at me; gnawing. It wasn't entirely unpleasant, like a teething baby or the kiss of fish, tickling, but the bites soon became violent, as if the baby had grown teeth and the fish had become piranha that, in turn, became my old moldy grandmother beating me for not rescuing my beautiful mother, who ran naked from the captain as he chased her into a copse as if he were Bluto chasing Olive Oyl. "Eat your spinach," grandmother was saying, but I couldn't afford spinach. "Look, he's gaining, he's gaining!" she said as the bites acquired the ferocity of bees. Woody and Peck tried to get it for me, but the man kept getting in the way. Laughing fiendishly, he unleashed Rudy on them. "You're next, bird dick," he said, "I'll find you!" Rudy had become a guillotine. A fun-house organ accompanied the man's laughter, but the sting and the bites hurt for real. I woke up in a nest of ants clawing and scratching. I couldn't see anything though I could feel myself covered with bites. The insects were all over me, and brushing them away, I stood up to survey my new situation. An old derelict had made a fire in an oil drum by which he was warming himself against the early morning chill. "Well, I'll be a 'coon's cousin and a monkey's uncle," he muttered, scratching his head, "I ain' never before in my life seen no flyin' ants like dem lil' critters!" He stepped closer, peering. I stepped back quickly so he wouldn't bump into me. "Lawdy, lawdy," he said, "look at how happy you done made de ants! Looka' dere, dey is walkin on air!" Fishing a pint of port from a tattered overcoat, he uncapped it. "Dis is to de marvelous," he said taking a swig. He returned the bottle to a pocket and singing, went back to warming his hands. The song struck a familiar chord: King Pleasure: "My Little Red Top." I realized my ass had been in the dream too—screaming at me from a rock named Moody.

So here I was, yet a fugitive to be sure, but now, thanks to the Lucan, I was at least an invisible fugitive. I hadn't thought of it until then, but I suddenly wondered if by some other miracle I had recovered my humanity or at least the shape of it, and poking ever so tentatively and tenderly around my sore and swollen ears discovered I was still a member of the genus *canis domisticus*, though it didn't matter much because, as nobody could see me, how could I be defined? Going over the implications of this, I realized that given the peculiarities of my situation, I was much better off than I had been with the blind man or with Woody and Peck. I was pretty much free to come and go as I chose, to make my investigations and discoveries unnoticed and—if I was really lucky—to get my ass alive out of whatever predicament it was in right now, alive, if it was still alive. I left the river walking west on One Thirty Eighth. Coming to Lenox, I turned south and headed for the florist's shop. I wasn't too surprised to see the new girl. I didn't know if Eva had gone to Rio, given her propensity for the truth, but she had gone somewhere, and after giving the shop a thorough investigation and finding nothing of note, decided out of a perverse curiosity to check on the blind man. Approaching the house, I saw it was sealed with the yellow tape the NYPD uses to denote a crime scene. He was nowhere around. Crossing Seventh, I saw him at the corner of One Twenty Fourth with a cane and a cup containing a dozen or so pencils. Wherever Lil' Eva was, I hoped she would get hers.

Figuring my invisibility would allow me at last to see the great James Moody, I headed towards the Apollo in a better mood than I had been in in some time, though I was yet again to be disappointed as, when I got there, the great man had gone. By now I was rather hungry. I figured what the hell, I might as well just go right on into Frank's and slop up a T-bone and a couple of chops, maybe some prime ribs on the house. I had done that and was about to leave when a man come in with a yellow-complected man with a goatee and alto saxophone. "So what's up, Johnny? Still working for Duke?" he said after the maitre d' had shown them to their table. The yellow man with the goatee and the alto was none other than Johnny Hodges. I figured I had better stick around.

"'The Duke to you, pasty face," Hodges said. "What'd you wanna see me for?"

"What's with the names, Johnny," the man said. "I heard you were a gentleman; that's not the way gentlemen talk; they sit down, they're civil, they enjoy a glass of wine together, a good meal. I like your music, Johnny, that's why I invited you here. Okay, 'the' Duke, whatever, he makes great copy, but you, you're the virtuoso and how much billing does he give you, how much creative space? All right, you got 'Prelude to a Kiss,' 'Black and Tan Fantasy' and 'Koko' maybe, but how many suites has he created for you where you actually get to soar? Come with us, Johnny. We'll make you a star in your own right. That's what you deserve! You keep the copyrights, who cares! The world just needs to hear your music, Johnny."

The waiter came, took their orders, brought them drinks and went away again. A piano trio was setting up. "Yas, yas, yass," an announcer said, "Here she is folks, de wunnerful, de one and only Miss Nellie Letcher!"

"I'm gonna fix your little red wagon," Miss Letcher sang, a song I could definitely identify with. She sang well, as she usually did. When she had finished, she went into a Fats Waller number. The two men had fallen silent for a moment, listening. I moved closer so I could hear them above the music. The lady had a great idea in those lyrics; I was going to fix someone's red wagon myself.

"Look, Johnny," the man was saying as the waiter brought their food, "I'm offering you a deal here!" They had ordered the two-inch-thick New York-cut steak with tails that Frank's was famous for, with mushrooms and julienned potatoes.

Hodges waited until the waiter left, cut a piece of his steak, popped it into his mouth, chewed slowly and swallowed before answering. "Sure sounds like it," he said taking another mouthful and chewing, "but the thing is, I like what I'm doing. Of course, the Duke writes for me; have you been listening? I'm usually right after the introduction. 'Come Sunday,' I am the introduction. So what if he doesn't write for me, personally, he writes for the ensemble, and I like working with the ensemble. That's the sound I like: Big Sid or Sam kickin' it. The big band. You listen to me. I love Harry Carney and Frog, Lawrence Brown. Bubber Mylie. Those are the cats as far as I'm concerned, those are my boys, mister. I'm with the Duke."

The man hadn't touched his plate. "I hear some of you people are calling him 'the Maestro,'" he said.

Hodges said, "Who cares what Rome likes? You guys can't come in here and just take over jazz, I don't care how many records you produce! By the way, I heard about what you did to Wardell Grey and that kid from Kansas City."

The man waved it off. "Forget about that, Johnny."

Hodges tossed down his drink and stood. "Forget about Charlie Parker? Are you nuts? I could never do that!"

"Johnny, Johnny, look" the man said, "you don't play bebop!"

"That's all right." Hodges gathered up his things. "Bird lives!" he

John Farris

said as he turned and left. "Thanks for the dinner, though I can't say I haven't had better."

The man muttered, "Insolent yellow nigger. Swing, huh? I'll make you swing all right."

Pushing up from the table, he walked to the phone. I followed. "Nah," he said when he had gotten his party, "Nah, nah, no. He wouldn't come in; I didn't even get a chance to discuss the copyright deal. He insisted on calling him, 'the Duke.' Yeah. Yeah, said he was 'the maestro,' yeah. You know what to do, call up the Count. See if you can't get that guy Lester whatshisname. What? He won't talk? Okay, they wanna swing, huh? Listen, get Zoot, get Getz, give Getz the money. Eager? Nah, not Eager, he's too eager. He's gotta swing too. Bop? We'll 'bop' him all right. He'll be 'bopped' all over when I get finished with him! Get out the monkey. All right, the Monkees, that sounds like a good idea for the future!"

Hanging up and throwing some money onto the table, he left the restaurant with me following close behind. This man was into everything. Now he wanted to steal jazz. What did this monkey mean, "monkey"? Something from the cave tugged hard at me: Dr. Petoit, the voice of "the thing" saying, "junk." The Lucan on the soapbox had said it too: " ... he will give you a monkey ..."

Hailing a cab, he got in with me scooting in before. He gave an address in midtown. The driver sped south on Eighth and entered Central Park. "Hey," the man said, "what is that smell?"

The driver said, "What smell?"

"It smells like you got animals in here," the man said.

"Maybe it's where you're going," said the driver. "If you hang around with animals, sometimes the smell goes with you."

"Oh, yeah?" the man said. "What d'ya mean?"

The address he had given was in the park itself, at the zoo. We pulled up in front of the monkey house, where he paid the driver. "Watch out for your mouth," he said, "and maybe you'll get a tip."

"Gee thanks, mister," the driver said, his eyes lighting up. "Mum's the word with me! You can bet on it!" He sped off, up the winding road of the park and was gone.

The monkey house was an ornate Greek Revival structure modeled on classical Indian architecture that smacked of the baroque, made of red brick and concrete with graceful arches over massive bronze doors that sported two grinning brass monkey knockers. It was many gabled, with chimneys belching a thick, sweetish smoke that hung over the park disguised as clouds. The aroma reminded me of the cave, Catherine and Chiang. Grabbing a brass monkey by the paw, he knocked three times.

The sound reverberated through the monkey house like a Chinese gong. He had knocked twice more before a voice said, "Hey, hold your horses, I'm comin,' I'm comin'!"

The door swung open to reveal a heavyset gorilla. Pretty sure the bulge in his chest was not strictly anatomical, I stepped carefully around him. "Ohh, hi, Boss, it's you!"

"'The' Boss, stupid," the man said, poking him in the chest with an index finger for emphasis. "Get it?"

"Okay, okay, " said the gorilla, "anything you say!"

Quick as a flash, the man pulled the whip he'd taken from Lash LaRue and lashed the gorilla severely with it. "Just in case you don't understand," he said, "who is 'The' Boss!"

I hated to see a wild mountain gorilla treated like that. The man had him completely cowed, buffaloed, tamed, under his control.

"What is the law!" he said to the trembling beast, "What is the law!" He looked like Edward G.

The gorilla looked like Boris Karloff. "You're the boss!" he said, cringing. "Believe me, I know about pain!"

Pain, that word struck a chord as deep as the one the monkey knocker had sent through the monkey house. There was a children's petting zoo next door. I wondered, if by hook or crook my ass just could ...

"Okay," the man said, "just so you know. Who's here?"

The gorilla rubbed his back gingerly, saying, "A few of the boys." He dusted himself off.

"Good," said the man.

I followed them silently down a long corridor, off of which were rooms of cages filled with howling, screeching monkeys. They continued past these to one that was obviously a meeting room for war games where several people sat around a large conference table. They stood when we entered. "Be seated," the man said. "Let's get right down to business."

The gorilla positioned himself at the door, arms folded across his mighty chest.

"Boys" was hyperbole, a misnomer, as there were a couple of women present, and Lucans. I shouldn't have been surprised to see her, but one of them was none other than Lil' Eva, Lil' Eva, "the frail so nice they named her twice, Lil' Eva, Lil' Eva." That was two strikes against her as far as I was concerned. So she hadn't gone to Rio after all or, if she had, she had come right back. I had to admit she looked stunning in her new outfit. The men were Huey Long, Estes Kefauver, and DeLesspus S. Morrison, the Mayor of New Orleans, whose picture I had seen in the newspapers many times, accompanying stories about the Crescent City. It was rumored of him that he was more than cozy with the wise guys in his town. I'd have bet a fat man it was true.

"The Goldiggers will come to order," said Lil' Eva. "Do I read last week's minutes or what? I'm new at this."

"Never mind the minutes," the man said. "I suppose you've all heard about Hodges. He wouldn't come in."

Lil' Eva said, "I coulda told you that. If I couldn't git 'im, nobody could."

The man glared hard at her. "Why don't you go play Take Your Clothes off for Money," he said.

"Aww, Sam," said Eva, "why I always got to play de prostitute? I'm tired of playin' dat game! Ain't you got a new one f' me? Why come I can't just sit here and take minutes?"

"Then just take the minutes and shut up," said the man. "When I want to know from you, I'll ask. Where's Petoit?"

Petoit. The picture had become more clear.

"He's back dere foolin' wid dem monkeys," said Eva. "Dat man sure do love messin' wid dem. De other day, I caught him playin' wid his own! Spankin' it."

The man said, "Good. Good, that's why we hired him. We're going to need them. We're going to have to turn them loose. I think Petoit's experiments have proved we can do it through jazz. We'll get the copyrights, all of them. Let's see: distribution, that's where you come in, Huey. Do you think you can handle that?"

"You can count on the great state of Louisiana," the governor said. "They ain't namin' that thruway after me for nuthin'!"

"You, Morrison?"

"Don' worry about it, Sam," the mayor said. "I cover the waterfront. I'll cover the town. Hey, where ya at? I'll infect everybody that passes through the parish."

The man rubbed his palms together. "Great," he said. Drifting into gleeful reverie, his eyes blazed with his sinister intent. "Get the Doctor, Eva," he said.

"Me?" said Eva, "I'm takin' da minutes. Why I got ta go git 'im? You know I don't like that man!"

The room fell quiet. Eva rolled her eyes toward the glass ceiling. "Sam," she said, "you knows I just hates it when he tie me up! I told you—"

The man's tone was paternal, "Just go get him, Eva."

Eva was near tears. She said, "But what about my skills?"

"I was not aware that this was a filibuster," the man said, fingering his whip. "I don't want to spank you, Eva."

Eva sighed. "I'll go, I'll go, but I'm tired," she said. "I don't like this. I never did like a monkey man."

She was gone only a minute when her screams brought everyone, including me, running to the main gallery where Dr. Petoit conducted his experiments. "Sam, Sam," Lil' Eva said, "some of the monkeys got out; they done escaped!"

He said, "Where's Petoit?"

She pointed to the doctor's inert body in a corner near an open cage. "There," she said. "I think he done died!"

"Accidents will happen," the man said, calmly. "Give him a saline shot. That ought to bring him around."

After they had managed to revive Petoit, they sat him up against a cage that held a giant tree sloth. The man said, "What happened?"

"Fantastic," Petoit said, groggily.

"Good, good," the man said, "that's great news." He told him about the plan to use the monkey on the jazzmen. He asked, "Do you think it will work?"

The doctor laughed. "There's nothing short of death that can stop these animals." Noticing Eva, he said, "Why Eva, how are you?"

"Nah, uh,uh," she said. "I ain't ready f' dat; don't you be doin' no testin' on me! I told you de last time —" She struggled some as the others held her down while Petoit adroitly administered the injection. After a moment, her struggles ceased and she nodded euphorically. "I told you de las' time ..." she said, "I told you de las' time ... mmm, I sure do feel good ..." Her voice trailed off dreamily. She started to hum a little tune.

"I believe, gentlemen," said Dr. Petoit, "Eva is in the land of Oobladee."

The gathered politicians clapped; made the usual speeches. One of the Lucans asked if he could get a piece of the action. "Sure," said the man, "that is exactly why I invited you to come in with us. My dear fellow, I was thinking of making you a full partner, no more of that junior stuff for you buddy; you can have as much of the action as you want!" He asked if the Lucan had a marketing strategy.

"I got brothas everywhere ready to do anything I say: Buffalo, L.A., Denver, Cleveland, everywhere," he said, grinning.

"Well," said Dr. Petoit, "since imitation is the most sincere form of flattery, I suggest you try it. I suspect you'll like it."

He tied a piece of rubber surgical tubing around the Lucan's bicep, thumped his forearm expertly and injected him. After a second or two, the Lucan slumped forward, comatose.

Another Lucan asked what would happen if he didn't come out of it.

"Then you get his share," the man said.

"I think this is the last of the salt," said Petoit, about to administer a saline solution.

With a rapid motion, the Lucan tripped him. Falling from his hand the instrument broke open on the floor. He said, "You just killed your buddy."

"That's all right," said the Lucan. "There's plenty of buddies where that one came from."

My old Grandmother had said, "There is no honor among thieves."

"'The maestro', ha," the man said. "The criminality of that is the grandiosity of the notion. Now, we are certainly going to need more mules than that." He had pointed to Eva. "What about that ass?"

My floppy ears of a great, invisible hound pricked right up.

"His brain is just about the right size,' said Petoit, "I think he'll do just fine. He's certainly got the strength of one; hell, two, and what a stomach on him! It's like a balloon already. I am pretty sure he'll be able to take anything. The only problem is I haven't been able to revive him yet. He is still in a coma."

The man said, "So, what's the prognosis? Will he survive?"

"Sixty/forty, though, as far as I can see, his system is absolutely heroic. I've given him all the solution we had on hand. We'll have to order some more."

I could not believe what my floppy ears were telling me. Was I hearing right? Was he talking about my ass, my own precious ass, comatose? Comatose was beyond mere pain, it was limbo. According to my information, mules had to be sterile. Had they sterilized mine? Talk about your Nazi bastards. His next words heartened me somewhat.

"That jackass is such a prick I want him to be fully conscious of what is happening to him," he said. "I won't perform the procedure until he is awake. That way if he gets caught, he won't be able to plead the ignorance of a dumb beast." He laughed, "He'll be as guilty as sin."

The man laughed with him. He said, "Good."

This plot had more twists than a pretzel. Here they were trying to make a mule out of my old ass, and sterilization was the only way I knew of to do that. They were going to sterilize the poor animal and the only thing between it and that operation was the fact of it being out cold; talk about a rock and a hard place! I was going to have to do something and I was going to have to do it quick, muy pronto, but what? The man appeared to have formidable organization; all I had going for me was a vague myth about jazz that seemed about to explode, a comatose ass and my invisibility. So far this last had seemed to be my greatest asset, my strongest suit. I thought about getting rid of them all right then, but I needed to know more about this monkey business: exactly how it worked, how many people were involved and exactly who they were. Besides, Petoit had said he'd have to administer more of the solution if my ass was to survive. I myself did not know the procedure nor was I sure that if I did, I would be capable of carrying it out. I would need him around for that.

The man asked, "And where is Rudy? Where is my dog?"

"The last I seen him," the Lucan said, "he was in de back, dere, chewin' on a monkey."

The man, Sam, exploded. "A wha? A monkey? I have told you a thousand times never, but never, to let her near those animals! Oh, my poor puppy! You! You're responsible for this!" Pulling out the whip, he lashed the Lucan grievously. It appeared he was going to kill him until Petoit stepped in.

"Sam, Sam, don't kill him; we're going to need him!" he said gently.

"What, oh yeah," the man said, out of breath, his arm weary at any rate. He put away the whip slowly. "Snake," he said, "you're lucky. But don't you think I'm going to forget this." He pointed to the gorilla. "You," he said. "Go and get my dog."

The gorilla exited, returning in a moment with a nodding Rudolph. It was hard to believe this was the beast that had menaced me, that had savaged Woody and Peck, it was so like a toddler resisting the sandman. The man was livid. "You son of a bitch," he said to the bleeding Lucan, "you'd do that to my favorite hound? Take this!" Pulling a pistol, a licensed .38, he shot the hapless snake six times. He reloaded the chamber and emptied it again. "You heard him," he said to Petoit. "There are plenty of those where he came from. You," he said, turning to the gorilla, "give me my dog. And go get another one."

Handing Rudy to him, the gorilla asked, "Another dog?"

"No, stupid," he said testily, "another of those Lucans. They seem to be all used up around here."

"Sure thing, Boss," said the gorilla.

The man said, "What did you call me?"

"'The' Boss," said the gorilla, quickly making his exit.

"And don't you forget it. Oh, my poor, poor doggie!"

Rudolph was too zoned out to bark. That was good, I thought, what if she/he had smelled me?

"It's not too bad," said the doctor. "Look at me; I've managed to survive, haven't I?"

The man said, "You be careful. Do you hear me, do you?"

"Sure, sure," Petoit said, backing off, his arms extended before him defensively. "We'll get him some treatment. Delaudid ought to do it; if not, there is something new being worked on by some of my colleagues in Kentucky called naoline that produces acute psychosis in the case of recurrence, not to say relapse."

"Do what you have to, Doctor, but don't you dare give my Rudolph naoline! I heard what it did to those monkeys down there. It reduced 'em to blathering idiots at the sight of the stuff! I can't have my dog like that; you'd better do better than that, and you'd better do it quick! Do you hear me, Petoit?"

"Sam, Sam," Petoit said, "watch your pressure! Of course, I hear you. We'll try another treatment."

"Petoit, if my dog dies ..."

"Sam," said Petoit, regarding him coolly, "we're not talking about death here, we're simply talking about a condition. Chronic, that is, lingering, perhaps, but the actual rate of mortality is random."

"Petoit, you had better cure my dog or I'll have you cured over a low fire. How did it happen in the first place, Petoit, you tell me how!" the man said sternly.

"It was an accident," said Petoit. "I had achieved the right potency, and, well, you know as much about the rest of it as I do myself."

"Well, you see to it that it doesn't happen again, do you understand me? I can see right now I'm going to have to have some laws drafted and enacted here! Petoit, your head might just be in one of them, so you had better be damn careful, you hear?" He handed the dog to Petoit who laid him on a pallet next to his worktable. "You heard me, Huey, Dee, I want laws aimed specifically at this kind of thing; I want to prevent a tragedy like this from ever happening again to my dog!" A great tear rolled down his furrowed cheek. "My poor poopie!" Running over to the worktable and pushing the doctor away, he fell over Rudolph sobbing uncontrollably. When he had pulled himself together sufficiently, he said to Petoit, "Go get the others!"

Humbled by his reduction to mere gofer, Petoit sidled out like a crab, chin on his chest. He returned with Allen Dulles and his brother; Hoover, two newcomers by the name of George Bush and "Wild Bill" Donovan and some others I had seen in the cave, in their ties with grinning skulls and crossbones and other finery, representatives and titular heads of governments large and small, both ancient and new. Ethiopia was represented by the "Lion" of Judah, His Majesty, Ras Tafari, the Emperor Haille Selasi, resplendent in the uniform of a nineteenth-century cavalry officer, with a sabre at his side and a copy of the Old Testament under his arm.

"Okay, Ras," the man asked, "did you check on what I asked you to?"

"Sure thing, Sam," the emperor said, adjusting his pince-nez, "I believe it's right here. Let's see ..." He leafed through the book, a special, gold-leafed edition in Aramaic, "I should have marked it. Oh, yes, here it is right here, 'Genesis,' Chapter Twelve, I believe."

"Wait—" the man said, "do you 'believe', or is there a precedent?"

"Here it is," said His Majesty, "Chapter XII, as I thought. Here's the verse. Mmm. I'll just quote the pertinent part: "Let us go down and confuse them."

"Point of clarification there, Emperor," the man said, "exactly who is the 'us' there? What are our rights?"

"It appears to be you, Sam," the Emperor said, "as far as I can tell: U.S., 'Uncle Sam.' You have the right to confuse and confound 'them.'"

"All right," the man said, stopping him. He turned to the assembled group. "Now, you all know who 'they' are, guys, go out there and confuse them. I want everybody to take enough monkeys to get the job done!"

The group filed out, chatting among themselves. This was much bigger than anything I had dared imagine. Not only did they have the law on their side, they also had my old grandmother's terrible Lord. There were so many of them I couldn't go after them all, and anyway, I thought, what would happen to my old ass? I decided I would stick around. Pretty soon I was left alone with a nodding Lil' Eva, a penitent, trembling Petoit, the man and Rudolph.

The man said, "All right, Petoit, now cure my dog."

I watched carefully over his shoulder as the doctor took Rudolph through a primitive version of the twelve-step program, the very first, I believe. When I had learned what I thought was enough of the technique, I set out rather anxiously to find John.

CHAPTER EIGHTEEN

The monkey house was positively labyrinthine, and appeared to be laid out like a five-pointed star. I had seen a similar building in Langley, Virginia, but, aside from the points of the star, the corridors angled and looped in an endless maze, and pretty soon I had lost all sense of direction in the dreary sameness of them. There were countless doors, though those I tried were either only painted on the wall or opened onto brick walls; designed, it seemed, to confuse and mislead, and though I could hear the monkeys everywhere howling and screeching and screaming, there was not one clue as to where I might find my ass other than somewhere in limbo, and I was despairing of ever finding it when who came striding along purposefully, an iron ring of keys in one hand and a box of syringes and the solution in the other, but Doctor Petoit, with Eva trailing behind uncertainly. "Hurry up, Eva," he was saying, "we don't have all night, you know."

"But, Doctor," Eva said, "I keep tellin' you."

"You keep telling me what, Eva?" said Petoit.

She said, "I don't do no donkey acts!"

"And I keep telling you I just need you to take your clothes off," he said impatiently. "That's all!"

"But—"

"Eva," he said, "do you want your shot or not?"

"You gonna give it to me, Doc?" she asked plaintively.

"Sure, I'm going to give it to you, but only if you act right."

"Okay, I'll do it. I'll do it jes' dis one time! You gonna give me my shot, huh?"

I followed them back the way I had come to one of the doors I had tried that had led to a brick wall, where the doctor, removing a device from his pocket, aimed it at the wall, which swung open to reveal a heavy steel gate. He unlocked this and we entered into what seemed to be an operating room in the middle of which was my ass, strapped to a gurney. The light in there was overwhelmingly like that of the cave. Having prepared the solution and injected John, the doctor ordered Eva to strip completely when he awakened and to keep his attention with some lewd postures he suggested. As he turned to demonstrate one of these, I grabbed up a surgical hammer and put his lights out. I had never hit a woman before nor have I ever after, but figuring Eva was in a special category all by herself, I cold-cocked her too, before she had time to react. John was yet groggy as I chewed through the restraints, but I managed to get him both on his feet and wide awake by calling out his name. "John, John," I said, "hey, old buddy, it's me, Lucius!"

His long black ears of a jackass shot straight up and his dear, donkey eyes widened in astonishment as he looked around wildly.

"Here! Here, John boy," I said reaching out to touch him. "It's me; I'm here; I'm just invisible, that's all!"

He brayed uncertainly and jumped when I touched him, the long ears of my little burro shooting straight forward.

"It's true, it's me," I said. "We don't have enough time right now for me to explain it all, John, but we have got to get ourselves out of here, pronto!"

Being a burro, John knew what "pronto" meant. He shot straight out the door and ran smack into a brick wall so hard he almost lost consciousness again.

"Steady, boy, steady," I said, and realizing I myself had no idea how to get out, nosed through the inert Petoit's pocket until I found the device and what seemed to be a floor plan, and pretty soon we found ourselves stumbling out into a starry night.

Spring had come softly, and the dank smell of humus mixed in with the thick, cloyingly sweetish odor of the smoke belching white as clouds from the many chimneys of the monkey house. The peculiar sounds made by those inhabitants of the zoo that were nocturnal in their habits and the thick white smoke combined to give the place a sense of extrasurreality, and it wasn't until we had gotten some distance away that the regularity of night crept in with no more than its usual din of katydids and crickets and the shine and screech of traffic from the perimeters of the park. I could see the handle of the Big Dipper pointing north, and followed it.

As glad as I was to see John, I realized that with his added presence, I could jeopardize the advantage of my invisibility as I had absolutely no idea what to do with him—where to put him, where to keep him—when I hit on what I thought was a reasonable enough plan, given my options: securing John behind some bushes in the Ramble, I sprinted quickly over to Central Park West where I hopped onto the back of a southbound cab. I hopped off at Forty Sixth, in front of a good make-up shop I knew of there. Smashing the glass when no one was looking, I snatched some red body paint. I was out of there and on the back of a cab headed north before the alarm sounded. Sprinting across the park, I got back to the Ramble just in time, as two rather gay fellows had become inordinately interested in John. I gave them a good scare. "If you touch my ass, I'll maim both of you," I said distinctly, sounding as much like James Cagney as I could manage, as menacingly. Startled out of their wits, they took off screaming. When they had gone, I took the body paint and painted John red all over. My black ass was a fugitive, not this red one. I had remembered that from my days with Woody and Peck in the Village. My plan was this: I would introduce John into the clubs uptown as a talking ass act. That was pretty classy I thought, and as long as he didn't play the trumpet in that distinct style of his, that would get us in where we needed to be.

Exiting the park at Fifth Avenue, we passed the notorious Riviera, where the great Chano Pozo had gotten taken off the count some years before, it was said, over a drug deal gone bad. I figured that with its shady reputation, the Riviera was as good a place to start as any. I wasn't wrong about that.

The place was dimly lit, smoky, filled with habitués of the jazz world and those that supported and preyed on them: Lucans and other offbeat characters hustling contraband, stolen goods and goods purchased wholesale from downtown around Orchard and Allen, purported to have been stolen to give them more glamour: wristwatches and rings, suits, coats and shoes, as well as items that had been lifted from the supermarkets: fancy-cut steaks and chops. They also sold heroin. Other drugs were purveyed, notably cocaine and marijuana, but it was the trade in heroin that I was interested in, though with John, as was usual, it was another story. Aside from the required burn-scarred mahogany bar and red booths on the side, there was a small stage that stood out in the general, smoky gloom of the place, lighted as it was by a small bank of frisels with pink and blue gels over them. A small, five-man combo played from this, and when the alto saxophonist took his solo, I recognized that sound. It was Jackie, the kid from the record shop; older now, heavier, but him. When after intermission the trumpeter, Kenny Durham, I believe it was, didn't return for some reason and Jackie asked if there were any trumpet players in the house, John was up and on the stage straight away, before I could object. The other musicians looked him up and down, the disdain in their eyes barely disguised, and as Jackie called "Straight, No Chaser," my ass romped through it like Wilbur Hardman. He called "Fours" next, and John went through that like Miles Davis. He called

"Parisian Thoroughfare," and "Hot House," and John went through them like Clifford Brown.

The crowd stomped and whistled. They cheered for more. The other musicians straightened up, tensed to play. Jackie looked a bit envious. "Yeah," he said, "I hear all them other cats, but where is your sound at, huh?" He called "A Long Drink of the Blues," and John, stung, tore into it like only he could. It brought the audience whistling and stomping to their feet. .

Jackie said, "Hey, wait a minute, Jack, I know that sound. Is your name John? Is that red coat by any chance, a dye job?"

I hurried to the stage as fast as my long, hairy legs of an invisible hound could carry me. "Psst, Jackie," I whispered, "lay out man, be cool!"

Jackie said, "Who, hey, what is this!"

I said, "Jackie, it's me, Lucius! You can't see me, but I'm in deep trouble!"

Jackie said, "If you who I think you is, you always in deep trouble somehow, so what's new, Gates?"

I explained to him I didn't want anyone to know who my ass was. If anyone found out, it would be curtains for me and jazz. I told him nowadays we — the old ass and I were certainly one — went by the name of "Red." When I told him as much as I knew about what was happening, he suggested we go over to the Park Lounge to see Billie Holliday.

By the time we got to the Park Lounge, it was too late; she had died just hours before. Jackie was devastated. *First Bird, and now Billie.*

I heard she had been visited by some shadowy guy with a package as she lay in the hospital, and just after this suspicious visit, she passed. Thinking about that scene in the park, I couldn't help wondering if what'd been in that package was connected somehow to those simians, and leaving John to root for himself (which he was doing a pretty good job of anyway), hopped a couple of cabs to Metropolitan Hospital to see what I could nose out.

It was easy enough to get past what passed for security there, and soon I'd made my invisible way of a miserable hound to the record room where they had everything she'd ever done in the world: the stuff with the Basie band, Shaw — when, up at Clark's Monroe House, her voice had been innocent as a tear, a Lil' ol' girl in a print dress with puffed sleeves she'd gathered at the waist with gardenias — the failed marriage she toured through while her voice cracked and broke in places she had to be put it back together in organza with needles, like a rag doll somebody had loved damn near to death, places her eyes had to be pinned before she could go on again and again like a "Little Red Top," which she

never sang, but which she might have for all she went spinning and spinning till she just had to drop, going round and round, going for the moon
and never getting there until somehow, broke and cracked like the vinyl
of some of these records in the record room of the Metropolitan Hospital, but nothing concerning her last visitor other than the fact that he
had brought flowers, white gardenias, and some fruit.

The "fruit" struck a chord: strange, bitter, the fruit of poplar trees,
cottonwood.

No evidence of who he had been. In point of fact, the pronoun itself was an assumption; "it" could have been a "she." A Lucan?

From what I knew of him, the man himself could not help being os-
tentatious. He would have called a press conference. Announced his
intentions to the *World-Telegram*, the *Sun* and the *New York Times* as a
scoop. The *Herald Tribune*, the *Daily News* and the *Mirror* would have
picked it up later, running front page pictures of his dog at her funeral;
his imprimatur. There was no evidence of that; this had been done on
the sly, furtively, in the dark by some person or persons of unknown in-
telligence, origin or shape beyond obviously shifty. A bag person. Willing to eat with the buffalo soldiers. Some pig. Chicken. Cornball. Lil'
Eva came to mind. Would she stoop so low? Would she? Of course,
she would. Eva was a "get-down" woman. Raised on limbo. Cut her
stick from the cane, the blind man told me she had told him. How low
was low? How far would she go was the question, thinking she had
gotten away with something dark. I listened to Billie over and over
there in that hospital going round and round in that record room until
it hit me like a big brass section: back to him. Now that she was a zombie, where else would she go? Find him and I'd find her, and vice-versa.
Now that my ass was safe with Jackie and the fellas, and I was invisible and therefore invincible, I could confront him. Beside the individual grief he had brought me I owed him for Woody and Peck, and now
and certainly, if indirectly, for Billie. For my beautiful mother and my
old grandmother. For what they had tried to do to my ass. I would take
it up with him.

Leaving the record room with great reluctance, I bayed a teary
goodbye to the great lady. An attendant came running up immediately.
"No dogs allowed," she said, astonished when she saw no one. The
sound I'd made was deeply mournful, like what the riverboats made
being sucked down the Mississippi, involuntary, a leaden lament pre-
saging the dirge to come after. I shouldn't have been at all surprised —
I simply was not conscious of the impulse — it had brought the attendant
double-timing, as it shook the windows in their frames. I am not too
sure if it was my baying that did that, or Frog's obbligato on a rendi-

tion of "Billie's Blues," a good bit. I hadn't made a sound like that since being shoved the awful news in that improbable hellhole of the deaths of my beautiful mother and my old grandmother, the switch-hitter who would've asked me to stop making so much noise. The misericordia. Made eerily ashamed of my grief, invisible as I was, I made my way out of there without too much more difficulty. Why I say "too much" is because, after descending easily enough in an elevator large enough to accommodate a platoon of gurneys, I crossed the lobby just as a janitor was mopping the floor. The fellow's eyes bulged and his dark skin blanched as I passed. Quickening my gait to a lope, I made what I must say was a cowering dash for the door, realizing as I did so that from now on I was going to have to be extraordinarily careful around water while making it to the curb with no further mishaps. I realized, too, that I had as yet no rational plan for the success of my objective beyond the vow made while uttering that bloodcurdling howl, which was that I was going to make both that man and Eva and any of those sorry Lucans that got between us suffer serious hemorrhaging. I set out for Central Park at a good clip, not even bothering to stop for a cab.

CHAPTER NINETEEN

Not then one hundred years old in its present boundaries, the truth about this great metropolis of ours is that it is in a state of constant renewal, and the sound of 10,000 jackhammers chattered and pounded away in my ears: the electric company, the gas company, the water department, the Department of Highways, private developers, wrecking crews, made a symphony in steel, *an iron sonata*, a suite for asphalt and cement-mixers, a pavane for riveteers; every street in disrepair or repair, every other building being sandblasted, and made aware of the problem presented my plan by the incident in the lobby, I had to dash suddenly, unexpectedly into traffic at times only after feeling the fender of one vehicle or another as it crept past me, down the uneven streets, and was made aware of another disadvantage to this invisibility business: how could I be seen in traffic? If I didn't see something coming, that was it, slow as it might be; due to my very invisibility, it would roll right over me. I would've been a dead hound, lying stiff in the road, tongue lolling between my huge canine teeth of a dog, stinking, bloated after a few days, drawing flies as I'd drawn ants by the river. Detours made a maze of a simple trip across town and somewhat south, and before I knew it I was in Battery Park. When I looked up again, I was at the George Washington Bridge, being shuttled east towards the Bronx, nudged by indifference. There I was, not even in the bureaucracy, being given the runaround. Spuyten Dyvil, Chelsea, Inwood, Marble Hill, Queens, Brooklyn; tongue hanging out. I'd only just begun and already I was disoriented, tired, sleepy; added to which I was ravenous as I'd not eaten a thing the whole of that miserable day. Being shunted towards Queens, I caved in to instinct, and in the full glare of a late afternoon sun, in bumper-to-bumper traffic, I hopped into the back of an opportune Brunckhorst's Provisions truck and wolfed down a couple of links of knockwurst, a couple of chops and some shell steaks with the ends on. The driver, alerted by a signal in his cab, stopped there in traffic and came around to investigate, but by then I had finished two more sausage links and exited, almost belching in the man's puzzled face. He asked the driver directly behind if he'd seen anybody going in the truck, getting a blast of horn for an answer; to which the Brunckhorst's driver responded with a blast of his own of verbal abuse, which caused the tow truck driver—it was a tow truck—to exit his vehicle, saying to the driver of the Brunckhorst's vehicle, "Yeah, whaddya wanna make of it, pally?"

A chorus of horns drowned out the man's answer, but pretty soon they were going at each other pretty good. Brunckhorst, smaller, slighter, absorbed the most punishment, though, pound-for-pound, pretty scrappy. Other drivers leaned harder into their horns or left their cars or delivery trucks to hoot at the tow trucker, who, pressing the advantage of his weight, knocked the smaller man down. Another driver joined in and pretty soon there I was, stuck in a traffic jam in Queens. When the driver of a city bus joined in, I hopped the bus, figuring anything was faster than walking—or running, which I had been doing—and, tired as I was, pretty soon fell fast asleep and into a dream where I was being chased by the Man. Moody was in it, pointing to Jack McVeigh, who pointed to Slim Gaillard. Billie was alive, Bird, Chano Pozo, a guy named Wardell Gray was having his eyes put out in a desert somewhere; the blind man asking, "Did I git 'im, Lucius, did I git dat rascal?"

I awoke thirsty as hell, still in the same traffic snarl. Noticing a watermelon truck, the driver of which was standing on the side watching the melee with obvious glee, I climbed into it, and pretty soon had refreshed myself, rinds and all, belched, stretched my long, lanky legs of an invisible hound and ambled over to the side of the road where I took a healthy, if foul-smelling dump, which I had, by now, learned to cover somewhat by scratching and throwing up dirt onto it, only I did it with my forepaws rather than my hind legs, like a dog. Stretching again, one hairy leg after another, and yawning the characteristic yawn of a dog, I ambled over and lay down, chin on my crossed forepaws, to watch the melee. Should I have felt some moral culpability? How could I have, given my condition?

A couple of days of this and soon a squad car arrived to break it up and, after six or seven months or so due to contract overruns because of the intermittent shortage of materials, not even my doing, as in said condition how could I have fenced anything, everything returned to normal, only now there was construction farther down the block, and after the intersection, more detours. Area merchants, outraged by what they called "pork barrel," complained of business suffering because deliveries were late or short or nonexistent, particularly choice cuts of meat, which I was responsible for, as, hey, it was there, and I had to live. What was I expected to do, open a can of dog food?

People kept coming and going all the while, boarding and de-boarding the bus, on their way to jobs, returning home to anxious, inquiring spouses, late because of the bus or casually watching the melee, but only rarely got involved. Somebody was always watching the melees, but only rarely getting involved. Somebody was always larger than somebody else. Whose fault was that; not mine, you bet your ass. Mine was lost somewhere; I hoped in Harlem, in jazz. I was stuck in Queens. While it might have seemed I was put off my pur-pose, I was, in fact, scenting people, nosing around for the slightest clue as to the whereabouts of the man and Lil' Eva, but nothing. Dur-ing that whole time, I saw not one Lucan. There were none on Queens Boulevard in Forest Hills; they didn't even deliver out there. Once I thought I saw that Peter Lorre character and Dr. Petoit, but, on closer inspection, realized it was neither of the two; close, but not close enough. As there was not too much else going on, I went to the movies a lot, imitated tough guys; Alan Ladd in platform shoes, a toupee; ac-culturated myself. I now imitated the very same matinee idols that'd hauled my ass and I out of the Hudson kicking and screaming; honed my skills; noted the flaws that ultimately defeated them, like James Cagney when he made the decision to go up the water tower in *Pub-lic Enemy* or Welles' decision to let his boys loose in *A Touch of Evil*, though, in point of fact, I personally had nothing against his charac-ter; hey, what was that gringa Vivian Leigh snooping around south of the Rio Grande for anyway, didn't they already have California, Texas, Arizona, Colorado and that euphemism for a slap in the face, "New" Mexico; not in Nogales, baby, making the fatal mistake of re-alizing too late that Charlton Heston had the advantage of being Moses as well as El Cid; what could one rum-runner and a bunch of hopheads do against an army like that, those odds; and what about my own, on top of what had happened the last time; I was already one down. One down with one more to go; talking like them, their syntax, their articles in a situation where I was dressed like that, in a Hom-burg, pinstripes and a double-breasted overcoat like a banker, smok-ing cigars exactly like Rico smoked them in *Little Caesar*, one deliberate puff at a time, with pinky ring, which reminded me incon-gruously of one I saw on Ethel Waters when she is raped by this triv-ial character, and out comes Jeanne Crain cross-dressing as gentry; poor Ethel never really recovered from that, who could dance with Mr. Sissle in *Chocolate Babies on Parade*, hot dandy Eubie Blake in ul-timate white tie, leaning on the ivories until she had her breakdown and had to be born again. I could not believe my eyes when I finally got out to Queens and, looking up, saw Central Park.

Coming up on the zoo, I noticed there was construction going on there, too. The Monkey House was closed for repairs. I was taking in this latest wrench my dubious fate had tossed at my machinations when I realized that all this time I had been on a tangent; reflecting stereotypes, reacting; hey, why should those monkeys have gone back to the zoo? No, they were out there in the world somewhere, acting like normal people. Teller, Petoit, Dulles, Hoover, Chillingsworth, the Senator, pick a city. They could have gone anywhere. The realization that the scent was cold settled onto me like a net: all this time I had gotten nowhere. I would have backed out right then and there, but where would that have left me? All this time I had not thought about my own condition too much, I mean, as such, the question of my physicality. What about my own humanity? Was it retrievable independent of the Man? This invisibility that was my defense, my weapon, was it also my fate? Was what the Lucan had given me irreversible? It had only been my desperation that'd driven me to magic in the first place and now here I was definitely stuck out here in the metaphysical realm; the Man's fate and Lil' Eva's and mine bound together in this hideous parody of a relationship, perhaps irretrievably, irrevocably. I would always be able to eat, find myself a place to sleep somewhere: all I would have to do would be to completely renounce my ass, repudiate it, and I would be safe from the authorities for as long as I lived. While I couldn't really blame it for anything, it, nevertheless, was all there was at this juncture to tie me to my reality. Scratch my ass and I would be free of all the baggage, period. All I would have to do would be to come to terms with the status quo, accept my situation, which would have been roughly defined as canis domesticus (invisibilis). Even if I found the man, made him confess and somehow got rid of this pronouncement the Presley kid had placed on me, would that help me in the case of my invisibility? On the other hand, suppose it just wore off and I lost even that advantage before I ever got to those two.

I had been sitting by the lake looking at what would have been my reflection but which, due to my peculiarity, was no more than a couple of mallard ducks, when I realized that what I was contemplating was tantamount to suicide. Sure, I was alive, but what was I without my ass, a complete nonentity with no more substance than a couple of ducks. Angrily, I kicked a stone in the direction of the birds, sending them scudding across the water, further distorting what would have been my face if I had had one. Give my ass up? No, I would never do that, rather, I would, so to speak, become one myself as his greater talent (if I were to be completely honest with myself) and my invisibility would only naturally reduce whatever I would do or say to his level in people's eyes. That was the condition: face the fact that if I embraced John I would no longer have the anonymity of an invisible dog. No matter what I would say or do from that decision on would be defined by who, and what he was, and what was that? A stubborn jackass. That was the deal. What I further realized was how much time I had wasted looking for them. I could waste much more, the rest of my life, maybe, or I could play my hand. I could make them come to us. The way I saw it, I had all the aces.

I was smart enough this time to trot over to Central Park West where I hopped a cab back up to Eighth Avenue and headed for the Paradise. My old ass would be sure to go for this as much as he loved publicity. To upstage me, to be the star; he would go for that like a seat in the Ellington band. With my luck, I half expected the place to be closed, but there it was, its red and blue lights bright as the promise its name implied or, at least, Christmas. There was even some music going on, but it was coming from the jukebox, dreaming of Slim Gaillard, "Hit that jive, Jack; put it in yo' pocket 'til I get back; I'm goin' downtown ta see a man; I ain't got time ta shake yo' hand," along with a few desultory customers nursing their gins and tonic, their scotches with soda, while staring absentmindedly at themselves in the mirror. Having no idea of what to do or where to go next, I decided to just cool my role here and wait and see who would turn up. As I could not afford the luxury of asking the barmaid, a henna-haired, mocha cafe-colored beauty with what appeared to be an expression of perennial boredom, for any info, nor could I just order a drink (though I was tempted to, if only to get that expression off her face—I hate to see pretty women so full of themselves and what they imagine everything and everybody else to be, forgetting the blankness imposed on my own countenance as a result of my condition). I decided instead on a little diversion, knocking a bottle of cheap rye whiskey off the shelf and, taking advantage of the patrons' attention to her magnificent rear as she tidied up, to snatch myself a couple of man-sized pulls from a handy bottle of Jack Daniels.

"Whoaa, what happened there, Milene?" one of the customers asked, up on his elbow greedily taking in her every move.

"I dunno, Harry," said she, "I must not of set it up there right, although I really do not remember pourin' any of this stuff. I must be losin' my mind."

"I ain't been drinkin' it, that's for sure, not how I like my gin; that's all I been drinkin. You, Lou?"

"Not on my account," said the other man. "I drinks scotch, that's all I been payin' for anyway."

"I don't know why, if you can't tell that's what I been givin' you, fool. What's the matter with you? Ain't you got no taste buds? Don't you start talkin' 'bout me cheatin' you!"

"Then the bottle just took a mind to fall, I guess, 'cause I sure ain't seen nobody here but us since you opened. Less you count that jackass, Red."

The barmaid straightened up at the same time that my ears did. "Now don't you go callin' him no jackass, you hear, Lou?"

"No, well, that's what he is, ain't he?"

"To tell you the god's honest truth, I just don't like to think of him that way, that's all, and I don't really like it when you be thinkin' of him that way either!"

"Well, Milene, I'm a man. Now you tell me, what other way I am supposed ta think of him, Milene. I knows you is sweet on him and he sounds pretty good on his instrument and all of that, but you tell me, what else in the world way am I supposed to think of him?"

"What he is, Louis, that's all."

"And what's that, Milene, huh? What."

"Well—" said Milene.

"What!"

"Well, a mule."

"Wha— Oh yeah, a mulatto."

"You're just jealous, Louis, and you know it."

"Oh boy," said the one called Harry, "here we go again. I'd better get myself a drink!"

"Why should I be jealous, hey, Milene?"

"You'd be surprised, Louis; you'd be surprised."

"You know what Milene, I bet I wouldn't."

The Basie Band kicked in. Jimmy Rushing's opulent voice floating disembodied, across the room. "I've got a mind to ramble; I've got a mind to go back home."

So old John was up to his usual. Here I had been scratching and sniffing trouble, wagging my tail in the dirt, shoveling shit, worried about whether he was going to be a drag, if he was managing to even feed himself properly and, from the sound of it, he had fallen into the schmaltz kibble. It seems we all have our faults, but being disposable to women had never—since I had known him—been one of his. I agreed with Harry. What was there to be surprised about? While Woody and Peck had both been initially attracted to me, he certainly had lost no points with either of them when that Luke had shown up with his antics. I mean, I'm a big dog and all, but, when everything is said and done, John was a pretty big donkey. I'd never really thought about the "atto" angle, though, in terms of breeding, just how much is couched in that term or, in fact, if it actually applied to John — I didn't know what his parentage was, but he had always been black to me, ever since that man had, advertently or inadvertently, introduced us.

"You know," said Harry, echoing my thoughts, "I ain't never thought about it like that, but it do make it just about right, don't it Louis. Sound somethin' like another mule been kickin' in yo' stall."

"Harry," said Louis, stung, "I want you to tell me how in the world I could be worried about Milene here and some goddam jackass? And as for what he calls that trumpet of his, why, that is just a passing fancy, and you knows what they says about that, hey, Milene?"

"Louis, tell me baby, why must you always be so old-fashioned, always so black and blue, and then turn right around and tell everybody you deserve a break 'cause you white inside?"

"Old-fashioned, Milene, is that what you think of me: old-fashioned? Well you just wait till that jackass comes waltzin' in here. I will put a good old fashioned New Orleans cow-walkin' on him. Chicago. King Louie, remember? Do you think he kin beat that? Where is he from, a Georgia cotton field? Harry, do you hear this I have to put up with: old fashioned! Zeke Biliken. Me, Louis. King Louis, ain't that right, Harry?"

"Well, Pops, I would never call you that, but you know how these contemporaries is, my worthy constituency. I'm not like that. I stand with the Count. Not them, what do they care about swingin'. They call it 'lynchin.' No, they is be-boppers and they don't want to know nuthin' about nuthin' else."

Milene said, "Now you know that is not true about Red, Harry; you can't categorize him like that. Sure, he is your contemporary all right, but I have listened to him many a night in here for most of the last year and I can tell you, contemporary or not, I do not see him as being stylistically limited. That mule makes good reference. He certainly refers to you, Louie, but he does not defer. And I do know that for a fact, because that is what he told me."

"King Louis." "Pops." Was this who I thought it was: the great Armstrong here at the Paradise on One Hundred Tenth Street and Eighth Avenue! Things were looking up, but while this was certainly the best opportunity I'd had yet to get some solid information as to the phenomenon or phenomena that created jazz, I couldn't ask him a thing about it without tipping my hand. I would have to go through, as per my usual, my old ass.

"Is that what you heard for true, Milene? Well, you just wait till he brings his old hirsute butt with the long ears of a jackass and the tail of a mule shufflin' on in here, and I will put the same thing on him that the great god Apollo put on that ass from Syria, Alepo, or somewhere like that, I think it was. I am going to flay him. Skin him alive."

"Louis, please, for my sake, don't try that!"

The great trumpeter looked at her sulkily and sucked his teeth. "Try, try hell—"

"Please, please, Pops, baby, don't."

He was pitying her now: "And why not?"

The barmaid said, "Because I don't want no trouble in here, Louis. I do not wish to see your own flayed body laying on this barroom floor."

Louis turned apoplectic: "What! You just wait till he brings his old rusty-dusty in here."

Milene looked at him derisively. "Rusty-dusty" she said. "Well, the way I see it from here, he might be a bit 'dusty' if you wanna call him that, but he is not 'rusty.'"

Louis must have been stung pretty deeply as he would not let it go. "Rusty-dusty. What is his name, Red? Well, when I get finished with him, his moniker is gonna be just that: "Ol' Rusty-dusty Ass."

"Oh, yeah," said Milene, "I'd like to see that day."

Louis straightened up. "Oh yeah," he said. He got up and walked to the window, pointing past the red and blue lights to the sky. "Look at it."

Harry said, "Whew! Give me a drink, Milene, I have got to be ready for this."

The barmaid poured his drink. I took advantage of their preoccupation to down myself another slug.

"Whoo," said Harry, "you better watch that Jack. I swear it look like it gettin' ready to fall."

Milene walked over to where I had placed the bottle. "No," she said, examining its placement, "It's all right." I was standing right next to her. She smelled good.

"I must be seein' things," said Harry. "I could have sworn I seen that bottle move."

The Jack was starting to warm me up pretty good. I had not smelled a woman like her this close since that girl in the park back when I had first met John. Calloway's "Minnie the Moocher" was on the juke. I wanted to dance with her. I had taken a few tentative steps by myself when John walked in. He looked a lot different than when I had last seen him. He was more mature; his chest had filled out; he seemed more confident of himself, supremely confident, and was accompanied by a group of musicians that I found out later included some of the younger cats from Texas and the West Coast. He wore a pork-pie hat and walked in with a swagger. "Red, oh, Red, how is yo' doin's baby?" the barmaid cooed. At the group's approach she had come around the bar, and now stared somewhat dreamily into my ass's eyes. She adjusted his tie: a wide, blue and red polka-dot affair with a Windsor knot worn over a pink Mister B, the collar of which was open down to the second button revealing a snow-white ribbed t-shirt. He wore a canary-yellow, double-breasted suit with a box-back and high-draped trousers, the inverted triple pleats of which culminated in creases sharp enough to cut paper. These were pegged narrowly around the ankles and rested on a pair of shoulders already as broad as the Spanish Main. It was a zoot suit cut from at least twelve yards of cloth, a magnificent raw silk affair that would have suited a plenipotentiary. I had never seen him looking so good. He had the air of a prince, a peer of the realm. He smiled, revealing an upper-right cuspid sheathed in gold and a diamond incisor. It lit up the room. He gave her the kiss I wanted to give her. The barmaid said, "Oh Red, you send me, Red, you really do. Your customary, I suppose, honey?"

He nodded, releasing her from what seemed like a death grip. She went back around the bar and mixed him a screwdriver, a drink the whole country had suddenly gone wild about, made with orange juice and Russian vodka, a legacy I suppose of the just-then burgeoning cold war. Sipping from this, his soulful eyes seemed to say, "And how are your feelings today?" He'd indeed changed a lot. I had never known him to drink.

"Har-ry, what's shakin?" said one of the group, a tall, lean young man with the accent of an Oklahoman who carried a trumpet case tucked under his arm like a baton.

"Ain't nuthin shakin'," Harry said, "but the peas in the pot, and they wouldn't be shakin' if the water wasn't hot. Cherry, you?"

"Oh," said the one called Cherry, grinning to reveal in his turn a gold-capped left-upper cuspid and a diamond incisor, "ain't nuthin' shakin but the leaves in the trees, and they wouldn't be shakin' if it wasn't for the breeze!"

The group cracked up at this, slapping thighs and palms. Only Louis was not laughing. "Hey, say," said one of the others suddenly noticing him, "wait a minute; wait a minute; say, ain't you; ain't you—"

Louis looked grim as if he had just eaten something he couldn't quite stomach. All he said was: "Don't say it, boy, if you can't play it." The room got very quiet except for the jukebox. Louie Jordan. "Junko Pardner." The record ended, punctuating the shock of the sudden silence.

"Wait a minute; wait a minute, boy; why I was just tryin' ta pay you a compliment."

"Then you should know you can't pay me nuthin' but some cash. Save the rest of it for your own account."

"Pops, I heard you had a big mouth."

"Do you want to lodge a complaint?"

"I might," said the younger man.

Louis said, "And what about that jackass over there that somebody said played a trumpet. Bugle, maybe, like the rest o' them army mules."

John had been sipping his drink and staring languidly into the barmaid's eyes, oblivious to the rising tension in the room around him. I don't know if he had heard what had just been said, but if he did, he gave no indication that he had. To his credit, he didn't blink an eyelash. "Hey," said Louis, "didn't you hear me; what do they call you, Red? Well, I'm callin' you out!"

The rhythm consisted of drums and bass with no piano. There were two tenors, an alto saxophone, a trombone, four trumpets including John and Harry, plus Louis, who had gone outside to a waiting car and returned with an instrument. It was as if it had been planned. Removing the horn from its case, he squirted a drop of oil on each valve and fitted the mouthpiece to it after which he shook it up and down like a jigger so that the valves moved freely up and down in their casing. He said, "Call one."

Whatever it was they played, I had never heard anything so postmodern. Atonal. The horns played sounds, whoops and shrieks and shudders whereas Louis would moan and strut. It was as arhythmical as a heart attack, the drummer avoiding the traditional pulse of the bass and the ride, instead playing whistles and a saw, timpani, marimbas and an enormous kettle drum so huge a five-foot stepladder was required with a pair of mallets as large as sledge hammers which produced a tone like a felled tree in a rain forest, while the bassist played arco with a frenzy, at times singing wordlessly along with a line like Slam Stewart or Major Holly, the difference being that the voice was at times in the same pitch as the instrument, while at others it was produced an octave above or even below. Louis was a professional, sticking to his regimen, sounding as though he were being dispatched through a time-tunnel, the stuff he had played with Joe Oliver and with the "Five," and the "Seven," as if he were being sampled onto what the rest of the group was playing. I hadn't known that John was playing like that, his outfit making it appear anachronistic, asymmetrical.

"That ain't no jazz," said Louis. "What's that y'all playin'? What key is that?"

The younger man said, "No key, Mr. Armstrong."

"What tune is that?" said Louis.

"No tune, just ramblin'."

"No tune ... no key ... no rhythm. You kin say that again. Milene, you like that stuff?"

"I'm crazy 'bout it, Pops," said Milene, "It gives me goosebumps."

Louis said, "No tune. No key. No rhythm. No wonder y'all ain't got no customers in here."

It was much later before I got a chance to speak with John, because, though I followed the barmaid and him to her home after the set, what they did there together was so personal I could not get a word in edgewise. I could not help thinking that they reminded me of nothing so much as a couple of worms. After a couple of days of this, Milene, pushing my grass-eating ass away, gasped, "Stop, oh, please, stop. I can't take it anymore."

John looked hurt.

"Oh no, baby," she said stroking his long, hairy ears, his long rope of a tail, "don't be mad with me; don't sulk; I am just a big girl after all, Red, and you are some donkey."

She stroked his magnificent member dreamily and gave it an affectionate kiss. My own groin grew warm. I felt a stirring there I had not felt since our party days on Morton Street, and the stronger this feeling became, the more my bird began to glow, until pretty soon it was a very visible fire-engine red which in my growing preoccupation with it I noticed before Milene did. My bird, it was visible! My apprehension diverted my libidinal impulse: the more my ardor cooled, the more my bird faded until very soon it was as transparent as the rest of me. The whole phenomenon had the appearance of a firefly on a still and sticky June evening, but I was glad the woman had not noticed it; it might have frightened her, a firefly big as a bird! Maybe she would have tried to kill it. Or worse, maybe she would have had John, me being unrecognizable to him there in the half-light, take it out with a hoof. I made a mental note that I would have to be careful of that, make sure I found myself in no situation where my libido was not under strict control.

Milene said, "Red, honey, ain't you hungry? I'm starvin' to death!"

The ass shrugged and nodded. As I had noted, he had been ingesting copious amounts of grass. It's a funny thing about the weed. Sometimes it enhances the appetites and sometimes it inhibits them. I myself have found it to be a most wonderful aphrodisiac, and it was no doubt a contributing factor to John's stamina and invention, though it seemed to have suppressed his desire for other nourishment.

The woman said, "Well, honey, whaddya want?"

The animal, pulling on a long fine blade, shrugged again. Smoke wreathed his ears until it became a corrugated halo.

"Lemme see what's in there," said Milene, grabbing a frilly housecoat. I wished she hadn't done that. Her body was beautiful. I envied John. As to the kitchen, I knew what was in there—a big fat goose egg.

They had been at it for days and there hadn't been much to begin with. She looked like the type that ate out a lot, though it did appear that she or somebody around did like to cook, as fine copper and cast iron pots and pans hung from the ceiling on hooks, and spice racks were full of exotic spices such as turmeric and coriander, cumin and cardamom as well as the more common ones like salt and pepper, but oh, how many varieties of pepper! And a veritable forest of fresh herbs grew profusely in little pots. There were reproductions of famous paintings that had food as their subject; still lives of fish and capons, pigs with apples in their mouths. I loved that kitchen. It was so baroque. I imagined a profusion of cooks in whatever they call those hats and aprons wrestling hams into ovens, sides of beef turning on spits. The range was big enough for an ass. Strings of garlic and onions and dried peppers hung everywhere.

"Oh, damn," she said eyeing the empty refrigerator, "I could have sworn I went to the store. Didn't I go to the store? Oh, Red, you make me forget everything! I guess I didn't. You know the god's honest truth? I wouldn't know where my head is half the time if you didn't screw it on for me. I'm gonna have to run to the store but"—she sniffed her armpits—"oh, god, I smell like an animal! I'd better shower first." She gave John another big kiss on the nose and padded off to the bathroom. She reappeared after a few moments dressed in a flowery muumuu that disappointed in how it hid her figure. I was already looking forward to seeing her without it once more. She wrapped her hair with a small silk scarf. She had the cutest nose I had ever seen on a human. "Back in a moment, hon," she said, disappearing through the door, a wicker shopping basket slung from the crook of her elbow. So much for looks.

I whistled a little tune John and I used to play.

John, flexing his ears, sat up. He looked over his shoulder and around the room. I whistled another bar. He joined in slowly, in half time so the theme became a statement within a statement. I thought he sounded a bit automatic, but, when I got to the last bar, he restated the theme more brightly and jumped up out of the bed, his huge dong of an ass slapping against his knees, located me and gave me a hug and a peck on both cheeks, the way the French do. I said, "John, John, boy, how you been?"

I rubbed between his ears and nuzzled him in a gesture of affection. He gazed at me with that dreamy expression that said he was as whacked out as Cootie Brown in a rainstorm. It was Cootie's credo in such a situation to always keep the clouds well below you. John's dreamy eyes went round. He made a little "o" of his mouth, squared his shoulders and executed a little jig, finishing with a spin and a flourish. Throwing his head back, he laughed, revealing the gold cuspid with the diamond incisor, and nodded. Pulling himself modestly into his trousers, he excitedly gestured that I should check out Milene's apartment.

It was indeed a beautiful place, spacious and well-lighted, with high ceilings and hardwood floors with wide planking. It was located on Morningside at One Hundred Tenth, the large windows of which looked out onto the great golden dome of the Cathedral of St. John the Divine and Morningside Park below, with the tiny, tidy campus of Columbia University a few blocks to the north. Navajo Indian scatter-rugs added bright patches of color to the floor. The feeling of airiness was enhanced by the fact that there was not much furniture. What little there was was dominated by a thirteen- foot concert grand piano. It knocked my socks off, so to speak (because as you will recall, I wasn't in fact wearing any). I was amazed that my very own ass, old John the Black One, in truth, had acquired this extraordinary arrangement for himself, with space enough to dance around such a grand instrument. There were a few paintings on the walls by the artist Bob Thompson, red and green and blue colorfield compositions depicting white women as trees with apples for breasts and red devils devouring them, paintings that were not unpleasant to look at, and there were some black and white photographs, portraits of Monk and Ellington, others taken from concerts. John was beaming. He implied he had never felt less cramped in his life. He made me remember the Hudson. He tried to look me up and down, shrugged when he realized the impossibility of that and directed me a deep, soulful look meant to inquire about my own well-being, a look that wanted to say, "And how are your feelings today?"

"Ah," I said, slowly settling my haunches onto a throw rug and sighing, "it's a long story, John."

When I told him what more I had learned, he sat, shaking his great head of an ass, and when I got to the part about Billie, a great tear escaped from his eye. He seemed to ask if I had a plan. When I told him what it was, he turned gray. "Decoy," his look conveyed, "you want me to be a decoy for that man? Do you remember what he tried to do to me?"

I asked if he remembered Woody and Peck. I told him I realized the situation regarding my beautiful mother and my *Old Testament*, ear-grabbing disciplinarian of a grandmother was personal, as he hadn't known them, but Peck and Woody, especially Peck, they were his friends. I reminded him that the reality was he was a fugitive because of that creep and what he had done to them.

John implied that that was exactly what he wanted to talk about. Some things just were, he wanted to say, and that man was one of them, a condition of life. He also wanted to say he was sorry about our having gotten caught up in his trick bag due to my having panicked on hearing some little snot-nosed white boy sing about what I was or was not; ergo, a hound dog who, in the confusion of his new state, tripped the very latch set up by myself to keep the likes of that man out. His look now implored me to understand that he had always been what he was—no more and no less—and nothing nor anybody in this whole world, including that man, was going to change that. He practically begged me to understand that the dye job worked for him. He figured all he had to do was stay as far away from that man as he possibly could and everything would be solid. John never really was one for trouble. He wanted me to understand that he had a good life here with Milene; the cats came by and jammed, and Milene would cook. I saw that kitchen out there, didn't I? Well, that girl Milene could really burn, could really put the pots on, could do anything with oats and apples and carrots in it like he loved, not those nauseous guts I had made him eat for practically our whole adolescence due to my own—he wanted to emphasize "my own" here—association with that character Luke.

I reminded him that that very character had helped us escape from that prison and that he was yet helping me as it had been he that had shown me the way to be invisible, and that that was actually the way I had gotten him away from that evil Dr. Petoit back there in Central Park.

He shuddered in a way that seemed to say that all of that was behind him now, that he'd just be getting on with his life and he thought he preferred keeping it that way. Milene was the coolest frail he had ever had since a little mule named Jenny, and she would dig to have me around. Invisible as I was, I wouldn't take up much room; like I knew how the old adage went: out of sight, out of mind. We could jam, just like in the old days, and Milene would cook up a storm. What'd I say.

It was a tempting offer. The thought of living with that Milene made me dizzy. I could smell the perfume of her wafting from the bathroom, her musky odor with the slightest suggestion of animal about it, imagined her taking me out to the park downstairs and across the street, us running freely with the collar off me, playing "fetch" when nobody was looking, the taste of her hand on my tongue, the moist, yeasty smell of her crotch as I nosed into her, she rubbing my back, scratching it fiercely, my belly, grabbing me by my great, floppy ears of a hound as she leaned into me for a kiss. The very thought of it set my tail to vigorously wagging, my bird to glowing violently. John's startled look couldn't have conveyed more eloquently what he was thinking: "Good gracious, Gates, my, my! Is that you I'm looking at like that? Now lemme hip you to somethin, look here, buddy roll, if you gonna be invisible around here, you gonna havta put some shade on that shit." His discovery embarrassed me enough so that I recovered, and my organ—

fiery as it had become—faded again until it appeared to be no more than the image of a thunderbird on a Navajo throw rug. The incident sobered me; checked my headlong fancy. I was still pretty vulnerable. I let the verderous image of idyllic romps in the park fade as my bird had. Milene came back from the store so loaded down it had taken two grocery bags and a couple of carts to carry it all. "I guess your friends will certainly be comin' over, so I got enough. Lord, ain't nobody I know in the world hungrier than a jazz musician! Poor things."

Her communication with John was superb, and pretty soon she understood who I was, what I was, and how it was with 'em.

"My, Lucius, that's heavy. I mean it. But you know what? Let's eat something first. I'm starving."

She made oatmeal apple fritters for herself and my ass and provided me with a dozen eggs and a couple of cans of corned beef hash. When we had finished, she said, "A dog, huh? And judging from the amount of food he put away, he is pretty big. Well, I could use a dog. I have wanted another since my Poopsie died in that terrible accident. Hit and run. People can be so cruel." She looked sad at the thought. "Invisible, huh? Well, that's a twist."

John had left out the part about my wanting to get to the man and how I wanted to do it. As far as that went, I was back on my own, left to my own devices, without any cooperation from what mattered most to me in the world then, my own ass. I truly felt like a dog; albeit, a lucky one. Milene was the perfect hostess, unobtrusive, oblivious to my comings and goings, completely uninhibited by my presence. I used the occasion of her frank sexuality and that of their passionate and frequent lovemaking to practice better control over my erections, and pretty soon I could go anywhere with her, smelling her closeness in the park there—under the golden dome of the Cathedral of St. John the Divine as I had imagined—without revealing myself, and she would appear as a dancer, periodically pirouetting and squatting, lazily tossing a red or blue rubber ball that seemed, miraculously, to return by itself. Most nights, between gigs, the cats would come by to jam, and pretty soon word got around that my ass had acquired quite some handsome voice. A few of the in-cats like Jackie, for example, knew what was really happening, but bound by the propriety of my friendship with John and my tacit agreement to his condition, I became no more than that: his voice. This mantle of invisibility was to be mine forever. That aside, he was quite right, it was a great life, and the only difference between it and the old days was that instead of being seen in my rhinestone collar when we went out, Milene and he were the focus of all the attention, with his fabulous drapes, his jackets with the exaggerated shoulders of a gangster or a jazz musician, and everywhere we went people would stop and stare, stomp and whistle in appreciation of this lady with the great ass. Without meaning any disrespect to the memories of Woody and Peck and their music-making ability and what all else, the level was more intense, personal. I mean Woody could shake her tambourine and her maracas if she had to all night long, and Peck had known her way around a guitar and could toot a pretty mean pennywhistle when she got going, but essentially what we had been doing was hustling small change with a few good tricks thrown in now and then. The focus now was strictly on music, and we were laying down some serious sounds. With Milene as our agent, the gigs started rolling in. At first it was just local stuff, but in a short time we were going downtown, playing the larger venues like the Five Spot and the Jazz Gallery. It was hilarious in a way that we were now headlining at all those clubs that had previously barred my entry because of either my age or the shape I happened to be in. John appreciated that fact, too, with a chuckle, reminding me though that he himself had never had that problem as most of the people in the clubs at any given time were complete asses. Billed as the "Lady with the Great One," we played Philadelphia, after which we were on the map; Pittsburgh; Chicago; Decatur, Illinois, you name it: Pep's, the Royal, the Pershing, where we went on opposite Ahmad Jamal to rave press notices. *The Defender* said, "Great Act! Great Ass!" The Tribune said, "Beautiful ... music with contours!" and on and on. John was eating it up and I was lapping it up pretty much too, being the "golden voice" of the "Lady with the Great Ass." "Fabulous!" the *L.A. Times* said after an engagement at the Lighthouse in Hermosa Beach. Hedda Hopper said we simply had to be seen to be believed, and we all got a great laugh out of that.

We were at a club on Bourbon Street in New Orleans when I saw Eva. If there has been any place in the world we would have run into her, I should have known it would have been that one, as they served hagfish there, a delicacy that suited Eva to a "t" since that animal had the nasty habit of boring into the flesh of other fishes, using its circular, barbel-rimmed mouth to feed on their interior parts. So, sure enough, as big as day and twice as ugly, there she was—in the company of a man who was unknown to me— dining on a blackened version of this insidious predator who, with its underdeveloped eyes, blindly but efficiently devoured its victims alive from the inside out. The place also featured beer by the chamber pot, and she and her companion were obviously enjoying a couple of these with their meal. Except for the tired look of a zombie around her eyes, she hadn't changed much; she was still fascinating to look at, like a coral snake with its bright copper color alternating with bands of red and glistening ebony, or blood welling up like a jewel from a deep cut on the finger, beautiful, dark-red, and left to its own devices, potentially lethal; like an infection. Her companion resembled Sidney Greenstreet in *Casablanca*, with his white linen suit, panama hat and the thick-lidded eyes of a toad and great jowls that worked tirelessly up and down as their owner consumed fork after fork of the hagfish. Fortunately, I thought, John hadn't noticed anything unusual, as he had never met Lil' Eva, having been god-knows-where when I was going through that episode with the blind man. We had just finished a set and had one more to do. Eva and her dining companion were deep in conversation. I was trembling slightly as I went over and sat close enough to them to listen.

CHAPTER TWENTY

"**P**etoit," Eva was saying. "Desire."

"How much?" said Greenstreet.

"Depend," Eva said.

"On what?" said Greenstreet.

"Market," said Eva. "Supply equal demand. If I has to go 'roun' de worl' or even halfway roun' ta git dis shit, and you can't git yo' load off, we could git stuck. We'd have ta take a dousing. Mah man, da man, don't like ta git wet, see?"

Greenstreet grinned. He swallowed a great mouthful of fish by taking a swig from the chamber pot. The smell of the fish came powerfully with a belch. Taking up a napkin from his not-much-of-a-lap, he dabbed delicately at his mouth. A smaller eruption followed. "My," he said, "you'll have to pardon my digestion." He paused for a moment, pudgy hand resting on his distended stomach, gaping mouth gasping for breath, curiously like a fish himself, and went on: "I see," he said. "And so?"

Eva had been bringing a forkful of the fish to her own mouth. She stopped and made a face. "Ooooh," she said, "you got to do somethin 'bout yo'stomach."

"I am seeing a specialist on my return to L.A.," said Greenstreet.

I thought Eva showed an uncharacteristic concern. "You gotta see Petoit," she said. "He a specialist."

"I'm sure he is," said Greenstreet, after he'd taken another swig of the beer. He belched again, making a little face of apology. It was odd to see so small a face on such a large man. Eva wrinkled her nose, waving a hand in front of it. "It's the hagfish," he said, "I love it, as you can see, but I'm afraid it doesn't always agree with my constitution. Sometimes, it's as if I can feel the very teeth of the godawful things gnawing away at my innards."

Eva snorted like a horse. She said, "Dat's what dey do, you know. You gotta have the stomach for 'em. Dey ain' never bothered me." She lifted her blouse to show him a little mound of a stomach that looked to me as if the creatures were breeding there.

Greenstreet leaned forward in his chair, salaciously eyeing the patch of flesh she offered to his view. He caressed it suggestively with a pudgy hand. "Mmm," he said, licking his lips, his mouth suddenly dry. He took another draught and wiped his mouth. "How much?" he said.

"Fuh what," asked Eva, "a consultation with Petoit or dat other thing?"

Greenstreet straightened and cleared his throat. "Let me make one thing perfectly clear," he said. "I have no intention of ever consulting with Dr. Petoit regarding any of my medical problems. I have my reasons for that, not the least of which is that I'm Jewish. I'm afraid I have some information concerning his treatment of those of his patients that happened to be Jewish during the war. I wouldn't dare go to him in that capacity. Could I trust him?"

"Always treated me," said Lil' Eva.

Having finished her meal and wiped her jewel-colored mouth, she removed a shell-shaped compact from her purse and, eyeing her reflection, dabbed gingerly at the mascara around her tired eyes of a zombie. Satisfied, she fished up a tube of lipstick and applied a fresh coat, outlining the deep vermilion with black. Surreptitiously, but not enough so that it escaped my watchful eye of a bloodhound, she scooped something up from the compact with a fingernail and passed it across her nose, which she wiped with a puff. She licked her lips and returned the puff to its case, which she snapped shut, returning it to her purse with a sigh. "Always treated me good," she said. Her eyelids began to droop as her facial muscles began to relax.

"You are not Jewish," said Greenstreet.

"Ain't I lucky," said Eva. "How much you got? I kin git all you kin handle."

"I'm talking about a considerable amount."

Eva had begun to nod. She straightened up with a jerk. "How much is dat?" she said. "We talkin' numbers here, ain't we? Don't be coy. Is you ready to deal, or what?"

"I mean, a considerable amount. I'm talking about a couple of tons."

"A couple of tons? Wow, dat's enough to supply de whole West Coast." She slipped back into her nod; pulled herself out of it, vigorously scratching at a thigh. "Mmm," she said, sniffing and wiping an eye, "Coupla tons ... yeah, we kin do dat. How much did you say?"

"Two tons," Greenstreet said patiently.

"Das right," said Eva, "two tons. Das what I thought you said. Two tons, das enough to supply de whole West Coast fer a week."

"You mentioned that," said Greenstreet. "You're repeating yourself, Eva."

Eva jerked up and out of her euphoria. "Repeating myself ... repeating myself." She turned away, saying to no one in particular, "Repeating myself, he says I'm repeating myself. It's my mouf' and it's my dope, and it's good, too. You want it or not?"

She had enunciated the gerunds carefully, mocking Greenstreet.

He said, "The ball's in your court. How much?"

Eva said, "Now who repeatin' theyself? Ain't but twenty six letters in the alphabet. Circles and lines and loops dat all goes de same way. Can't help but repeat yo'self. Has you ever tried to say somethin' widdout repeatin' yo' self?" She grunted at her own cleverness, sensing she had him at a disadvantage, that he knew nothing about linguistics.

"Eva," said Greenstreet exasperatedly, "numbers, come on, give me a number!"

"De same thing! You see dat?"

Before Greenstreet could answer, Milene signaled that the set was about to begin. I decided to sit this one out. The band, consisting of ourselves and a pick-up rhythm section, slid into "Cherokee." It took my ass a moment to realize that I wasn't on the stand, but when it did, it extended the introduction for a couple of bars before going to the melody on his own. It was a small thing, but we hadn't rehearsed it that way with the rhythm section, and perhaps because of the pianist's not being experienced as he might have been, it threw them off for a couple of bars. John coasted until they caught up before launching into a scathing solo.

Scratching, Lil' Eva said, "Dis here music is awful." She made a face.

"It's the rhythm section," said Greenstreet. "I have to tell you that that ass is brilliant. I have never heard a jackass play like that before. Most of them sound like army mules. What is the name of this band?"

I almost liked Greenstreet.

"I donno," said Eva, "I ain't come in here for no music. I came here ta eat dis fish. Sho was tasty, wasn't it?"

I enjoyed it very much, thank you, as much as I could, given my constitution. But, please, I have to tell my associates something."

Eva looked like this was the moment she enjoyed the best. "For you," she said, "30 million. Pure China white."

Greenstreet whistled. "30 million, that's a lot of money!"

"Comin' outta Viet Nam. Cost a lot ta git it."

A sly look crossed Greenstreet's countenance: "Viet Nam, huh? Well, now that I know your sources, why don't I just get it myself?"

If a zombie can laugh, Eva did. "Don't you even try it," she said. "You will come back in a body bag. Mah man has got dem Hmong peoples locked up pretty tight. Dey likes heads, you know. If somebody was ta tell 'em to dey might stick yours on a pole. Burmese, too. You think it's a lot o' money; raise yo' prices. It's good dope. Any junky kin look in the mirror, see dat right away. You kin look in the mirror, see dat right away. You kin even give 'em less. Dey'll go f' it. It's just like a baby's kiss."

I liked your demonstration," Greenstreet said earnestly. He signaled for the waiter. The band was playing "Polka-dots and Moonbeams." John tried singing, and, unable to articulate the verse, made onomatopoetic sounds, some practically scatological. It was very funny. The crowd laughed and stomped and whistled its appreciation.

"Check, please," Greenstreet said to the waiter, who approached bringing them a complimentary drink of something that, to my delicate nose of a bloodhound, smelled suspiciously like cat piss. Taking a sip, Greenstreet shuddered and grimaced, setting his jowls in motion like the wipers at an automatic car wash; something I'd only recently become familiar with as Milene had just bought a car, driving wherever we could when we were touring, just so we could have our privacy, avoiding a situation like one that occurred on the way to Pittsburgh from Philly. Milene had neglected to buy me a ticket or just figured she could save on one, and the god-damned bus filled up so I had to stand all the way there, enduring the puzzled stare of passengers bumping into me in the aisle if I did not find a way to dance around them, with the consequence that I was really too tired to be at my best by the time we got to Pittsburgh. John liked getting loaded and watching the wipers jiggle over the soapy windshield. As to the beverage, Eva did not drink hers. She was nodded out. Greenstreet shrugged, downed it, shuddered, and paid the check. He took Eva gently by the arm. "Shall we go to my place for a nightcap while I make the arrangements?" he asked.

"It's yo' call, daddy," she said. "Nice of you ta ask."

I made the decision to follow as he steered her into the humid July night.

It was about ninety degrees and sticky, and the smell of magnolias and jasmine hung in the night air, reminding me of the odor at the florist's shop. A hansom cab stood at the curb, harnessed to a mangy, swaybacked horse that was wearing a straw hat (with a daisy in it) and diapers. Greenstreet steered her towards this and gave the hack an address in Jackson Square. I hopped onto the back, riding with them through the French Quarter as I perched over a swaying water bucket. I wondered if we were going to see the man; for as slimy as Greenstreet was, I knew he was just a tentacle.

Where we went was to a seedy hotel in the square. The building faces a statue of Jackson himself (up on his pedestal, arm upraised with that ubiquitous sword in it) and the Mississippi River. I had never seen that water before, except in pictures. It looked positively animal, alive and purposeful, its deep brown shoulders contoured with muscle like a roustabout, its surface like deltoids, oil-slicked from the tankers that pushed up from the gulf to Memphis, and the ubiquitous shrimpers. It could definitely have been a man, like in the song, though, as muddy as it was, you could see that it was a young man, still cutting its channel, surging to make its mark on the earth, and it could take you down. Hugging a guitar to his side, a young black man, as muscled as the river, sang to it, entreating it in a rasped, breaking voice, not to encroach on his property. His head turned from left to right and he stomped his foot to the rhythm as he plucked and strummed, recalling his earlier travels and misfortune. It was a six/eight rhythm straight out of Angola, and it made me realize that I was definitely coming to know what it was I was looking for. Moody himself must have heard this, and somehow out of it had come the philosophy that had led to the great treatise, "Moody's Mood for Love." All of this was bathed alternately in red and black as a blinking neon sign cast its intermittent glow on the inky night, stitching the words, "Seedy Hotel" letter by letter as if reluctant to reveal itself. To the left of the hotel was the international fruit and flower market.

Greenstreet paid off the hack, and he and Eva went inside. I followed them past a mimeographed and crudely lettered sign tacked to the entrance that read, "Alberto Melendez, come home, your mother miss you," into the lobby where a seedy-looking clerk dressed in harlequin red and black that varied from the usual pattern in that, instead of having triangulated patches of the two colors evenly distributed over his attire, his was simply red on one side and black on the other; so that when he faced right, he appeared to be wearing all red, and when he turned left, all black. The costume seemed to have been worn forever. The clerk was in the middle of the lobby—whose general décor, including the one attempt at elegance among the plastic potted plants, a patch of plastic orchids that gave off the sickly sweet smell of meat that had just begun to rot, as Raymond Chandler had put it—and looked up when we came in. He gave the pair the once over before he said laconically, "Evenin,' Mr. Oleo, where ya at?" to Greenstreet as we approached.

Greenstreet said, "Good evening, Eddie. Any messages for me?"

The clerk said, "None since you left, Mr. Oleo." He handed over a key and went back to the book he'd been reading, Stendahl's *The Red and the Black.*

A self-service elevator carried us up to the fourth floor where they got off, and I followed them down a narrow corridor —which looked as if it should have been too long for the actual dimensions of the building or as if it were a photograph that had been taken through a twenty eight millimeter lens with a beat up camera—to room 412 where Greenstreet attempted to insert the key, though it would not turn the lock no matter how he jiggled it. Inspecting the key, he said, "God damn it, that idiot gave me the wrong key. Wait here, I'll be right back."

It was a full twenty minutes before he returned, during which he found the door leading to the stairs to be locked. "Oleo," the desk clerk had called him. I was sure that wasn't his name, as he had mentioned that he was Jewish, and "Oleo" sounded Italian or even Irish, depending on whether or not you put an apostrophe between the "o" and the"l," and how you pronounced it. The clerk had pronounced it "Ohhleo," like margarine. I was sure it was an alias, just like everything else was around here.

Standing alone with Eva and not chewing her to bits right then and there like a boxer about to lose a fight was one of the most difficult things I have done in my entire life, but I managed to do it by concentrating instead on a spider struggling to build a web over the Exit sign, which I had first thought was a pretty wrongheaded thing for a spider to do, as they were supposed to love the dark, but pretty soon I saw that the arachnid's efforts had a cunning logic to it that almost had to be more than instinct, as whatever moths and other circling insects, which had been attracted to the feeble light of the Exit sign, soon found themselves trapped in this wily hunter's silken net. It should have been the mayor of New Orleans, whose best effort to clean up that town had been to diaper the horses of the hansom cabs.

By the time Greenstreet returned triumphantly waving the key, the spider had raised a family, though a lizard —I think a chameleon—was creeping towards one of the kids. "I am never going to stay in this hotel again," he said. "It was recommended to me by an associate. I'm not sure it is a healthy place. It seems to smack of miasma. And that clerk, why, he looks like a checkerboard! Well, here it is, such as it is, be it ever so humble."

I was glad he had returned, as I had to go to the bathroom and knew from experience my shit was not invisible. He inserted the key, and this time, mercifully, it worked. Throwing the door open, he invited Eva into what looked like hell. There were mushrooms growing everywhere there was a crack, and there were plenty of those. It reminded me of the Lower East Side of Manhattan in how ailanthi grew alongside these in profusion, but there was also cypress, the trunks of which were split and rotted, crowns blown off by hurricanes. Creeping vines of kudzu covered the walls, coursing across the floor like a carpet. Lightning had obviously just hit during a recent storm, and here and there the scorched and blackened trunks of trees still smoldered, sending up spumes of smoke and embers when the boiling sap would cause the fibers of the wood to burst with the heat, giving off what light there was. Fortunately, there was enough cover for me to take a dump, the smell of which blended easily with the fetid air.

The ever-petulant Eva said, "Hey dis here is sho some dump!"

I looked around guiltily, relaxing when I saw she was talking about the place itself and not the fresh and steaming result of my own exertions, which had already begun to draw flies.

"The heat is good," said Greenstreet. "That's about it. The only problem with that is it is not needed, not so much of it at any rate, and wouldn't you know that with the first-class, four star rate I am being charged here, the thermostat doesn't work, though all the smoke does help keep the mosquitoes away. That was the one thing I worried about. I can't stand the little assassins, can you? Anyway, the fan works. Let me turn it on." He threw a switch and a wide-bladed wooden ceiling fan began to creak slowly and laboriously around and around, circulating the close air. "Shall I give us some light, or is this sufficient? It is a bit, well, quaint, isn't it."

Eva snorted. "Dis place too country fuh me, and I'm from Beauford, South Calina. Gennul Beauregard was from dere."

Greenstreet rubbed his pudgy hands together. "Is that right? Well, what do you say we have something to drink? What would you like, oh —" he slapped a pudgy hand against his forehead. "You know what? Actually I have only some bourbon, and, unless you like it neat, I will have to have something sent up."

"Bourbon?" Eva wrinkled her nose in distaste. "I might could use a ginger ale or somethin'. You right about dis heat."

"Ginger ale. I'm afraid there's none of that. I'll have to have that Eddie bring us some."

By the time the desk clerk brought up a tray of drinks and some ice, we had grown mushrooms, which I hadn't noticed in the general gloom of the place, though the sharp-eyed clerk noticed immediately. Mistuh Oleo, suh?"

"What is it, Eddie?"

"Is dat yo' dawg dere, suh?"

Looking around, I saw no other dogs besides my no longer quite so invisible self and that the desk clerk was pointing to none other than me.

"Hey," Eva suddenly said, aroused from her drug-induced stupor, "'cept fuh dem mushrooms, dat damn hound over dere look familiar."

She cocked her head of a harpy like the predatory bird she resembled, and stared hard at me. "Wait a minute. Wait a minute." Her eyes narrowed suspiciously as she turned to Greenstreet. "Wait a minute heah. Oleo, is dat yo' dawg?"

The clerk said, "Animals is against the rules, suh."

I almost had to laugh at that. All the reptiles and swamp rats and spiders in here and what not, and this man was ready to discriminate against me.

Greenstreet's heavy-lidded eyes widened in surprise. "Why, no, Eva, I have never seen that dog before."

"Well, I has. Dat sorry houn' right dere mus' be de one I'm thinkin' he is. Yeah, I is sho' of it, even wid dem mushrooms all over his sorry ass. De man want 'im. Git 'im!"

My "ass" was not sorry nor was it covered with mushrooms; I was. The fungi had not grown on the humans like it grew on me, perhaps because my hirsute condition made me a better host. I couldn't scrape the accursed things off fast enough. They were miniature, spongy landscapes that were oddly not grotesque enough to disguise me. I needed some pepper, and not just any pepper, I needed some Tabasco sauce.

Greenstreet lunged for me, but I evaded the fat man easily, running through his legs as he reached for me, knocking him down. Eva was too stoned, but the desk clerk, who was wiry thin and quick, with the bulging eyes of a reptile himself, snared me. Luckily, the smoke had begun to irritate me some, and I snapped viciously at him, making him let me go.

"Oh, dat's de one. Dat's de one all right; I am sho' of it. Lemme call de man. Git 'im!"

When Greenstreet went for the phone, I nipped him, but viciously, on the ankle. He screamed and grabbed his bruised ankle. "That is a vicious cur," he said. "Get him off of me; call somebody!"

"There ain't no point ter try ter call nobody right now, suh," said the clerk.

"Why not? Why not? Why not?" Greenstreet said, his voice rising hysterically with each entreaty. "Get him off me!"

I was only growling. "You are going to get yours, Eva," I said, though I was so angry it sounded like a bark.

"Das him; das him; das him," said Lil' Eva. "I would know dat nasty growl on 'im anywhere! I'm a call de man. Git 'im; don't let 'im git away now."

"Sorry, suh, but dere really ain't no point."

Greenstreet screamed, "No point! Why not, for god's sake?"

The desk clerk said, "'Cause ain't nobody on de switchbode. Heah I is up heah wid y'all."

"Well, get down there, goddamn it; get down there right now! If that horrid cur touches me once more, I am going to sue the dogshit out of this establishment, do you understand?"

"No disrespect, Mistuh Oleo, suh, but dat would probably be all you could git; see, de chain done broke — 'gone broke' as you Yankees say — I jus' keep dis place open 'cause I don't know whut else ta do, Mistah Oleo. You kin see we half in de red." He pointed to his seedy harlequin suit. "I ain't been able ta buy my own sef' a new suit since all o' dis here stuff began. If I could afford me uh new suit, don't you think I'd have me one?"

"Just go downstairs, Eddie, and plug in, and don't wait for that fucking elevator, use your key and open that goddamned Exit door!"

"Sorry, Mistuh Oleo," the desk clerk said contritely, "but I leaves dat key at de desk, gonna haveta wait fuh de elevator."

"Just get down there, you godamned idiot! Why should the Exit door be locked and the key at your desk!"

"Sorry, suh, but peepers steals 'roun' heah. Dey'll steal anything ain' locked, even a door."

Eva was trying to sneak up on me with a piece of tree branch while I kept Greenstreet at bay. I turned and snapped at her. She screamed and dropped the branch. It was a hefty piece of wood that could have broken my cranium of a fungus-covered hound had she managed to hit me with it, but she was the type that would only come at you from behind. I ran at her and she retreated. I stood over the weapon lest Greenstreet or the desk clerk get any funny ideas, inhaling the smoke and snarling. It was a good thing I hadn't any pepper or I would have torn them up right then.

"Get down there, Eddie; get down there!"

"Yes suh, Mistuh Oleo, yes-suh-ree-bob! I wonder how he got in heah when dat do' was locked. He scratched his head, gazing at me in disbelief, the sorry spectacle of a mushroom-covered invisible hound in a fleabag hotel in New Orleans holding a couple of dirtbags at bay or was it the other way around?

It was a Mexican standoff. I hadn't quite planned it this way, but this was the way it was happening. Eva was going to call the man. He would be coming here. I let her get off the phone and waited, snarling.

The number she called was busy. "Keep tryin', Eddie," she told the clerk, "There is somethin' in it fuh you."

John Farris

I didn't see the mugs when they came in nor what it was they hit me with, but when I woke up I could not move as I was wrapped pretty tightly from my shoulders to my knees in some hawser that was probably from one of the tankers as the heavy smell of petroleum emanated from it, making me nauseous. I'd only felt that nauseous once before in my life, and that had been in the hellhole. I had a headache and I couldn't put my paw on it to feel it, but I was willing to bet a broke-dick dog I had a pretty nasty knot on my head right next to where hound dogs usually have them. I probably looked like a goat in a rug that looked like a pig-in-a-blanket. It took me another moment to realize that I was in some sort of vehicle and we were in motion, slow motion, because as the vehicle turned or stopped or started, I felt a gentle tug at my center of gravity as if I were experiencing a free-fall, floating as I had done when I had tumbled from the nest. There was another odor on top of the petroliated hawser, a sickly-sweet smell that my delicate nose of a tied-up, groggy hound soon identified as that of orchids. There was also the fragrance of gardenias and carnations. It was a mixed bouquet, and I figured I was either in a florist's truck or a hearse. The great, sensitive ears of a mushroom-covered, mummified hound told me it was most likely the latter, as I could hear the strains of the second line—the trumpet, the clarinet, trombone and tuba—which somebody was listening to on the radio, but no, this was live: "Didn't He Ramble," "St. James Infirmary," "I'll Be Glad When You're Dead (You Rascal You)." The trumpet sounded like that woman from the Preservation Hall Band, with her husband, Edmund, playing the stick. If what I thought I was hearing was so, it was likely that it was the funeral of some dignitary, as the Hall family didn't come cheap. The only ones who were able to have these two toot them into the ethereal were politicians and oil people, the owners of the cane plantations, and the shellfish processors. As more of my consciousness returned, I could see I had been lain beneath the blossoms of what was most likely a flower car, and peeping through the tangle of stems and leaves and blossoms, I could see the blue sky and imagine the white clouds in it. The heat was overbearing, adding to my general discomfort. As fond as I was of the Halls and the Preservation Hall Band, the music wasn't doing anything for me. Shaking my sorry head of a wrapped-up and soon to be delivered hound in disgust at my predicament, I snagged my great canine tooth on a few strands of the hawser, tearing them as I pulled free. The petroleum on the strands tasted foul, but the strands intrigued me. I had always had good teeth. My old switch-cutting grandmother with the heart of the *Old Testament* had made me brush and floss them after every meal. I thought of her now, how she made me sit quietly at the table and eat whatever providence had placed on my plate, whether I appreciated it or not, and keeping my lolling tongue of a desperate bloodhound out of the way as best I could like I used to do when she had given me green peas and carrots or zucchini and stood tapping a freshly-cut switch against a palm like a quirt, watching me to make sure I had properly chewed and swallowed my distaste, I began chewing my way through the petroliated hawser. It was a good thing my old grandmother had been there or I would not have been able to do it, but pretty soon, between the saliva that ran copiously from my jaws and the patience of a termite, I had freed myself of the hawser. Now that I was out of that hellacious swamp, the fungi came off easily, and with just a bit of vigorous scraping, I was soon invisible again and sat up to get my bearings. There was a cemetery dead ahead, filled with blue and white mausoleums, which made the place look like an unincorporated township of the dead. The procession turned into this, winding past the tiny houses where the owners slept their eternal sleep until we got to one with its great brass door covered with blue fleurs-de-lis, which was thrown open as if in anticipation of its occupant. It wasn't going to be my funeral. The priest looked like a Lucan.

Ignoring what I had presumed to be the hearse bearing the deceased, he walked over to the flower car where I sat next to where I had been tied, and pushing aside the gardenias and the orchids, looked in. "Doggone!" he said in the direction of the driver, "Hey, he's gone." The tune "Long Gone From Bowlin' Green" came to my mind.

"What?" said the driver. "Nah, dat cain't be; I thought I tied 'im up pretty good!" He came around to look. When he didn't see me, he examined the rope. "Doggone, it look like he done chewed clean thru dat rope," he said. "I'll be damned!"

The priest said, "You don't know how right you are, the man ain't gon' like this."

Eva came up dressed like a mourner. It was funny to be looking right in her face knowing she didn't know what the fuck was going on. She looked puzzled, there in her chintzy ante-bellum widow's-weeds. "What's going on?" she demanded, having noticed the look on the priest's face.

"The dog, he's gone, doggone it; looks like he chewed right through that rope."

A look as black as the clothes she wore crossed Eva's face. "What!" Pushing aside the blossoms she saw the limp rope. She sifted frantically through the pile of mushrooms. When she came up with nothing more she said, "Goddamn it! De man gon' be mad as hell." Pulling a derringer from a black bag she carried, she shot the driver right between the eyes. He almost collapsed onto me. "Bury him," she said to the priest.

The ceremony was brief. It threatened rain. Lightning flashed in the southern sky. The rain was going to mess up my plans. Wherever we were going, I did not want to be making muddy footprints. Figuring I'd better take no chances, I decided to hotfoot it back to the Quarter to let John and Milene know I was all right. I'd let the case wait until after the rain.

I got back to the Hagfishery just as it started coming down good. The band was leaving the dressing room. I whistled our little tune to John as they approached the stand to let him know I was on the scene. We did a great set.

Back in the dressing room, Milene was not happy. "Lucius, where in the fuck have you been?" she demanded when the three of us were out of earshot of the others.

"Errand, Milene." I told her I'd had an errand to run.

"You could have told us," she said. "What kind of errand took a week?"

I was shocked. I'd had no idea of how long I'd been gone. I said, "Actually Milene, I saw this woman I found irresistible. I followed her home."

"You?" she said incredibly.

"Yeah, me," I said.

"Lucius," she said, "that's creepy! Ugh." She was in a pretty foul mood. "Tell me something. I ain't never thought about it before but do you watch me while I'm in the bathroom, Lucius? Do you watch when John and I are making love?"

"Sometimes I admire you while you are in the shower. What's wrong with you, Milene? I missed the gig, is that the end of the world?" I looked helplessly at John, but he couldn't see me.

"That's it," said Milene. "I have had enough of this shit. You almost got us fired. Red has got a reputation to uphold; I got one too. You, who knows who you are? That's why you don't care. We're leaving in the morning."

The morning. They were leaving in the morning. It looked like it would rain all night. I wanted to wait till the ground dried. I said, "I can't leave in the morning, Milene."

"What do you mean? We got a gig in Seattle, Washington! You 'sposed to meet the rhythm section at 11 for rehearsals. I ain't gonna go through this shit again. If you can't come with us, if you can't make the gig, you're fired."

John was noncommittal, as usual.

I thought for a moment. I thought for a long moment. I didn't know about Milene, but John was my ass. I could always make it up to him. I couldn't leave yet. I was so far and yet so near. "I have to do this, Milene," I said, "or do you know what?"

"What?"

"My voice will never be right anyway. Nothing will be right."

She gave me what would have been a long, searching look. She finally said, "Lucius, I know you a little bit better than I think you give me credit for. You see, I know you're lost and have to find yourself."

She had me there.

"I don't really understand what happened with that Presley guy. I'm not really sure how one lil' ol' song from one lil' ol' white boy could have made you lose so much confidence in yourself."

Coming from her, it was a low blow, and it stung. "What do you mean, Milene? You think I don't have any confidence?"

"Look at yourself."

"You know I can't do that, Milene, why would you ask me to?" She was making me very uncomfortable. I could feel my long ears of a low-down hound burning.

"And why not?"

"It's my protection, Milene."

"From what, Lucius? From what?"

I said, "That's exactly where you have me, Milene. I wish I knew. I'm trying to put it together now. I try to explain it to myself every day, but so far I have not come up with any satisfactory answers. I can't explain it to anybody else because nobody will listen, and if they do, all they hear is me barking. Or me whining. Or me snarling. Even you, Milene. I try to explain it to you, but finally you only hear me when I sing. Yes, Milene, when I sing. Because I can't really say it otherwise. I don't really understand it myself."

She studied the general area where I should have stood before her, the very picture of a young man. "Is that why you sing, Lucius?"

"I don't think so, Milene, but it certainly is what I have to sing about. And, in a way, it is a good thing nobody really understands me."

"Why d' you say that?"

"Because both John and I would be exposed in a heartbeat, and what good would that do him or me, or you for that matter, since you love him so much? We really are fugitives, Milene. I know you find that hard to believe given what has come to be our everyday lives and all, but that really is a disguise he is wearing after all. His name is John, not Red, and he is wanted by the man."

"What for, some grass?

"No, Milene," I said patiently, "for murder."

"But you didn't do it."

"Well, you try explaining that to somebody. See if they'll listen."

She sighed. "All that is very depressin' to think about, Lucius. You know John don't like to think about it."

I was so hurt that she had chosen to attack what I had considered to be the very heart of my integrity: my case, as my mind had put it. So that I should not have lost it along with the rest of me, I almost said the obvious, though the fine instinct of a hound made me not do it. John's reluctance to think was the result of breeding that dated back to the dawn of civilization, not too long after eohippus made his first appearance on the earth. Evolved as he was, it was a component of his condition, as to think too much was a part of mine. As long as it was in front of his face, what did he care? And if confronted, I had come to know well that his usual reaction was to turn tail and run. Oh, he'd kick a little bit, though that was about it. His willingness to go along with just about anything would invariably kick in, except when it came to my affairs. That was when nothing else would do except what he himself was involved in, which usually had to do with his own anus. But what could I do but love him for that? I suppose, in the end, that was where his supreme confidence emanated from. If sometimes it smelled like a fart, so what? All he knew how to do was let it all hang out. He could make music out of it. If I myself had cared to do any research into the matter, I could have found royalty in his background; and that, simply put, was what he acted like, my royal ass.

"You weren't with a woman last week, was you Lucius? I can smell a woman on a man even if he is an invisible hound, and all I smell on you is gas."

"I was, Milene, I was with a woman that it seems to be my destiny to be with right now. Can't you smell the fragrance of the flowers? She likes gardenias."

Milene said, "Like Billie?"

"No, Milene, not like Billie."

"And you went home with her?"

I almost laughed. "No, Milene, we went to a hotel."

"I don't think I like her, Lucius. I don't think she's good for you. You sounded so sad when you said that."

"I am not generally given to hysteria, given my lot." I told her about my background, the part even before I met John when I was being brained by my supposed brother, trained by my grandmother — though I was so wild that even she couldn't train me — and kept by my beautiful mother.

"I hear a lot of bitterness in there sometimes, Lucius, forgive me for sayin' this, but it almost sounds like you didn't really really love them all that much."

If her intent was to make me squirm, she did. "Not love my beautiful mother and my old switch-hitting, cane-cutting grandmother? I don't really understand what you're getting at, Milene," I said.

She looked rather penetratingly at what would in other more felicitous circumstances have been me. "Lucius, please forgive me for saying this — I'm only saying it because I really do love you — but all your cachet about them, at least what you said to me just now, sounds basically platitudinal. I mean, ain't you got any real feelin's about them, some description besides adjectives that are ultimately emotionally stunted?"

"The lash, Milene, the whip, the cane. None of them are very endearing."

"Ah, Lucius, Lucius, Lucius. Is that ... is that why you can't really love women?"

That said, what was there for me to do but become defensive. "Wow, that's some analysis, Milene; you're in the wrong business. You should have me on a couch somewhere. You are entirely wrong about that. People usually describe relatives in platitudes. It's usually others they are really brutal about. No, I have always loved women, but I have always loved them from a considerable distance, in the, so to speak, abstract."

When we got back to the hotel, we drank till the sun came up reddening the blue-black Louisiana sky, commiserating with each other over fate and fortune (mostly mine). There was much backslapping and many sloppy kisses and, when it was time for them to make their flight, I rode with them to the airport. The driver of the cab on the way out looked like a Lucan. Transformed, he would have been an orangutan, with the long stringy hair, the thin lips and pink skin of an octoroon. I didn't like the way he said, "Where to, folks?" cigarette dangling carelessly between the Mason-Dixon line of his lips, and when we got to the airport without any mishaps, I was relieved, though the skycap that approached for the luggage had the look of a Lucan, a fat slug of a man from which the sweat rolled off like a secretion to reduce any friction in his path. I was paying strict attention now, but other than these two I saw nothing more suspicious, and we said our teary good-byes before they boarded their flight. I was going to meet them in Oregon, and failing that, back in the Apple for a trip to Europe. I watched as the plane taxied and took off into the by now azure and cloudless Louisiana sky, climbing like a bird with its wings flapping slightly to lazily circle the airport before heading west at an altitude of about four thousand feet. Thinking that was a bit low for a true flight, I watched in horror as the whole left wing fell off, sailing like a surfboard to the ground while the rest of the plane fell twisting like a maple seed after it until it too reached the ground, exploding in a giant orange and oily black fireball on contact. I watched, drained, too stunned to move as an evil black plume of smoke twisted skyward nearly to where the plane itself should have been, and hung there like a giant rain cloud where before there'd been none, and I heard the urgent sound of the sirens as they ululated at about C sharp and wailed at about G, warning everybody out of the way as they raced towards the scene. A horde of taxis followed them, and I grabbed one of these.

CHAPTER TWENTY ONE

Coming up onto the scene of the nightmare, I stumbled blindly from the checkered cab I'd clutched onto for my own dear life and watched numbly, unable to make sense of it, as the fire crews threw a storm of foam on the bits of burning swamp scattered over a two-mile radius which was all that was left of my oldest and dearest friend, my very own seemingly indestructible, lovable if a bit too stubborn for what ultimately was his own good smart ass as well as to his girlfriend, the very beautiful Lady Milene, and I didn't know who-all or what-all else. My curiously detached mind of a bloodhound could not help making a comparison to that scenario at the Seedy Hotel except that in this present case, after all the foam had settled on the oily, cottonmouth-infested waters, there was nothing much left in there that was recognizable except for one giant engine that rested on the hellishly deceptive, placid waters like an aluminum bubble. With all the foam on it and around it, it looked like a giant Christmas bauble lying in a field of snow, but what a gift accompanied it. The foam kept me from inspecting it too closely as I did not want any of the trouble I'd had back in Greenstreet's room; who knew how many sharp-eyed "Eddies" there were in this crowd. I was having enough trouble with mosquitoes as it was. When after the most heartbreaking hours of my miserable life of a troubled human being transformed into a hound dog and made invisible by sympathetic magic it was finally ascertained that there was irrevocably nothing left except the engine, then the fire crews and the medical people went off leaving only the transportation safety people and the officials of other concerned agencies, everybody except the IRS, to sift through the swamp as if they were sieves for clues. I had my own ideas.

As luck would have it, if, indeed, it could have been called that — as the song goes, if it was not for the kind of luck I was having, I wouldn't have had any luck at all — I caught a cab back that was being driven by the same orangutan of a hack with the thin, bloodless lips of a Mason-Dixon Line that had driven the three of us out to the airport with what looked like the very self same, half-smoked cigarette butt dangling carelessly, with such simian élan and insouciance, and right beside him in the passenger seat was none other than the very same fat slug of a skycap that had handled the luggage for the flight. They didn't look too sad.

"Good job," the driver was saying.

"Yup," the skycap said disinterestedly, slapping at a horsefly that kept circling his bald, glistening pate and settling and resetting on his eyelids.

"Where'd you learn that?"

"School of the Americas." He'd produced a toothpick and was laconically chewing on it. "Don't you ever light dat cigarette?"

The driver said, "Nah, I'm tryna' quit smokin'. School of the Americas, huh? Good school?"

"The very best. We try to keep it out of the newspapers. We usually succeed until it's discovered kinda' late to do anything about it that some less than delicate military operation in the hemisphere had been prepared for at that hallowed institution."

"Prep, huh?"

"Nah, far from it. Not even the Ivy League, but, hey, when you think about it, look at it carefully, you'd see they couldn't get along without us. The sob sisters, we call 'em."

"Even Harvard?"

"Hey."

"C'mon, whereya at now? Yale? I thought all you guys came out o' there."

"The only one that really compares is George Washington University."

"You don't say? And why is that?"

"It was named after a soldier. The commander-in-chief of the colonial army. He was a guerrilla who took his tactics from the red Indians. Those divinity boys up at Yale and those business administrators up at the 'Big Yard' could never have stooped to the level of the half-naked pathetic bunch of savages he'd conquered to learn nothin' off 'em, and how to survive on the Potomac and how to use Prospect Park for cover. Those guys up there prefer the bully pulpit to the bloody one."

"It was certainly pretty smooth. What'd ya use, gelignite?"

"Nah, not that. Gelignite would have caused an explosion."

"Hey, I get it, too suspicious, huh?"

"You got it. What I used was an extremely corrosive acid made from the digestive organs of a certain Brazilian salamander capable of going through aluminum at the rate of a cubic inch of water passing through the locks of the Panama Canal. And, as it is a natural substance, the compounds of which disintegrate completely after only a few seconds exposure to air, indistinguishable from so much vapor, it is therefore untraceable. All those aeronautics boys from the FAA and the transportation safety gonna be able to conclude is stress syndrome. Ya' see, them lil' buggers' juices produce the same effect on the metal as the most stressful condition: metal fatigue."

It was late night again. The driver had pulled up in front of a nude dancing joint on Royal and cut the motor before I did a very mindless thing. I tore both of their rotten throats out and left them sprawled across the blood-drenched front seat in attitudes of grotesque surprise. The orangutan had thought the slug was suffering an attack of some kind, and he had sat and watched helplessly, horrified as his comrade died the death of a barnyard animal he deserved, and I turned on him for the second time in my life and cold bloodily ripped out his carotid artery and severed his jugular. Neither of them had made a sound.

The name of the nude joint was "Miss Lil'y White's." With a name like that, if I had been in any discernible shape, I'm sure they would have tried to keep me out.

The decor was cedar, as if they were afraid of moths, and photographs of a petite, boyish blonde with her curly hair cut close everywhere hung in every conceivable place. What in this blonde reminded me of Peck was that she had the fresh-scrubbed look of the Ivory Snow Girl, and she really needed no clothing as freckles covered her bare skin as thickly as tattoos. I had to strain my eyes of an interested hound in the soft red glow of the place to make sure it was not she, though I was taken aback by the resemblance. It was not too far-fetched to have thought it might have been Peck as the Chicagoan had certainly passed through the Crescent City, the Big Easy, on more than one occasion in her career, and she had been certainly compelling enough to have gotten herself star billing anywhere she went. I assumed these pictures to be of Miss Lil'y herself, as along with the motif of the cedar and the photographs were lilies of every conceivable variety in every conceivable shade of white, including the one great gilded calla that sat on a cedar lowboy in front of mirror in a lounge where table dances were offered the individual, leering customers, not exclusively male, if exclusively white, and lap dancing in which the dancer was allowed to sit facing her patron with her two hands clasped tightly behind his (her implied) neck if the tip was gratuitous enough.

It had been a long time.

A butch type in tattoos and motorcycle leather had ordered a couple of bottles of champagne and was waving over a long-limbed, pert-breasted beauty with a long chestnut mane to her table. I decided to join them before my bird began to glow.

The dancer had lush, cushy-looking lips that parted into an easy smile that revealed her slightly crooked teeth as she spotted the hundred-dollar bill the butch was waving like a semaphore. "Ah got all o' dis heah fuh you, and honey, if ah like whut you got, there eeis plenny mo' where dat came fum. Whereya at?"

The dancer, grinning some more, ran her tiny triangle of a tongue over what I was sure had to be the plushest lips on Royal. Royal, hell, in the Crescent City, the Big Easy. Her voice was all silk and kitteny. "Hi there, sweetheart," she purred. "Welcome to Miss Lil'y White's. What's yo' name honey? Why, is this yo' fust time heah?"

"Sho' eeis," the butch said. "Ah'm fum Bogaloosa and ah'm jus' comin' out."

The butch wasn't bad looking. She had great muscle tone and fine bones though her lips were a little too thin and her nose a little too sharp. She said her name was Canine. I had to laugh. For some reason, I thought of Needle-nose, the sparrow. "Ah'ma gonna put all of dis heah money and some mo in uh great big wad in mah pants, and you kin have much o' it as yuh wont, is dat awraght wid yew, ba-by?" The dancer delightfully grinned her assent. "Mah name is Kitty," she said.

It was a good thing I had spent all that time up on Morningside Avenue watching John and Milene work out as I am quite sure it was only that experience that enabled me to keep my bird from glowing like a searchlight as I waited for them to go through the preliminaries, and the butch had ordered another bottle and gotten drunk enough and wet enough for me to join them though, as I think about it now, it probably would have gone unnoticed in that red light. Knowing this was going to take a miracle as far as timing went, I waited until Canine had slipped her well-oiled finger into the dancer's ample rectum, and the dancer had retaliated by throwing a fierce Georgia-grind as she sucked cherries from her neck by the bowlful before I carefully nudged the butch up on one cheek and slid my waiting thirsty bird into the dancer's willing, grateful cunt with a whoosh.

"Ooh, ooh, ooh, oooh," she exclaimed, grabbing what she thought was the butch by the back of the neck but which was, in fact, the back of my great hairy neck of an invisible bloodhound, "Canine, honey, ah, ah sho' do love yo money!"

The butch was so drunk and so excited by the passion aroused in her by the lapping action of my long, hungry tongue of a bloodhound in her ear she thought it was her own prick that had the dancer whooping like a High Plains Indian and gyrating in her lap as if she were grinding the corn and mashing the pemican for her man's long trip to the Happy Hunting Ground, and didn't even mind when my growing boldness and complete mastery of the techniques I'd learned at the hands of the expert Woody and the divine Miss Peck and those I'd learned from watching my poor but equally well-trained donkey and his lost, lamentable lady Milene made me quite firmly boogie my way out of the dancer to ram my great ramrod of a bird up her own narrow behind. "Oh, Kitty, Kitty, Kitty," she moaned, "Yew got da grand prick of uh big dog!" And sat for me obediently, wagging her tail and barking like the canine I assumed she had named herself.

She didn't even mind when I took it upon myself to lead them into the techniques and practices that formed the five-pointed star, using my four paws and tail to bring them into the exercise, or when I howled like a mourning Irisher when I took them to the pretzel. I was right about the dancer's lips, and I ground my own lipless mouth of a bloodhound against them, resting there as if I were resting my very soul on Buddha's couch, and as she shook her head from side to side, they slowly parted enough for me to slip my great engine of a bird between their incredible softness into the wetness of her throat in an exercise I had perfected on "the street." Using a circular breathing technique, she took in great, heaving gulps until my hairy balls were bouncing against her thrusting chin. I didn't at all mind Canine's little toadstool of a clit against my rear end, but when she tried to introduce her fist into it I had to close up shop, though the dancer did mind when I gently guided the offending appendage into hers. It was the one good deed I was going to do for the day. After all, the butch was paying for it, but she was not worried about her money now, as I was giving her as good as she got. "Oh K-K-K, Kitty, K-K-K-Kitty, Kitty," she stuttered between her moans and rebel yells, "ah, ah, ah, ain', ain', ain' had no idea it was go-go be like this, h-honey," as we brought ourselves to a great shuddering climax.

"Oh mah god," she said suddenly sitting up from where we had fallen to, beneath the table and gratefully planted a kiss while examining the dancer's well-developed clit, "Honey, whut yew kin do wif dis Lil' thang yew got down heah between yo' laigs oughta be a daggoned state secret. Yew, yew, yew know whut, Kitty? Ah, ah, ah thank dat fuh sa fust time in mah whole cotton-pickin laif ah done fell in love." Her gaze was tender as she looked into the dancer's eyes.

The dancer's smile was as wan as if she'd just given birth, and there were tiny beads of sweat over her exquisite lips as she leaned over to give the butch a grateful kiss. "Oh, Canine," she said softly, her hand on the butch's cheek, caressing it like a crystal ball. "Is dat fuh true?"

"Oh Kitty, Kitty, Kitty," Canine said, her chest heaving mightily, the blood rushing to her own cheeks, "ah wont yew ta know fuh sho' dat truer wouhds ain' nevah been spoken. Kitty, baby, whut kin ah do fuh yew tuh prove mah lov fuh yew?"

"Move in wif me and be mah fren'," said Kitty. "Do fuh me whut yew jus' did fuh me all da time. Tell me, would dat be too much?"

"Oh no, Kitty, oh no." She ran her fingers through the dancer's chestnut mane.

So, although they didn't know it, I had made a couple of fast friends. I knew I would have to visit with them frequently, at least until I had finished my investigations, so that they could get the big bang out of this relationship they sought, otherwise, you know what they say: "the first time can be the best time."

It was a good thing too that we'd all gotten in our orgasms when we did as Canine had no sooner finished what she'd been saying when a couple of Crescent City rollers walked in. They weren't in uniform, but were immediately followed by a dick in a panama hat.

"Halt," said the younger roller, "stop everything dat we ain' supposed ta see in heah! Cease it and desist raht now. Deh has been a mudah raht outside de do', in fact, two of 'em. Anybody heah see anythin' suspicious?"

The sullen crowd, annoyed at having its pleasures interrupted, said nothing. The other roller said, "Anybody here come ovah heah inna taxi?"

People reluctantly raised their hands.

"De lieutenant gonna wanna have a wuhd wid y'all."

"Sheeit," said Canine, "what all eeis goin' on now! Ah though dis heah joint was a respectable place, but muhduh?"

"It is a respectable place, Canine, ah wouldn't wuk heah if it wudn't," said Kitty, pouting somewhat. "Didn't happen hear, did it? Happened outside. Cain't blame de establishment fuh whut go' on outside, kin yuh?"

Canine said, "Oh honey, yew raht, ah sho' am sorry ah said dat." She offered the dancer a mollifying kiss. They were thusly embraced when the younger roller walked up and poked Canine in the behind with his stick. She said, "Whut da fuck?"

I knew she was already sore back there. She had, after all, a rather small behind. I liked them that way. As I thought about it, she was built sort of like that first girl I had ever met, the one in the park. But that would have been too neat. From what I could see, my life didn't have that much order.

"Hey," she said, "whuts ya do dat for!" She sounded out the consonant perfectly, and had supplied the correct vowel.

"Ah thought ah tol' y'all da lieutenant was heah. De agreement wid Miss Lil'y White is dat when he is heah all y'all is tuh observe de exact letta' of da law. Why, if he was tuh observe yew behavin' like dat, ah'd have ta close da place down; take all y'all down ta central bookin'. How yew like dem apples?"

The butch said, "Sheeit."

The lieutenant approached, giving the girls the once-over. I did ditto for him. He was a ruddy-faced fat man with the broken capillaries of a dipsomaniac who kept removing his panama and wiping the sweatband with a handkerchief (that was as limp as my bird at the moment) before replacing it onto his bald pate. He had a somewhat harried look, as if he were not really in charge. He turned to the roller. "And whut d'we have heah?"

The roller, in a typical, studied police action, tipped his hat back with his stick. Ah dunno, Lieutenant, a coupla' bu, I mean, a couple of bitches, ah guess."

"Ah see," said the lieutenant, wiping the band of his hat and replacing it at a raffish angle. He tugged his seersucker into place and straightened his tie. He reminded me enough of the captain to have been his brother. "Evenin' ladies," he finally said. "Whereya at? How y'all doin' tonight?"

Canine said, "Well, ah was doin' fine suh, till yo' man theh poked me wid his stick." She emphasized the word "man." Put a bad connotation on it. I was going to like her.

The lieutenant looked at the roller and winked or it could have been that he had a tic. "Oh, did he now. Well, ah'm mighty sorry 'bout dat, Miss ..."

"Canine."

"... Canine, fuh any inconvenience he might have caused you. He is not heah ta do that. He is only heah ta do his job, ma'am. May I call you that?"

Canine said, "You call me Canine. I ain't no madam, and don't you go tryna pin me wid dat."

The lieutenant held his pudgy hand up in a gesture of defense. "Didn't mean tuh imply that, Canine, in fact, at this point, ah'm not tryna' imply nuthin'. Ah'm ony lookin' at the facts so fur as ah know 'em raht now, and the fact is a cabdriver and a skycap got themsefs muh-duhed tonaht not fifty yards fum wheah we standin' now. Had they throats torn out like a dog. The blood was fresh when mah man came up on 'em, and they was still warm. Probably jus' beginnin' tuh congeal now, which means the killuh coulda' come in heah. Do yuh happen tuh know enny dogs, Canine?"

"Not tuh mah knowledge, Lootenant. 'cept fuh huntin', ah nevah liked 'em too much."

The lieutenant leaned over towards Canine and sniffed delicately. Wiping his hatband, he said, "Well, yuh smell like one."

"Ah beg yo' pardon, ah'll have you hosswhupped," Canine said. "Mah grandaddy owns uh swamp. Do yew unnerstan'?"

The lieutenant eyed her suspiciously. "How much acreage?"

She tossed her head and proudly lifted her dimpled chin. "20,000. 20,000 acres o' pure Lousiana swamp. Sits on anotha' 100,000 owned by otha membas o' da family. Pristine. Black wid oil. Yew talk 'bout yo' gasoline inna watah; well, whut ah'm talkin' about eeis pure gunk, da dead bodies o' dinosaurs. We'uns eeis Cajuns. Mah acestus came heah tuh escape religious puhsecution and received a land grant from Louis. Mah great-gran 'daddy fought eein da Civil Wauh. Mah gran 'daddy eeis fightin' eeit steeil, dey won' no surrendah fuh heein'. He is a cunnel today. Muh daddy would be faghtin' eeit too, but he died in WWII, a much decorated pilot."

The lieutenant said, "And whut side wuz he on?"

"Why, ah'm surprised at yew, Lootenant, owwa side, o'cose. He died over da Nomandy Invasion."

Turning to the roller, the lieutenant said, "Write that down."

The roller looked confused. "Whut, suh, dat she smell like a dog?"

The lieutenant waved deprecatingly. "No, no, not that, the fact that huh gran'daddy got 20,000 acres. The chief is runnin' fuh reelection real soon. Maybe he might like tuh make a contribution."

"Anytime, Lootenant, how eeis dis heah?" She offered him a five hundred dollar bill.

"Why, ah thank you very much gracious lady," said the lieutenant, taking the bill and looking around. He folded the bill deftly and slid it into the sweatband of his panama. He replaced the hat and turned to Kitty. "And yew, Miss ..."

"Kitty."

"Hm," said the lieutenant, "how very interestin'. I nevah thought o' that. A cat coulda' done it as well. You happen to know enny cats, Miss Kitty?"

"Hate 'em."

I was glad the dancer had said that. In no way did I want the distraction of cats.

He sniffed at her suspiciously, taking her through the same regimen he'd gone through with Canine. Fortunately, she had made enough in tips to offer him a sizable contribution as well. Thanking her in the name of the chief and himself, he removed his hat and again wiped the sweatband. It was then that I understood all the swiping with that handkerchief.

He asked that the ladies please not leave until he had completed his investigation. They were pretty much upset, but his request suited me just fine as I figured his queries might offer me a stellar chance to find out more of what I needed to know and at the same time not lose the ladies. The sordid truth was just when I needed every bit of my concentration focused on the task in front of me, blind circumstance had led me to love—and this so soon after the deaths of my companions, my comrades. Talk about your complications.

What I learned from the lieutenant's routine was that running for public office could be pretty lucrative, though the "elect" seemed to be contributors themselves, the selected, those soon to be relieved of their burdens, made to feel so deliriously happy they would not be arrested tonight that they gave and gave and gave; all they could afford in some cases, in others, all they had; but they gave no information because what did they really know about anything, they were just out to have themselves a good time, before this they were on Rampart Street and the day before that on Beale or Central Avenue listening to the niggers playing their peculiar music, or they had been at the Shrine of the Saint Cecilia praying that it wouldn't happen to them that night, or taking a bath, mentioning all this because this lieutenant insisted on knowing all the facts right down to the last tiny detail, which meant exactly how much you ate, what it was you ate and where, as well as with whom you ate it; if, indeed, it was a gift, and at what time; this last for the *Register*, for in the meantime a reporter from that journal had shown up toothpick in his mouth, palmetto porkpie hat with a red paisley band thrown back on his head like a yarmulka, as well as one from the *Times-Picayune*, who both asked some variant of the same question over and over without getting much payoff. They wanted to know what every single solitary star looked like over Alabama last night, who was that whistling "Dixie" till the lights went out, where had the last bone been picked, the last candle flickered and died. It continued as the pudgy lieutenant kept wiping his hatband, while thanking his current informant for his patience and contribution, or hers, which as far as the both of us were concerned, wasn't actually much as I myself certainly was not speaking to the lieutenant, I was only listening, and what I learned from him was something I had already suspected about any city: governance was a bitch; the man's job was practically impossible. I suppose the whole idea of the modern city-state is something like being born, which in turn must be like being a great big turd being flushed through a humungous toilet: one minute you're on this incredible journey to somewhere, and when you look up, here you are, this little piece of shit in a giant cesspool. At least that was my experience, and whether these people the lieutenant was questioning knew it or not, it was theirs too, just by the definition of their having been here, at the "scene of the crime," so to speak. I had learned that if you blinked and you were driving too fast, you missed the town completely, and were headed for the graveyard.

By the time the lieutenant had finished his little tour around the premises, his head was seriously hung to one side as if he were discouraged or tired or loaded or all three, as he was certainly staggering somewhat. "Thibideau," he called to the other officer, "tell those two reporturs to get out of heah, goddamnit, they're impeding mah investigation, and tell the rest of them they are not allowed to leave till ah am satisfied. Oh, and Thibideau—-"

"Suh?"

"See that Filipina ovah theat, send huh ovah heah wid a coupla' bottles o' that there good champagne. You heah me Thibideau, the good one, mind yew."

The girl he pointed to was incredibly beautiful, with the wide sloe-eyes of a doe and hair as glossy black as a raven's that hung almost far enough to cover her nakedness but not quite, though she was only about twelve years old if that and looked slightly confused, as if this were the very first time she had found herself completely naked in a roomful of total strangers and she didn't know quite what to do with either the bottles she clutched to a chest that was just beginning to bud breasts that were like two points on the antlers of a young buck, stimulated, I suppose, by the chill of the champagne, nor the fat man with the bald head she was being directed toward. When she had reached the table at which he had sat himself, she stopped and stood anxiously. The lieutenant removed his hat. He handed it to the waiting roller. He said, "Take this heah tuh da station-house and wait theah fuh me wid it. Yew be kehful wid it now, y'heah? Now dem numbahs is in muh head."

The roller looked disappointed that he was not going to get to watch, but pleased that at last he was going to be allowed to arrest the cash. "Sho' thang lootenant," he said, leaving with a wistful backward glance at the girl.

The lieutenant ran his thickening tongue over his lips. Though the handkerchief had been wet, this was the first time that I'd actually seen him sweating and now he generously patted his brow with it. Closing his eyes, he shuddered, uttering a great sigh as if he had come already, and belched.

CHAPTER TWENTY TWO

After a moment that seemed like an eternity, the lieutenant looked up. "Mah name is Grosz," he said. "Das Grosz. Some people call me 'der' or 'die,' though all o' those ain' nuthin' but ahticles, some definite, some not. In awduh tuh avoid thuh mos' definate uv 'em, you kin call me 'der.' It is an expression uv endeahment. Ah have come tuh be quat fond uv yew. Ah hope ovah tahm yew will do thuh same for me, mah deah. Yew have thuh wide, sloe eyes uv a doe. Ennybody evah tell yew 'at?"

He was positively fawning.

The girl, uncomprehending, shook her head.

"Un biche, je comprez?"

Her soft, frightened eyes widened even more, and she shivered a little from the chill of the champagne bottles she yet clutched to her chest like a pair of lifesavers.

"Don' be afraid, mah deah, ah'm not gonna huht yew; heah, ah'll take those." Gently, he took the bottles and placed them on the table. The girl's unblemished skin was covered with goose bumps. He gave her arms a quick little massage and dropped his hand as if he were nervous himself. She didn't stop shivering. He beckoned a waitress over who wore a little cotton tail as if she were on loan from the local playboy club. He said, "'Scuse me, miss, but would yew git me a intuhpetuh ovuh heah?"

The waitress had the hardened look of a veteran. "Ah buleeve thuh guhl speaks ainglish, suh; all she need is some tahm tuh git used tuh yew. In thuh meantahm, ah kin bring yew somethin' else tuh look at, somethin' with mo' seasonin.' She sin' nuthin' but an appuhtizuh. She is new heah. This ain' but huh fus' tahm."

The lieutenant let out a little sigh, closed his eyes and shuddered himself as if he had come again. He opened them slowly and looked around, orienting himself among the plethora of flesh that was at his beck and call. He said, "Thankyuh, honey, that would be mos' kind uv yuh, but ah buleeve she'll do quat fahn fuh mah puhpuses, so long as she unnastans. Yew sho' she unnastans ainglish?"

"Quat sho', suh, ah huhd huh jabbuhrin away wid some o' thuh guhls when they brought huh in, suh.

"Whut did she say?"

"Suh, she was sayin' somethin' 'bout huh rahts bein' vahlated, somethin' 'bout how she got heah. Said somethin' 'bout how she desuved a faih hearin', suh, pahdon me, suh, but ain' that a scream?"

"Please, honey, yuh'll ony frahten thuh po' creatuh, and whut good would thet do thuh po' boy or thuh county insofah as cleanin' up this heah mystery?" the lieutenant said. "Now, sweetie, ah wonts yuh tuh keep this heah whut ah'm 'bout tuh tell yuh unduh yo' hat, ah mean yo' tail, but those two boys whut was muhduhed? They wudn't jus enny two ol' common coons y'know, even though they mighta' looked like it to thuh untrained eye. Uh uh, them coons, ah mean, them boys wuz a coupla operuhtives fuh thuh man. The main man. Thuh Chief uv Opuhrashuns. One uv 'em went to uh very exclusive school at considuble govement expense. Thas' why this heah investuhgashun go' havta' be so thuruh."

"Mah lawd," said the waitress, appalled. "Opruhtuves, huh? Well, would yuh buleeve that! And raht outsahd thuh very do' theah lak uh coupla' barbarians! Whut will these heah rasculs go aftuh next. Soon no job wull be sacred, naht yo's naht mahn, nobody's. Ah mean, whereya at!"

The lieutenant dryly cleared his throat. He said, "That will be all, Miss, thankyuh, and remembuh wuht ah said, unduh yo' tail, yew unnastan'? Now, do yew have uh tip fuh me?"

The waitress pursed her lips. She drew herself into the very picture of a board and saluted gravely. "Yew kin bet yo' bottom dolla' on me, suh; all fuh one and one fuh all."

She leaned over and said something in the lieutenant's ear that made the broken capillaries in his face go royal. Removing the only article of clothing that she wore, the tiny tuft of cotton at her rear, she dropped it into his ample lap, where it quickly disappeared into the folds of cushion. The lieutenant wiped his brow and turned his attention to the girl. He was too involved in his investigation to notice the waitress whispering excitedly into the ears of the wait staff until the whole room was buzzed, bright. Their voices rose with their excitement. An old bugger shouted "Allelulia! At last, at last, thuh lam' am come."

The lieutenant looked up surveying the room and glowered darkly. "Who wuz that that said that!"

The young roller pointed the bugger out.

"Well, lock him up, and remove that waitress from the premises entily. Take huh tuh thuh hutch. Give huh uh thud dugree buhn."

Nobody noticed the old bugger being hauled off to the hoosegow, but the pathetic screams of the waitress attracted some attention.

No one asked, "What'd she do?"

No one said, "Ah dunno; ah dunno."

Someone did say, "Wull, she nevuh did have much o' no ass noway, leastways not fum wheah ah cud see thuh thang. She nevuh did dance with me. Stuck up, ah guess."

The lieutenant did say, "Awraht, y'all, now lissen up! Ah am ony go' say this one tahm, afta' which ah'm go havetuh crack some knuckles." He waited till the room was quiet before going on. "Ah wont all y'all heah tuh know thet this heah is offishul. Ah wont it tuh be absuhlutly quat heah" — he doubled his fists and his head shot forward — "or ah'mo have y'all chawged wuth obstructin' justus. Y'heah now? All o' y'all. Ah mean it now."

The room fell silent. Someone dropped a pin that sounded like a toll. When the ambiance was to his satisfaction, he gave his brow some swipe with the handkerchief and turned his attention once again to the girl. "Ah wontstuh fully apolagize fu thuh innerupshun, mah deah, ah dew hope yew wull fo'give me, but yew see, it is ony uh slaht mattuh uv thuh law put intuh place tuh keep thuh populashun trim and effishunt."

No one dared laugh at the irony of his great girth. He sighed once more, shuddered and closed his eyes slowly like a narcoleptic. When he'd recovered his composure, he gave himself another great swipe of the handkerchief, dabbing at a certain spot on his pants until it was practically dry. "It is called in Latin (which is no mo' than thuh langwidge we encode thuh tenets we choose tuh live by in), *coitus intuhruptus*, and is ultamutly fuh yuh own puhtecshun. Why, honey, yew have no ahdea whut cud happen tuh someone as young and tenduh as yo'self in un city as sinful as N'Awlins. It is mah own theory thet it has somethin' tuh dew wuth thuh watah, thuh moon's effect on the Mississippi drives 'um crazy: all them floods, the muskeetas, thuh gennul effluvia. This heah law wuz desaned tuh puteck putty babies like yo'sef fum yo'sef. Dew yew unnastan', baby? Ah am ony heah tuh hep yew, do yew unnastan' whut yew standin' unda? Yew standin' raht heah unduh thuh law, yuh see, ah am ony thuh law-wahd, theahfoah ah am bringin' yew thuh wuhd. Befo' we go on heah, ah havetuh ast yuh this: dew yew have uh lawya, thet is, ah yew repasented bah ennyone?"

The girl shook her head slowly and a tear fell silently down her cheek.

"Good," said the lieutenant, "very good. Thet mean yew ah completely at mah muhcy. Whut's yo' name, chile?"

"C-C-Conchita," the girl stammered, and once she started talking, she didn't stop. Seems she'd read the dictionary from cover to cover like Malcom X. The only problem was she didn't know any more than the lieutenant or the rest of them knew. She knew what each individual word meant, but when she put them all together they tended to lose all meaning for her like a story she'd read about a guy who'd gone to the Museum of Modern Art and gotten lost because he didn't know how to read a map. She had lost that story but went on and on like Sheherazade, which was too bad for the lieutenant, because as far as I was concerned, he didn't have 1,001 nights left on the planet. When I got tired of his antics, I was going to drop him like a heart attack, I was going to drop him like they dropped my ass out of the sky, like a piece of pork. I was going to clean out the barrel.

The lieutenant appeared to have come again. When he regained his senses, he said, "Oh mah, Conchita. Conchita, it has uh nahce rang tuh it. Seem like ah hud it befo', like a lullaby, a lyric, maybe a lyre when you are finally and irrevocably fu—ah mean plucked bah thuh raht, talented finguhs."

He held up a damp, pudgy hand, the fingers of which were as limp as a surgeon's in a scrubroom waiting for an attendant to give him the glove. "Is theah ennyone who wonts yew besahds me? Whut language is that? Tell me, tell me, baby—whispuh in mah eah, please. (Ah happened tuh heah uh ol' nigruh sangin' thet one day long 'bout when ah wuz yo' age. Ah didn't know what it meant way back then, but ah thank ah sho' do now.) Conchita, what in the wurl' does it mean?"

The child, suddenly sensing that, young as she was, she was in charge, shushed him none too gently. The soft, defenseless look in her great, sloe-eyes of a frightened doe was now the unblinking stare of a hunting falcon. She began to slowly circle him like a shaman going round the earth going round the sun, or a mongoose circling a snake, or like a boxer circling his opponent so the opponent cannot get off a proper punch, and as she went around and around, she sang this little ditty: "*It means a little shellfish, which I am; and you have brought me out of my shell.*"

You had to give it to the girl. Her voice was hypnotic as heroin itself. It reminded me of the Great Lady singing "Gloomy Sunday" or Hercules putting Argus to sleep. Talk about a natural. She was so good at it that before long every eyelid in the place was drooping, including the four of Canine and Kitty, who mumbled along with the beat. I didn't understand the words as in the place of an interior pronoun she substituted an exterior one so that it went like this, "Sunday is gloomy, in shadows YOU spend it all," instead of "Sunday is gloomy, in shadows I spend it all." Figuring that she would be all right and that the newfound objects of my affection—albeit for different reasons—weren't going anywhere anytime soon, I decided to check out the rest of the place. I wanted to give Kitty and Canine a little kiss on their cheeks and maybe something more, though I realized that would only have been a waste of my time and theirs, as by now they were far beyond knowing what was happening to them or anybody else.

A china-white carpet led up a grand bank of stairs to a mezzanine where there was nothing much except more of the flowers, including a rare white poppy called *drusis papever*, and more pictures of the woman I assumed to be Miss Lil'y White. The second floor was more interesting, reminding me of an old joke I heard back when I was in knee pants about a guy who dies, and going to hell, is asked by the devil behind which of the corridor of sealed doors would he like to spend eternity, and his choice lands him in the deep shit because he thought he heard the sound of lovemaking beyond one door, and in the same way, there were the sounds of lovemaking behind a corridor of locked doors, though nothing I hadn't heard already, back on the "street," so I continued on to where the carpet ended at the third floor.

There was not much light up there and compared to the rest of the place it seemed shabby and dusty, as if it were not used very much by the general public, like an attic where old toys are kept along with the family treasures and not a few secrets. The bare wooden floor was not the only departure from the general decor as up here were none of the flowers, and the one door was painted lime-green, and there was a little gold star on it. Feeling I might be getting someplace at last, I leaned against it with my great shoulder of a hunting dog and found it locked, though not too difficult to pick with a toenail. Nosing it open with some caution, I quickly entered a suite that was obviously Miss Lil'y White's personal domain as once again there was a profusion of the flowers, including the gardenias, which gave off a most incongruously heavenly fragrance. It was not too hard to understand why Billie had loved them. In place of the photographs were paintings of the woman, some in modern style, and while this might have been Miss Lil'y White's, somebody had a serious penchant for black art, as I recognized the palette of Norman Lewis in one of them, and a lot of the sculptures were African; from what I could tell by smelling the wood, the good stuff from Benin State, maybe five hundred years old, as well as bronze weights similar to the figurines I'd had seen at the junkyard back when I was stripping, before I had become a dog—black men on little asses, women pounding yams—and on closer inspection realized that some of them could very well have been mine as some obscurantist had taken the trouble to remove the foundry numbers as well as the initials that would have identified the artist—or as was more likely, the artists that had created them—though as my sharp detective's eye of a hound could see as I examined them, they were not being used as mere ornamentary even now, as the tiny bits of yellow dust that clung to them were not ordinary dust-motes, they were—so far as I could tell without a jeweler's glass and my kit—24 carat gold, used, I suppose, to gild the great calla downstairs in the lounge, which must have taken a lot of it, as there was solid gold everywhere: in bricks, in bars, in discs, in nuggets that had been fashioned into earrings and necklaces, anklets, bracelets and watches and finger rings with great stones in them, cat's-eyes and moonstones and lapis lazuli as well as the more precious diamonds, emeralds and rubies. As with the weights, I was sure I had seen some of this stuff before, as I thought I saw some remnant of my own craft, though these things had been carefully reworked. So this cache had ended up in New Orleans along with Lil' Eva and the man. So Miss Lil'y was obviously a Gold Digger. I wondered if she could have been a Lucan as well, as that would have explained the penchant for African objets d'art, the Baule and Dan masks that hung on the pastel-colored walls. The woman that entered from a bedroom was the living representative of the subject of the photographs, and, except for the fine dusting of freckles that covered her everywhere that I could see from her head to her toes like an armor of tattoos, she had the well-scrubbed look of the Ivory Snow Girl and bore no mean resemblance to Peck. The woman had to be good-looking. I hadn't seen legs like that since Peck's were wrapped around my ass. The problem was the mound of fur the woman cradled in her arms was not the soft, silky part of her anatomy that seemed so familiar to me; it was a Persian cat, and it hissed when it smelled me and jumped out of the woman's arms, running straight for me, tail in the air, scratching and biting. There was nothing I could do to avoid bleeding all over the place but to snap back. The cat let out a scream like a baby and leapt at least five feet in the air, all the while spinning like a roman candle, each hair of his coat at attention as if their owner had been exposed to an electric socket and came down hissing and kicking like a karate expert. The woman, who I took to be Miss Lil'y, said, "Beauregard, Beauregard, what in the world is wrong with you!"

Like I said, I did not want to bleed so I waited until he had descended almost to the level of my crown and gave him a good stiff roundhouse of my own to the solar plexus that I calculated would take all the air out of him and sent him flying across the room like a well-served tennis ball where he came down still spinning to collapse in a furry heap in a spray of gardenias that stood in a corner.

"Beauregard, just look at what you did to those flowers! Is that any way to behave? Oh, my god, you've knocked yourself silly this time, haven't you, Beauregard?"

She sounded like Peck.

"Beauregard, oh, Beauregard, are you all right? Speak to me!"

She ran to the animal and bent from the waist to pick it up. She was wearing a blue chiffon shorty nightgown that, as she bent to the cat, revealed a well-rounded behind and the always interesting fact that she wasn't wearing any drawers. I knew that behind as well as I knew my own ass. How I knew it was Peck's for sure was that once when we were fooling around with some really kinky sex I had nipped her just a little too hard back there with the result that she bore a little scar on her left buttock that looked like a strawberry crescent. Underneath all the freckles I could see this scar. Staggered, almost swooning from the sweet bouquet of the gardenias and this revelation, I quietly tipped over to the yet bending woman where I put my delicate nose of a practically overwhelmed hound close enough to her behind to clear up this enigma for me, and the oh so familiar smell of her juices proved beyond the shadow of a doubt that the woman who now went by the rather un-compromising name of Miss Lil'y White was none other than the one I had spent a couple of years with. On my poor, dear late lamented ass; the one I thought was dead, and whose murder we had been blamed for. I had to sit down a moment. The cat began to stir.

"Oh Beauregard," said the woman that I now knew was certainly Peck. "Oh you poor, dear pussycat, are you all right?" Kneeling, she took the cat to her breast, nuzzling it. The animal whimpered.

She had always liked animals, but I did not like the smell of this. Of all the people in the whole round world, what was Peck doing down here in New Orleans with all my gold? As glad as I was to see her, I had to wonder what she was doing alive and, if she was alive, where was Woody? As I remembered it, the two women were inseparable as a Siamese plug. Was she alive as well, and if she were, why was my own ass dead and I a fugitive? I had never known Peck to have a flower fetish. Maybe the Lil'ies went with her new routine, but what was she doing with all the gardenias? Fortunately, all the fight had gone out of the cat, and though it glanced wearily and uncomprehendingly in my direction, it did not make a further move toward me but seemed con-tent to just let Peck—the peculiarly resurrected Peck—fondle it. Blissed out, it began to purr and, after a moment, she put it down and began to straighten the mess it had made of the flowers. I wanted to ask her about the mess someone had made of my life and what con-nection she had to this club, but was somehow I was afraid of what she would tell me. I thought the cat was asleep. I didn't know any different until I felt its claws deep in my back like daggers aimed at the very mat-ter of things. When its fangs went into the back of my neck, I let out a howl like the great Chicago bluesman I never was: Arthur Cruddup.

Ain't that a great name? Cruddup. It sounded like "shuddup." I believe that's why he changed it to the Mighty Wolf. The "Back Door Man," Howlin' Wolf. Changed his religion. Made people change theirs. I learned in that moment to dance like St. Vitus.

Miss Lil'y White cum Peck said, "Lucius."

Loose as my skin was, this cat knew very well how to get under it. I ground my teeth in pain and said, "Listen, Peck, get this goddamned beast off my back. Get its teeth out of my neck now."

"Lucius, I can't."

Of all the things under the sun that were curious about this situation—this *menage a trois*, if you will—this answer was hardly the least of them. "Why not, Peck, why fucking not?"

"Because, you know how cats are, Lucius. They have little minds of their own. They do exactly what they want to do, which usually has everything to do with what you might not want them to do at the moment." I executed a step that the great Fred Astaire learned from one of the little Nicholas brothers. Under the circumstances I could have hardly been more cool. "Peck," I said, dancing to beat the band, "if you don't get him off me right now, I am going to roll over on him. Do you love him?"

"Of course I do, Lucius. He is the only pet I've had since losing you and your friend John."

"Well, Peck, I am going to crush him like a Dixie Cup."

"Please don't do that, Lucius, please don't."

"Well then, get him off me and I mean now."

As Peck started toward us, the cat, tail straight in the air like a baseball bat, took off into the bedroom like a shot. Peck quickly closed the door and turned. "There. Now you don't have to kill my cat. Beauregard is about the only company I get these days."

"How did you know it was me? As you can see, I'm invisible now, and I have never howled like that before."

"We only slept together for a couple of years, Lucius. I would know that voice anywhere." She rubbed her buttock. "How could I forget? Did you know it was me? How did you know it was me?"

"This might sound funny, Peck, but you smell the same."

"I'm going to take that as a compliment."

"Believe me, it was meant as one. How did you get here? Where is Woody?"

"She is really gone. How I got here is a long story. It's really complicated."

"A real movie, huh?"

"You might say that Lucius, a real suspense flick."

"Well, play it for me. I hope I have lots of time. But do me a favor. Leave out the suspense. I'm afraid it's killing me."

"I can imagine. It killed Woody, Lucius. It almost killed me. I almost don't know where to begin."

"You might try at the beginning. First things first. What happened to Woody? How did she die, and why did I get the blame for it?"

"I don't know what happened to her. When I found her, she was already dead. I figured whoever did it was probably looking for me. That was when I became Miss Lil'y White." She pointed out her freckles. "They're not real freckles, Lucius, they're just tattoos."

All the memory that came flooding back, my eyes of a hound going over that yet innocent looking flesh without a crease or a seam in it, though something did not jibe with the evidence of my eyes. Reluctantly tearing them away from her voluptuous body, I fixed my gaze on a Fang mask in back of her close-cropped head. "Peck, so far you haven't surprised me. For the sense of a continuum and an authentic relationship, I want you to do that without throwing me a curve. Where'd you get the gold?"

"Oh, that." She looked at all the loot and laughed. "Most of it is not mine. It was here when I got here. I don't own this place, Lucius. It is only an example of a fairly new marketing concept called a franchise. All I actually own around here is that cat you were about to kill a moment ago. I don't even own my own body anymore nor, really, the name I go by, as you know. The few things I do own I've worked really hard for: that Fang mask you're looking at. That Senufo bird. I admit that is a particularly good one, but I had to have it." She pointed to an eight-foot-tall, ironwood figure of what might have been a stork, its wings outstretched, a six-foot snake dangling from its two-foot beak. "Guess why I had to have it, Lucius? No, no, no, don't guess. I'll tell you. I had to have it because it reminded me of you. To tell you the truth, Lucius, that cat in there is not nearly enough for me. I suppose that between you and John you have ruined that for me. C'mon, that little cat? Nothing I get around here is actually enough. Oh, I get off once in a while; wouldn't lie about that; I wouldn't be what I am if I didn't know how to make myself come sometimes, but, mostly — I hate to say it, Lucius, but it's true — I just fake it for my clients. You know how this business is. I like to make them happy, but when I myself am truly happy, I'm dreaming of you. You and John, of course. Where is he anyway?"

I was glad she asked me that, and was equally glad I couldn't show it. My voice was flat; emotionless. "Oh, he's ... he's around ...might be here later."

Her eyes widened. "He is? Oh, Lucius, Lucius, I don't believe you, you're kidding me! Ohh, that would be great, the two of you again! But all to myself, no disrespect to the memory of poor, dear, murdered Woody." She paused, then clapped a hand to her forehead. "Oh, but Lucius, I just remembered, he can't really come in here unless he is invisible like you. Is he? (That's a neat trick, you know.) Because if he's not, he can't. This is still the south, you know. Governors here stand in the courthouse door or the schoolyard with pickaxe handles. Churches are bombed to dust. Everything is color-coded, because that's the way the brain functions here. And I don't get to get out much. Nowhere to go, anyway. They tell me this is the best game in town. But you, you can come as much as you like, but you can't stay here, Lucius; that cat in there is so jealous, and I wouldn't want you to have to hurt him. But do come, say you'll come to me Lucius, often. Please. You see," she managed to blush behind the freckles, "I still love you, whatever that means. Adore you."

If my donkey had not been involved, I would have been on top of her, plowing away like a big dog, but, instead, I steeled myself. "Flattery will get you everywhere, Peck, but tell me some more about this franchise business. If you don't actually own it, who does? Who do you get your franchise from?"

"I don't know him, Lucius. I've never seen him. I answered an ad in the newspaper, and I drop the money in that pneumatic tube over there, where, god, Lucius, does it ever disappear quickly. Practically faster than the speed of light. I don't know where it goes."

"How do you know it's a man?"

"I just assume it is. I don't know many women in the management end of this particular branch of the business. This is not a straight whorehouse, you know. This is a dancing palace. You can't see it from here, but do you feel the boogie in it?"

I couldn't feel anything. That little girl down there must have had them all knocked out. "What about the flowers, Peck, you never used to go in for 'em, candy either."

"Just a motif, Lucius, like the rest of it."

"So you don't really know anything, do you?"

"Never said I did, Lucius, never said I did. I am just an empty vessel. A dumb bitch with a hole, waiting for someone to fill it up. Anyone. Preferably you, but if you can't do it, I've got a book. I've got a cat. I've got a bed that, while I can't call it my own, I can sleep in. Or, if I don't feel like sleeping, do whatever I want to do. Watch television, though I don't really like to do that. But I don't know anything. Listen to what Confucius has to say about me: "The receptive brings about sublime success,/furthering through the patience of a mare. /If the superior man undertakes something and tries to lead, he goes astray,/but if he follows,/he finds guidance./It is favorable to find friends in the west and south, /to forego friends in the east and north./Quiet perseverance brings good fortune."

The word "book" rang a bell. Peck lit a candle. With bravado, its flame threw a yellow glow across the room. The heavy, heady scent of gardenias filled the room with a rush, anew.

"Do you like these, Lucius?"

"What's that, Peck—"

"These candles."

"Another courtesy?"

She touched the bow of her lip with a tongue I knew the taste of, how seductive it could be. "They're from Asia, I think. I don't really know."

"Tell me about the book, Peck."

"That's not fair, Lucius—"

"What's not fair?"

"Lucius, you know, if I am not anything else, I am a professional. The information in that book is privileged. It is based on a contract of faith. Confidentiality."

She was talking numbers and I knew it. I needed to have a gander at that book. I knew that in order to do that, I was going to have to relax. I was going to have to make her feel good. I had to take another angle. I could feel myself getting cocky. "Well, can you tell me this: do you know a man named Petoit?"

"Petoit?"

"Yes, Petoit. He's a doctor."

Before I got to the second syllable as I spelled it out, she blanched. She ran that tongue over those lips. Her answer was reluctant. "Can't say that I do."

"This might sound crazy, but when was the last time you've been to a doctor, Peck?"

"I'm clean, Lucius. I'm certified. How about yourself?"

"I'm getting there."

"What happened, Lucius, what happened to you?"

Maybe I shouldn't have done it, but I just could not resist the joke. I said, "I think it was something I ate."

"How curious," Peck said suddenly staring off into space, "how very curious, something you ate." Turning her full attention to me again, she went on: "Where'd you eat it, Lucius? What kind of food was it?" I realized I had made a mistake. Peck never could take a joke any way but literally. The only way she made up for that with me was in bed. She was so good there I usually forgave what I knew could be her curtness, ascribing it to being no more than the natural dominatrix in her. This time I lied. "Korean, Peck, kim chee," I belched. "I got it at a little restaurant—a stand, really—in LA. I had gone to Little Tokyo to do some shopping."

Her eyes narrowed. "Is this why you asked me about that doctor, what was his name?"

Something made me want to throw her off the track, as if our corporal situations were reversed and she was the scentor and I was the scented, the one being brought to bay. It wasn't hard to say that this was one of the smartest women I knew. "I guess you don't get to hear much music anymore, let alone play it."

"Lucius, I know you. You are being deliberately irrelevant. John is the one who is supposed to be like that, not you."

I decided to go for the gold. If I was right about her, I couldn't be telling her any more than she already knew. If I was wrong, then it would be information she could use. "He is an associate of that guy who is after us. A Frenchman. Vichy. Killed a bunch of Jews during the war by pretending to treat them for various ailments after he'd hidden them. Cute guy. No, I wouldn't be going to him for a stomach ache. That man killed Woody, Peck; he let his dog do it. And, and I lied to you a moment ago. John won't be coming by here. You won't have to worry about him queering your deal."

"Why not, Lucius? Why'd you lie to me about a thing like that? Why if he were to walk down Royal at five o'clock some afternoon, I'd be glad to wave at him from the window like those women used to do from the Jefferson Market Jail. You can tell him which window to watch for. Tell him what I'll be wearing, about the tattoos, I mean."

"Can't, Peck," I couldn't keep a lump out of my throat. "he's dead."

Peck's hand went to her own. "John, dead? No. No. That can't be true. Dead? When, Lucius? How, how?"

"Was on his way up to Seattle to make a gig. Plane. It was no accident."

"No, no, no, no. Not John. You think he killed John, too?"

"And my mother and grandmother, and Billie Holiday. In different ways, but he did it." I gave it all I had. "Now do you see why I have to take a look at that book? There could be something very important in it."

I had to wait until she stopped snuffling. When whores cry. "Lucius," she said, sniffing, "the thing about that book is—"

"*Peck, the man is trying to kill jazz!*"

"No, he can't do that. He can't."

"Try telling him that."

"But, but records, performances all the time! You ... you said John ... John was on his way ... way to a gig." Her blue eyes filled to the brim with more tears.

"Yeah, and look what happened to him. He ended up in a swamp. Alligator meat. Wasn't enough left to bury 'im. What about that book, Peck?"

"It's got a device on it, Lucius, a device put there by the Crescent City police department, put there to control the traffic. Whenever it is opened, a signal goes off. Cameras roll. And if they happened to see anything at all suspicious, they'd be here quicker than you could say Jack Flash. You can bet on it."

"But Peck—"

She dabbed at her eyes. "What"

"Look at me."

"What. I don't see anything."

"That's right. And they won't either. I'm invisible, remember? All you'd have to do would be to open it. Look your numbers over. What's to see?"

"They send my clients to me. All of them."

She was starting to irritate. "Then what's the point of having a book, honey?"

"There has to be a book. I don't know, something about western civilization. There's always a book. You have to have one or you can't operate. Been that way ever since the Bible. Everything those girls did was known, every trick turned, jotted down and duly noted. With a system like that, why should you worry about jazz?"

"It's history, Peck, history has a way of being linear; you don't really know who was turning those tricks back there. Things get all mixed up in the hopper. You want a good example of that, just look at me. I mean, look at me the way I was when you met me."

"Lucius, I'm starting to get tired. I can't follow all of this. You are beginning to sound like a didact. Didactics bore, particularly in art. Too many sweeping statements. Vague references. Broad generalities."

If Peck knew what was going on, she did a good job of concealing it. The honey must have worked because she asked me if I would make love to her now, for John's sake. In a way, I should have known better.

It was like an opera. *Bouffe* except for all the dead bodies. As Peck ground her own quite vibrant body against me, I could not help thinking about Woody's ; cold as she had never been, stiff as Gertrude and Alice doing the log, the ophidia. Funny. Peck had always been the stiffest of the two, and now here she was writhing against me like an anaconda while poor Woody was as stiff as a board. Anaconda. That was a snake, wasn't it? But Peck? The little freckle-faced blonde with the fresh-scrubbed look of the Ivory Snow Girl? I had never thought about it before, but all of a sudden here I was wondering if this little blonde, who had me going like the Bronze Buckaroo turned dog, had any snake in her. I know she had had, as a matter of fact, quite a bit over on Morton Street, but I suppose I had assumed that to be no more than a temporary situation: she had always had such an aversion to them, at least for as long as I had known her until then. Thinking about it now I realized the revulsion she might have felt might have been no more than the effects of a certain law of physics: "Like and like repel." Still, except for how she hung on to my bird, devouring the poor thing like a tree viper, there was nothing to my eye that was snakelike about her, not the flutter of her eyelids nor her silken skin. A snake? If she were, it would be without a doubt the best-kept secret since Warren Harding. I dug my rough, unpared nails into her skin all the way to the pads of my forepaws. Peck, cum Miss Lil'y White, let out a yelp as if she were about to have puppies.

"Lucius," she whimpered, yet throwing me a supple curve even as her eyes widened with the surprise of pain, "honey, that hurt!"

I couldn't feel a scale anywhere. The pupils of her now wide eyes were round as two blue moons. The thin twin jets of blood with which Luke had offered up his last testimony back there in the blind man's room had been black as ink. The tiny yet thick droplet that now welled up from Peck's white shoulder was red as Mars. She had draped herself around me like a flag, the pink tongue with which she had uttered those words a monolith. If there had been a faint hiss, it was attributable to nothing I would fathom beyond the beyond the dog in her.

My abstractions had the effect of cooling whatever ardor I had managed. After nuzzling my hairy neck for a bit with lips that were, if a bit thin, nevertheless a fact, she said, "Lucius, what's wrong?" It was less a hiss than a whine.

Forming the words with my own pretty lipless mouth of a hound, I heard myself saying, "I don't know, Peck. I've been thinking."

Grabbing onto my bird, she manipulated it sulkily. It was no use. Disentangling herself, she sat up. "About what?"

"Well, you know, Peck, about John." I lied, while examining her carefully for any sign of the blemish. I managed a quick tug at the delicately pink shells of her ears as best I could with my nubby paws and found them for all my exertions seamlessly attached to her head. It was, in terms of my desperate hypothesis, another negative. So far as I know, snakes definitely did not have ears; at least not like Peck's, that seemed to perk up, her eyes narrowing as she regarded me.

"John? I think about him too. A lot. I told you that. Especially in situations like this. John, as I recall, didn't think much; except about music or maybe about how to make me, you know, come, Lucius."

She knew how to sting like an adder.

"It was a hell of a way to go, Peck."

"What? On the way to a gig? Think about that, Lucius. It couldn't have been so bad. Hey, wasn't that the way that guy—what was his name—Clifford died? John was crazy about him, wasn't he? You know what they say: imitation is the most sincere form of flattery."

"Brown," I corrected her, "died in an automobile accident."

"Automobile, airplane, they were both on their way to a gig, weren't they? They're both dead, aren't they? C'mon, John must've loved that. I don't know. I can think of only one other way he might like to have died ..."

"How is that, Peck, tell me."

"Think about it, Lucius, would you mind dying now?"

"Why, Peck, you going to kill me? How would you do it: strangle me? Would you squeeze me to death?"

"Oh, don't be silly." After a moment she said, "No, I meant a heart attack. Wouldn't you love that? You wouldn't have to think about it at all. It would just happen. Wouldn't that be divine, Lucius?"

"And what about you, Peck? How would you like it?"

"I don't know, Lucius, people have to die, don't they? I guess it wouldn't mean any more than that I died the way I lived. Giving people pleasure and taking it."

It was good to know that if what I was thinking was right, she wouldn't mind. I said, "Tell me something."

"What do you want to know, Lucius?"

"Tell me everything, Peck. How did you and Woody meet?"

"You know all of that."

"Tell me again, and try not to leave anything out."

"My god, Lucius, you are sounding more and more like the pathetic protagonist in a cheap pulp fiction novel by Jim Thompson: *Savage Night, A Swell Looking Babe, Population 1,200*. Worse than that. I had never thought that possible. Why would you put me in this situation, this position?"

"Didn't put you here, Peck. Found you here, remember? This is your favorite position. According to you, you wouldn't mind dying in it."

"That has an ominous ring, Lucius. Why, what are you really thinking? Say, are you threatening me? I thought we were friends. I don't like to feel threatened."

"Tell me, Peck."

"Oh all right," she said, "but why don't we have some music. And let me fix us a drink. It would be too tedious without it."

She made drinks and pressed a button. Chick Webb. Ella singing, "When I Get Low I Get High," and then "King Porter Stomp." She went through that whole litany about Chicago. Nothing much that hadn't been in the newspapers. She emphasized the casual brutality of her childhood, in which slaughter was a tradition. A way of life. The coppery smell of blood in her nostrils. Even now, she said, she could hear the terrified squeal of swine in her sleep. The confused lowing of cattle. Hundreds of thousands, if not millions, of sheep bleating in sheep terror on their way to the little gate. She was never to use the term "executed."

Even the parish priest was in on it; there had been blood in the font at her baptism, lamb's blood, as was the "wine" served to the congregation at Communion. Her first menstruation had occasioned a psychotic episode for which she had to be hospitalized; thinking it the result of what she had consumed, she had refused Communion after that and was sent away to school.

I said, "And Woody?"

The school, she said, had been a reform school. She had met Woody there at a Baptist convention. Instead of a confirmation, she had had a conversion. It'd been Woody who'd helped her with that. She said I certainly knew the rest.

"And snakes?"

That got a rise out of her. She looked confused. "What about them?"

"Any in the old family tree?"

She laughed. "Is that what you think? Why Lucius, my folks were not exactly liberals. Snakes were not even allowed in the slaughterhouse. Never allowed the dignity of even gracing our table. Why if my daddy had caught one crossing our threshold, he would've blown its brains out. Now you, they would've loved you."

I shuddered as she said this, thinking of poor Luke back at the blind man's. They were really between a rock and a hard place. Worse off by far then any dog. Worse off than even my ass, black as it was.

"Why did you have to come here, Lucius?"

I felt woozy.

"The truth is, Lucius, I grew up in a prison. According to my father, my mother was a snake. Sometimes he called her a bitch. I never met her, but if the latter is true, Lucius, I'm sorry ... I can't ... I could never let you out me."

CHAPTER TWENTY THREE

I awoke choking and gagging, hearing the words "lucumi" and "cumbia." I didn't know what they meant. I didn't even know if I could spell them correctly. "Lucumi" and "cumbia": they were in no dictionary I'd ever seen, though I did vaguely remember a recording by the great Charles Mingus called "Cumbia and Jazz Fusion" that I seemed to recall was an Afro-Colombian jazz suite. 'Lucumi,' it was obvious, was possessed of the l-u-c root that was related to me, the name I had chosen to appear under, though maybe I was just a "Pet" after all, because I could see I was strapped down once more to a gurney like the one I'd been strapped to in the hellhole with the "Thing" or the one at the Monkeyhouse poor John had been strapped to, and I had Lil' Eva Lil' Eva, Petoit, Teller and the rest of them standing around me.

The only ones that were missing were the man himself, and curiously, the Axe Man, as he was from New Orleans, the Crescent City, the Big Easy, where the very formal music known as "jazz" was born, giving everybody the heebie-jeebies. The heebie-jeebies: If I wanted them, it looked like I had them: J. Edgar, Luciano, Chillingsworth, Lawrence Welk, Buck Rogers and His Rocketeers in the Twenty Fourth Century, the Masked Marvel (a lot of them were yet masked), Disney, the Wizard of Oz, the Pope, Farmer Gray, Perry Como, Betty Crocker, Paul Whiteman, Howdy Doody, Superman, Roy Rogers and Gene Autry, Desi Arnaz (Babaloo, meester?), the Nelsons, Estes Kefauver with the Dulles Brothers, Bing Crosby, Bob Hope, the Mc and Mac boys, McCarthy and Mac Arthur, and all of them, all of America's heroes, its icons, or maybe they had me. And what was very different about it from yesterday was that they could see me too, undesirable as that might have been to my vital interests and I suppose to theirs too, as that might have been why they wanted me, to get rid of me. I didn't see Peck. My stomach felt curiously empty, more empty than it'd felt since I'd swallowed whatever it was that the Lucan had given me. Lil' Eva, Petoit and Desi Arnaz stared down at me in a way that was almost friendly.

"There," Arnaz said, "You see. It worked. A guy back at the hotel showed me that. He had a little reservation as to its efficacy over here, as what he showed me is from Nigeria, and he thought what the Lucan used might have been from Caguey or somewhere else in the Caribbean."

"My my," Eva said, "ah ain' knowed nuthin' 'bout dat stuff. Dem black cocks and dem puah whaat heifuhs, de piebald sows mah ol' mammy 'ud be creepin' tuh duh bahn wid blood and chickun feathuhs all ovah huh when she'd come creepin' in, dem strange wuhds, dem strange wuhds ah huhd huh muttuhin' out deah in de moonlaht, ah nevah luhned de meanin' uv 'cose de ol' biddy said ah nevuh wud luhn nuthin' no way no 'count as ah wuz; de goobah dus' she sprinkled on de broom and roun' de do' lak roach powdah when she got tahd and wonted mah ol' 'bacca chewin', bib-ovahvall wearin', bad farmin' alcoholic' daddy tuh see ef he mought could fin' his ol' way tuh Highway 61, and ah thank she gib 'um duh keys, bu ah nevuh did fahn out ef 'e did, 'cose we ain' nevuh got so much as uh pos'cahd fum 'im aftuh dat. Uh uh, we 'uns wuz raised Christian sho as dey hung dat whaat man fum dat cross and we got tuh eat dem biscuits. Uh, uh, chile, dat is too much monkey bidness fuh me tuh be involved wid, lak de song say. Hey Petoit, say, Awnaz, y'all lak' Chuck Berry?"

Petoit said, "*Eva, the Babalawo is busy*. He has to concentrate on this little matter at hand. Please try not to bother him with irrelevancies." He rubbed her head, patting it like the dog she was, far more of one than I had been in my entire life. "I know you are a good Christian; let's see how long you can stay one."

"Aw," said Lil' Eva, "y'all don' nevuh pay me no tenshun. Treat me lak ah wuz uh dawg. Ah ain' no dawg, deah is de dawg layin raht deah, see 'um?" She pointed to me. "Yew wont tuh fuck wid somebody, yew fuck wid him, yuh unnerstan'?"

Petoit did not bother to look up. "Eva," he said, "do you want your shot or do you not want your shot? Now you know the man said I could withhold it from you at anytime."

Eva drew back. I could see what I can only describe as panic rising in her gorge. "Widhol' mah shot, ah doc, yuh wudn' do dat tuh me, wud ya?"

"I would, Eva."

"Aw no, doc, " she whined like the dog she wouldn't admit she was, "don' do dat tuh me, please don' do dat!"

The doctor raised his eyebrows. "No?"

"Uh-uh, doc, please!"

Petoit said, "Well Eva, you know what to do."

"Now?"

I had to watch with what great gusto, which I'm sure was pretend, she performed fellatio on him. When she had done this to his satisfaction, he wiped himself off. He zipped his fly and pointed to Arnaz. "Now, Eva, do the babalawo. I didn't like that little outburst."

Arnaz waved the pathetic Eva off. "No, thank you, I'm fine," he said. "I don't indulge."

Petoit's eye's widened. "Forgive me Padrino, but you, a Cuban? Where is your obligatory machismo?"

The appropriator of "Babaloo" for mass consumption on CBS Television kept staring at me. "It's Lucy."

"My god, man, I'm sorry," said the Frenchman.

"That's all right buddy, don't feel sorry for me. I make a lot of money, TV, you know."

Petoit said, "I suppose that's some compensation. However, I myself am French, know what I mean, comprez?"

The babaloo ignored him.

Shrugging, the doctor said, "Ooh, and Lucius, at last, how are you! It's been so long since we've seen you. By the way, let me congratulate you, you look fine."

I said, "Where is Peck?"

"Peck, Peck? Let me see. Oooh, you mean Miss Lil'y White? Of course! You're old friends, aren't you? She had a few pressing matters to attend to, which entailed her going to bed. She is a working woman, you know. But don't worry, she left us here to tie up all the loose ends. You, Lucius, you are a loose end. Tell me, are we doing a good job, credible at least, non?" He tried the steel hoops that bound me. "At any rate—particularly the going rate—I'm sure she'll be back. You see, she has nowhere else to go. You must know she is the proprietress here. She is one of the herrinfolk. Put a lot of money into this establishment. Everything she had. And while the turnover is excellent, it is quite a labor-intensive operation. Anything can go wrong at any time, as I'm sure you of all the creatures on this earth must realize. You yourself, for example, put the fritz on one of our best operatives. We can't have you doing that. Nobody would make any money, and where would everybody be then? Turned out into the streets, begging. Eating from garbage cans. Now, you, you can't mind that. You're a dog. All you're used to is scraps."

"Thief! Murderer!"

"Listen as the pot calls the kettle black. We have quite an update on your exploits. A case in point would be that Bronckhorst's job in Queens. That was your handiwork, wasn't it? That watermelon truck. Your hairs were found all over the rinds. You took a shit right near there.

Then, Frank's Restaurant in Harlem, as well as several instances of assault. And, lastly, but not leastly, there were the murders themselves."

"You killed my ass!"

"An inconvenience. Your ass simply got in the way. Not very smart. You might even say, he did it to himself."

"What happened to my mother?"

"You know, I'm not too clear about that, but it appears she went off the deep end."

My stomach turned so sour I started to growl. I had to know. "And the old lady, my grandmother?"

"She went the other way."

"You explain that, mister."

"My, my, Lucius, demanding, aren't we? Still, as it was your grandmother, I suppose you do have a right to know. I admit I made a somewhat ambiguous statement. Let me clarify that. She was simply going north on a one-way street that went south. Fortunately, no one was killed but she and your mother. It was an experiment in robotics engineered by an associate of ours called High Tech. I'd say it was very successful. It worked fine. I couldn't have done it any better myself. Oh, Lucius, I could tell you some war stories."

"I bet. I know about you, Petoit, remember?"

He shrugged again pulling his shoulders up into his neck like a turtle before letting them fall like a hanged man. It was a very Gallic gesture. "You know what they say in mysteries of this sort about that: what good will it do you and, further, what is said about curiosity. I realize you are a dog, but in this case try to use your imagination a bit. Oh, if you will indulge me, while you think you know all about me, and I seem to know all about you, there is one little detail in your file I do not believe has appeared to date and if it has—you will forgive me—it seems to have escaped my memory. Tell me, Lucius—since we're giving away all our secrets—do you have a father? Just for the record."

I'd never heard of such thing. Talk about your investigators. After all the works these boys had done here on the earth, this man standing before me as I lay bound, possibly dying as Faulkner put it, didn't know my paternity from a hole in the ground. I had my doubts about him. This was beginning to sound like *Chinatown*, which hadn't been made then. It had been written, but I am talking about the big picture.

"Exactly where was that nest of yours located, that you fell out of? Was it higher than four stories, the projects somewhere? I bet it was someplace in the mountains, as with the coppery skin that could have been shining like gold if you had burnished it right and that number 12 hair of yours, you could be Jibaro."

I didn't care if he was a doctor or not, because, if he was, any treatment he was going to give me was going to be lethal anyway, and any thug in the world or lunatic could do as much for me in a sidewalk second without any of that expensive schooling I suppose the doctor had had. All you had to do was give him a gun. But I didn't want this Frenchman telling me anything about my gold.

"This captain at your training school — may I call it that? —told us you could have had quite a brilliant career as a singer, operatic, organic as a brass pipe; but all you seemed to be concerned with even in the midst of your correction was the whereabouts of your ass. Where did your ass come from, Lucius?"

"Too bad you don't have one yourself, Petoit, but then you never did have one. Look at you. Flat as the walls of a barn, but you can't keep the animal. What are you doing with my gold?"

"I am proud of you. At last, a question someone can answer. It's a simple one. Are you ready? We're keeping it. We're holding it in reserve. The Federal Reserve. Behind walls twelve feet thick and reinforced with cortisined steel that goes twelve stories down into the ground. This little bit is just for display. Ostentation. Make the customers feel good. Like they own a piece of the rock. And they do, Lucius, we relieve you of that. And you don't have to worry, because we take care of you. Look at that ass of yours. Even with such obscure and I'm sure humble beginnings. It's like Social Security. What's he got to worry about now? So just sit back and enjoy your imminent demise. Think of it as a free ride."

It was the most absurd economic plan I'd heard in my entire life: I pay dearly and draw a blank, a check my ass can't cash. "Yeah, I bet I can guess the architect of that one. Where is that pig now? Whose skirt is he hiding behind now that he's killed his own niece?"

"References, Lucius, though I understand yours, being what you are. If your are referring to who I think you are, you don't have to worry about that either, he'll be here soon enough."

If he had been another sort of person, he'd have made a good psychic.

The man himself walked in as if on cue. He wore a black Borselino, the wide brim of which was turned up in front in the Munich manner. An ankle-length leather coat was draped casually over his shoulders. The jacket of his pearl-gray camel suit was bloused and belted over a black shirt with a cobalt blue tie. Black gloves, a pair of black leather chukka boots and a white silk scarf that wound around his neck like a snake completed his attire. Rudolph strained at a leash snarling and snapping, his countenance horrible to behold, as if he had no fear and was a boxer (instead of a Doberman pinscher) being led into a ring with the sole purpose of annihilating his opponent, though I knew he was not a boxer because he didn't play fair. If there was going to be any fighting, he was going to use his teeth, like the bitch he was, with the six little teats. I wondered where his puppies were. I thought the man was overdressed. He thought he looked like a film director. Rosellini on the set. He's got all the angles. What moves where. He looked like somebody who thought he could lock the river down. Rudolph had gained weight but he was still quite a bit too narrow in the chest to do any damage to a great big hound such as I had become in the proverbial fair one—one-on-one—unfettered. He pranced like a pony out of hell. The man made a show of restraining him with some difficulty. The room came to attention and saluted. His gaze slowly swept the assemblage, coming to rest on me. He let out a chuckle. Handing the leash over to an aide, he removed his gloves and sauntered over to me, his movements stylized, baroque. "Well," he said looking down at me with satisfaction, "you led us on quite some chase."

I said, "How is your dopefiend dog doing?" I had a plan. It wasn't much of a plan, but I didn't have anything else. My ass was already a goner. I knew with the unerring instinct of a bereaved bloodhound that if I failed in this, it would be curtains for me too. I had to make him get these hoops off me.

The man said, "What did you say?"

"I said, "How is your dopefiend dog doing, motherfucker!'"

He laughed. "I know what you are doing. You're trying to get me riled up so I'll remove those hoops that have your carcass there where I want you, so you can prove you can maul up on my dog. You know what? You are a scream. To think I would get my ideas from you. Don't worry, Mr. Apulius, I have my own plan. I have quite a surprise for you. I found something I think you might like. Bring in the act," he said to a Lucan.

No matter what I was going through, no matter what alienation I felt, no matter what pain, what suffering I had gone through, I had never gotten compensated for it, but what happened next made me want to jump for joy, it made me want to shout, it made me want to holler and turn myself about, and had it not been for the six steel hoops strapping me down to that gurney I would have. The Lucan returned leading a donkey act. The donkey was John without a scar on him, though he did have that dazed look that was characteristic of him in situations that had nothing to do with music. The woman was Peck, who led another woman by a halter. That woman, who was none other than the gracious Lady Milene, had a slight bruise near the right temple, though, other than that, she was miraculously all right, if a little indignant at being in a situation she appeared to have no control over, chafed at being led. It was she who first spoke. "Lucius, what are you doing here? Are these the people you are involved with?"

I expected them all to walk in next, my dear mother and my old brush-cutting grandmother. Woody. Billie. Bird. Wardel Gray. Lester leaping, leaping morosely with a lid on, and if that were true, those two goons I'd taken off the register outside. If immortality was granted, the cardboard creatures that were assembled here like an evil deck of cards, each one representing the most (all right, arguably) hideous, heinous murderer imaginable, why wouldn't it seem logical the others would appear? Maybe I was dreaming, I thought, hallucinating. "John, John," I cried out, afraid I wouldn't hear that bray of his, but just the silence of my imaginings, "John, boy, is that you?"

John's ears half-heartedly shot up and dropped like a shrug the way they did when he was disappointed in something, like Rosamond's or Eeyore's. He looked annoyed with me.

I turned what neck I could to the man. "Is this some trick? Is this real?"

"Pardon me, but you've already remarked my ambiguity."

"I've learned you speak with a forked tongue, but what are you spearing now?"

"I'm surprised you're not more quick, Lucius, when you seem so intelligent. I mean that what you see before you now is both real and a trick. Right now the reality of them exists, but only at my pleasure. They move when I tell them to, lift a finger, wipe a brow, even bleed. I enjoy it when I can make people bleed, see the dark red liquid welling from a cut, quickly filling the fresh ravine of the flesh made by the cold, sharp steel of the knife to overflowing, and then dripping like thick raindrops, spattering the earth. I like to see bone and muscle, each nerve exposed. Dr. Mengele taught me that. To make lampshades of human skin. If you were to pinch them hard enough, Lucius, they would bleed. They're going to bleed all right, whether you pinch them or not. They themselves are a trick, as everyone who enters this establishment is a trick. The babalawo here knows that."

The babalawo nodded.

The man had me confused with all that double-talk. I no longer knew if what I was seeing had any more substance than a piece of paper, and I don't mean a piece of paper with lines on it and some circles, I mean a blank piece of paper. I felt like I had in the cave where I had met most of his supporting cast and though the "Thing" had told me they weren't real, here they were in all their glory: Edward Teller and the rest of them. I said, "John, John, you tell me. Are you real?"

I must have sounded pathetic. John certainly looked at me like I was pathetic.

Lady Milene said, "He's all right. What's not real is this situation you got us into."

I felt like giggling. "Milene, you're alive!"

"There ain't no question of that, you fool, the question is how long this bunch is going to let me stay that way. These people are killers, Lucius!" She burst into tears.

The man said, "Now, now, none of that. Oh, I'll explain. Your friends missed that plane. The lady unexpectedly went to the toilet on herself before they boarded. One of those little accidents nobody could have foreseen."

"C-can y-you b-believe t-this," Milene sobbed, "that s-shit s-s-saved m-me for t-this! Where are we, Lucius?"

They were real all right. Nothing could approximate that carping. I realized Milene could be like Xantippe, only I—like Socrates—was the scapegoat, and not John.

"We're at Miss Lil'y White's, Milene."

She pointed to Peck. "And is this who you missed the gig for?"

As bad as things were, I was glad I had missed it. "No, her." I jerked my large head of a hound toward the expectant Eva.

To say that Milene could be 'no nonsense' was to be putting it mildly. She said, "Lucius, if we ever get out of this, you will never work with us again. You hear me? I'm tellin' you!"

"Milene, it's not what you think!"

"And who is this one over here treatin' me like I'm her property!"

"Sorry, Milene, is it? We were never introduced. I'm Peck. Forgive me if I don't offer you my hand, but this is the South. Still, I'm glad to meet you, honey, 'mighty glad,' as they say in these parts, or 'right glad.'"

That "honey" struck a chord.

"Well, you know what, Miss Peck, or whatever your name is, I'm just sorry I can't—"

Peck flushed beneath the freckles. "Well, you don't have to get huffy with me, I just work here!"

"That's enough of that!" The man's voice had the ring of authority. Like a churchbell. The room fell silent except for me. Fuck it. I didn't feel I had anything to lose. I could hear the voice of the Mighty Wolf ringing in my ear: "Church bells toll fuh d' diamonds; church bell toll fud d' gold; jes' uh lil' spoon o' yo' precious love'll satisfy my soul. Some cryin' about dat … dat spoonful, some dyin' about … dat spoonful, evahbody's lyin' about … spoonful."

The man said, "You have everything to lose, but I'm going to tell you anyway, Lucius. I have you bound here for submission to certain of my agents. Peck here—Miss Lil'y White to you—is one of those."

I took a long soul-searching look at the woman who had been my lover, well, John's anyway. "You know, I thought—"

"I'm sorry, Lucius."

Clearing his throat, the man said, "I said that will be enough of the small talk, this bickering and apologia, I want it to stop, and I mean this very minute."

Peck's shoulders slumped. Biting her lip, she saluted. "Sorry, sir. Lucius, you must submit to me, now!"

She had never used that tone of voice with me before. That pitch, e flat above high c—above the range of the human ear—and it went straight to the dog in me. Unfolding its wings, my bird shot up like jackhammer. I heard myself saying, "Yes, Peck."

"You will obey."

"Yes, Peck."

"Naughty dog. Naughty, naughty, naughty. Just look at that. What is that? Aren't you ashamed of yourself? I mean, to want to end your whole life on a note like this. What is happening to you, Lucius?"

I felt no shame. The old bird was talking to me. Playing be-bop. "Cherokee."

Arnaz said, "Look, look what's happening to him, look! Interesting."

Petoit stared hard. "Very, very! I myself have never seen a case like this. In my experience, the process was always irreversible."

"Irreversible," muttered the man, "irreversible. Teller, come over here. Do you see this?"

Teller hurried over. "My, my," he said, "incredible! Not irreversible, what is this! I've never seen it either. Is this desirable? What elements do you suppose are at work here? Let's find out. Maybe I can split them."

Milene said, "Lucius!"

"Oh, my," said Peck. "Lucius, you're so-so cute!"

My ass looked unimpressed. I didn't know what they were talking about.

The man said, "It doesn't matter. So he's unique. So what? So, he's still dust."

Eva looked nervous. She said, "Honey, kin ah have mah shot now?"

Peck said, "Mmm."

Milene said, "Who is that? What's going on? What happened to Lucius?"

I didn't know who in the fuck they were talking about.

"Let's get on with it," said the man. "Whatever is laying on that table."

Eva said, "Ah don' give uh flyin' fuck 'bout d' niggah. Honey, kin ah have mah shot now?"

Petoit said, "Hush, Eva, not now."

Eva said, "Ah'm not talkin' tuh you. Daaaddy."

The man said, "Hush, Eva!"

Eva's nose was running like a clock. She had tears in her eyes. She shook like she had the ague. Dengue. Her teeth chattered like the music she couldn't stand, but without the feeling. Rudolph pranced nervously, tearing away at the carpet and whining until his toenails clicked on the hardwood floor.

"Wait, I can't concentrate," Peck said. "That dog is ruining my carpet! Can you make him stop?"

"Fuck dat dawg," said Eva. "Fuck dat carpet. Ah'm sick."

Nobody saw the Axe Man when he came in except me. He wore a plaid suit that was like the hotel clerk's, only it was black and white and squared. "Oh, baby," he said, gleefully rubbing his hands together as if he were trying to make a bonfire of them, his fingers long and curiously slender for a murderer's. "Whereya at? Whut's dis jazz heah all about?"

The man shot him a furious look. He said, "You're late."

"You know whut ah gats tuh say 'bout all o' dat jazz," the Axe Man stated, "way bettah late den nevah! Who dat y'all gats layin ovah deah? Niggah's in de cut, aint' e. Hey, lemme know somepin' on 'im: do 'e lak' jazz."

Peck said, "I'm sorry, I can't do this if there are going to be all these distractions."

The Axe Man looked over at John. He turned to me again. "Say, wull, ah'll be damned, looka dere. Ain'gats no hair!"

It was true. I could see it was smooth as an egg like a man.

"Ah needs uh shot," said Eva. "Ah needs it bad."

When he wanted to, the man could be like lightening. He had his pistol out in a flash. Leveling it onto Eva, he shot her in the head much like a famous novelist, who just died last week, shot his wife, Joan, down in Mexico. Eva went down like a cannonball. I did not like Cannonball. I had heard him once, with a guy named John Coltrane. I believe Miles Davis was in that band. I had never liked Eva, who had always been so sly. Lil' Eva, Lil' Eva. The frail so nice they named her twice, who could slip her hand in a blind man's pocket in the bat of an eye. She bled all over the off-white carpet. And the blood ran red, contrasting with the carpet and her black skin. She had been a pretty woman, but she came to a pretty bad end. I couldn't even feel sorry for her. I wasn't glad either. It was a mess no matter which way you looked at it.

Milene screamed.

Peck said, "Aw, look at the mess you made of my carpet." She could be so cold.

The man blew the smoke away from the barrel of his mean little pistol. He said, "I've fourteen more shots in here, who wants to go next?"

John batted a fly across the room with his tail. The room fell silent. Milene looked like she was going to faint, but steadied herself, rocking like a drunk. Nobody else moved. The man squinted an eye down the barrel of his pistol and said, "Proceed."

"From where?" said Peck.

The man said, "The top, Lil'y, take it from the top."

"Right, the top. Sorry, sir, Lucius, you must submit to me now."

Nobody saw the little Filipina when she came in. When she got finished singing her little song with its hypnotic refrain, they were all in a nod, and that was how we made our escape, following the Big Dipper north.

Not more than a few months later, I happened to read somewhere that the man himself was under indictment for some black bag job in D.C., and that a few of his operatives would go to jail. As for us: Milene, my ass and I, we were alive and that was it. America's heroes suddenly had their own troubles, for which I would like to think I was in some way responsible. A lot of them lost their contracts; their death grip on the landscape. Not all of them. I imagine some will always be with us.

Of course, when Milene booked our next gig, she never did say anything about any of that. I never did see James Moody.